No Compass
To Right

Book Four - Crater Lake Series

No Compass
To Right

Book Four – Crater Lake Series

FRANCIS L. GUENETTE

HUCKLEBERRY
HAVEN
PUBLISHING

Author's note: This book is a work of fiction. Names, characters, places and incidents either are the product of the author's imagination or are used fictitiously and any resemblance to actual persons living or dead, events, or locales is entirely coincidental.

ISBN
978-0-9940664-7-3 (Softcover)
978-0-9940664-5-9 (Kindle)
978-0-9940664-6-6 (epub)

Cover Photos & Design: Bruce Witzel

Huckleberry Haven Publishing
Box 309
Port Alice, BC
V0N 2N0
disappearinginplainsight.com

For my granddaughters: Emma and Britney
Many thanks for laughter, love and inspiration

ONE

Justin bent forward and rested his open palms on his knees. Robbie stopped beside him and grinned. "Are you twenty-three or fifty-three?"

Straightening up and catching his breath, Justin shouldered his hiking partner aside, "You won't be eleven forever, kid. Enjoy it while you can."

The cardio climb to the alpine meadow had been worth the effort. Turning one way, they saw rippling hills in shade upon shade of muted greys and greens giving way to flat lowlands; in the other directions were mountains as far as the eye could see. The various perspectives floated above the marine cloud which had filled the valley below with mounds of thick cotton.

Justin shaded his eyes and stared up at the summit of the highest peak on the Cat's Cradle. His boss, Reg, had explained the origin of the mountain's name. "The two peaks dip in the middle. They're both angled like a pair of goddamned hands. Get it ... cat's cradle, the kid's string game." Reg had worked a toothpick around his mouth as he said, "The name caught on because the whole damn area is crisscrossed with cougar trails. A regular happy hunting ground." He had jammed the toothpick back in the top pocket of his grey work shirt and chuckled as he walked away, pausing only to call back over his shoulder, "Enjoy your hike."

While they admired the view, thick cloud crept up to twist and swirl around their feet. Justin had studied the hike enough to know that the shifting wind driving the fog into the cradle between the peaks could block climbers from getting any further than the spot where he and Robbie now stood. The higher summit, as if mocking them, stood outlined against blue sky. But to get there they had to climb into the cradle and descend along a narrow ledge that was now obscured by the mist. Only then could they make the climb up.

Robbie placed a hand on Justin's arm to get his attention. He turned his gaze in the direction of the boy's. They watched as a black bear and two cubs ambled off into the gathering fog. Robbie tilted his head to study the retreating animals. His confident voice floated on the damp air, "They won't come back our way."

Walking through the tendrils of fog, Justin halted near the stone cairn that marked the summit of the lower peak. "Let's hunker down and wait. The fog might clear." He slipped out of his pack and dug inside to pull out the rocket stove. He got it set up and filled the metal canister from his water bottle. Passing Robbie an energy bar, Justin planted himself on a rock near the boy and they both waited for the water to boil. Robbie was quiet, hunched into his coat and he appeared, as he always did, to be easy in his thoughts. Justin admired that trait most about the kid. Now that the challenge of the hike was on hold, his thoughts bounced from one anxiety to another.

With his newly minted engineering degree in hand, he felt a strong pull to make this area his home. He could stay on at *Crater Lake Timber*. For all he knew, he'd end up back there one day but right now, he wanted a chance to apply his forestry knowledge on a larger scale. Then there was Lauren. She had made it clear over the phone that she thought his plans were ridiculous. Lauren wanted him back in Vancouver, but what job she thought he'd get there eluded them both. In her refusal to visit him, her exact words had been ... *and stay in that shed you call a cabin? I don't think so.*

Robbie pointed into the sky as he tugged a small sketch pad from his pocket. He extracted a pencil from the coil binding, flipped to a blank page and began to sketch. An eagle circled above, visible through a rip in the mist. The quiet was broken only by the scratching sound of Robbie's pencil. Justin sipped at his tea and waited, but it soon became obvious the fog would not lift. His voice mirrored the disappointment on his face. "We'll try another day."

Robbie shoved his sketch pad back in his pocket. He got up, shouldered his pack and made his way along the path through the eddying mist. Justin took a moment for one last view of the higher summit. As he turned, he moved forward quickly and grabbed Robbie's sleeve. "Hey ... that isn't the path. Geez, you'll end up head over tail down the cliff if you aren't careful. It would be great if your sense of direction were as finely tuned as your animal intuition."

Robbie grinned, "I wouldn't need you then, would I?"

The climb down was steep in spots but safe enough, traversing along a wide ridge. When they came out on flat ground, the smell of damp foliage filled the air and the wind pushed at them like a battering ram. The sunshine that had mocked them as it glinted off the higher peak of the Cat's Cradle was nowhere to be seen.

Justin zipped his coat up snug around his neck and smiled down at Robbie, "Cold up here for the middle of May, hey? Good thing we're nearly there."

"I'll be glad to see your truck and those sandwiches Izzy packed for the way home."

As they rounded a corner, the faded black Chev pickup, solid and comforting, sat where Justin had parked it in a wide pullout off the gravel road. He still felt stunned when he thought about owning a vehicle. Coming back to Crater Lake, he knew he would need wheels if he was going to be job hunting. Money was the problem. He'd planned to borrow Liam's old truck. Hopefully, after a summer of work, he'd have enough cash set aside to buy something of his own.

The evening he had arrived, Izzy and Liam had taken him out to the driveway and presented him with the keys to the truck. Liam had smiled, laid a hand on Justin's shoulder and said, "A graduation gift, kid. You deserve it."

"We got Craig Sampson to check it out. It's in good shape even though it looks a bit the worse for wear," Izzy had told him.

Justin worked with Craig's son, Mike, at the sawmill and he knew Mike's dad wouldn't approve any vehicle that wasn't solid. But in that moment, as he gazed at his own truck, he admired it like it was a shiny new model straight off the lot. He had choked up with emotion when he tried to thank them. A gift like this was what parents might give to help their kid out and since he had missed out on so many family milestones, having Izzy and Liam on his side meant more than he could tell them.

TWO

S ophie made a face and pushed her plate away. "I only like geen gapes."

Liam took a sip of his tea. "They didn't have the green grapes at the store." He emphasized the *r* sound. "Only red this week."

Sophie's lip came out and a stormy frown pulled down her dark brows. Izzy put a banana on the table. "Today we have red grapes or a banana. You choose." Her voice was calm but no-nonsense. Liam had never acquired such a tone and he admired it.

Sophie looked from the grapes to the banana before she said, "I only eat these many wed ones." She picked out three and reached for the banana. Looking down at Dante, their copper-coloured Irish Setter, she asked, "Dante like these ones?" She pointed at the red grapes.

"Don't you dare." Izzy pushed Dante away from the table where the dog hung out whenever Sophie was eating. "I told you ... grapes are bad for dogs."

Sophie cocked her head to one side and narrowed her small dark eyes, "I thought you say geen gapes bad for dogs."

With forced patience, Izzy replied, "All grapes, okay? Let's get moving now. We all have things to do." She glanced at Liam and caught him grinning.

Rising from the table, he stacked the lunch dishes. "Come on, Sophie. Eat that banana. We're going over to see Grandpa Alex and Cynthia and if you behave, Grandpa says you can play in his bus."

Izzy was running water into the sink as she asked, "You remember that I have my first client this afternoon, right?"

"We'll stay out of your hair. Don't worry." Liam glanced out the large window that graced the front of their cabin. He gazed past the diagonal lines of cedar decking, beyond the undulating trail flanked by apple trees in full blossom, over the calm waters of Crater Lake to a spot in the distance where clouds circled the lower regions of the Cat's Cradle. "I'm betting Justin and Robbie didn't have any luck with their climb."

"They'll both be disappointed, if that's true. It's the second time they haven't made it to the top." Izzy glanced sideways so she could see Liam's face. "Robbie's decided not to go to school in Dearborn. What do think about that?"

"It's up to him, Izz." Liam pulled a tea-towel from the drawer and began drying the dishes that were filling the drainer. "If he says he's sure he wouldn't like it, we better take him at his word. I have no problem carrying on with homeschooling. I enjoy it."

"What about Tabby?"

"No reason she can't stay and do the homeschooling, too."

Izzy returned to the subject of Liam's younger brother. "Robbie's doing well now, though ... isn't he?"

Liam reached an arm around Izzy and hugged her close. "You know he is. Are you worried about going back to work?"

"No ... the last two years have been amazing, but I'm anxious to get back to counselling."

"That's who you are and we don't want your new office to go to waste."

The last six months of Izzy's two-year break from work had been dominated by renovations. She had decided to combine a private counselling practice with a return to part-time work at Micah Camp and that meant she needed a place to see clients. They had plans drawn up to add a second floor to the workshop-greenhouse structure. At the same time, she and Liam had decided to enlarge the cabin to accommodate the many people it now housed. The counselling space had come together in a satisfying and relatively painless way. The inside renovations had been another matter – phases of excitement had alternated with periods of hair-pulling frustration. From plans, to material lists, to lining up the contractors, at times it seemed that the job would never end. She had told Liam that if she had to hear Reg Compton, their general contractor, with that toothpick bobbing in his mouth, telling her one more time that delays were inevitable on a project of this sort, she might scream and push the guy off a nearby deck.

Liam had laughed and warned her that Sophie would not take kindly to such action. Reg was one of her best friends and his bobbing toothpick only added to his charm. She would run to Reg, shouting, "Weg, Weg." Then she would take his gnarled hand in hers and tour the new rooms telling him where her bed was going and her bookshelf and her favourite stuffed animals. The way Sophie hung on Reg's every word cracked them up. With rapt attention, she nodded at the right times as he explained to her how a new window would go in this spot or how they couldn't build the wall until they put in the wiring. Though Izzy may have found Reg to be a frustrating contractor, he redeemed himself when it came to Sophie.

The renovations were done now and Izzy couldn't be happier with the results. They had built onto the front of the cabin, adding a bedroom and playroom for Sophie. That allowed them to reclaim the sunporch where the child had slept since her birth. And they put in a second bathroom upstairs. Izzy had used the spacious upper loft as an office for years, but with the new counselling space completed, she was happy to move all work-related materials out of the cabin. The loft accommodated the bathroom with room enough left for a comfy sectional sofa for TV watching. And they hadn't needed to give up the second-floor view of the lake she had grown to love.

"All I have to do is round up a few clients," Izzy told Liam as frown lines gathered between her eyes. "Beulah thinks Bethany should talk to me. She's concerned about her."

"Bethany is struggling, that's for sure." Liam's voice was resigned.

They continued working side-by-side in silence for a few moments, both caught up in their own thoughts of their friends next door. After wiping up the sink, Izzy turned to lean against the counter. "Has your dad put the final touches on that library bus?"

"You'll have to see it to believe it. It's something." Liam dried the last plate and put it away in the cupboard. "All pine inside. He even fit a small wood stove in the thing."

"Did he leave that big bookworm mural on the side?"

Liam nodded, "He said he had too much work inside to bother with the outside."

Around a mouthful of banana, Sophie added her opinion, "I like the wom."

Liam shooed her from the table. "I know you do, kiddo. Go and find your coat and boots. I'll be right with you." He turned back to Izzy. "He keeps saying he's going to talk to us about the encampment he's putting together out there."

"I'm glad he plans to talk to us since this is our property."

"But we have so much of it, don't we?"

She laughed and kissed him. "True ... we do. What does he have in mind?"

Liam chuckled as he headed down the kitchen stairs, "Probably setting up a warrior rendezvous. You know dad."

Shaking her head, Izzy promised herself she'd talk over this camp idea with Cynthia sooner rather than later. She did know Liam's dad.

ᴥᴥᴥᴥ

Standing in the middle of the living room, Bethany frowned as she rubbed her fingers over her forehead. She couldn't figure out where she'd put Sophie's birthday present. Her gaze was caught by the view of Crater Lake from the wall of windows that graced one end of the A-Frame. She let the distraction of the afternoon light skipping over the water capture her attention. Caleb always said - *A view like this ... it puts everything in perspective, doesn't it.*

Tears filled her eyes and rolled down her cheeks. She desperately wanted that perspective. She reached for a Kleenex. She'd received the results from her breast biopsy a week ago. The letter Dr. Rosemary had given her was right there, tacked to the side of the fridge with a strawberry-shaped magnet. Benign ... nothing to worry about. She should be celebrating. Beulah was happy enough for the pair of them. And yet, any little thing these days made Bethany cry.

Sinking into a chair, she drew her knees up to her chest and stared out the window. Time went by, clouds sailed past and the sun, when it shone through, moved steadily closer to the far mountains. Eventually, the ticking of the clock sank into her thoughts. She took a moment to recall what she had been doing.

She located Sophie's gift on the shelf in the bedroom closet - a large, brightly coloured carrying case filled with crayons, markers and paints. Placing it on the table, she wandered through the kitchen pulling open drawers until she found scotch tape, scissors and a pen. She spent another ten minutes searching for the birthday card she had purchased the day before. Then she remembered it was still in her purse.

Staring at the table, she frowned - wrapping paper. She got down on her knees and dug through all the lower cupboards of the cabinet that stood by the wall. She was looking for the bin that held such things. Rocking back on her heels, she brushed her shoulder-length blonde hair from her face. Since returning to her life at the A-Frame from her small apartment in Victoria, she hadn't been able to lay her hands on a single thing. Beulah seemed to have moved or misplaced every item Bethany went in search of.

She located the bin on the shelf at the top of the broom closet. Back at the table, she chose a large blue sheet covered with arching rainbows. Her mother had loved rainbows. A small stained glass one had hung from the window of her mother's room in the seniors' place. It was now out in the bakery catching the stray rays of May sunshine and spinning them around the work space in a prism of colour. The tears started again and Bethany gave up the battle to control them. Going back to Kingston to bury her mother had been hard. She had felt weighed down by so many memories and few of them were good.

She had been surprised at how well-attended the funeral had been with folks from the home and a handful of her mother's Bingo friends – women Bethany remembered from when she was a girl. Somehow, her mother had managed to stay close to friends through all those years.

Bethany's experience had been so different. She had no living thread to connect her to the past. No one could bear witness to the girl who had grown up in the run-down house in Kingston. Her younger sister, the wild one, was long gone now. No one could corroborate her memories of the teen years of sexual abuse at the hands of the neighbour, Mr. Malone, for whom she babysat every weekend. No one could testify on her behalf to the unwanted pregnancy and the pain-wrenching delivery. No one could help her recount the revolving door relationships marred by so many kinds of abuse that had filled the years until Beulah found her and brought her here.

Bethany swiped at the tears on her cheeks. She had worked hard to put these things behind her. She was home; she had her life with Beulah, their organic bakery business and a host of opportunities in front of her. And she had her health. Beulah kept telling her that was all that mattered.

Leaving the wrapping paper and gift on the table, Bethany went to the bedroom and curled up in bed. She closed her eyes and drifted away into a familiar fantasy. By some type of magic, she could be someone else, living a different life, far from here, far from anything and everything she had ever known. To escape was all she wanted.

THREE

Alison pulled off the gravel road at the Micah Camp sign. She slowed the car to a crawl and set on the seat beside her, the map she had printed from one of Izzy's emails. The paved entry, just past the sign, led into a circular drive that widened in front of the chalet-style main building. Off to the left, a narrow service road wound its way past a maintenance shed and over to the Airstream travel trailer that was to be Alison's new home.

Deciding to park her car at the trailer rather than move it later, she pulled in beside the shiny bullet-shaped abode. It sparkled in the sunlight that flitted through the branches of the surrounding trees. She hoped the door was unlocked. Faced that morning with a less than clean bathroom at the *Dearborn Hotel*, she had skimped on her morning routine. She'd like to get in the trailer, have a long, hot shower and lie down for a nap. She hadn't slept well the night before. The bed had been so-so and night after night in strange beds was taking a toll on her. She got out of her car and went up the steps to a small porch that brought her to the trailer door.

The knob turned in her hand and the door swung open. Half-inside the entry, back lit by the slanting bars of sun wavering through the tree branches, she let her eyes adjust to the darker interior. She was so busy taking in the colour-coordinated, compact space that the sounds she was hearing didn't register. She stepped further inside and had a clear view of the double bed at the far end of the trailer; the curtain that separated the bedroom from the rest of the trailer was pulled aside.

Alison's brain lit up with information she felt incapable of decoding. She stared at the long, smooth back of a naked woman whose body was arched and whose firm buttocks slapped against the groin of the man she was straddling. A strange sound came out of Alison's mouth.

The woman twisted to stare over her shoulder. She froze, in mid-stroke. Her eyes met Alison's. Beneath the naked woman, the man's hips continued to buck and thrust. "Don't stop now. Are you trying to kill me?" He gasped out the words.

The woman whipped her head around and slapped at the body beneath her, "Jeremy, stop it. Stop. We have company." Swinging her leg over the man's body, she collapsed onto the bed. She jerked the corner of the bedspread to pull it around herself and over her head.

Alison clutched her hand to her chest and opened her mouth to speak, but no words came out. She gaped as she stared at the man's naked body spread-eagled on her bed. By the time her gaze had crawled up to his face, he had risen on his elbows to stare at her.

He came to life, vaulted off the bed and hopped from one leg to the next as he pulled on a pair of checked shorts. His head disappeared inside a fluorescent pink T-shirt he plucked from the edge of the small night table. The tight garment rode up his midriff. "Oh, Jesus," he gasped as he stared at her, "Don't have a heart attack. Calm down. I can explain."

Alison's voice screeched out at a pitch that could have curdled cream, "What are you doing in my bed?" The moment the words were out of her mouth she knew she sounded like one of the three bears. A hysterical laugh rose in her throat and she tried to choke it off.

The man moved forward a step towards Alison as he yanked his long, tangled hair into a ponytail. The muffled voice of the woman under the bedspread stopped him. "I thought you said she wouldn't be here until tomorrow?"

"Don't freak out. I'm a teacher here," he told Alison.

The woman on the bed rose onto her knees and the bedspread slipped to the floor. "Get my shirt off this minute. You'll stretch it out of shape," she shouted. "It's brand new."

Alison backed up with her hand up in traffic cop mode. All she needed was a whistle around her neck to complete the picture. Her back hit the door jamb. She turned and stumbled outside and down the trailer steps.

✻✻✻✻

"I won't do it and you can't make me." Tabby leaned a jean-clad hip into the counter and ripped at the peel of the orange in her hand. The bright-pink, striped T-shirt she wore set off her dark skin and spiral curls.

Brigit continued to bread pork cutlets and place them in rows on the tray in front of her. She did a mental count of how many more she needed. Micah Camp's thirty-six residents, young people who liked to eat, plus assorted staff meant a lot of food preparation. Without raising her voice to her daughter, she said, "Watch it, young lady. You're skating on thin ice with that tone." She took a deep breath, then added, "We can talk about it more tonight. I don't want a scene with you while I'm trying to work."

Tabby tossed her orange peels in the compost bin and banged the lid shut. "You can talk, but I won't be listening. I mean it, Mom. I'm not going to school in Dearborn and that's that. You'd have to drag me there by my hair every day." She popped a segment of orange into her mouth. With eyes flashing and nostrils flaring, she appeared to be daring her mother to come up with a response to that challenge.

Brigit's frustration with her daughter disappeared. Tabby looked the way she had when she was a toddler, stamping her small feet and demanding to have her own way. Brigit turned and busied herself covering the tray of meat with plastic wrap and moving it to the walk-in cooler. She didn't want to ruin the young girl's dignity by laughing. When she came out, she leaned against the counter and watched her daughter finish eating the orange. The two of them had reached a stand-off, no doubt about that. These must be what the magazines called the tween-age years. The way Tabby was behaving of late – the dramatic, all-or-nothing statements, the sulks punctuated by bursts of temper and the many door slamming exits – seemed more like a resurgence of the terrible twos.

The latest locking of horns between them was caused by Brigit's suggestion that Tabby should at least consider going to school in the community of Dearborn as opposed to carrying on with the homeschooling she had been doing at Crater Lake for the past two years.

In the turmoil of their arrival in this isolated spot, straight from a bustling Haitian community in Toronto, Brigit had been relieved that she did not have to cope with getting Tabby to and from Dearborn every day for school. And Tabby had thrived on the attention from the adults in the tight-knit community. Brigit couldn't complain about her daughter's progress. Liam was an innovative and creative teacher who used in his instruction all that the natural environment of Crater Lake offered; the tutoring Tabby and Robbie got from Gordon, the camp's math instructor, challenged both the kids to excel.

Academics was not the issue. Brigit studied her daughter's slim but maturing body and wondered how kids could grow up so fast. Lately, the idea that Tabby needed some girlfriends had captured Brigit's attention in a big way. The problem was that Tabby saw no need for any friend other than Robbie. Her refusal even to consider going to school in Dearborn was final, because Robbie wouldn't go.

Brigit had nothing against Robbie. He was a great kid. She saw as much of him as she saw of Tabby. The two were inseparable. They studied together; they had activities together. Tabby stayed at Robbie's; Robbie stayed at their house here at the camp.

Brigit hadn't given the relationship between the two of them a second thought until shortly before Tabby's eleventh birthday. Her daughter had her first period – an expected occurrence, one she had prepared Tabby for. Brigit wasn't an emotional, clingy mom, but she had caught herself feeling weepy over this rite of passage that marked the beginning of so many changes in a young girl's life. Her tears took a back seat to her surprise when she overheard Tabby telling Robbie the news. He had replied that he could tell something was different. Robbie had a keen intuition about people.

One day last year, when he and Tabby were passing through the kitchen, he had stopped and stared at Brigit. Then he had said, "What's wrong?"

Brigit would swear that she had done nothing to give away the fact that Tabby's grandpa was having bypass surgery that morning in faraway Toronto. She hadn't wanted to worry her daughter when the statistics pointed to a great outcome. She had said, "There's nothing wrong, Robbie. Why do you ask?"

Tabby had looked from Robbie to her mother and then both kids had leaned against the counter and stared Brigit down until she had told them everything. Later, as the two of them left the kitchen she overheard Tabby say to Robbie, "It was her light, right?" Robbie had nodded. The two of them had developed an obscure way of communicating that excluded the rest of the world.

Brigit's musings about Tabby came to an abrupt halt when a strange, panic-stricken woman careened into the kitchen. Her reddish hair was drawn up on the back of her head and a pair of glasses swung wildly on a beaded chain around her neck.

Brigit's gaze went from the distraught woman to Tabby. Mother and daughter stared at one another with the same look of startled surprise – their dark, sweeping eyebrows were raised on wide foreheads.

The woman choked out the words, "I'm looking for whoever is in charge. Your director, where is your director?"

Brigit walked over to steady the woman by taking her arm firmly above the elbow. "I'll show you to his office." She led the woman out of the kitchen, across the dining room and pointed down a hallway, "It's the glass doors on your right."

Roland rose from behind his desk as the woman pushed open the glass doors and came to a stumbling halt in the middle of his office. Nick Anderson, who had been in mid-sentence, frowned and closed the file in his hands.

Both men stared as the woman gasped out the words, "I'm Alison Kirk."

"Roland Campbell. You've taken us by surprise, Ms. Kirk. We understood you were not arriving until tomorrow."

Nick dropped the file on Roland's desk and moved towards Alison, speaking slowly, "Why don't you sit down, Ms. Kirk. You look as though you've had a fright. Can you tell us what's wrong?"

Alison stared back and forth between the two men. She stuttered out the words, "There were people in my trailer –,"

Roland did up the button of his suit jacket and stepped forward. "People? Why would there be people in your trailer?"

Alison's paleness began to suffuse with a deep-red colour that started below the neck of her sweater and rose in a steady wave over her face up to a point where it blended in effortlessly with the colour of her hair. "People ... people in the bed," she gasped.

Nick's frown deepened. His voice remained calm, "Is someone hurt? Did someone hurt you?" Alison stared at the floor but didn't answer one way or the other. She held a trembling hand up to her throat as if any further words would choke her.

Roland asked, "What were the people doing?"

A new wave of colour swept Alison's face and Roland gave an almost imperceptible shrug of resignation. "Were these people having sex?"

"In my bed, on my clean sheets," Alison whispered.

Nicks eyebrows shot up as he muttered, "Oh, for the love of God."

The sound of a quick knock preceded Jeremy's face peeking around the edge of the glass door to Roland's office. "Nick, can I talk to you out here in the hall?"

Alison visibly shook at the sight of Jeremy. As Nick left the office and disappeared around the corner, Roland directed Alison to a chair. "Take a seat, Ms. Kirk. I will attempt to get to the bottom of this situation." Roland excused himself and left Alison digging in her pants pocket for a Kleenex. Her red hair and the two bright spots of colour on her cheeks made her look surprisingly like a Raggedy-Anne doll.

Roland found Nick leaning against the wall next to Jeremy. He gazed at Micah Camp's computer tech teacher decked out in a scooped-neck, pink T-shirt that hardly reached his navel. Bold black print declared – *Yoga Moms Rock.* "What the hell is going on?"

Nick gestured with his thumb at Jeremy, "Out with it, man."

"It was me. I was in her trailer." Jeremy coloured slightly.

Roland stared at him, "In her trailer and from what we are to understand, in her bed on her clean sheets. This is your place of employment. I'm assuming you have your own home in which to conduct your sexual liaisons."

"The woman is one of my computer clients from Dearborn. She's married and I can't bring her to my place. I have my girls with me right now."

Roland shook his head in disbelief. "Get that ridiculous T-shirt off and escort your female friend off the property, immediately."

Nodding his head, Jeremy watched Nick and Roland walk away. He then turned and rushed down the hall for the side exit. The less time he spent in the building the better.

Pushing against the door, Jeremy almost bowled over the camp's French teacher. He watched helplessly as Paula stood staring at him. Her long earrings, bright-red twisting helixes, swung against her cheeks. The smile that had started to crinkle her dark eyes disappeared in a look of confusion. Jeremy slapped his forehead in frustration, once, twice, three times for good measure.

"Why are you wearing that shirt?" she asked him. She moved away from him and the door as she brushed a strand of dark hair from her face. "You look like a nutcase. Why are you smacking your head like that?"

There were no words. With hands outstretched as if he were the crucified Christ, he backed out the door, bowing like a court jester as he went; then he turned and ran.

Jeremy had been trying to land a date with Paula since the moment she started working at Micah Camp. He thought they had a lot in common. They were both single parents. He remembered meeting Paula years before, when she would come to the camp with her mom, Josie, who ran the paper and soap making shop. The business provided the camp residents with work experience. Back then, Jeremy had been one of those residents trying as hard as he could to get his life together.

So far, Paula hadn't given him the time of day. Jeremy supposed she considered him a once dorky kid turned equally dorky adult. She probably thought he was a total loser because his marriage had failed and he could imagine that her mother affirmed that idea. Instead, Paula had set her sights on Micah Camp's trauma counsellor, Nick Anderson. Jeremy would have bet his computer shop in Dearborn that nothing was going to come of her dream of landing that guy.

Well, any chance of picking her up on the rebound was down the drain. News of his little romp in the trailer was bound to spread around the camp like wildfire. All he could do now was try to mollify the woman he had left naked in the new career counsellor's bed and hopefully, in the process, find his own frigging shirt.

※ ※ ※ ※

After witnessing yet another of Tabby's dramatic exits, Brigit had settled down in the corner of the dining room with a cup of coffee. Roland came through the large doors escorting the red-headed woman over to a table that commanded a sweeping view of Crater Lake. He pulled out a chair and the woman sat down. Spotting Brigit, he walked over and gestured back to the woman at the table. "Do you have some time to keep our newest employee company? She's had a shock and she might be more comfortable debriefing with someone other than her boss."

Brigit stood up, nodded and crossed the room. She was burning with curiosity to find out what was going on. "Can I bring you a cup of coffee? Or maybe a pot of tea?" she asked.

The woman looked surprised and nodded, "Tea would be lovely. Thank you." She reached out her hand, "My name is Alison Kirk. I'm the new career counsellor." A tear formed at the corner of her eye as she spoke.

Before Brigit could return to the kitchen, Gordon came into the dining room. He sat down at the table and reached across to grab Alison's hand in a firm shake. "I gather you are the new career counsellor. I'm Gordon McKenzie, the math teacher." Alison's lack of response didn't faze him. He turned to Brigit, "Did you say you were bringing tea? I'll join you both."

Later, with the tea poured and a plate of cookies on the table, Gordon placed his cup on his saucer and looked at Alison. "You might as well come out with it. The place is abuzz with your entrance. Tell us what happened. You'll feel better if you get it off your chest."

Alison's lower lip trembled, but she took a deep breath as she met Gordon's gaze. "I have no idea why I panicked the way I did."

With Brigit and Gordon encouraging her, Alison told them what had happened. Brigit was hard pressed to hold a smile in check at the absurdity of the situation that Alison described. "Don't be so hard on yourself," she told the woman beside her. "You must have been exhausted from the trip ... being on the road all by yourself and staying in motels for days. No wonder you wanted to settle into your own place."

Gordon patted Alison's hand, "Obviously, it was a shock to walk in on such a scene. Jeremy is a generous fellow. He volunteers his time here, you know. But he did show an astonishing lack of discretion in this case." Alison's face turned a deep shade of red at the mention of Jeremy's name and Gordon patted her hand again, "Now, now ...,"

Brigit stood up. "I better get back to work."

Gordon followed suit. "I'll walk you to your trailer, Alison." At the startled look on her face, he said, "None of that. Best to get back on the horse that threw you. If you're planning to stay and work here, the trailer is to be your new home and I've heard it's quite nice."

Brigit touched Alison's shoulder and added, "Stop by the kitchen anytime if you want to chat. I live here at the camp with my daughter, Tabby. I'm sure we'll have lots of opportunities to get better acquainted."

FOUR

"The bishop stood by me. He sent me to a decent treatment program ... four months. But there's still more to get at. Drinking is always just a symptom." Izzy watched as the man across from her raised his eyes to hers. His were blue like the colour of the lake on a cold, bright-sky day – a blue so deep she had to look twice. He spread his hands in a gesture of acceptance before going on. "For me it's the loneliness. Occupational hazard. Loneliness seems to be an integral part of the priesthood." A rueful smile lifted the corners of his mouth. "I suppose it should be in the vows - something like - I accept the burden of isolation, the hours of unbroken silence and the weeks of solitary confinement inside the prison I must erect, brick by brick, around myself." He sat up straighter in his chair. "I've been a priest for fifteen years. I came at it as someone who had lived a full life – I'd been in the forces, worked a bunch of different jobs. I thought I knew what I was doing."

The unspoken question in his voice caused her to ask, "What made you choose the priesthood?"

"I grew up Catholic. The church meant a lot to me when I was younger. I drifted away in my teens." His expression was distant as he looked inward. "After I came out of the forces, I went to university. I was working on a degree in criminology. I was going to be a cop. Summers, I worked construction, flying in and out of small communities up in northern Ontario. Heading back to Eliot Lake on one of those trips, the plane went down." Izzy watched his hands tighten around the arms of his chair. "The pilot and the other guys from the crew were all dead. It was surreal ... I was hardly even injured. There I was, all alone, stumbling around outside, staring at the wreckage of the plane and those dead bodies and trying to figure out why I was still alive. To be

17

honest, I wasn't sure that I was. And I didn't spend more than a half an hour stuck there ... out of nowhere these quads roared up. Two guys were fishing at a nearby lake and had watched the plane go down." Kieran shook his head, "In the days after the crash, I couldn't stop thinking about why I had survived. Was it where I had been sitting? Something about the plane? There didn't seem to be any logical explanation. The fact that it made no sense bothered me more than anything else. So, I imposed my own order on it. I became convinced that there must be a greater plan for my life."

Kieran's mouth twitched up at the corner. "It sounds trite when I say it now and believe me, my spiritual director at the seminary practically laughed me out of his office when I told him I felt I had been chosen. I think his exact words were – *you and a hundred other psychotic misfits.* But I was in too far by that time. The church had become a comfort, so I stayed the course. After my ordination, my first posting was as a university chaplain. That ministry suited me. Parish life was more of a challenge." He gave a half-shrug before adding, "I suppose the drinking snuck up on me."

His last words faded away to silence. Izzy plumbed the space between them, gently – more by instinct than by using any method she could describe. The lack of words now felt comfortable, right for this point in the session. She allowed the silence to thicken and deepen – her body language remained open, her eyes were ready to meet his. As she waited, she let Father Kieran Galloway's presence in her new counselling space touch her. He was in his mid-forties. He had dark hair speckled with grey and slashing dark eyebrows. Deep frown lines formed between his eyes when he was thinking, as he was now. Dressed casually, in jeans and a pullover sweater, he didn't look at all like a priest.

His frown deepened as he rose from the chair to wander the large, second-story room that sat atop the workshop-greenhouse building. He stopped by the window to take in the view – into the greenhouse below, out over the expansive garden and beyond, at Crater Lake glistening in the afternoon light. The sound of chimes moving in the breeze came through a side window which was open enough to fill the room with the outdoor smell of growing things.

Izzy continued her silent vigil as the priest stopped to admire the art work on the walls. Turning to her, he said, "I saw my destruction coming from a great distance. I watched its approach with something I can only describe now as fascinated curiosity." He returned to his chair and looked at her with interest. "Have you ever been out on the open water in a small boat?" She shook her head. "When it gets rough, you watch the waves, slipping into the troughs and riding out the crests. You're waiting, wondering if the next one will be the one that swamps you. When that wave hit me, I watched the water pouring over the sides of my life. I gave myself up to it. I let it sink me." He paused and stared down at his hands. "I remember the strangest feeling then ..."

As his words stopped, Izzy knew this was a different silence – one to be probed. "What is it you remember, Kieran?"

"Relief. I surrendered to the inevitable and a crazy reveling in martyrdom – going down with the ship and all of that." He spread his hands again. "The relief soon gave way to less-than-salutatory feelings and behaviours. I thought the day I lied to one of the parishioners, telling him that the last three bottles of communion wine had fallen out of the box and broken on the floor of the sacristy, might be rock bottom; it wasn't. That came several Sunday's later when I got up to preach my homily. I pitched over the lectern and fell down the stairs that led up to the altar. I needed five stitches to close the cut I got over my eye when I hit the edge of the front pew." He pointed to a scar that snaked across the top of his eyebrow. "I'm sure old Mrs. Craig is unlikely to forget that experience. She always got to church early to grab the front pew." He lapsed into silence.

"You mentioned that the loneliness of your life contributed to the drinking. Is there more to it than that?" Her tone of gentle curiosity took any confrontation out of the question.

He exhaled a deep breath and stared out the window. "Yes, of course."

"Are you ready to delve deeper?"

"Yes, definitely. One of the first items on my list of things to do when I arrived in Dearborn was to find a counsellor. I wasn't sure who would be available in such a rural area, but your credentials plus the fact that you're out of town and not part of the parish make this arrangement a perfect fit for me." He smiled and his face changed completely. Any trace of self-pity or gloom was banished in the way a stiff breeze could send the clouds scudding off into the distance. He was an attractive man. "It doesn't do for the priest to air his dirty laundry in front of the congregation," he added with a twinkle in his blue eyes.

Izzy acknowledged his humour by returning his smile. "I've got a few forms for you to fill out before we finish up today's session. I'd like to take time now to hear about strategies you remember from past counselling."

"You want to know how I'm coping." His face took on the thoughtful look she had already seen several times in the past hour. "I need to make connections with people in the parish and the wider community. I'm working on a plan for that. I'd be content to sit down with a good book in the evenings, but I know I need to accept invitations, join some groups. The daily running I do helps with a variety of issues. And I like gardening."

Kieran got up, walked to the window and swept his hand out to indicate Izzy's garden. She rose to join him. "What you have here is amazing. The yard around the rectory in Dearborn is a mess. I understand the last guy was getting long in the tooth for outside work and he didn't like anyone else poking around. There used to be a greenhouse, fruit trees, some decent perennials, but it's all overgrown now."

"It's always nice to meet a fellow gardener, if only to be in touch with someone who understands the work involved."

Looking down through the glass to the interior of the greenhouse, Kieran said, "Your bedding plants are huge. Did you buy them in Dearborn?"

"No ... we had a stretch of great weather in February and I was off work then so I planted everything from seed. Now that I'm back to work here and at Micah Camp, the gardening must take a backseat. I should have had a bunch of those planted outside by now."

"What is Micah Camp?"

"It's a residential care facility that specializes in working with young people transitioning from high school to the next stages of their lives."

"Where is this place?"

Izzy laughed, "A convenient location for me. Just down the road." She walked back to her desk and located a sheaf of paper, "After you've finished filling out these forms, I'll give you a tour of our garden. I have two rhododendron cuttings ... one is the most gorgeous cotton-candy colour. They're all potted up and looking for a new home and you'd be doing me a big favour if you took a few of those bedding plants off my hands.

⚜⚜⚜⚜

Kieran pulled his car into the open carport attached to the mobile home that served as St. Bertha's rectory. Contrary to what several of the diocesan priests had told him, the trailer wasn't akin to a railway transport car. An older fellow had pulled him aside and assured him that a city parish would never consider housing a priest in a dwelling better suited to a refugee camp. Well, Kieran had his own ideas about the priests who hung onto the plum parishes in the city, lining their pockets with the stipends from funerals, weddings and baptisms and spending their spare time on the golf course.

This place suited him. He'd made do with less. The rectory was a modern two-bedroom home with a side addition that contained a large porch and an office where he could meet with parishioners. It was next door to the church and it sat on a good-sized lot on an upper level of Dearborn's tiered town. He had a great view of the ocean waves rolling along like Royal Lipizzaner stallions, flinging their manes out in the strait beyond the harbour.

He hauled the rhododendrons and the tray of bedding plants Izzy had given him from his trunk to the run-down greenhouse in the corner of his yard. The door of the small building was hanging on its hinges and a few panes of glass on the windward side were missing. But the concrete floor was solid and the benches that ran along each side of the six by ten structure were in good shape. He spent the rest of the afternoon outside, working and stopping occasionally to enjoy the view. A neighbour's old tom cat sat on the top of the fence and watched him with typical feline disinterest.

In the shed he found a pile of scrap wood and a roll of plastic. He'd brought his own tools and he was glad about that. He wouldn't have wanted to rely on the random assortment he found scattered around the shed. He did some preliminary work on the greenhouse door, knocked together a few wood frames, stretched the plastic over them and set them in where the greenhouse glass was missing. He had located a hose which he hooked up to the tap on the side of the trailer and ran into the greenhouse. Next, he rolled the lawnmower out of the shed and set to work tuning it up. He'd get the grass cut the next day.

It wasn't until much later, when he was sitting in his quiet living room after turning off the evening news, that he thought about the something more that had contributed to his drinking. He had lost Sean and he couldn't come to grips with the gnawing emptiness and the guilt that his brother's death opened in him.

Growing up, he and Sean had been close – barely eleven months apart in age, they shared a bed for all the years Kieran had lived at home. They hadn't had an easy childhood with a father who drank and a mother who struggled with depression. Too many times, the food was scarce and complaints were met with a thump to the head. Kieran was always running interference for Sean and giving over half of whatever was his for his brother. He couldn't remember ever loving anyone else in his whole life.

He hadn't wanted to go into the forces because of having to leave Sean; his excuse was ridiculous and they both laughed about it. They were grown men, after all. But the years they had gone their separate ways had not proven kind to his brother. Sean had bounced in and out of employment; he was constantly broke and down on his luck. He died in a downtown Toronto flophouse protecting a young girl from her pimp. The guy had pulled a knife, stabbed Sean and left him to bleed to death in the dirty hallway.

Kieran had travelled to Toronto to bury his brother. He presided at the funeral Mass himself. The church had contained a handful of people who had called Sean friend. They shared stories that depicted a man who had died as he had lived – a friendly guy who was always willing to lend a hand. Kieran had preached on the gospel of John, chapter fifteen, verse thirteen. *Greater love has no one than this: that he lay down his life for his friends.*

His words seemed to resonate. Months later, he received a letter from the girl Sean had died to protect. His willingness to stand up for her and the price he paid had turned her life around. She was off the streets, cleaned up, back home in Hamilton and working at a Tim Hortons. She thought he might want to know. Like maybe Sean's death meant something.

Sean's death had meant many things. Kieran's grief and guilt became the pry bar that opened the doors of the past and each one led deeper and deeper along the dark hallways of his mind. Drinking became a handy and necessary solution.

FIVE

Mike watched as Wynter swiveled the ring on her third finger so it glittered in the candlelight. She gave a satisfied sigh and raised her eyes to meet his. Empty dessert plates and coffee cups littered the white linen on the table at *The Sea Shed* restaurant. Leaning toward him, she whispered, "I'm so happy. Promise it will always be like this."

"I'm glad you're so easily pleased." Mike's eyebrow quirked up at her as he added, "We're living in my parents' basement and sometimes my mother makes me so angry that I stomp out in the middle of dinner. I sure hope things are going to get better than this."

"I'll get your mom to like me. You'll see." She sat back in her chair. "Are you sure about having Justin for the best man instead of Zach?"

Mike made a face as he dug in his pocket for his wallet. "Like I want that showboat brother of mine stealing the limelight at my own wedding. No thanks. Justin's a good friend and I want him to stand up with me. Zach can be an usher."

"And what are we supposed to do about Lauren?"

"If Justin wants to bring her, he can. But the way I hear it, they're fighting all the time."

"I wonder how it will be with Lisa-Marie as matron of honour and Justin as the best man. She never talks about him. I think they must have fallen out somehow."

"Well, I don't think it would be any better for her with Zach as the best man. She did dump him a couple of summers back. The whole group of them can get over themselves for our sake. How does that sound?"

Wynter grinned. "Sounds good to me." She reached for her sweater from the back of her chair. "I have something I want to show you. Can we drive down Beach Road when we leave here?"

"It isn't even dark yet and we do have a nice bedroom." He dropped some cash on top of the bill. "Even though it is in my parents' basement. We hardly need to drive down Beach Road."

"Oh, you're a funny guy." Wynter nudged Mike in the ribs as they left the restaurant. "Just drive. I'll tell you where to turn."

Staying with his parents was a concession he had made to his mom who had looked aghast at the idea that he and Wynter would get their own place before they were married. What would people at the church think? Mike didn't give a damn what anyone thought; but all the same, he had given in to her suggestion that Wynter stay with them.

It had been too much for him, though, when his mom had suggested Wynter occupy the spare twin bed in his sister Hannah's bedroom. Mike's dad had intervened, throwing his hands up in frustration and stating in no uncertain terms – *it's up to Mike and Wynter to decide where she sleeps and Helen, you and I can either respect their decision or watch them find somewhere else to live.*

For all the good will of Mike's gesture, his concessions weren't yielding any results. His mother was driving him around the bend with her conviction that Wynter wasn't the girl for him and with her nonstop meddling in their wedding plans.

Wynter pointed and said, "Here, right here."

Mike signaled and turned the truck into the driveway of Dearborn's only mansion, an iconic place known as the Lady Brit. As he opened his mouth to speak, Wynter held her finger to his lips, "Shush ... enjoy the show."

Light flickering off the ocean waves in flashes of molten yellow deeply tinged with red, set the house ablaze in tone upon tone of gold. The cedars that marched at intervals along the edge of the property leading to the beach slowly darkened to black as the sun disappeared behind the mauve-tinged mountains.

Mike stared across the truck at Wynter. "Okay, the sunset was something. But why are we here?"

"Do you know why they call this place the Lady Brit?"

"Never thought about it. I know some crazy guy barged this whole damn thing up here in the 50s. Must have had more money than brains."

"This house was built in the early 1900s. It's in the colonial revival style and has been kept in stunning condition. The man certainly had money. He was one of the first independent loggers in the area. He had the house moved here for his wife."

"Oh, let me guess. Her name was Brit."

Wynter smiled, "Britannia to be exact. He must have loved his wife very much. After he died, she kept the place up for ages. When it got to be too much for her, one of their kids ... an architect ... came up with the idea of dividing the house into apartments and selling them separately. It's run like a co-op."

"Parking here feels creepy." Mike glanced around. "We look like peeping Toms."

Wynter went on as if he hadn't spoken. She pointed to one side of the large, dark entry, "There are two apartments on that side. Dr. Rosemary lives in the top one. The bottom unit is owned by one of the forest companies and they use it as a guest house so no one's even living there most of the time. The architect kept the entryway and the grand staircase intact. You access all three units from the original foyer. The apartment on the other side is both floors, three bedrooms and three bathrooms, plus that large attached gallery on the main floor that you can see off to the side."

"You sound like a real estate agent." Mike felt his face settle into a frown. He tried to relax, took a deep breath and went for a neutral tone. "What are we doing here, Wynter?"

Reaching in her bag she drew out a set of keys, opened the truck door and got out. "Come on. I'll show you."

Moments later, standing in the empty half of the converted mansion with the last light of the day streamed through the large windows and making the hardwood floors gleam, Wynter leaned back against an arched doorway and took Mike's hand. "You can see why I fell in love with it, right? The minute I saw it, I knew we had to live here."

With hard-to-conceal admiration, Mike ran his free hand along the solid wood banister that graced the curved stairway. Working at the sawmill since he was a kid, he had become familiar with wood. The wide crown moulding that circled the high ceilings, the decorative wainscoting that gave way to glossy white paint shining even in the low light of evening ... were all real wood, beautifully maintained. He could only imagine how the place would look with sunlight streaming through the windows. They were saving to buy a house in Dearborn. But the type of house he had in mind bore no resemblance in size, stature or price to the Lady Brit. "This place must be worth a fortune. How on earth did you end up getting the keys?"

"I was ordering a cappuccino at *The Kitty-Cat Café*. That big marmalade tabby was sleeping right in the front window. I adore that cat. We should have at least two cats." Wynter paused to grin at him. "Anyway, I was supposed to meet your mom and the lady from the florist to talk about flowers for the wedding, but they weren't there yet. Instead, I spotted Darlene sitting with some woman whose outfit screamed real estate. They were talking about the Lady Brit."

Mike tried to focus on what she was saying, but as she wandered the large room twirling strands of her thick wheat-coloured hair through her fingers, he was swept by the white-hot urge to grab her and make love to her. She was beautiful. This feeling was quickly replaced by one of disbelief that he was engaged to marry Wynter Snow – a girl whose photo had graced the pages of several magazines.

There was nothing special or even particularly noteworthy about him. He worked at *Crater Lake Timber*, just a regular guy who never went to college. He rarely left his small town, hadn't seen much of the world. He'd spent his life playing second fiddle to his popular, younger brother, Zach.

From the moment he began dating Wynter, Mike hadn't been able to see how a guy like him had any future with up-and-coming fashion model, Wynter Snow. As the time for her to embark on her exciting career had approached, the whole interlude of having her in his life began to seem like a bad joke – one with him as the tired punchline ... *left behind Mike.*

On their last date before she was to leave, while they were parked down here at the end of Beach Road in the same truck he drove today, he had told her that they should break up. A long-distance relationship wasn't for him. Her talk of coming back to visit and having him come to see her was nothing but that – just talk. He had told her, "Those possibilities are things a girl like you says to a guy like me. You want to let me down easy."

He remembered the silence and the shocked look on her face and the large tears that had slid from her eyes. She repeated his words – *a girl like me* – and asked him what kind of girl he thought she was. Did he think she would sleep with him and then run off and never think of him again? Didn't he know she loved him? Didn't he love her? She assured him that nothing he could say would make her even consider breaking up with him.

He let her assure him that she'd only be away for a year, though he believed that the day he said goodbye to her was the last day he would ever see her. But she kept in touch, she invited him to come to Cuba for Christmas ... she was doing a photo shoot there. Wynter let him see that the job of modeling was nine parts hard work and one part glamour and she kept right on loving him. His memories of their time in Cuba could leave no doubt on that score. If ever there had been a honeymoon before any talk of a wedding, Cuba had been that for them.

After one year, as she had promised, she came back to Dearborn. That first night, at the same table they had just occupied at *The Sea Shed*, she had asked him quite pointedly – *what comes next?* He had asked her to marry him and she had said yes. The smile on her face lit up the whole restaurant.

He tuned back into her words. "You know the way all the streets here are tiered down towards the beach? I've seen the roof and the top of the Lady Brit from the sundeck of your parents' house – the sweeping roof lines and the matching chimneys and the way the sun gleams off the upper windows. I was always curious about this place. It seemed too grand for Dearborn, but as soon as I saw it close up, I realized that it belonged utterly to this stretch of beach."

She walked over to him, took his hand and led him through the arched doorway, into the gallery with its bank of windows facing the water. "When I realized that Darlene was talking to the real estate woman about the Lady Brit, I listened in. The woman said that half the building – a huge apartment – was going for a song. It had been on the market for over a year with no takers. I sat right down with them and asked the price." She smiled as she wrapped her arms around his body and snuggled close, "The woman was pretty scathing to me. She said, in this snotty voice ... *We aren't talking about a rinky-dink apartment. This is half of a fully restored heritage building – almost 3000 square feet. I'm sure it is out of your spending range.* Darlene cracked up. She told the woman ... *Best listen to this young lady. The way I understand it, she not only has drop-dead looks but she's got some money stashed away, too.*"

Mike watched the waves crashing up against the nearby beach and smiled at the perfect way Wynter imitated the real estate lady's high-pitched voice and then Darlene Evan's booming one. His mom always said there wasn't much about Darlene that didn't boom. Mike had known her for years. She was a town councillor; her husband had been the mayor of Dearborn when Mike was growing up and Darlene also served on the Micah Camp Board of Directors. She had been a steady presence at the many meetings his mother hosted around the dining room table of their home and when he was at work at the sawmill, he'd seen her coming and going to meetings at the camp.

"I want us to buy this place." Wynter's serious tone made him consider Darlene's remarks about Wynter's stashed away money. The money she had from her grandmother was something he tried not to think about. He found it hard enough to wrap his mind around the reality of marrying a girl who looked like Wynter without throwing in the fact that she was a wealthy catch.

He pulled her close and slid down the wall to a sitting position on the floor holding her tightly against him. He stroked her hair and when he spoke, he was only stating a fact. "You want us to buy this place with your money. That's what you really mean because we could never afford it with what I've put aside and on my wages from the sawmill."

He felt her body tense. She glanced up so she could see his face as she spoke, "You always said I was to make my own decisions about that money and my decision is that it is our money. Why shouldn't we spend it on a beautiful home?"

Trapped by his own words, Mike took his time responding. "I wanted you to have that money in case someday you changed your mind ... about me."

She sighed and cuddled close to him. "Oh, Mike. Just tell me ... do you think you could love this place? Can you see us living here?"

Mike nudged her off his knee and levered himself up the wall. He grabbed her hand to pull her up beside him and then walked back to the windows. They could hear the waves crash against the beach and then the crunching, slithering pull of the small rocks being tugged back by the surf. He reached over and tipped her face up to his. "Everything great in my life happens when I can hear the sound of the waves." He smiled at her, knowing she was remembering the camping weekend out at Side Bay on the west coast, the first time they had made love. "My dad always says – *happy wife, happy life.* You love this place and it will make you happy. Given that, I'm positive I'm going to love it, too." He drew her into his arms and kissed her. As she stepped back, he frowned. "How we'll explain this to my mom, is another thing."

Wynter laughed and the sound bounced off the walls of the empty room. "You worry too much about your mom. Come on, I know you're anxious to pick Zach up and get out to Crater Lake for Justin's Friday night poker game, but first let me show you the bedrooms." And the sexy way she looked back at him as she led him up the stairs to the second floor of the Lady Brit left him no doubt as to what her showing might involve.

SIX

Lisa-Marie pushed Tyler's arm away. It had come to drape over her at some point since he had conked out. As usual, he was hogging most of the bed. She sat up and pulled a sheet over her naked body. Her heart-shaped face settled into a frown as she looked back at the man in the bed. His muscled, well-proportioned form was laid out in all its splendour. She wanted to feel like the earth shook when they were together and sometimes she came close. She knew her friend Maddy would raise an eyebrow at that remark and tell her ... *close isn't exactly the point, is it? You're not playing a game of horseshoes.*

Lisa-Marie brows drew together with irritation as she gathered up her clothes and headed for the shower. Later, wrapped in a silk robe she had picked up in Rome from the discards of Wynter's photo shoot wardrobe, she curled up in a chair near the window and reached for her iPhone from the edge of the table. She texted Izzy to let her know she would be there first thing in the morning and to thank her for having the red Jeep left at the *Dearborn Hotel.* From the window of the hotel room, she could see her vehicle sitting in a lonely corner of the parking lot. She had avoided spending time at Crater Lake for most of the last two years, but now, when going home was so close, the desire to be there was almost more than she could bear.

She glanced over at Tyler. Being in Dearborn with him was an opportunity that had come up quickly and was too good to pass up. She had met Tyler in Rome. At the end of her internship year in London, she had picked up some freelance photography work with a travel magazine. When Wynter's modeling schedule brought her friend to Rome, Lisa-Marie flew there and they spent a wonderful few days together seeing the sights.

29

One afternoon, Tyler, a fellow Canadian, had gravitated to their table at an outdoor sidewalk café where she and Wynter were drinking wine and enjoying themselves. He was a hot-looking, black guy from Vancouver who was straight off a job with a film crew that had been doing a documentary about the Coliseum. The three of them had gone dancing with a bunch of other people and, at the end of the night, Tyler had insisted that Lisa-Marie call him whenever she got back to Vancouver. Since they were circling the fringes of the same business, maybe they'd be able to help each other out. This final comment had been accompanied by an irresistible come-on smile.

A couple of months later, back in Vancouver, she had called him. They had met up at one of the many coffee shops that lined the streets near Maddy's west-end apartment where Lisa-Marie was staying. Maddy was conveniently away on one of her regular trips to San Francisco to be with Jesse. Tyler told Lisa-Marie he'd had a tip about a director who was looking for a rugged, pristine wilderness location for a movie. A brutal bear attack seemed to figure prominently in the plot. Tyler wanted to draw up a proposal for scouting locations on the Island. He'd heard a crew had already been chosen to look at settings in the Rockies.

In the sidewalk café that afternoon, Tyler had dropped his closely cropped head into his hands and moaned. When he raised his coffee brown eyes to meet Lisa-Marie's, he admitted, "I want to do this, but I'm shit at pulling a proposal together and I don't know anything about the Island." He suggested they team up. He'd do the filming; she'd do the photos. She assured him that the north Island could be perfect. The day ended with the two of them in bed and she didn't regret it at all.

They got the job, largely based on Lisa-Marie's organizational skills and photos, but she had to admit that Tyler's tight jeans and T-shirt had appealed to one of the two guys doing the hiring. Tyler knew how to play that up and his tactics hadn't hurt. Such was the business, it seemed.

Since that first night, she and Tyler had spent most of their time together. Right before coming to the Island, they had stayed at a rambling house rented by a foreign film crew. They were a raucous group and the house was party central. She was okay with their accommodations; her travels in Europe had gotten her used to bedding down in odd locations. She was careful to turn a blind eye to the times Tyler disappeared with various friends. She knew lines of cocaine would be on any surface they could find. That was his thing and she had no plans to become his keeper.

She took her battered journal from her bag. Opening it to a blank page, she began to write.

30

Dear Emma:

I know what you're going to say ... I should be sleeping. It has been a long day. First ferry out of Vancouver, the drive up the Island, all the location stops. I got some amazing photos and I think Tyler's film footage of the logging road out to Zeballos has quite an eerie quality. I could almost see a scary bear attack happening on that road.

I can't sleep. I'm sick to my stomach with wanting to see Sophie. It's always like this when I've been away from her for a while.

And, to be honest, I'll be glad to take a break from Tyler.

I know ... it's more than that. Justin's at the lake and I can't have Tyler around when I see Justin again. It's all too awkward.

Lisa-Marie tapped her pen against the page as she read over the last words. Her gaze strayed out to the parking lot and she watched a man with his arm around a tipsy woman in heels heading for a truck. The woman was laughing as she leaned into the man. Lisa-Marie remembered her seventeenth birthday celebration right downstairs in the *Dearborn Hotel* bar. It had been Justin helping her to the car after she'd had more than her share to drink. So many memories of Dearborn and Crater Lake included Justin.

Staying away for the last two years had been about avoiding him. She still burned with humiliation when she remembered how she had begged him to choose her and not Lauren. But the night Lisa-Marie had spent with Justin – a night when the earth did move – hadn't mattered to him at all. Her pleas had fallen on deaf ears. He had stayed with Lauren.

According to Maddy that decision was costing him. Lauren was all wrong for him and Lisa-Marie had told him as much. She hadn't returned to Crater Lake the past summer when she knew he would be there, asking instead that Izzy bring Sophie to Vancouver. She recalled with pleasure the wonderful month she had spent alone with her daughter in Maddy's apartment, swimming at nearby English Bay and playing at Stanley Park. She had come home with Sophie only when she knew Justin would be back at university. But he was finished school now and had moved into Liam's old cabin for good. There would be no avoiding him.

She closed the journal and tucked it back into her pack. She wanted to do what all the self-help books advised – let go of the past; move forward, not backwards. How could she do that? Everything about going home to Crater Lake connected her to the past like a chain that, link by link, bound her to the place and the people she loved.

Getting up, she stretched and returned to the bed. She nudged Tyler with her hip to get him to move. Regardless of what was to come, she couldn't wait to be home.

⚶⚶⚶⚶

Mike and Zach, each loaded with a six-pack of beer and a grocery bag of assorted snacks, clumped down the overgrown trail, along a worn boardwalk that led to the cabin Justin had stayed in every summer for the last three years. Knowing that their approach up the steps and across the creaking boards of the covered porch was announcement enough, Mike opened the door without knocking. From behind him, Zach called out in a loud voice, "The Sampsons have arrived. Let's get this poker night happening."

Justin rose from the rocker by the unlit woodstove. "About time." On his way to the table, already set up for the night's poker game, he added, "Ethan's been salivating like one of Pavlov's dogs waiting for the two of you to show up with the food."

Ethan laughed as he rolled up his sleeves and adjusted the green visor on his head, "More like panting at the thought of the money I'm going to be taking off the bunch of you he-men losers." He crossed over to the counter and dug through one of the grocery bags. "I hope you got the gluten-free pepperoni this time."

Mike shoved Ethan out of the way with his shoulder so he could get to the fridge. "Ya, ya ... we got your special-order text message." He twisted the cap off a beer, grabbed a bag of chips and headed for the table. "Reg's truck is still up at the sawmill and the light's on in the office. What do you suppose he's doing there so late?"

Digging into a bag of pork rinds, Zach spoke through a mouthful, "We gotta get a work party together one weekend and come out here to help you clean up that trail, Justin. It's a mess and you've got a couple of punky boards on the walkway and a loose step." He took the deck of cards and started shuffling.

Ethan divvied out the poker chips with one hand and pointed from Justin to Mike with the other, "Reg told me you two guys are a couple of lazy assholes and because of the pair of you screw-ups, he has a bunch of paperwork to do."

Pouring a generous slug of vodka into his plastic Star Wars cup, Justin topped it with 7-Up and headed for his spot at the table. "Without Mike and me, Reg would be chawing on that toothpick of his so hard he'd crack his jaw." Sitting down, he asked Mike, "How come you're late?"

Grinning, Zach poked Mike in the ribs, "Ya, big brother ... tell them why we're late?" He smacked the cards down on the table for everyone to cut for the deal. "It sure wasn't my fault. I was ready on time."

Mike took a long pull from his beer. "Wynter wanted to show me an apartment she has her eye on." He won the cut and began to deal.

Zach elbowed Mike again, "The way the two of you looked when you came in, I don't think it was just an apartment she was showing you." Sorting through his cards, Zach said, "First he stomps out in the middle of dinner and drags Wynter with him. He leaves us stuck with Mom ranting and raving. Then he comes back a couple of hours later looking like he's died and gone to heaven."

"Give me a card," Justin told Mike. "Where is this apartment?"

As a card slid across the table, Mike said, "It's in the Lady Brit."

Justin whistled softly, "That big mansion down on Beach Road?"

Moments later, fanning his winning hand out, Ethan reached for the pile of chips in the center of the table. "A mansion would suit Wynter." He looked over at Mike. "You're hitting way out of your league, man. There's no easy way to say it."

Zach crunched up the pork rind bag and threw it into the garbage can near the table. "Mom will blow a gasket when she hears you guys are buying such a fancy place."

A frown chased across Mike's face, followed by an angry shake of his head, "I guess if it was any of her business, I might give a shit."

Ethan smacked a card down in front of Mike. "As exciting as your family life is ... and believe me, I'd love nothing better than to discuss your mama all night ... we're here to play poker, so let's get on with the game."

A few hours later, with empty beer bottles littering the counter and a large pile of poker chips sitting at Ethan's elbow, he stared at Justin and said, "Answer her text or turn your frigging phone off. That chirping is driving me nuts." Ethan chomped off a chunk of pepperoni. "Why do you keep reading all the shit she's sending you if you don't plan to answer?"

Justin turned his phone off and tossed it in a high lob over their heads towards the sofa. "Satisfied?" He stared at Ethan for a moment before he said, "Just another day in paradise, my friend."

Mike waited for Justin to finish topping up his glass from the vodka bottle on the edge of the table before he said, "This paradise of yours ... the seismic activity seems to be getting serious."

Drink in hand, Justin reached for the cards. "A guy as happy as you are right now, Mike ... I'm not going to talk to you about how fucked up a relationship can get."

Ethan chugged his beer and said, "At least you have a relationship. I have come to the sad conclusion that I am not going to meet Mr. Right at Micah Camp." He grimaced, "Or even Mr. Right for the night. Two years of watching couples hook up and head down to the boat shed is starting to fray my nerves."

Eyeing Ethan, Justin said, "Why the hell are you still there? Most kids are on their way out of Micah Camp after a year. Don't get me wrong ... Reg will be headed for his coronary way faster without you working in the sawmill yard. And, aside from the irritating fact that you almost always win, you're an entertaining guest on poker night."

Picking at the label on his beer bottle, Ethan said, "It's a good thing for you I'm pretty loaded right now. I'm sort of sensitive on the subject of my extended stay at the camp and I wouldn't want to have to punch you for bringing it up."

Zach chuckled, "You're a cheap drunk, Ethan. What have you had ... three beers?"

"I'm wiry, boyfriend. I don't have the hollow leg and fat head you do." He put his bottle down and crossed his arms over his chest as he rocked back on his chair. "I can't get into a decent dance school no matter what the hell I do and my parents said I had to stay at Micah Camp or move in with one of them. Since I don't have any money of my own, except what I make at the sawmill and take from you guys, it's Micah Camp for me." He batted his lashes, "Not while I have a breath left in my beautiful, gay body would I move in with either of my parents."

"For your information," Zach told Ethan, "Me and my fat head are doing just fine."

Mike eyed his brother, "Ya, right ... installing internet satellite dishes makes you a regular captain of industry."

"It's a step on the way, bro." Zach tipped up his beer to drain the bottle before he added, "Hey, did you guys hear that Lisa-Marie is working with some film company that's scouting for movie locations up here." Mike glanced at Justin and saw his jaw tighten. Zach kept on talking. "I saw Lisa's Jeep parked at the *Dearborn Hotel* this afternoon but didn't see her around. Apparently, she's all hot and heavy with this black dude she's working with ... name's Tyler."

A well-placed kick under the table had Zach turning to his brother and asking, "What the hell?"

Justin sat forward and stared at Zach. "Lisa-Marie told you that?"

"Well ... she didn't exactly tell me."

"Then how are you so well-informed?"

"Facebook, man. It's all out there on Facebook. I'm not sure how you resist it."

Justin drained his glass before responding. "I don't want to know what I don't know, Zach. That's how."

SEVEN

R oland studied the amber-coloured scotch that rolled around the bottom of his glass. "What on earth could that woman have been thinking to blaze a trail across the entire camp in such a state? I confess, the way she looked, my first thought was that she'd come upon a massacre."

Nick relaxed into the armchair across from his boss. "Izzy recommended her for this job, right?"

"All I can say is that Ms. Kirk's credentials checked out."

"You'd think a trained counsellor could tell the difference between a crisis and a roll in the hay." Nick stared at Roland for a moment over the rim of his glass. "You joke about a massacre, but things like that can happen when you least expect them and getting information as quickly as possible can save lives."

Nodding in agreement, Roland took another drink. Nick had a point. Three years ago, not so long that Roland was likely to have forgotten, a gun toting young man had stalked the whole area bent on killing his ex-girlfriend – a Micah Camp resident. His hostage taking at Izzy's cabin and the death that followed, proved that bad things could happen – even in a quiet, wilderness setting like Crater Lake. "I don't mean to be facetious, Nick. I understand that crisis situations occur."

Nick finished his drink and asked, "Did you see Jeremy's partner in crime?" He smiled. "She certainly filled out that pink T-shirt better than he did."

Roland reached for Nick's glass and from the kitchen where he was doing the honours, he heard Nick ask, "How are you adjusting to the bachelor state? Where is Jillian off to this time?"

Returning to the room, Roland said, "University of Toronto. She's teaching right through to the end of the summer. It will play havoc with her writing and she'll be a wreck when she returns. She hates teaching." He gave a hidden sigh of relief at Jillian's extended absence. Since the moment she arrived at Micah Camp, Jillian had been a force in Roland's life that he was relieved to put on hold now and then. He settled back in his chair and changed the subject, "How is your research going?"

Nick had managed to bargain his graduate thesis on school shootings into a published book deal and lately, had submitted it for entry into a PhD program at UCLA. Roland listened to his response. "Izzy's return to work is good timing for me. I want to be on campus down in California for part of the summer.

"Sounds like you might have another book deal in the making." Roland spoke in a matter-of-fact way. Succumbing to anything like professional jealousy was pointless. Research on trending and often grisly topics was currently the rage in academia. He responded to Nick's indirect request for time off. "I see no problem with your taking unpaid leave." Changing the subject, he asked, "What's happening with you and our French teacher. She couldn't take her eyes off you at the last staff meeting. I hear through the resident grapevine that you two are an item."

"I was worried this would happen." Frustration settled like a shroud over Nick's face. "I've been out with Paula a couple of times ... nothing serious from my side of things. Then out of the blue, I got an invitation to dinner at Reg and Josie's. I tried to get out of it, but it's not like you can make up an excuse around here. Everyone knows what everyone else is doing."

"Awkward ..."

"I'll say. Between Reg swearing like a trooper and going on about board foot price of lumber, Josie grilling me like she was doing a job interview and everyone mooning over Paula's little boy ... it was a long evening." Nick gulped at his glass as if to erase the memory. "I have nothing against kids, but I don't see myself in a step-daddy role. It's obvious Paula's looking for more than I am. I'll have to find a diplomatic way to extract myself from the whole thing."

Roland pointed his glass at Nick to emphasize his words, "Diplomacy is the key, Nick. I do not want to be looking for another French teacher. They're hard to come by."

Nick's changed the subject as he said, "Is it your understanding that we're at the end of all this expansion? Don't get me wrong ... I love my new cabin, but living in a construction zone for months on end is getting dreary."

Roland couldn't have agreed more. In two years' time, Micah Camp had gone from eight resident cabins to a dozen. Nick should appreciate his new cabin. The building was nicer than Roland's. Even the cook had a larger place than he did. Unexpectedly, she had brought a daughter along with her. Retaining a cook who was willing to live at Micah Camp was something the Board of Directors did not take lightly. They were more than willing to shell out the funds to provide her with decent accommodations.

The small cabin their previous cook had occupied – the one Jillian had first stayed in and converted to a research office when she moved in with him – had been renovated to be used by guests or staff members who had to spend the night. Roland had suggested that the new career counsellor move in there. Darlene Evans, Micah Camp's Board Director, had other ideas. Instead, she recommended that Roland give up his cabin to the career counsellor and move into the luxurious suite on the second floor of the main camp building. He had refused to consider such an idea. He valued his privacy far too much to live in the same building that housed offices, classrooms, dining and recreational facilities. To say nothing of thirty-six residents coming and going at all hours making the place, as Darlene was fond of reminding them, *just like home*. The airstream trailer had been Darlene's plan B.

With the increasing number of residents, the changing selection mandate, on-going funding concerns and resolving staff issues, Roland had enough on his plate to welcome a break from dealing with contractors, tradespeople and the endless mud. "From your lips to God's ears," he told Nick as he finished his drink.

❧❧❧❧

As the credits began to roll and the haunting music took over, Robbie hit the stop button on the DVD remote. Tabby frowned at him from the chaise lounge of the u-shaped sectional sofa and clasped her hands over her heart. "I love that movie and that song."

He knew she did ... geez, this must be the fourth time they'd watched *Titanic*, both dutifully covering their eyes for the nudity during the painting scene. Robbie knew Tabby cheated every time, though, not because he cheated but simply because he knew. He grinned over at her, "I still say she could have moved over and let him on that chunk of wood." He leaned back and pushed Dante with both hands. "Get back to your own spot, you mutt." He softened the command with a vigorous scratch behind the dog's droopy ear.

"He'll never move if you pet him." Tabby plopped over onto her stomach and let out a huge sigh. "Rose's mother was so bossy. Reminds me of someone I know." She cocked her head to one side and put her finger to her lips, "Shhh ... did you hear Sophie?"

Robbie pushed Dante back again and rolled off the sofa to spring up on his feet and walk over to the railing. He looked down to the main floor of the cabin and across to the stairs that led to Sophie's new bedroom. He didn't hear anything. Izzy and Liam were out on the cliff deck and they'd asked Robbie and Tabby to keep an ear out for Sophie. "Nope, nothing." He returned to the sofa and threw a pillow at Tabby. "Your mom's not bossy."

"Ya, easy for you to say. She isn't forcing you to go to school in Dearborn."

Robbie brushed Tabby's concern aside. He didn't want to think about anything changing. "Tell her why you don't want to go."

Resting her face in her hands, Tabby stared at him and he watched as the light around her shifted subtly, changing colours. She was upset now. "My mom doesn't understand. She doesn't notice the way people look at us." She glared at Robbie. "Don't even say it. *They might be staring, but it doesn't mean anything.* They stare at us because we're different and it will be even worse at school."

Because of the staring, he'd had to tell her about the way he could see light around people. The light – so many patterns and colours – told him what people were feeling. For as far back as he could remember, he'd been able to do this. She had thought people stared because they didn't like her and Robbie, didn't want them around or worse yet, wanted to hurt them. Most of the time, the stares didn't mean any of those things. Robbie was First Nations and Tabby was black and together or separate, they stuck out in the town of Dearborn. Even the kids on the reserve in Cedar Falls stared because Robbie was Mi'kmaq and Tabby was as different at the reserve as she was in Dearborn.

One day, Tabby told Robbie's dad how the native kids stared at her. She didn't get it. Why would people who got stared at themselves stare at her? Alexander had laughed and said – *we Indians are an equal opportunity people. We're likely to stare at anyone who hasn't been in our family back a few hundred years. It's a matter of survival.*

The reality of being different was the reason he and Tabby were content to stay put at Crater Lake. No one stared here because, in one way or another, everyone stuck out.

Tabby rolled over to her back and looked up at the sloped cedar ceiling over her head. "Do you ever think about your mom, Robbie?"

"Ya ... not like every minute or anything, but I don't ever want to forget her." His mom had died when he was eight. She drowned when the lobster boat she crewed sank near their home on the reserve in Burnt Church. He'd never even met his father before the day Alexander had shown up at the reserve after the funeral to pack Robbie up and bring him across the whole country to live with Robbie's older brother, Liam. And Izzy. He remembered those early days when he had hurt so much with missing his mom. He'd had nightmares of drowning. But then at the end of the weary days of travel, he found Izzy and she had his mother's light and he could breathe again. It wasn't the home he had known, but it was enough like coming home to help.

"I wish I knew who my dad was." Tabby sighed again. "My mom won't ever talk about him and that isn't fair. I mean I could pass him in a store or something and not even know him."

"I don't think you need to worry about that in Dearborn."

She tried to give him a stern stare, but soon they were both grinning. "Hey," she said, "do you remember when we were at my grandparents' house in Toronto last summer and practically every person on the street was black like me?" He nodded and she said, "I bet one of those men was my dad." She paused before asking, "We belong here, right?"

Tabby had asked this question of him since the early days of their friendship. Asking was like the way a troubled kid would touch a rock in her pocket for comfort or sing the verse of a familiar song in the dark. "Yes, we do." He jumped off the sofa and stretched. "Izzy says you can't sleep in Lisa-Marie's room tonight because she's cleaned it all up and changed the sheets."

"I've got my sleeping bag, I'll sleep here." She sat up and looked around the room. "It sure is different up here now with the bathroom."

"By different you mean great, right?" He headed for his room, calling over his shoulder, "I'll sleep out here, too. You use the bathroom first and I'll grab some pillows." Stopping in the narrow hall that led past Lisa-Marie's room to his own, he stared across the railing to the large windows at the front of the cabin.

Watching him, Tabby asked, "Is there an animal out there?"

Robbie laughed, "Nope, just squirrels in the roof again."

❧❧❧❧

Izzy glanced at her phone and then tucked it into her shirt pocket. "That was a text from Lisa. She'll be here first thing tomorrow. She's says thanks for bringing the Jeep in for her."

Liam squatted near the small chimney stove that sat on a square of raised firebricks in the corner of the cliff deck. He set a chunk of wood on top of the embers and rose to rub his hands free of debris. He leaned against the railing and checked the metal sheet that circled the back of the stove. Frowning, he glanced over his shoulder to Izzy sitting on the swing bench that dominated the center of the deck. "I'm going to have to spend some time repairing this. The metal sheeting is coming loose in the corner."

As he sat down on the swing, Izzy stared at the chimney stove that Caleb had gotten for her so many years before. "I wonder if it's time to replace the whole thing. We could put in a sort of semi-circular stone fire pit and carry the brick right up the back." Izzy stretched her legs towards the fire. "I'm sure we could find someone in town who does brickwork."

Liam draped an arm around his wife and pulled her close. "Haven't had enough contractors wandering around here yet, hey? Speaking of building projects, the plans for Sophie's play house came in the mail today." He chuckled as he said, "I think it incorporates all her requests."

"A boat with a sail and a flag and a slide and two swings underneath, one with a tire."

Liam laughed, "All included, but I nixed Robbie's idea of a zip-line from up behind the koi pool to the play house."

"I guess more building means Reg will be hanging around again."

"You know Reg ... he'll be around to deliver the wood and I've got to get him to bring the machine down to clear a spot behind the kitchen. For the actual building, Justin and I will be able to handle most of the work." He stared at the flames licking up around the log in the fire. "I'm worried about Reg."

"Worried he might choke on his toothpick or swear himself into a stupor?"

"He's working long hours at the sawmill and he seems more obsessed than usual with production. I mentioned the other day that he's getting a bit old for tromping through the woods with a chainsaw and he said – and I quote – *do you think a fucken thing is going to get done right around here if I don't do it? I don't have time to waste on molly-goddamned-well-coddling old-man arthritis or the shit storm coronary Josie says I'm bound to have.*"

"Sounds like Reg. He's been tromping around the bush most of his life. I'd be more worried about the guys that work there and have to put up with his badgering every day than I'd be about Reg."

Liam knew that despite Izzy's disparaging remarks, they'd both been grateful when Reg came along to manage *Crater Lake Timber*. After Caleb died, the woodlot and sawmill had suffered and Liam wasn't the type of guy that could make the business the going concern it had been. He had given it a try, that first year when everything seemed in danger of falling apart, but he was no Caleb, though he now lived in the house the man had built with the woman who had been his wife. One of Caleb's favourite baseball expressions came back to Liam – *life does have a way of throwing those old curve balls.*

The pumpkin orange glow of the fire spilled heat and light over the small deck. The sound of sap popping and sputtering filled the still night. The cliff deck, cantilevered out over the dark waters of Crater lake, felt like a cocoon sheltering them from the blackness beyond where mountains met water with no defining line between the two. Leaning forward to poke at the flames with a long metal rod, Liam asked, "Are we ready for Sophie's birthday party?"

"I think so. Beulah is picking up the cake from Helen tomorrow. I need to wrap Sophie's gifts. I thought I'd wait for Lisa to do that with me." Izzy shook her head, "Liam, how on earth can Sophie be three already? It seems like only yesterday we were waiting in the hospital for her to be born."

Liam remembered how, three years ago, the reality of Sophie had almost rolled him down like an animal caught in the high beams of a transport truck. Before he and Izzy had been together, he had succumbed to a weakness other men would probably understand though he surely hoped most wouldn't condone. He had known the morning after, before the cold grey light of dawn lit the sky outside his cabin, that what he had done was wrong.

Lisa-Marie, not even seventeen years old, had paid a huge price for Liam's failure to find another way to help her the night she had shown up by his bed, naked and distraught. That price was Sophie. When Izzy first discovered the truth, before they knew anything about a baby, her judgement of his behaviour had been as severe as Liam thought it would be. Somehow, they managed to weather that storm and start a relationship.

When a pregnant Lisa-Marie had shown up on their doorstep, Liam had nearly lost his way. Izzy had been the one to step up to the plate. She had done everything in her power to help. Having forgiven him for the couple of hours Lisa-Marie had spent in his bed, Izzy felt no need to throw the consequences of those hours in his face. He had been stunned by the degree to which she met every challenge with grace and generosity. She nurtured Lisa through the latter stages of her pregnancy, the labour and delivery like the girl was her own daughter. And she opened her arms to the baby. All she had asked was that the two of them adopt Sophie – make the child their own. And though he owed Izzy much, he hadn't been able to agree to that. He could never be part of taking Sophie from her mother, even though that's what Lisa-Marie seemed to want at the time. And that, too, Izzy got over.

Against all odds, the whole group of them had become a family. He and Izzy began caring for Sophie, allowing Lisa-Marie to return to the life of a high school senior and later, to follow her career dreams. They made it possible for Lisa to be a part-time mother to her child. And into that mix, along came Liam's father with Robbie in tow. *Here's your little brother, Liam.* Izzy had taken Robbie in, too.

Liam had much to be grateful for and he did what he could every day to honour that reality. Family had come to him in his late forties and he cherished each moment of it. As his thoughts gathered around that idea, he said, "I'm glad Fiona will be here soon. I've missed her."

Izzy snuggled close against Liam's side, "When I saw Rosemary last week, she sounded confident Fiona can handle anything the medical practice throws her way. Do you think she'll arrive in time for Sophie's party?"

"She wasn't sure the last time I talked to her. I notice you made sure to get your appointment in with Rosemary before she left."

Izzy shifted on the swing chair so she could look up at Liam, "Fiona hasn't been a doctor for very long. And she's your sister. I prefer to be poked and prodded by the doctor I'm familiar with." Settling back against Liam, Izzy said, "I wonder what happened between her and Nick. I know he visited her when she was finishing her internship time on the downtown east-side, but he never mentioned her again after she left Vancouver to go back to Toronto for her residency. That silence says a lot. They may not have parted on friendly terms."

"She's hardly kept in touch with any of us, Dad included. He threatened more than once to fly out there and see her, but she always said the same thing – she was busy with work."

"Becoming a doctor is time consuming. I wonder if it will be awkward for Nick ... Fiona coming back here."

"She'll be busy and staying in town so I can't see how they'll have too much to do with each other."

"Unless he needs a doctor," Izzy told him. "I heard that he's had a couple of dates with Josie's daughter, Paula."

"She used to come to the camp with her mom all the time, right?"

"Yes ... now she's our French teacher."

"Are she and Nick likely to turn into anything?"

"I doubt it ... she doesn't seem his type." Izzy reached for the large teapot at her feet, covered in its thick, cable-knit cozy. "Want some more?" she asked Liam. He held his cup out and she refilled it and then her own. "Alison is due to arrive this weekend. I'm looking forward to working with her. A career counsellor for the camp is long overdue."

A breeze had come up, rippling over the water and rhythmically lapping small waves against the rocks below. They finished their tea and the fire burnt down to a bed of shimmering red edged with gold. Izzy shivered and wrapped her sweater around her body. Liam glanced at the watch that he'd worn every day for the last four years – it had been Caleb's and the weight of it on his wrist was a daily reminder of the times spent with the best friend he'd ever had. "It's getting late. Is Tabby staying over?"

Izzy rose from the swing bench. "Yes, and I hope Robbie told her to stay out of Lisa's room. I don't want to remake that bed." Walking back to the cabin with Liam at her side, she stopped suddenly. A scrabbly, scratching sound echoed down from the dark side of the cabin ahead. "Did you hear that? Those squirrels are making that roof into their own personal townhouse."

Liam chuckled, "I thought you had made your peace with life in the wilderness."

"Squirrels are rodents. You know that, right?" She shrugged with what could be construed as resignation; Liam knew her better than that. Sooner rather than later, he could imagine them contemplating a roofing project. Approaching the back steps, Izzy said, "You take the dogs out while I check on the kids."

"It will take me awhile. Pearl is having a hard time with the stairs. It would probably be faster to carry her up and down, but she won't let me. She looks at me like I'm betraying her and the other day she growled at me when I tried to help her."

Izzy stopped and wrapped her arms around him, molding her body close to his and rubbing the small of his back for a moment. "None of us is getting any younger, that's for sure."

EIGHT

Lisa-Marie left a note for Tyler on the night table, stopped for a large coffee at the Petro-Canada on the way out of Dearborn and made the tight turn onto the gravel road to Crater Lake before seven a.m. The road cut a swath through trees that reached for the rose-tinted sky on one side and a sea of green branches that banked down cliffs on the other. As her Jeep rounded sharp corners, sparks of light off the moving water below glittered in her eyes.

Braking suddenly, she watched a deer and two dappled fawns skip across the road from the cover of the trees on the high side. They disappeared down the slope as if they had never been there. She gripped the steering wheel a bit tighter and gave thanks that the drive had become familiar enough for her to enjoy but not so familiar that she let her attention wander.

The trip brought back a host of memories. Liam had taught her to drive on this road. She had sprawled in the back of Izzy's Highlander clutching her hand and timing labour contractions as they bumped along this road to get to the hospital in Cedar Falls. She and Wynter had seen a cougar right around this corner one night when all Wynter could talk about was whether Mike would ever notice her.

Lisa-Marie was sixteen the first summer she came here. She had been shuffled off to stay with Auntie Beth and her partner, Beulah, because her grandmother could not deal with a suicidal teen. She had met Justin and imagined she'd found something worth living for. He had been near the end of his time at Micah Camp and was working in Izzy's garden. Liam had given Lisa-Marie a journal which she named Emma after a feisty heroine of classic literature. She had filled the pages of her diary with dreams of Justin. One

45

night, when she finally acted on her feelings and lured Justin down to the beach, he had pushed her aside, called her a kid. In desperation, she swam out into the cold, night waters of Crater Lake. After she managed to get back to the shore, she had really messed things up when she demanded from Liam the only kind of comfort she understood. But she couldn't think of that night as a total mess because then she would wish it had never happened and then she wouldn't have Sophie. Events, like a row of dominos, stretched behind her; if she removed one tile, they would all go down.

Nearing the top of the steep drive that led to Izzy and Liam's cabin, she passed the chain link fence that barricaded the yard around *Crater Lake Timber*. She could hear no whirring of large saws this early in the morning; except for the ever-present sound of the squawking stellar jays, all was quiet. Gripping the steering wheel, Lisa-Marie maneuvered the Jeep down the hill that ended in a tight hairpin curve before the roadway straightened out. The trees, tops swaying in the breeze, formed a canopy leading her forward. Moving light flashed and hinted at the lake beyond.

It still took her by surprise when she passed the drive that veered off to the left. The sign at the T crossing was new. Mounted on a gnarled chunk of old wood and pointing down the road towards Cynthia and Alexander's cabin, it read – CRAZY HORSE WAY. Under, in smaller lettering were the words – WELCOME TO THE SALTBOX.

Pulling the Jeep in next to Izzy's Highlander, she could see Caleb's old Dodge – a truck Liam would never give up – and next to it, the newer GM Sierra Izzy had forced him to buy. The familiar vehicles were joined by a black Chev she'd never seen before. She let out a deep breath as if a part of her that was pushed down deep whenever she left here could finally be released. She was home.

She filed away for later contemplation her impression of the new top floor to the workshop-greenhouse along with the images of the early morning dew clinging to the muted pink, red and coral rhododendron flowers. They rested amid waxy leaves on bushes that rose out of the garden at regular intervals like heavily bejewelled ladies. Some were squat and wide while others towered high with arms waving. They begged to be photographed, but that would have to wait.

She avoided the cabin's main door off the garden that would have had her creeping past Liam and Izzy's bedroom. Instead, she crossed the drive, ran up a few steps, passed the koi deck and entered the cabin through the side door to the kitchen. Everything was quiet inside as she had hoped. She took a moment to catch her breath as she stared at the lake through the geraniums that bloomed in luscious disarray all along the window ledge. She walked through the galley kitchen, glancing quickly up the stairs that led to the upper floor. Her room would be ready, the yellow walls and the sunflower bedspread would bathe the space in a warm glow of colour.

She walked down the three stairs that led to the main floor and caught her breath. The sunroom, straight ahead through the French doors at the end of the dining room, was back to looking as it had the first time she'd been given the grand tour of the cabin. She quickly scanned the inviting collection of comfy chairs, cushions and hanging plants. One summer, the sunroom had served as a photography workroom for Edward, Izzy's father. Next, it had become Sophie's nursery.

Before heading through to the living room, Lisa-Marie leaned close and stroked her finger across a small indentation in the frame on the door that led to the sunroom. The bullet that killed Edward had lodged here in the wood. Her heart twisted as she remembered the kind, older man who had accepted a hugely pregnant young girl into his space, who had encouraged her to follow her dreams of being a photographer and who had helped launch her on her fledgling career.

She walked on into full view of the newly completed renovation. Along the front of the cabin, the entire length of the living room, ran a wood railing giving way in the middle to three wide stairs that led down to the new playroom and Sophie's bedroom. The floor-to-ceiling glass that had once formed the exterior wall was gone; the open concept and tall windows in the playroom helped to compensate for the loss. She took in the room with its assortment of toys – a mini kitchen complete with oven mitt hanging from a hook, a small table and chairs, a colourful plastic castle, a doll's cradle and high chair. Bins lined one wall and a shelf overflowing with books lined another.

She tiptoed down the stairs and across the playroom to the bedroom door, nudging it open with a gentle push. Sophie's fine, black hair fanned out across a pillowslip adorned with fish swimming in a sea of bottle green. A large mural covered the wall behind the bed – an under-the-sea cornucopia of fish and shells and a forest of green upon green seaweed. Pearl, Liam's golden retriever, lay asleep on the carpet beside Sophie's bed. The dog had been her daughter's faithful companion, guardian and sometimes nursemaid since Sophie had been born. Pearl opened one eye and her nose twitched while a low whine of recognition escaped her mouth. Squatting down for a moment, Lisa-Marie kneaded behind the dog's ear in slow circles. Pearl had also been her first companion at the lake.

Standing up, she noticed the framed photo on the night table – she and Sophie were building a castle in the sand near English Bay. They were looking up with big smiles and the ocean and clear blue sky were rolling away behind them. Lisa-Marie slid under the covers and spooned close to her daughter in the bed. She breathed in the Sophie smell that in these first moments of coming together threatened to overwhelm her with emotion – love and wonder and loss all mixed with equal doses of guilt and joy. The child stirred and muttered something under her breath as she turned. Her eyelids fluttered but allowed only a glimmer of the dark-as-midnight eyes beneath. The sweeping arc of her perfectly formed eyebrows rose as her arms stretched over her head and she yawned widely. She stared and whispered so softly Lisa-Marie had to lean in close to hear, "Mama ... it is weally you?"

Lisa-Marie blinked away tears. "Yes, baby. It is really me."

Sophie's arms went around her mother and she burrowed her body close. They held each other tightly for a moment and then Sophie pulled away to reveal a big smile on her face. "Izzy tell me you coming to my pawty. And," Sophie paused for emphasis before she said, "her say you binging me pesents."

She grinned at Sophie's inability to get around the *r's* and leaned in to tickle the child, "Yes, tomorrow will be your birthday. Lucky girl. And there will be lots and lots of presents. How old will you be?"

"I be this many." Sophie studied her hand as she raised three fingers and held two down with her other hand.

❧❧❧❧

The cabin was swept clean of the previous evening's male debauchery. With the door open to air the place out, Justin sat on the covered porch. He angled the lawn chair so he could catch glimpses of the lake through the thick trees. One of the first things he wanted to do around the place was thin out the trees that obscured his view. He needed more light. He had big plans for the cabin and his future.

Zach's idea of a work party was a good one. He could get one of the fallers from *Crater Lake Timber* out at the same time. He'd get the trail cleaned up, fix the boardwalk and repair the back stairs. Eventually, he wanted to close in the porch he was sitting on, knock out the cabin wall and turn this space into the kitchen. Then he'd need a new deck. He'd make sure it wrapped around the front of the small cabin and cantilevered out over the cliff. For all of that, he'd need money.

He glanced up at the satellite dish Zach had installed on the side of the cabin. They'd had to choose the spot carefully to get a sight line through the trees. He frowned. The dish meant he now had internet, telephone service and the ability to text and fight with Lauren at any time of the day or night. Talk about a mixed blessing.

Going over the litany of problems he and Lauren were having was pointless. Their relationship had somehow jumped the rails of the shared track they had been travelling and now they were each moving along what seemed a parallel route. Whether they would get back on the same track or whether the rails would veer further and further apart, Justin couldn't predict. One thing he now knew for sure was that the track they had shared for the last three years was her route, not his.

In his peripheral vision, he caught the flash of a squirrel's tail bouncing across the faded boards of the deck. Seconds later, the only evidence of the animal's existence was a rippling of branches in a nearby tree and the squirrel's chattering backtalk as it scurried higher.

He recalled Zach's words from the night before about Leez. Her actions were none of Justin's business, period. End of story. He hadn't seen Leez for almost two years and though, in those first months after they parted, he'd tried to call, text and email her, she had never responded. And since the mere mention of Lisa-Marie's name made Lauren bitchy cold and over-the-top sarcastic, he stopped trying to make contact.

One day, in a fit of guilt, he had confessed to Lauren about the night he had come back to his cabin convinced that she was cheating on him. He described how he had drunk too much and slept with Leez. Huge mistake ... telling Lauren ... and he guessed that sleeping with Leez had probably been a mistake, too. Lauren threw his infidelity in his face over and over while clinging self-righteously to her own virtue. It crossed his mind, on more than one occasion, that she might not be as innocent as she let on. But to accuse her would only bring a screeching tirade down on his head. She'd say – *isn't it just like a guy to accuse his girlfriend of what he himself is guilty of?*

He pushed thoughts of Lauren and Leez out of his mind and reached into his pocket for a folded envelope. A couple of days ago, Beulah had caught him as he left the sawmill and handed him a bunch of mail. Among the flyers and junk, had been this letter. He smoothed out the paper and studied the name above the return address – Dr. L. Michaels. He went inside and put his coffee cup in the sink. He pulled on his shoes and tugged a sweater over his head.

Shutting the cabin door, he walked down the porch steps and headed out on the trail that ran along the cliff. Crossing the bridge over the tumbling water that dumped into Crater Lake, he walked by Izzy and Liam's guest cabin and carried on to the edges of their huge garden.

Izzy was on the path, wearing work gloves, shoveling bark mulch out of the wheelbarrow and dumping it around the base of a large rhododendron bush. Without allowing himself the time to reconsider, he cleared his throat loudly to get her attention. When she turned with a startled look on her face, he said, "I have a problem that I need to talk about. You're looking for counselling clients, right?"

Izzy pulled the gloves off her hands and smacked them on the side of her leg a few times. Several expressions flitted across her face. After a moment, she nodded slowly and said, "This isn't my usual work attire, but okay."

Following Izzy, Justin went through the door of the new covered entrance on the side of the workshop. As she led him up the staircase, he recognized the mobility seat that Izzy's father, Edward, had used to move up and down to the sun porch. It was firmly attached to the wall on the far side of the staircase; its metal gliding track shone in the light that came through windows that marched along the length of the wall near the exposed beams of the roof. Those beams carried on into the large, bright room over the workshop.

Izzy headed towards a door on the far side of the room. "I'll just wash my hands. There's a small kitchenette right behind that screen. Fix yourself something. I got a fancy, new coffee machine the other day. There's cream in the fridge."

Justin punched a Tim Hortons coffee pod into the machine and while the hot water whooshed into the mug, he wandered out into the large room. He'd never seen the garden or the lake from this height. The view was stunning. The attention to detail in the room made his mind veer back to ideas for his cabin. From the warm tones of the cedar on the ceiling, to the tall windows; from the muted shades of the carpet, to the neutral colours on the walls that served as a backdrop for the framed Monet posters – everything worked together to please the senses and calm the mind.

He was admiring the view when Izzy joined him with the coffees. "Shall we sit?" she asked him.

As he settled into the wing-backed chair across from her, Justin said, "I'll pay you for any sessions we have." He frowned for a moment before adding, "How much does counselling cost?"

"I'm not going to take money from you." Izzy sipped her coffee and smiled. "You're family. You can be my first pro bono client." She looked at him for a moment. "The whole family thing is an ethical issue. Let's say ... as an example ... that you had come to discuss Lisa-Marie. It would be hard for me to remain objective."

"Well, no problem, then. I'm not here to talk about Leez."

"Okay," she took a deep breath. "Before I review confidentiality, I need to check in with you about how we left things at the end of our last counselling relationship."

Her gaze was level, her tone reassuring and Justin was surprised that even though so much of his and Izzy's lives had changed over the past four years, he still cringed with a stab of humiliation at the way his younger, vulnerable self had fallen for her. She had taken the lion's share of the blame for the situation – telling him that it had been her responsibility to confront what was happening. She hadn't because she had enjoyed the attention he paid her. That admission should have helped but it hadn't.

His silence now didn't seem to faze her. She went on, "I also want to clear the air about the resentment you had towards Liam and me when you found out about Lisa's pregnancy. We've never discussed that either. I think time has resolved both situations, but if we're going to embark on a new counselling relationship, I don't want to make assumptions."

"I made my peace with Liam long ago. I don't accept all of his actions but, hell ... I don't accept all of my own when it comes to Leez either; so who am I to judge?"

Izzy nodded, "And what about me?"

"Those times were so long ago ... everything has changed. I'm here because counselling helped me before and I need help again." He pulled the envelope out of his pocket and tapped it against his leg. "I got this letter last week." He passed it to her. "It's from my mom's psychiatrist. A couple of months ago, they put my mother on a new medication and she's come out of the fog." Izzy examined the return address on the envelope before she pulled the letter out.

Justin got up and paced in front of the windows as Izzy read the short letter. His hands clenched at his side, he was blind to the rippling blue of the moving water out on Crater Lake. The sound of Izzy refolding the letter brought him back to the present and he returned to his chair. She passed the envelope and its contents back to him as he said, "My mom hasn't known anyone or responded to anything for almost ten years. After all this time, she's ...," he unfolded the page in front of him and focused on the words, "... aware of her surroundings." He glanced up at Izzy, "That's got to be awful. I've been to that place where they warehoused her and it is stark." He stuffed the letter back into the envelope. "She remembers the accident, she knows that Angie's dead and she's asking about me." Gripping the arms of the chair, Justin shook his head in disbelief, "I'm not supposed to try to see her, she's not ready. Who the hell is this Doctor Michaels to tell me that?"

Izzy leaned forward, "Okay ... take a deep breath. Let's talk about that." She waited a moment for Justin to regain his cool. "The doctor says you can write ... your mother wants to hear from you. It sounds to me like she's worried about you. She's got to be struggling with an emotional overload – grief, guilt, shame."

"What about me? I want to see her." He knew he sounded like a little kid, but he couldn't help it. "I've wanted that for so long. The possibility of seeing my mom again was the only thing that kept me going all those years in the group homes."

"That's normal. Reading between the lines of the psychiatrist's letter, I'm wondering if she thinks your mom is in danger of relapsing if the emotional load gets too intense."

"I can't just go about my life like nothing's happened." His knee had started to jitter.

Izzy got up and went to her desk. She pulled a pad of paper and a pen from the drawer. "No, you can't do that, I agree. You need to write your mom a letter." She pointed to the chair by the desk, "Sit over here and start writing. This isn't the letter you'll mail, okay? This is where you'll write out everything you feel – good and bad. Later you'll write the real letter."

While Justin poured out his heart on the paper, the sound of the pen scratched along. As he wrote non-stop, slashing out some words and writing in new ones, Izzy finished her coffee and enjoyed the sound of the wind chimes out in the garden.

Raising his head after about twenty minutes of frantic writing, Justin ripped a sheaf of pages from the lined pad and folded the bunch in half. He came back to his chair and slumped into it. Izzy smiled, "Feel a bit better?" To his nod, she added, "I'll get in touch with Dr. Michaels and explain that you're in counselling with me and ask for any other information she can give me about your mother's treatment plan. There's no guarantee she'll say anything, but it's worth a try."

"That would be great. I thought about phoning the doctor's office, but I wasn't sure I would be able to stop myself from blasting her."

"Well, that wouldn't help. Let me handle it. Spend some time reviewing what you've written here today and figure out what you need to tell your mom. Come back and see me next Saturday and we can talk about some of the feelings that came up on those pages. By then, I should have heard from Dr. Michaels one way or the other." As they both got up, Izzy made a face, "I forgot to go over confidentiality with you. I'm rustier after two years off than I thought."

Justin smiled, "No problem. I remember the spiel."

As she walked him to the door, she asked, "You'll be at Sophie's party tomorrow, right?"

"Wouldn't miss it. I got her this cool aquarium for her bedroom with some flashy Angel fish. Hope you and Liam don't mind."

Izzy smiled, "Not at all and Sophie will love it."

❧❧❧❧

"You neva catch me, Mama." Sophie's voice rang out and her high-pitched giggle preceded her as she hurtled down the garden path. With her head turned to watch behind her, she ran right into Justin.

"Whoa, there." He swept the child up into his arms and followed her gaze to the bend in the path where a sprawling lilac bush blocked out much of the garden beyond. Lisa-Marie ran around the corner; her honey-coloured hair flew back from her face. She skidded to a halt when she saw Justin and he watched as a neutral, closed expression quickly replaced her look of shocked surprise.

Sophie wiggled to get down. She reached for Justin's hand and dragged him towards Lisa-Marie, "Mama ... look ... I find Justin." The child looked behind her at Pearl ambling down the path. Stomping her small foot, she called out, "Come, Pewl ... come." Sophie trotted along the trail with Pearl near her side and Justin and Lisa-Marie fell in behind them.

Justin cleared his throat and glanced to the side to catch her eye. "It's good to see you, Leez." He was stunned at her sudden appearance, though he realized he shouldn't have been. Feeling emotionally raw from his session with Izzy, his first reaction to the sight of Lisa had been straight-up need. He wanted her to throw her arms around him and hug him tightly, to stand back and look at him the way she used to. "It's been too long." He knew he sounded lame ... like stating the obvious would help, but he couldn't think of what else to say.

"Hmmm ... well, I'm home now, so we'll be running into each other all the time." Resignation chased coolness as Lisa-Marie kept her attention on Sophie's meandering steps from side to side along the path in front of them. The child stooped to examine a bright red salal leaf that had fallen in the dirt and then picked up her pace when she saw Liam at the end of the garden pushing a wheelbarrow.

Sophie began to run, calling out, "Liam ... I want a wide."

Liam stopped to wait for the child, waving to Lisa-Marie and Justin as he called out, "I'll take her with me. I'm heading over to the guest house to look for my good pruning shears. I think I left them there the other day." He watched Pearl struggle down the trail. "Stay, Pearl. Lisa, can you keep her in the garden?"

Lisa-Marie called out, "Sure." She touched Pearl's faded-red collar and turned the dog towards the small garden house. "I'll wait here for you guys," she said as Liam helped Sophie into the wheelbarrow. Sitting down on the wide step of the porch that led to the glassed-in structure, she tried not to flinch as Justin sat down beside her. She kept her gaze on Pearl who had sunk down on the path to relax in the warmth of the late morning sunshine. The uncomfortable silence between her and Justin caused a physical pain in her chest. She threw some words out to ease the discomfort, "What brings you over here on a Saturday?"

Out of the corner of her eye, she could see his knee start to pump up and down in an un-Justin-like show of tension. "I was having a counselling session with Izzy."

Any pretense of distance between them disappeared as she turned her head to stare at him. "Why?"

"Thought I should help her out with her new practice." Lisa-Marie's eyes narrowed. He pulled the envelope from his pocket, extracted the folded paper from within and handed it to her. She took it without looking away from his face. "Read it."

She unfolded the letter and scanned the few short paragraphs. "Oh, my God ...," she whispered as her hand dropped to his knee.

Words tumbled out as he took her hand in his, "I need you to be my friend, Leez."

For a moment bitterness overwhelmed her and she pulled her hand away. "What about Lauren? Have you talked to her about this?" She waved the letter in his direction without looking at him. She didn't want him to see the tears.

"She doesn't know anything about my mom. I could never talk to her about this."

Lisa-Marie passed the letter to him and placed her hand back on his. That old temptation to be the one Justin needed was too strong. The painful chapters of their respective pasts, dragged out, examined and shared with one another, made his request for her friendship inevitable. She'd never forget the anguish in his voice when he'd told her about his little sister's death. Angie had been three – the same age as Sophie was now. The child had ridden her trike out of the driveway into the road while her mother knelt in the dirt of the flower bed weeding and Justin played in the tire swing in the back yard. Angie had been hit by a car and Justin, who had heard the screeching tires and was on the scene in moments, could do nothing to help her. She died in his arms. Justin's mother had never recovered from the shock. She sank into a catatonic depression and ended up being hospitalized. Justin, reeling from his sister's death and his mother's defection into a world of her own, spent his teen years in a series of group homes. Micah Camp and Izzy's counselling skills had turned his life around.

Sophie's voice could be heard long before she came into sight, clinging to the sides of the wheelbarrow. "Mama ... I hungy." Pearl perked up her ears and rose slowly on trembling back legs.

Lisa-Marie let go of Justin's hand and stood up. She took a deep breath, searching beyond his careless good looks that had always been her downfall to see the suffering under the surface. "You told me once we'd always be friends and I stopped believing it. I see now that you were right. Too much holds us together." She turned to look back down the path. Liam had lifted Sophie out of the wheelbarrow and the child was running towards her. "I better go and feed my starving daughter. My cell phone number is the same. Text me or call anytime."

NINE

Beulah pulled the wood paddle loaded with the last of the pizza crusts from the outdoor oven. Steam billowed around her and the yeasty smell of bread filled the fresh, morning air. She balanced the laden board on her shoulder and steadied it with one hand as she came up the two steps that led into the bakery building. Stacking the crusts onto the racks to cool, she glanced out the open door to enjoy the sound of the stream at the end of the clearing as it roared along the bank to rush past the bakery and the A-Frame cabin. Near the streambed, she could see the green fronds of the many-shaded ferns swaying in the mist thrown to the side by the thundering water. A raven with shiny-black wings spread wide, swooped to land on a snag that jutted up near the cliff where the water dropped down into Crater Lake. The bird preened its feathers while it squawked loudly.

Beulah had expected that her wife and bakery partner would make an appearance this morning. Bethany usually enjoyed the slower pace of Saturdays when they switched from baking loaves of organic bread to making the pizza crusts. As Beulah placed the last of the crusts on the rack, she stretched and rubbed the small of her back for a moment. She reached behind her head to loosen the knot on the black bandana that covered her short spikes of grey hair. Shaking the folds of the fabric out, she told herself to face reality. Bethany was in a serious slump and without some type of intervention, she was unlikely to improve. They'd been down this road before.

Beulah felt a combination of worry and exasperation all rolled into a tight ball that lodged itself in her gut. She knew Bethany's trip back to Kingston to bury her mom had been difficult. But she had insisted on doing it by herself. Beulah had held the bakery together while Bethany threw herself into her last year of school in Victoria and revelled in her newfound independence. Beulah kept to herself the opinion that her wife was taking on too much with studying full-time, being away from home and dealing with the loss of her mother. Bethany made it clear, in large and small ways, that she wanted nothing of her partner's smothering. Beulah had no choice but to accept that her efforts to love and care for Bethany were being so harshly judged ... and rightly so. Too many years of their relationship had been spent with Beulah calling all the shots. So, when Bethany refused to slow down for a moment through her entire health scare and wouldn't admit to a single worry, Beulah decided she had no right to tell her wife how to cope.

But, thank God, it had all worked out. The thought of Bethany having cancer and losing a breast had Beulah considering, on more than one occasion, that she should get down the bottle of whiskey that was kept in the cupboard over the sink. She'd sat in Rosemary's office and told the doctor she'd gladly change places with her partner – the surgeons could lop off both her breasts for all she cared. They'd never been of much use to her. She couldn't bear for something like that to happen to Bethany, to say nothing of the consequences of a terminal cancer. Beulah had been left confused and frustrated when Bethany didn't seem to rally after the positive news in Rosemary's letter.

Beulah glanced at her watch. She had a couple of hours before she had to deliver the pizza crusts to Dearborn. Maybe she could tell Bethany what had been on her mind for the past few days. Izzy had her new counselling practice up and running. It was time for them to make use of the resource.

Bethany was curled up in the chair in the living room of the A-Frame. An open book lay in her lap, but she was staring out the window to the lake. Hearing Beulah come through the door, Bethany turned her head away from the view. "I didn't know it was so late." She shrugged hopelessly, "I kept wanting to get up and come out to the bakery. I couldn't seem to make myself." Tears glistened at the corners of her eyes.

Beulah waved her hand, "Doesn't matter. What are you reading?"

Looking confused, Bethany glanced down at the book in her lap. "Oh ... *Divisadero* ... for the next book club. I usually love Michael Ondaatje, but I can't get into this one."

Beulah walked past Bethany to wash her hands vigorously at the sink. She dried them on a hand towel hanging on a rod at the end of the large island that dominated the kitchen space of the A-Frame's open floor plan. "Should I fix us some lunch?" she called over to the living room.

Bethany's shrug of disinterest contributed nothing to Beulah's enthusiasm for the task. She walked into the living room and sat down on the sofa. She tilted her head towards the wrapped gift on the coffee table. Spiraling, brightly coloured ribbons adorned it and a card was taped to the top. "I see you got Sophie's gift ready."

Beulah smiled as she did whenever she thought of Sophie. The kid was a barrel of laughs, striding around with Liam's old dog, Pearl, at her side in the company of one or more of the many adults who doted on her. She had a rolling kind of stomping walk that cracked Beulah up. Sophie acted as though she owned the entire area all the way from Justin's cabin at the far end of the point, past Izzy and Liam's huge place, Alex and Cynthia's saltbox structure, the A-Frame with the organic bakery behind it and right onto Micah Camp sprawling along the far point. "Lisa-Marie should be back today. And Arianna will be here next week. It's starting to feel like homecoming."

Bethany nodded more out of the need to agree than in actual agreement. Beulah studied the woman across from her for a moment. This didn't seem to be a good time to mention her counselling idea. She felt sure her suggestion would cause Bethany to weep and wail about her life being so unfair. Neither of them needed that.

Slump or no slump, Bethany was still beautiful. Beulah looked now at her partner's curvy body, her thickly fringed, blue eyes and her blonde hair cut in a complimentary shoulder length style. The combination never failed to grab Beulah's attention. She rose and walked to Bethany's chair. She reached out her hand and Bethany took it. Pulling her wife to her feet, Beulah said, "Come on ... I'll wash your hair before we have lunch. That will make you feel better."

※∽※∽※∽※

Helen stopped at the base of the wide steps that led up to St. Bertha's church and caught her breath. She'd come up the hill at a brisk pace and she didn't want to rush into the building puffing like a steam engine.

Pushing open one of the wood doors, she took a moment to admire the inset sections carved with a variety of symbols – a fish, a cross draped with a robe, a simple loaf, a chalice of wine. The parish had fundraised its way through many a bake sale to commission and pay a local artist to create these doors. They had been worth the effort. Having lobbied so long for their own church, the parishioners of St. Bertha's wanted to put their best foot forward. What better way could they do that than by drawing attention to the front doors of the church?

Helen stopped near the holy water font, taking in the entire space in one sweeping gaze – the altar directly in front of her on the other side of the room, the rows of chairs separated by the center aisle, the doorways that led, on one side, to the kitchen, coffee room, and bathrooms, and on the other, to the sacristy. The building bore a stillness she usually found comforting when she arrived here Saturday afternoons. Today, that stillness meant a church empty of priest and nothing set up for confessions. She was too surprised even to dip the fingers of her right hand in the holy water and make the sign of the cross.

Father Mysner always placed a comfortable armchair in the space between the altar and the sacristy door. A discreet, portable screen blocked the view from his chair. Helen always imagined the priest on the other side of that screen, prayer book in hand, meditating on passages from scripture as he waited for his penitent parishioners. She shook her head at that image. He could have been finishing up last week's New York Times crossword for all she knew; it didn't matter. He had shown up.

On the first Saturday of their new priest's time at St. Bertha's, he was nowhere to be seen. The screen she found so comforting, as she sat saying a prayer and gathering her thoughts, was also absent. Turning, she left the church and walked around the corner of the building to peer over to the rectory. An emergency could have called their priest away. Her heart began to pound and her breathing shallowed out to short gasps – perhaps a car accident, maybe someone injured or dying at the hospital in Cedar Falls. She stood helpless in the grip of a steely fear that had held sway over her emotions for months.

She regained her composure with difficulty and refocused on the task at hand. Her eyes widened when she spotted a man who must be Father Kieran Galloway. She knew all the men in the parish and this man, bare-chested in the rectory back yard was not one of them. The unseasonably warm, May sunshine beamed out of the sky on their new priest as his muscles flexed and his wide shoulders strained to push a lawnmower through the thick grass. As she stared, to her horror, he looked up and spotted her. The low chugging and growling of the lawnmower ceased immediately. He stepped from behind the machine and pulled a shirt from the fence post on which it was hanging. He wiped his face on the garment and came towards her at a brisk pace.

Tension rose up Helen's spine to her neck and flowed down to her toes. Her entire body stiffened and became strangely taller. She backed up a step as the priest swung open the gate that separated the rectory yard from the church grounds. He couldn't be thinking of walking over and talking to her without his shirt. The whole idea was so beyond the beyond that she watched him approach, not quite believing what she was seeing.

He pulled the shirt over his head. He was close enough now to stretch out his arm to shake her hand. When she stepped back without raising her arm to return the greeting, he pulled his hand back and laughed. "Grass stains. Sorry about that. The lawnmower seized up on me a few times and I had to flip it over and clear the blades. Maybe we should forego the handshake for now. I'm Father Galloway. What can I do for you?"

That question certainly took the cake. Maybe he could get in the church and do his job. She blushed at directing such a sarcastic thought towards the priest. Clearing her throat, she looked at her watch and explained, "I'm here for confession. St. Bertha's always has confession from one to three on Saturday afternoons."

The priest gave a small shrug, "I didn't imagine anyone would show up. Confession is not exactly on the hit parade of sacraments." He must have noted her disapproval of such a flippant remark. He paused to run a hand through his hair. "I thought I would see anyone drive up and be able to come over to the church, if needed." He waved his arm towards the rectory lawn, "I wanted to get this grass cut while the sun was shining. Beautiful out today, isn't it?" He looked towards the church parking lot. "You must have driven up when my back was turned. Where did you park?"

She couldn't believe her ears and she tried to force the shocked look from her face. Did he think he would trot over to the church to hear a confession dressed like that with grass stains on his hands? She forced herself to speak through the shock because now he was looking at her with concern behind his ready smile. "I walked over. I always walk. I don't drive."

"Oh ... well ... that's great. Walking is great exercise. I'm a runner myself."

For heaven's sake, she wasn't here to discuss the merits of walking or running. "I noticed that you didn't have the confession screen set up. Perhaps no one told you where we store it. Would you like me to arrange things while you get cleaned up and changed?" She knew her tone had veered into the one she used when her intention was to correct her sons, Mike and Zach, without seeming obvious. Well, at least she hadn't fallen into the tone she took with Hannah. To talk that way to a priest, no matter how oddly he behaved, would only add to her list of sins to confess.

She watched as Father Galloway stared down at his grass-stained jeans for a moment before he said, "I don't know anything about a screen. If you're here for confession, why not come over to the trailer and have a cup of tea? We can sit out on the deck and enjoy the sun – kill two birds with one stone."

Helen felt her eyebrows rising so far up her face that she wished, for one wild moment, that she could see her own expression. She backed up a step and looked quickly at her watch. "Oh, good grief," she gasped out, "Is that the time? I'm running late." She spun on her heel and walked away, picking up her pace as she went.

She heard Father Galloway call out, "Wait ... I didn't get your name." Helen raised her arm in a backward wave and kept on walking.

❧ ❧ ❧ ❧

Kieran drove along the street, peering at house numbers. Finding the right combination, he signaled and turned into the sloped drive that bordered a well-kept front yard. The lawn was weed-free and bright green. The circle of earth around the base of a large ornamental plum that drooped with deep-pink blossoms was neatly dug around the edges and the grass was tightly clipped along the fence line. The Sampson house had curb appeal. An inviting sidewalk, flanked by beds of bright yellow and orange marigolds, curved towards the entrance.

Soon after ringing the bell, Kieran heard the stomping of feet. The door was flung open and he was greeted with the hearty handshake of a man who, he assumed, must be Craig Sampson. Before getting out of his car, Kieran had reviewed the small file card he had brought with him. Father Mysner had left him a box of such cards on the desk in the rectory office. The old priest had employed an outdated method of data keeping, but one that proved effective. The card had the names Craig and Helen Sampson penned on top in a neat script, followed by their address and phone number. Under that were written three additional names – Michael, Zachary and Hannah. On the back of the card were a few brief bulleted notes – Helen, social committee, fundraising; Craig, Christmas and Easter only; no dogs or pets.

The husky man with salt and pepper hair was dressed casually in jeans and a black golf shirt. He stuck his hand out and pumped Kieran's as he said, "Hello. Craig Sampson. You must be the new priest. Come on in."

Inside the entry, the house smelled of roasting beef. Kieran felt overdressed in his charcoal grey trousers and matching shirt with its short sleeves and white clerical collar. He followed Craig up the carpeted steps to the main floor. Large windows and a wide deck provided the same stunning view of white-capped waters that he enjoyed from the rectory. A young man with a head of sandy-blond curls sat hunched on the sofa. He was drinking a can of beer as he tracked the hockey action on the large, flat-screened television.

"Zach, come and meet Father Galloway." Craig turned to Kieran, "This is our son, Zach."

The young man stood up and smiled as he readily shook the hand Kieran offered. "Nice to meet you, Father. Are you a hockey fan?" He pointed to the television, "The Kings are kicking St. Louis' butt."

"Let's get the man a drink before we grill him on his hockey allegiances." Craig laughed and said, "But I'll warn you, Father, this house is a Toronto Maple Leaf non-bashing zone." Zach rolled his eyes and Craig continued, "Never mind him. Kids these days ... they don't understand team loyalty. What can I get you, Father? We have beer; or would you prefer a Scotch? That was always Father Mysner's favourite."

In that tense moment, Kieran regretted not anticipating the offer of a drink and preparing a good refusal. He cleared his throat and said, "No thanks. I'll pass for now." He registered the small wave of discomfort that sloshed between him and his friendly host. The awkwardness was fleeting, but Kieran knew he had better get used to it. Being social would inevitably involve such unspoken nuances of behaviour. He turned to Zach and said, "I'm usually a Canuck fan, but for these semi-finals, I've got my money on the Devils."

As they stood and watched the back and forth action of the game, Craig took a drink from the beer in his hand and said, "Helen will be out in a moment. She's putting a few final touches on things in the kitchen." He gave Kieran a quick glance and then focused back on the TV. His boisterous voice dropped a couple of octaves as he said, "Helen's had a hard time lately. The death of those kids at Christmas ... she took it hard."

Kieran had no idea what Craig was talking about. Before he could ask for a clarification, he heard footsteps coming up the stairs and Craig saying, "Hey, you two. Come and meet Father Galloway. This is my son, Mike and his fiancé, Wynter. Grab yourself a beer, Mike, and get Wynter a glass of wine."

Kieran turned to see a young man who shared his father's dark hair. He was holding the hand of a girl who had the most stunning violet eyes Kieran had ever seen. Greetings were given and received and small talk revolved around the hockey game. When Mike returned from the kitchen with the drinks, a woman followed closely behind him. Fluffing her hair and smoothing her dress, she said, "Make sure you get a coaster for that can of beer, Mike. And grab one for Zach as well."

Craig moved towards the woman and draped an arm around her shoulders, "Ah ... here's Helen. Do you want a glass of wine before dinner, sweetheart?"

Kieran had the time it took Helen to cross the room to cover his surprise at having to confront the woman who had made such a hasty exit from the church parking lot earlier in the day. She glanced at him from shoulders to feet and the look on her face told him that she approved more of his attire this evening than she had this afternoon. She stuck her hand out and said, "How nice to meet you, Father Galloway. We're happy to welcome you to our home and to St. Bertha's parish." As their hands met, he noticed the way she scrutinized his. Though he was tempted to ask if she saw any lingering signs of grass stains, he decided against such a comment. Instead, he chose to play along and act as if the earlier meeting had not happened.

Helen turned to her husband, "I'll wait to have wine with dinner. Haven't you offered Father Galloway anything?" And so, the whole uncomfortable *no-thank-you-ritual* was repeated.

A door slammed down the hallway off the living room. Helen stopped speaking mid-sentence and turned towards the sound. She frowned and her face became stormy as a girl who must be Hannah, sauntered into the room wearing a pair of shorts and a long, open, silk robe over a bikini top. Her head of blonde curls was bent as she texted rapidly on her phone.

"Go back to your room this minute and get dressed in something appropriate for dinner." Helen's reaction was immediate.

The rapid movement of the girl's fingers continued for a moment, then she jammed her phone into the back pocket of her shorts, taking her time as the slinky fabric of the robe was pushed back to reveal her tanned midriff. As the garment swung back into place, she stared at her mother. "I was unaware that we had started dressing for dinner. Let me see," Hannah cocked her head to one side and put her finger to her chin. "Shall I wear my sapphire silk or my cherry red gown?" She looked over to her father and asked, "Can I have wine, Dad? Since this dinner is such a formal affair and all."

"You most certainly may not," Helen cut in.

Hannah appeared on the verge of directing another remark at her mother when Craig spoke up, "Do what you're told, Hannah. And cut the smart talk."

As the girl turned and flounced back down the hall, Helen called out, "Do not bring that phone to the dinner table or else."

When they moved into the dining room, Kieran was seated to the left of Helen and across from Mike and Wynter. The roast beef, delicately seasoned gravy, oven-baked new potatoes and vegetables were delicious. His large first helping had brought a slight smile to Helen's face. Yard work was doing wonders for his appetite.

After having to refuse wine with dinner, Kieran glanced across at Mike and Wynter to ask, "When's the big day?"

Wynter's smile was as stunning as the rest of her. "September fifteenth," she told him.

Helen looked Kieran's way and said, "I have my heart set on a church wedding, but it is hard to convince young people of the importance of tradition and ritual. You must see that type of obstinacy all the time, Father."

The sudden anger on Mike's face went unnoticed by his mother, but Kieran saw Wynter move her own hand to cover her fiancé's fist where it lay clenched on the tablecloth. The looks they exchanged conveyed much. Not for years had Kieran seen a young couple so smitten with each other and their obvious affection for one another made him want to smile. At the same time, it hollowed him out. Maybe this was the reason he had kept to himself in the past. Standing on the sidelines looking in was painful. Whoever had said – *life is not a spectator sport* – hadn't had much experience with the priesthood.

Helen glanced at Wynter and then back to Kieran. "Wynter has given up world travel and a modelling career to marry our Michael and settle down in Dearborn."

Again, Kieran watched as Mike's hand flinched. Wynter only smiled serenely as she said, "I feel like I'm the big winner in that exchange." Kieran had no trouble believing that Wynter had been a model. She had that kind of photo-perfect look. But the thing that elevated her mere physical appearance to real beauty, in Kieran's opinion, was the joy that filled her every word, glance and movement.

Kieran smiled at the young woman and asked, "Do you live here in town?"

An awkward silence descended on the table in the same way a squall of rain dumps sheets of moisture on the coast. Into the sudden quiet, Helen said, "Wynter is staying with us until the wedding. She has a bed in Hannah's room."

A muscle in Mike's jaw twitched and Kieran could tell by the way Mike flinched and stared at Wynter, that she had kicked him under the table. Up to this point in the meal, Hannah had maintained a sulky silence. At her mother's remark, she leaned forward to look past Zach to her mother. "Do you seriously think Father Galloway gives a rat's ass where Wynter sleeps?" She turned her blue-eyed gaze to him. "For the record, Father ... Wynter does not sleep in the bed in my room, though my mother is only stretching the truth since she did make quite the production of offering Wynter that bed."

Craig responded immediately. "Language, young lady. And we could all do with less of your smart talk. Apologize to your mother and to Father Galloway."

Hannah mumbled something that might have been the word sorry; it was hard to tell. To Kieran's relief, Zach, who seemed oblivious to any tension, launched into a description of his educational plans and his summer job. "I can get you a good deal on a satellite internet dish, if you're interested, Father. The speed of the connection will blow you away."

The conversation around the table continued to lurch along through the rest of the meal. Craig offered to put Kieran's car on the hoist in his garage anytime. Mike showed a glimmer of interest when Kieran talked about running.

Helen was returning to the table with a tall cake adorned with fresh fruit and whipped cream when Craig asked Wynter, "How is the search for your dream house going?"

Mike tried to catch Wynter's eye but she didn't notice. She smiled at Craig and said, "We're going to buy that place in the Lady Brit that's been vacant forever."

Helen had almost reached the table. She turned so abruptly to stare at her future daughter-in-law that the glass serving plate in her hand tipped. The cake did a slow slide off the plate and onto the table where it made a squishy, plopping sound; not stopping there, its thin layers skidded past one another in all directions. In its short flight, the dessert had managed to send Helen's wine glass spinning end over end to the floor in a spray of red wine that barely missed Kieran's trousers.

"How can you imagine that you could afford something like that on Mike's salary?" Helen's voice was shrill. She looked at her son. "This is how it starts. Living beyond your means. I told you she would never be satisfied to be a sawyer's wife, didn't I?"

Helen's words had a greater affect on the family gathered around the table than the flying cake. Craig half rose from his chair with his hands flat on the table surface. A warning tone crept into his voice as he said his wife's name.

Hannah made a sound of disgust and Zach lowered his head, muttering, "Here it comes."

Mike got up from the table. He put his hand on Wynter's elbow and pulled her up next to him. "You did tell me that. And it was bad enough when you said it behind Wynter's back. God, Mom, are you trying to drive us right out of here?" He grabbed Wynter's hand and headed away from the table.

Wynter's voice could be heard as they left the room, "Mike ... stop, we should go back. I'm sure your mom doesn't mean that."

A moment of weighted silence passed as Helen stared at the ruined cake. Then she made an odd choking sound and her eyes filled with tears. Her hands went to her flaming cheeks and Kieran had a fleeting impression of Munch's painting, *The Scream*. Thankfully, Helen did not scream. She spun around and left the room.

Hannah looked at her father and said, "You see, I told you, she's totally cracked." She pushed her chair away from the table and exited the house by way of the kitchen.

Zach reached around Kieran with his plate and used it to scoop up a large chunk of the cake. "Still tastes good," he said around a mouthful of dessert.

Kieran rose from the table. "I think I'll get going, now."

Craig nodded. "I'll walk you out."

ЖЖЖЖ

Beyond the small circle of light, shadow upon shadow banked away into the distance. Alison stood on the porch of her trailer and breathed in the heady scent of trees and damp undergrowth. She had never before experienced the impenetrable quality of the dark. The sudden hoot of an owl made her jump. She shivered, crossed her arms and slid her hands up and down the sleeves of her sweater. Glancing at her watch, she turned and walked inside, closing and locking the door behind her.

She had spent her first full day at Micah Camp on her own. Not hiding out, exactly, but avoiding the main building. She skipped breakfast. For lunch, she finished up the beef stew from the dinner tray Brigit had kindly sent over the previous evening. The trailer had a well-appointed mini kitchen with an assortment of supplies. Cup-a-soup and crackers had made a fine supper.

Her goal for the day had been to keep busy. She had taken some time to pull boxes of career counselling files from the trunk of her car and to review several screening tools and activities that had worked well for her in the past. She'd organized and re-organized her clothing. Everything she'd packed needed ironing or hanging or folding. And she'd cleaned the small trailer. The bathroom had come in for a special brand of scrubbing.

All she wanted to do now was sleep, but she was anxious about the moment she would turn out the lights. She stared at the bed. The day before she had tackled the mattress like a dog gone mad with a chew toy, flipping it and shaking it out. The bedspread had gone in a black garbage bag; she would find someone to deal with it on Monday. She located clean sheets and pillow slips in the neat, fully-stocked closet tucked behind the curtains that hung to one side of the bed. For all her efforts, her first night had not been comfortable. She hadn't slept well.

She got into bed and the silence settled around her like a shroud. She felt pressed flat into the bed with the weight of it. Forcing herself to relax, still her breathing and stay calm became an exercise in futility. She couldn't stop her thoughts.

Alison had never thought of herself as a prude. She had led a sheltered life – had gone to an all-girls high school and had lived at home while she attended university. Bradley had been the first man she dated and the only man she had ever slept with. The scene she had witnessed in her trailer yesterday had shocked her to her core. Her mind kept going over it like a video on slow play – frame by frame by frame. She burned with embarrassment and something else she couldn't even name.

How on earth did she end up in such a situation? Not very long ago, if she had been asked to describe her life in three words, she would have said – stable, steady, straightforward. She was working in a job she'd held for over ten years doing career counselling at a private school. She had two grown children who were out of the house and, oh what a lovely house it was in a quiet neighbourhood with a mortgage newly paid off. And she had a marriage that had lasted into its second decade. She was about as stable and steady and straightforward as a person could be. Until Bradley pulled the ground of her life right out from under her feet and left her scrambling to find anything to stand on.

She recalled the day her world had tipped over and she had fallen, like Alice, right down a rabbit hole. Bradley had picked her up from Mass. Though he had converted to Catholicism when they were married, he was not the steady church-goer she was. That day, he had suggested they head out of town for brunch. She remembered exactly what they both ordered. She had the southern omelet and fresh salsa loaded with cilantro. He had the eggs benedict like he always had the eggs benedict wherever they went for breakfast. She had been seated near the window and the view had taken her breath away – a field of canola coming into bloom, yellow as far as the eye could see. She loved the prairies. Lots of people wanted to get away from the place where they had grown up but not Alison. She was a prairie girl through and through.

She had been sipping her coffee – a blueberry blend that was pure heaven – when Bradley had looked across the table at her and said, "I want a divorce, Alison. I've fallen in love with someone else."

She had stared at him like he was speaking Klingon. No fewer than three times, she had asked him to repeat what he had said. For some reason the meaning of his words wouldn't register. Then he said, "I've never wanted to hurt you but now, before it's too late for both of us, is the time for honesty. I know you have never enjoyed the physical side of our relationship and I've tried to be okay with that. But I'm not. I want more. Leslie makes me feel like a man and that matters to me. Both the kids are out of the house and making their way in the world. I feel like my time has come."

In retrospect, she supposed she should have seen it coming. There must have been signs of his discontent over the years. But she had never picked up on anything. When she remembered the stupid way in which she had stammered out questions that morning, at the restaurant table with the beautiful view of a sea of yellow canola out the window in front of her, her faced burned with humiliation. *How on earth could you fall in love with someone else? For pity sakes, we've been married twenty-two years, we have two children, we're Catholic.* As if any of those things would have stopped him.

He had been kind but firm; he had made up his mind. He had already arranged to move out of the home they shared. He told her he was going to meet with the kids in the city that night and tell them.

Their children took the news surprisingly well; they felt sorry for her. At the same time, they understood that their dad had a right to move on with his life. Luke had held her hand the way he used to when he was six years old and told her, "I know this sucks, Mom, but Dad says he's going to treat you fairly ... he promised us that." Sarah, who was studying to be a nurse, was adamant that her mom needed to get on with her own life. That would be the best way for her to cope.

Alison had taken leave from her job and had holed herself up in the house. All she had wanted was for everyone to leave her alone so she could stay in her night gown all day, scream, cry and rant at the injustice of it all. She hadn't a clue what life she was supposed to get on with – this *was* her life. She was angry. Her kids didn't understand and after a few weeks they stopped coming around.

She was furious with Bradley and that fury made it impossible for her to tell him how wrong he had been about her all those years – she had enjoyed the sex, she just hadn't known how to show him that. And he certainly never helped her figure that out. Well, let him go ahead and think he wasn't man enough for her. Let him go and prove himself with Leslie. She didn't care.

Whenever she saw him, he stared at her with a sad expression until she wanted to heave a heavy object at his head.

She finally took her doctor's advice and went on an extended trip to see a slew of relatives, advising everyone in advance that if they wanted her to visit, they should not mention her marriage. When she had completed a trek that spanned three provinces, she opted for a cruise. While she was sheltered under an umbrella on the deck of the huge ship, she decided to make a complete break from husband, house, job and even province.

Returning home, she immediately displayed a for sale sign on the front lawn and sent out the email asking friends and colleagues for any tips on upcoming jobs. Getting Izzy's response had seemed like a miracle. Micah Camp was certainly far enough away from Saskatchewan and with accommodation thrown in, the position seemed perfect.

Now she was here; she was starting over. She had the chance to recreate herself. Effecting such a change would be all well and good, but she couldn't sleep for fear of where her thoughts would lead her. The reality of this fresh start grew more terrifying with each passing day.

TEN

Reg tipped back his chair and studied the overloaded desk in front of him. He had told Josie he was going fishing to cover the fact that he was here, in the *Crater Lake Timber* office, working on a Sunday afternoon. The rain would make it hard for him to explain why he hadn't caught anything.

He bobbed the ball cap on his head up and down a few times and leaned back a bit further as he locked his hands behind his head. He liked the office when everything was quiet. At times like this, he often thought of Caleb and how the guy had built up this business from nothing. In those early years, Reg had worked with Caleb when the whole operation was a couple of fallers and a wood mizer to saw logs. The business was bigger now. They were doing selective logging on the woodlot, using several machines at a time. The yard itself was larger and a selection of multiple saws allowed them to fill orders for everything from fence posts to siding.

Reaching for a toothpick from his pocket, Reg put it in his mouth. He was going to be sixty years old this fall. He didn't usually mourn the passage of time or rail about regrets. Shit happened and then you dealt with it. That had always been his credo. He'd shifted from job to job over the years, married, divorced and moved on. He had two daughters and he'd paid to get them through school. They were back on the east coast. One was a nurse and the other was a welder.

Since taking over the management of *Crater Lake Timber* and moving in with Josie, he'd felt settled. They bought a house together – the mortgage wasn't huge because Josie had a place in Dearborn she had sold and Reg had some money put aside. Still, he wasn't thrilled about being in debt at his stage of life.

They did well financially but they had expenses, too. They'd shelled out a shit load of money for Paula's destination wedding and when Josie's grandson, Noah, came along, she'd spent generously on the kid. Two years down the road from that fancy wedding, Paula's marriage broke up. In his day, you sure as hell didn't throw in the towel after two years of marriage. Then again, Paula's husband had been an asshole, plain and simple. No way her kid needed to grow up around a deadbeat dad like that.

Josie told Paula to come to Dearborn and move into their basement. That hadn't always been convenient, but what the hell. Having Noah around was a hoot. Reg had always got a kick out of kids. And Paula certainly wasn't scrounging off them. She was a French teacher and besides doing her job out here at Micah Camp, she subbed in Dearborn and Cedar Falls.

Paula sure as hell didn't have good instincts when it came to men though. From what Reg saw when they had Nick Anderson over for dinner, she was barking up the wrong tree. Shit, now he sounded like Josie. She liked to stick her nose into things. But he was willing to take the bad with the good. His partner was generous to a fault when it came to family and fiercely loyal, too.

Motivated by a desire to be debt-free, Reg had taken the cash he had set aside from the sale of his dad's home in St. John and dropped it into some investments that he thought would turn a handy profit. The commodity markets were strong and for several months his investment boomed. With the sound of the cash register dinging in his ears, he doubled down with the savings he and Josie had put aside. He should have seen it coming – that old wrath of God kind of thing. A couple of months back, his money-making plans tanked. He hadn't gleaned any extra income and he'd lost big on his initial investment. The loss was a bitter pill to swallow; it stuck in his craw. Unfortunately, it was also a pill that Josie knew nothing about.

He was wallowing in regrets now. To make matters worse, he'd spent a good deal of time acting as the general contractor for Izzy and Liam's renovations and providing endless consultations on Alex's bus project. He had been well paid for his work, but the moonlighting meant he wasn't beating the bushes and bringing in new business for *Crater Lake Timber*. He was behind the eight ball and working his ass off to make up for lost time. He'd driven a hard bargain on his last contract with Izzy and Liam, asking for a share of profits as well as his regular salary. They had agreed because neither one of them wanted to deal with the woodlot or the sawmill and they didn't need money. Reg shook his head. That had to be one hell of a nice position to be in. But a share of the profits wouldn't amount to much if he couldn't get the business booming.

He clunked his chair down with a thud and reached for a bottle of Rolaids from the desk. This goddamned heartburn was going to be the death of him. It crept up on him and slammed him with pain that wound around his body like a vise. He popped a couple of antacids and picked up a pen. Pulling his lined pad of paper towards him, he began to write rapidly. He soon had a list of at least a dozen leads. He tapped the pen on the edge of the page. He'd need a couple more kids from down at the camp. If he could make good on a few big orders, there would be plenty to do around here.

Concerns about future employees got Reg thinking about Justin. He knew the kid had his eye on a job out in the bush with one of the big forest companies. Justin had his industrial first aid ticket. He was good with customers and a whiz when it came to calculations. He could knock down the price of a complicated order without ever dipping into the profit margins they couldn't afford to violate. He was quick and he did his homework; he always knew the most recent board foot cost of any product they sold. With his engineering degree, he was a real asset up on the woodlot, too. Reg wanted to hang onto him, but right now, with his eye on the balance sheet, he couldn't afford what Justin was worth. He wouldn't stand in the kid's way though. Reg had already put out a bunch of feelers.

Well, shit, he told himself, this business is always the same. You get someone trained so he knows what the hell he's doing and then he goes out and finds a better job somewhere else. He pushed his way out of the chair and headed over to the shed where his saw sharpening equipment was stored. He'd sharpen a few blades and get his thoughts in order before he headed home to Dearborn.

※ ※ ※ ※

Brigit stood at the door of her cabin and tapped her foot, "Come on, Tabby. We're going to be late. I still have to stop at the camp and pick up my red bean casserole."

Tabby sauntered out of her bedroom, staring down at the pages of the book in her hand. "We won't be late. You're always saying stuff like that and we're never late."

Brigit stared at her daughter who was clad in a long shirt, a pair of leggings, ankle socks and runners. "I thought I told you to get changed."

Tabby looked down at her clothes. "What's wrong with what I'm wearing?"

"We're going to a party not a baseball game." Brigit looked at her watch, "I'll go and get the casserole and you go put a dress on."

Tabby sank into the living room chair and draped her legs over the arm. "I already got dressed up once today for church. I'm not doing it again."

With her hand on the door knob, Brigit said, "Meet me in front of the main building in five minutes and you better be wearing a dress. And brush your hair. Good grief, don't you care how you look?" As she walked down the steps, Brigit pretended she didn't see Tabby stick her tongue out and make a face. What on earth was she going to do with that kid?

Halfway across the camp, she realized the spattering of rain wasn't going to slow down. She sprinted to the side door of the main building and once inside, headed for the kitchen. She'd borrow an umbrella from the stand outside the front door on her way out.

Standing and waiting a few moments later, umbrella in one hand and casserole dish in the other, Brigit looked past the circular drive to the path that Tabby had better come walking down wearing a dress if she knew what was good for her.

She was taken by surprise when Nick came up behind her from the other direction. "Hey, Brigit, are you waiting for someone?"

She turned, "Tabby ... if she doesn't hurry up we're going to be late for Sophie's party. What are you doing on this rainy Sunday afternoon?"

Nick zipped up his windbreaker. "This weather sure came out of nowhere. I was out walking, trying to clear my head. I've been hitting the internet doing research since early this morning."

Looking at him with more attention, Brigit said, "Have you eaten?"

He chuckled, "Trust the cook to ask a person if he's eaten. I'm fine."

"You should come with us over to Izzy's. It's a party and there will be lots of food. It isn't good to spend the whole weekend with your head in the books." In response to Nick's doubtful look, she slapped him lightly on the arm, "Come on. All work and no play and all of that. It will do you good to be with people." Brigit turned at the sound of running footsteps.

Tabby jogged up to them, still dressed in her shirt and leggings with a yellow raincoat flapping around her body. She had Brigit's raincoat over one arm and was carrying a clear plastic garbage bag in the other. Sophie's birthday gift, complete with fluted tissue paper sprouting from the top was visible through the rippling plastic. Tabby smiled at her mom, "I brought your raincoat, Mom. And you forgot the gift. I put it in this bag to keep it dry. Good I remembered it, right?" She hopped from one foot to the other, "We better get going or we will be late."

Brigit gave her daughter a look that she hoped conveyed a message loud and clear – *I will deal with you later.* She looked back to Nick, "Well, what do you say? Feel like going to a party?"

Nick smiled. "Why not?"

❦❦❦❦

Cynthia came down the stairs with Sophie's birthday gift in hand. Alexander had opted for books and they had picked out a set of three hardcover *Pete the Cat* stories. She called out, "Are you ready, Alex?"

"Just pulling this lasagna out of the oven."

She took a moment to stand in the middle of the building and admire her home. A wall of windows banking onto Crater Lake flooded the living room, dining room and compact kitchen with natural light. The other rooms on the main floor were under the long slope of the roof facing the trees. On one side of the foyer were two rooms, her and Alex's bedroom with its vaulted ceiling, and a stunning bathroom that seemed to open right into the thick forest; on the other side was a laundry/storage room. Up the stairs off the foyer, facing the water, were her writing room, an open loft area and a spacious guest room. Sophie was too young to sleep so far from them when she stayed over, but Robbie often bunked there, sometimes with Tabby tagging along.

Cynthia's contributions to the home had been in the areas of colour, fabric, shape and texture. Her tasks were made simple by pairing furniture, throw rugs, artwork and various objects with the warm tones of real wood and the gleam of glass. She had chosen earthy colours, heavy pottery and knobbly fabric. Her best find had been the weaving that hung behind the sofa – a tapestry of abstract trees, black and twisted, with flashes of vibrant purple foliage, sprinkles of white flowers swaying on delicate stems and splashes of yellow and red on the forest floor.

An arrangement of forsythia spikes sat on the dining room table and cast a yellow shadow in a circle all around the vase. She walked into the kitchen and enjoyed the green flecked colour of the counters, the gleaming faucet and the glittering lights that hung down from the ceiling. She sighed, she did love her Saltbox.

Together, she and Alex wrapped the hot casserole dish in a large towel and bundled it into a small, handled tote. Gathering up keys, slickers and flashlights, Cynthia looked around for the walking stick to take with them in case they had to whack something on the head and the air horn to have on hand if they had to scare something away. She'd leave it to Alex to deal with anything they might have to stab. He was the one who carried a knife. She smiled over at him, "I think we're ready."

74

Outside the Saltbox, Alex asked, "Do you want to take the trail or the driveway?"

Pointing to the trail that wound away through the bush with tantalizing views of the grey misted lake, Cynthia said, "Definitely the trail. The view's better. I hope Izzy wasn't planning on doing anything outside." She tugged on her hood as she spoke.

Alex laughed, "I'm sure she's lived around here long enough to know you don't plan anything based on weather." Out on the trail, the sound of the rain was amplified by its patter against the glossy salal leaves. "Only a few more days until our trip. Not regretting your decision to come along, I hope?"

"No regrets here. I half expected you might cancel because you couldn't drag yourself away from your library bus."

"Oh, come on, Cyn ... you have to admit ... it turned out well." Alex reached up and brushed aside a long wisp of old man's beard that hung from the branch of a yew tree at the side of the trail. A sudden smell of vegetation, alive and soaked with moisture filled the surrounding air. "I want you to be sure about coming along."

She linked her arm with his, "Two years ago, we did a trip together for fun. Last year, you went off on your own to do your work and I did the same. This year it's time for me to see what a native activist does when he's on the job."

"It isn't as exciting as you make it sound, I'll tell you that. We'll be meeting a lot of people, drinking a lot of tea and eating a lot of fish."

"I love fish."

"I'm looking forward to next year when I come along and see what a writer of medical crime stories does when she's on a working holiday."

"She doesn't like to be interrupted, I'll tell you that."

"It will be a great holiday for me. I'll lie around on a chaise lounge reading novels the whole time and be right on hand when you need to verify a sex scene."

"Oh, you," She shoved his arm. A slight breeze propelled the pink apple blossoms, plump with rain, to loosen a shower of drops over their heads as they made their way along the path that led to Izzy and Liam's deck.

❦❦❦❦

"Okay everyone, gather around ... time for cake." Izzy clapped her hands a few times and called out, "Where's the birthday girl?"

Sophie ran up the few stairs from her playroom where she had been serving tea from her new dishes to Justin, Robbie, Tabby and all her stuffed animals. Alexander reached down to pick her up. Sophie shook her head. "No, Gandpa ... you squish my pwetty dwess." She smoothed down the fabric of the full-skirted, cotton-candy striped garment and walked towards the dining room table. The closer she got, the more her eyes sparkled.

As the adults gathered around, Cynthia nudged Alex. "Really, Gandpa ... Sophie is three now." He laughed. Liam stood on the other side of his father and grinned at the joke, though he had to admit, he was somewhat amazed at the passage of time as he watched his daughter walk past him. A line from a Ralph Hodgson poem flitted through his mind. *Time ... you old gypsy man, will you not stay, put up your caravan just for one day?*

Beulah slipped in beside Bethany and dropped an arm around her. She squeezed her shoulder and leaned close to whisper, "How are you doing?" Bethany had been quiet during the party. The carefree nature of the gathering of friends had seemed to cheer her. Beulah had seen her smiling with real joy as she sat colouring with Sophie. Both pondered carefully their next choice from the case of crayons open on the table beside them. Beulah was relieved when Bethany gave her a quick smile.

Robbie and Tabby came up behind Sophie. They grinned and made exaggerated pushing motions with their hands as if to urge the child forward. Sophie was oblivious to it all. Brigit smiled at their childish antics. A birthday party brought out the kid in everyone. She admired Sophie's pretty dress while reminding herself that Tabby really needed a talking to.

Nick glanced at Izzy who stood beside him watching the child's slow march to the table. Catching her eye, he said, "I haven't been to a kid's birthday party since I was a kid myself." He chuckled, "Times have changed since the days of hot dogs and pointy birthday hats." She smiled and he caught himself admiring the way she so effortlessly managed a large, social gathering. She had welcomed him like an extra guest was something to be expected, supervised the serving of a large meal, moved the group along with opening presents and calmed a few childish tantrums – and she had done it all in a knockout dress with nary a hair out of place.

Watching Sophie come forward with all the dignity a three-year-old could manage, Lisa-Marie held her camera at the ready and was surprised to feel tears in her eyes. She looked over at Izzy and received a nod of understanding.

A white cloth covered the table and hung down in rich folds. Rainbow coloured confetti dotted the surface. The streamers that flowed from the large bunch of balloons attached to the ceiling swayed and cast a coloured glow. In the center of the table was the cake – shaped like a long snake striped with bands of yellow and green and complete with bright, black candy eyes and a flickering tongue made of red paper. The snake coiled on its platter with its head raised up on small blocks of chocolate that were shaped and decorated like the branch of a tree.

When asked a couple of weeks before her birthday what kind of cake she would like, Sophie had replied without hesitation, "I have a snake cake."

Izzy had frowned and said, "Are you sure? I was thinking maybe a butterfly or what about a big flower?"

Sophie shook her head, "No ... snake cake."

Liam caught Izzy's eye as Sophie clapped her hands in glee at the sight of the cake. He mouthed the words – *snake cake* – with a wide smile. He leaned over to light the three candles that sprang from the snake's back.

Justin lifted Sophie onto a chair and as everyone began to sing *Happy Birthday*, the child's small hands went to her cheeks and she stared around the table with a look of sheer wonder on her face. Soon everyone was clapping and urging her to blow out the candles.

With a stack of plates at her elbow, Lisa-Marie stood over the cake with a knife. She looked at Sophie. "Okay, birthday girl. You get the first piece." She pointed the knife to one end and then to the other. "Head or tail?"

As everyone looked at her, Sophie frowned. "Wobbie go fwst. I don't matter."

Robbie gave her a serious look, "Nope, can't do it, Sophie. Birthday rules. Hurry up and pick your piece so we can get ours." Sophie pointed to the tail of the snake. Nodding his approval, Robbie said, "Great, I've got dibs on the head."

As Lisa-Marie cut and served the cake, Cynthia leaned close to Izzy and asked, "Why does Sophie say she doesn't matter?"

"She started doing it while ago. I think it's a combination of *I don't care* and *it doesn't matter*. She's so sincere when she says it, too. You'd think she was a little martyr." As she exchanged a chuckle with Cynthia, Izzy heard the door in the kitchen close. Amid the clattering of dishes and the clinking of cutlery, the hum of conversation and the peals of laughter, no one else noticed.

A moment later, Fiona appeared at the top of the three steps that led to the kitchen. Her long dark hair was loose around her shoulders, hoop earrings swung near her face, her jeans were tucked into knee-high, leather boots and the white fabric of her shirt collar was vibrant against her brown skin. In the crook of her bent arm she held a sleeper-clad baby and over her shoulder she carried a diaper bag.

Like a wave in a curved pool, acknowledgment of her presence swept around the room with differing degrees of intensity. A series of conflicting reactions crossed Alex's face. Understanding and empathy chased after each other in Liam's expression. Robbie's features bore only acceptance. Izzy and Cynthia couldn't believe what they were seeing and the others felt confused at Fiona's sudden appearance. But the baby she held in her arms was a mystery to be explained, not a rock slide to be buried under.

All these reactions occurred in a heartbeat. Fiona's gaze had locked onto Nick. She walked down the steps and straight to him, jostling the crying baby up and down. Her eyes never left Nick's face as she said, "Meet your son. His name is Aidan."

Aside from the sudden gasps that followed Fiona's words, the room went silent. For Izzy, it was like the time Sophie fell down the back steps. A moment of stunned and absolute quiet passed before the toddler let out a piercing scream. Izzy only hoped, in this strange situation, that Nick was not about to do the same

He stared first at the baby's face and then at Fiona's. He backed up a step. His hands opened out in a gesture that looked like a benediction but his face was white and a small tick had developed near the edge of his mouth. Noticing the silence around him and feeling the sudden weight of the stares fixed upon him, Nick began to shake his head as if in denial. A moment later, he turned and strode quickly out the back door that led to the garden.

As the group in the dining room slowly came back to life, the steady beating of the rain on the roof competed with the noise of Aidan's plaintive cries. Sophie glared at the baby then looked at her mother. "He too loud, Mama. Maybe you tell him to go."

ELEVEN

C ynthia could hear Aidan's cries ramp up a couple of notches as Fiona carried him inside the Saltbox. The baby seemed at the end of what had fast become a short tether. He had been passed around the party guests to be petted and admired by everyone. However, when Liam had knelt by Sophie, holding Aidan in his arms and introducing the infant cousin to her, Sophie had stated her opinion firmly - *I no like him. He dumb.*

As Aidan turned red in the face and flailed his chubby arms in the air, Cynthia, Alex and Fiona had made their rushed goodbyes. Theirs was not as hasty a leave-taking as had occurred earlier when Nick left. Cynthia didn't think she'd ever seen such a look of shock on a man's face.

After staying outside for a couple of minutes to make sure the dog peed and didn't find some interesting smell to chase after into the dark trees, Cynthia stepped inside the cabin and walked through to the kitchen to put in the sink the empty casserole dish she had been carrying. Alexander was in the living room walking the floor with Aidan. He was struggling one-handed to get the baby's arm out of his jacket. Fiona sat in a chair digging around in her bulging diaper bag. "I have a can of formula in here somewhere. I fed him before we left Dearborn, but he seems to need to eat all the time." She held up the can triumphantly and then dug around some more until she produced a disposable bottle and plastic inserts.

Cynthia helped Alex free Aidan from the jacket and turned to take the feeding supplies from Fiona, "Here, let me get that ready for you."

In the kitchen, preparing the bottle, she heard Alexander cooing to the baby. "He looks just the way you did at this age, Fi," His voice took on more of the Alex-like tone Cynthia was familiar with when he said, "I'm assuming by Nick's reaction to your arrival that he had no idea about Aidan." Fiona nodded and Alex continued, "Cynthia and I will look after our grandson. You get your butt over to Nick's and see if you can repair some of the damage you've done. And take Johnny Lobo with you." Alex pointed to the German Shepherd that was curled up on a dog bed in the corner.

Cynthia pulled the bottle out of the microwave and checked the temperature of the formula on her wrist. She passed a flashlight and the dog's leash across the kitchen counter to Fiona. With the dog at her heels, the younger woman accepted them and made her away across the foyer and out the door.

Later, Cynthia sat in the living room's most comfortable chair with the baby snuggled in her arms. She was giving him his bottle. As he slurped away greedily, his sleeper-clad feet kicked out now and then. The two of them were alone because Alex had gone back to Liam and Izzy's to bring Fiona's rental car around.

Enjoying the silence and the baby's satisfaction, Cynthia had a moment to think. She was amazed at the ways this unusual family had twisted her securely into the warp and woof of its story. She smiled now as she considered Aidan's dark eyes. The oddball connections could still take her by surprise.

She'd had trouble enough wrapping her head around the fact that Alex had three grown children with one young enough to be his grandson. Although Alex made no distinction, Fiona wasn't his biological child. Even so, he'd been the only father the girl had ever known. To further confuse things, Liam hadn't seen hide nor hair of his father for almost all his adult life and Robbie's mother had sent Alex packing when Robbie was a baby. So, the only child he did much fathering with was Fiona. *Truth is stranger than fiction.* She couldn't have created a family like this if she had tried. No one would have believed her.

Coming here three years ago to rent Izzy and Liam's guest cabin, Cynthia had intended to stay just long enough to edit her latest novel. But then she had met Alex and her writer's curiosity was piqued. She wanted to learn the story of this guy who dressed like he shopped at an army surplus store and walked around with a large hunting knife on his belt. At that first dinner with the family, she had assumed Sophie, Robbie and possibly even Lisa-Marie were Izzy and Liam's kids. Cynthia had struggled to keep her mouth from gaping in shock when she learned that Lisa-Marie and Liam were Sophie's biological parents and that Robbie was Alex's son. Now she was part of it all and her commitment to making this family work was as strong as everyone else's.

80

She heard the door open and soon Alex came into the room, grinning at the sight of her in the chair with Aidan draped over her shoulder. She was patting the baby gently on the back and soon enough, he rewarded her efforts with a loud burb. Alex stretched out on the sofa and said, "Well, isn't this a nice domestic scene. I did not imagine, after our morning activity, that tonight I would see you in grandmother mode."

Ignoring her partner's wink, Cynthia sat the baby on her knee. "Where on earth is this little guy going to sleep?"

"I was going to suggest a dresser drawer, but Liam gave me Sophie's fold-up playpen. That should work for now. I left it in the kitchen."

Aidan started to fuss and Cynthia turned the baby to face Alex and the open room. She leaned his small body into her own. "Should we cancel our trip?" she asked as she stroked the baby's hair.

"I'll certainly make the offer, but I'm sure Fiona will refuse. She'll know the commitments I've made." He frowned, "People wouldn't understand why I didn't bring the baby with me."

"How is Fiona going to manage a baby and a demanding full-time job? Where is she going to stay? Who'll look after Aidan when she's working?"

"She wouldn't have come here unless she intended for Nick to play some role."

Cynthia's lips pressed together in a tight line before she said, "I know you won't want to hear anything against Fiona, but what she's done is damned cold ... not to have told Nick he has a son."

Alex frowned slightly, "Maybe ... I'm sure she had her reasons." He sat up, "You can bet that the next time I talk to Kate, she'll get a blast from me. Even if Fiona chose not to tell me, Kate should have."

With a shrug, Cynthia brushed that off. Kate was Fiona's mother. She and Alex had long since parted – Kate to be a tribal police officer and Alex to be a warrior. They occupied different sides of a native divide.

Since she and Alex were not going to be cancelling their trip, Cynthia made up her mind to share an idea that had occurred to her while she was feeding the baby. "Fiona and Aidan should stay here while we're gone. Izzy and Liam have Sophie's baby furniture in storage. We'll gather up some stuff and make a room for Aidan in my office."

Alexander raised an eyebrow in surprise. She never allowed him through the door of her office. She fiercely guarded the space and the privacy it provided. She stood her ground not only because as a writer she needed a room with a door, but because it represented the woman she had been before Alex – an independent female author who produced a book a year. She had travelled extensively and the only constant in her life had been the office space she set up wherever she landed. She shrugged and said, "I won't be here to use it."

Alex crossed the room to lean over his grandson and kiss the woman holding the boy. As he stood up, he said, "You are a singularly fine woman, Cynthia. I don't know how I got so lucky." He chucked Aidan under his chubby chin. When a deep frown darkened the baby's face, Alex held his hand up in a gesture of peace. "Okay then ...I'll get the playpen in here and we'll see if we can get this baby to sleep."

❧❧❧❧

"Aidan is cute." Tabby dragged her walking stick along the path behind her. She and Robbie were heading to Micah Camp to spend the night at her house.

"Sophie sure didn't think so." Robbie chuckled.

Tabby pushed into him with her shoulder, "Hey, you're an uncle. Lucky." She continued walking until another thought stuck her. "I can hardly wait to try out Sophie's play structure. Do you think it will take Liam a long time to build it?

"Better not with Sophie on the job." He made a face. "It won't be as good without the zip line." As they walked along, the ground of the path gave slightly under their feet. The sensation was like walking across a springy mattress. The whole area was fallen trees and roots covered over with years of built up debris – a network of interwoven ground that wasn't solid at all. Robbie watched the trail at his feet as he said, "Are you ready for the math test tomorrow?"

"Ya, but you can study some more in the morning before Mr. McKenzie comes in. He never gets to the camp before ten."

"You might not do better on the test than me."

Tabby laughed, "You know I will. I always beat you at math."

Robbie adjusted the strap on his backpack as he said, "I brought the next Harry Potter movie. Did you finish the book?" They had a deal that they wouldn't watch a movie until they had each read the book. That way they could discuss which parts of the story were exactly as they should be and which ones had been done all wrong. Tabby nodded, and Robbie asked, "You guys have microwave popcorn, right?"

"Ya, we have popcorn. Geez ... after eating that whole snake's head how can you think of popcorn?" Since the night a few months back when Tabby had come down with a sudden flu bug and thrown up a ton of popcorn, her attitude to the snack food had been less than enthusiastic.

Robbie felt the sudden, shifting mood of the girl beside him – subtle like when a quiet wind started on the lake and gently but inevitably changed the direction of movement for the entire body of water.

Tabby heaved a large sigh before she said, "If my mom forces me to go to school in Dearborn, I'm going to run away."

"Where to?" Robbie slowed his pace, curious to see where she thought she might go.

"I don't know. I'd go to your place, but that's the first spot she'd look." Robbie nodded. "Hey," Tabby said, "What about the library bus?"

"I bet your mom would look there, too." Robbie threw out an idea, "Toronto?"

Tabby looked doubtful, "Maybe ... but it's so far away. I'd have to steal the money to get there. And I'd miss you."

"I'd have to run away with you." Doing his best imitation of Jack Dawson from the *Titanic*, Robbie said, "Listen to me, Rose ... now that you've told me you're going to run away, I'm involved. I'm part of this. I wouldn't want to run away. It's going to be cold out on that road." He shrugged, "But, like I said, I wouldn't have a choice."

Tabby giggled. She nudged his shoulder, "Wouldn't it be so cool to live at that old library bus?" Shadows lengthened quickly in the failing daylight as they continued along the trail and the waning moon, an opaque shadow, hung in the sky above the tree line.

❧❧❧❧

Wearing her new, batgirl pajamas, Sophie stood on a small stool and stared at the fish darting around the tank. When choosing where to put it, Sophie had told Justin, "My fish like to see a lake." So, the tank sat on the wide window sill.

Lisa-Marie stopped in the doorway from Sophie's bedroom with the child's worn bunny tucked under her arm. Her gaze was drawn to Justin where he sprawled on the floor of the playroom. He was smiling and his warm brown eyes followed her daughter's every move. Sophie had received a variety of wonderful birthday gifts but Justin's presentation of the fish tank had been a real hit. Lisa-Marie's eyes suddenly filled with tears. She sniffed quietly, cleared her throat and said, "Come on, Sophie. Time to say goodnight to your fish. It's bedtime."

Sophie stared over her shoulder at her mother and then looked at Justin, "Fish sleep?"

Justin pushed himself up off the floor and walked over to scoop the child into his arms. "You bet. They sleep all night and they never try to get out of their tank." He glanced at Lisa-Marie and winked. Walking into the bedroom, he plunked Sophie on her bed and tickled her stomach.

The child giggled and rolled away. She sat up and said, "Mama, you wead this many books." She held up three fingers. "Because I that old now."

"Okay, but only three. It's getting late and you've had a long day. Do you want the new *Pete the Cat* books from Grandpa and Cynthia?"

Sophie nodded as she snuggled under her blankets and patted one side of the bed. "Justin, too."

He looked to Lisa-Marie for permission. She said, "The birthday girl's the boss." When they were comfortable on the bed with Sophie tucked in between them, Lisa-Marie and Justin took turns reading.

With the last book done and Sophie barely able to keep her eyes open, Justin leaned close to her and pushed her dark hair aside to kiss her forehead. She reached up and wrapped her arms around his neck in a hug. Lying back on her bed, she said, "I love you this much," her arms spread widely.

Standing up, Justin spread his own arms. "I love you more."

Sophie grinned and murmured, "Mama sing." Justin made to tiptoe out of the room but she raised her head. "No, Justin stay."

He sat down in the comfy rocker in the corner to listen while Lisa-Marie's voice caressed the sad lyrics of *Puff the Magic Dragon*. His own eyes drooped and he barely heard her get off the bed a few moments later. When she nudged his foot, he rose from the chair to follow her out of Sophie's room.

Closing the door gently, Lisa-Marie walked over to the fish tank and stared down at the gently moving fronds of plastic greenery. "It's a wonderful gift. I hope we can keep the fish alive." She glanced over at Justin. "I had a gold fish when I was little and it died. My grandma said – *go to the Five and Dime and buy a new one.* But I was devastated watching poor Goldie floating belly up on the top of the tank."

He smiled that smile at her, the one that had always made her heart thump. She felt the tears coming again and resisted the urge to throw herself into his arms. The whole day had been an up and down rollercoaster of emotion. This place, the people ... family. The experience was wonderful and overwhelming but there were still moments when she felt unsure about how she fit into all of it. Sophie was her child, clinging to her now in these early days of novelty at having her mama home. Soon enough, the child's regular routine would kick in and she would turn to Izzy and Liam and even Robby for her day-to-day needs. At three years old, a well-adjusted toddler, Sophie accepted her life. Her mother came and went. Izzy and Liam were her constants. This arrangement worked for Lisa-Marie. At the same time, it made her feel edgy and guilty. She felt as if the people around her were all waiting for her to do something, but they would neither say that they were waiting nor tell her what they expected her to do.

Justin moved closer and slipped an arm around her as they both focused on the fish. "We're going to be okay, Leez." She leaned her body against him, drawing strength from the circle of calm that surrounded this guy she'd loved for what seemed like forever. She knew he was rattled by his mother's situation and also by whatever was going on between him and Lauren. But Justin still exuded a strength and solidity that amazed and comforted her.

⁂⁂⁂⁂

"Nick, I know you're in there. Open up." As Fiona raised her fist to pound on the door again, it opened and she was confronted with Nick's six-foot-two, linebacker build, vibrating with anger and blocking out the light coming from inside the cabin. She met his hard glare, "Well, are you going to let me in or not?" He moved aside and she pushed past him. Johnny Lobo trotted along beside her. "We have to talk." She slipped her shoes off and glanced down at the dog. "Alex made me bring him." Unhooking the lead, she said, "Go lie down." Lobo obediently walked across the room, jumped up on one corner of Nick's sofa and curled into a tight ball.

Nick slammed his drink down on the end table so hard that the alcohol sloshed up and over the sides. "You've got one hell of a nerve coming over here and saying that to me. You're about a year late for what you and I needed to talk about." He dropped his body onto the free end of the sofa, crossed his arms and glared at her.

Fiona settled in the chair across from him, tucked her feet under her legs and studied her well-trimmed fingernails. Recollections of the last time they had been together filled her thoughts. She had already been pregnant with Aidan, almost sure she wasn't going to tell Nick but open to what might happen. They had met at a downtown hotel. She'd let go of the small, furnished apartment she'd rented for the six months she had interned as part of a mobile medical unit on the streets of Vancouver's downtown east side.

Those streets had thrown everything they could at her – from the violence of murder, sexual assault and vicious behaviours of desperate people preying on one another, to the literal stench of street life radiating from rotting feet, infected sores, putrid bodies and toothless mouths. And despite all of that, she had recognized community there and had witnessed acts of humanity that had made her curl up and sob when she was finally alone in her room.

Nick's visits had been her lifelines to sanity. She couldn't wait to pull him into bed and feel his body against hers – his clean, strong, whole flesh. It seemed her life depended on the pounding excitement of such encounters. On the streets, every minute, life and death were waging a war for supremacy. All she knew was that when she was with Nick, she had a huge appetite for life.

That last day, through the long afternoon of love making, she had sensed an ultimatum lurking in the contours of his body. Later when they strolled to a nearby pub for dinner, his questions had hinted strongly at commitment. *What will happen when you return to Toronto for your residency? When will I see you again?*

She couldn't let herself think about her upcoming residency because she had no idea how she was going to manage. The pregnancy was bound to slow her down and the baby would make an appearance as she was due to complete her certification exams. She simply wouldn't accept reneging on the demanding schedule she had set for herself. She had come too far and worked too hard to slow down now when the finish line was in sight. Making any kind of commitment to Nick was impossible. In those moments, as he made demands on her, she felt herself moving beyond any consideration of him. Something had to give or she wouldn't survive what was ahead. He was the thing she could let go of and she did. She had scrawled a note on a napkin when he was in the men's room and walked straight out of the pub to hail a cab. She went directly to the airport, abandoning her suitcase in the hotel room they had shared.

Draining the glass at his elbow, Nick asked, "How do I know the kid is even mine? The last time I saw you ... oh, wait ... I didn't see you. You left me a note on a pub table. That's how much a year of being with me meant to you."

His tone was bitter and though no one was going to believe her, she had never meant to hurt him. "You know he's yours because I say he is. I have no reason to lie about who fathered my son."

"Why now? What brings you back here now?"

"I'm doing a four-month locum in Rosemary's practice. I'm surprised no one told you."

"You are not a subject people discuss with me." He rose and began to prowl the small cabin, from the sofa, past the table and chairs, across to the French doors and back again. On one such circuit, he stopped and said, "You decided to drop in at a kid's birthday party and spring the news on me."

"I hadn't thought to give you the news in that particular way, but yes, I did plan to introduce you to your son and no matter how I might have done it, the experience was going to be a shock."

Resentment now reigned supreme. Nick barked words at her. "I seem to recall you not wanting to have a child with a white guy. Isn't that what you told me? What the hell happened?"

Fiona snapped. Her nerves were stretched to taut wires by the trip and worries about the grilling she knew was still ahead with Alex. She got up and faced Nick from across the room. The sofa acted as a convenient barrier between them. "Do you think I planned it? Do you think I wanted to be vomiting my way through fifteen-hour work days, getting so big I could hardly get around a hospital bed to do rounds? Do you think I wanted all my colleagues looking at me like I had to be the most backward squaw that ever left the reserve? Do you think I wanted to be sneered at for having come so far and then not having had the sense to keep my knees closed for just a little while longer? Do you think I planned any of that?" Fiona's hands had clenched at her sides as she spoke. Lobo raised his head and whined softly.

"Did you know you were pregnant the last time we were together?"

"Yes ... I knew." He would eventually do the math, so she might as well own up to it.

"You know what ... screw you, Fiona. Forgive me if I don't feel sorry for you because being pregnant and becoming a doctor was so hard. You could have had an abortion."

"Yes, I could have." Her words dripped ice. "I chose not to."

Gripping the back of the sofa, Nick leaned forward as he spoke, "And what the hell did you do with the kid after he was born? Prop him in a corner as you worked?"

"Ha, ha. He was with my mom." Fiona took a deep breath. Going on like this with Nick was pointless. She knew from experience that whenever they argued, they were prone to ramp things up to the explosion point. For a moment, she was tempted to push him. Those explosions had often led straight to the nearest bed and she hadn't been with anyone since she and Nick had parted.

Stifling an urge that would only cause more problems, she called out, "Johnny Lobo, come on." The dog jumped off the sofa and came to her side. She snapped the lead on and straightened up to face Nick. "Aidan and I are here now. He is as much your child as he is mine and the fact that you have only now found out about him doesn't change that. Being at the clinic and on call, I'm going to have a demanding schedule. You and I need to work out how we're going to deal with Aidan. I'll be staying at Alex and Cynthia's for the next couple of days. Come over when you're ready to talk."

As Lobo came up the steps to the deck of the Saltbox, his tail wagged wildly from side to side. Going straight to the rocking chair, the dog nuzzled Alex's outstretched hand. "Hey, boy. What have you done with Fi." He scratched behind the dog's ears, "I can't see Nick asking her to spend the night, though you never know with those two." He caught sight of the jittery beam from the flashlight at the bend of the trail.

Fiona dropped the dog's leash on the small table between the two deck chairs and sat down. "Let's get this over with, Alex. It's been a long day and I'm tired."

He continued to pet the dog. "Have you heard that Kris Kristofferson song, Johnny Lobo?" Glancing her way as he scratched behind the dog's ears, Alex saw Fiona shake her head. "It's a classic ... a tribute to John Trudell. I'll play it for you someday." Staring out to the dark lake, Alex said, "I'm not going to lecture you, Fi."

She sat forward, resting her bent arms on her knees and cupping her face in her hands. "Why not? You always do."

"A lecture is hardly what you need. I can see you're more than tired. Your spirit is low." An owl hooted, sending a forlorn sound from the trees behind them.

Fiona slumped back in her chair. Her relief was palpable. "I'm better than I was. I had four days off after wrapping things up in Toronto and before flying here. Mom was going to give me a crash course in baby care, but she took one look at me sitting in the kitchen like a zombie and she put me straight to bed. She said Aidan wouldn't be safe in the arms of a woman who couldn't string two coherent sentences together. I slept almost the entire time."

"Your mom is a good woman."

Fiona yawned and stretched her arms over her head. "So, no lecture. What then? You've got something to say."

The dog, ignored now for the moment, stretched out on the deck and laid his head on his paws. "If you need us, we'll cancel our trip," Alex told her.

"No ... I wouldn't ask you to do that. Nick and I need to figure this out. And besides, what would Cynthia say?"

"It was her idea." He straightened in his chair. "You and Aidan can use the Saltbox while we're away. It's a good place for him. You both need family. Liam and Izzy will help you. And it's close for Nick."

Fiona tilted her head to the side as she considered the idea. "I'll have to stay in Dearborn when I'm on call, though." Then she shook her head, "What about Arianna? I know you told her she could stay here."

"I'll figure out what to do with Arianna. You focus on what you have to work out with Nick." Alex stood up as he said, "Don't be proud, Fi. When you need help, ask for it."

The sound of Aidan crying came from inside the cabin. Fiona's shoulders slumped. "How's he been doing?"

"Sleeping for the past hour. We've got the playpen from Liam and Izzy's. We planned for you to be in the guest room upstairs. There's plenty of room for Aidan to bunk in with you for now."

She stood up and studied her father. "You wish I had told you ... about Aidan." A sudden gust of wind made the trees creak and groan. The wind chimes hanging from the corner of the deck swayed together and apart and tinkling notes echoed over and over. Lobo raised his head and whined a quizzical sound.

"You're a survivor, Fi. If I taught you anything, I taught you that. I won't deny it, though ... I was worried about you." He rose and opened his arms. She stepped into his embrace. Hugging her close, Alex said, "You're here now."

✈ ✈ ✈ ✈

Izzy slipped into the bed next to Liam. She pushed her pillows around and shifted onto her side with her elbow bent to rest her head on her hand as she studied Liam. He was lying on his back with his arms bent and his hands folded behind his head. She gave him a rueful look. "Fiona and Nick have a baby. Your family ... never a dull moment, hey? Did you know about Aidan?"

Liam shook his head, "I was as much in the dark as everyone else. My heart goes out to Nick right now. He looked like he'd been hit by a freight train."

"I thought Fiona might have confided in you."

"No ... seems like she didn't tell anyone. Dad was stunned when she walked in. That isn't like him."

"Did you see Robbie's face? He knew right away who Aidan was. He doesn't talk about it much now, but he still knows things."

"It's second nature to him. He doesn't need to talk about it."

89

Dropping her head to the pillow, Izzy said, "Sophie was so cute the way she poured over those plans for the play structure. She's going to love the whole process of seeing it built as much as she'll enjoy playing in it. What a kid." She laughed softly in the darkened bedroom. "I thought she'd turn herself inside out when she opened that package with the little tool belt inside. When did you find time to make that?"

"It wasn't easy, let me tell you." Liam rolled over towards her as he said, "Having everyone home and together today was good ... it felt right." He pulled his wife into his arms. "Fiona's going to need our help, Izz." She nodded against his chest and he added, "It will be fun to have a baby around again.

Wrapping her arms around him and moulding her body to his, Izzy made a small snorting sound. "I don't know if fun is exactly the right word. I'm sure we are in for an interesting summer."

"Well, given that," his hands wandered from her shoulders down across the soft fabric of the camisole top that clung tightly to her breasts, "we'd better take advantage of the energy we have now."

TWELVE

F inishing up a ten-kilometre run with a good stretch of brisk walking to cool down before he reached the rectory, Kieran thoughts turned to yesterday's homily. He had been preaching on John, chapter fifteen, verses nine to seventeen – one of his favourite gospel passages. He had told St. Bertha's congregation that this biblical passage was the basis of his personal theology. *Love one another as I have loved you* – the greatest commandment. He shared the excitement he felt when he had discovered this was the gospel reading for the first Sunday Mass he would share with them.

He advised them all to use this great commandment as a litmus test for the rules they lived by, including any church rules that might need their scrutiny. He had joked that he often thought people who subscribed to WWJD thinking – *what would Jesus do* – might be on to something if they stopped and considered what Jesus meant when he said love one another as I have loved you. Then Kieran had gone on to challenge his listeners to think about the types of things Jesus did to show his love – to consider how he sought out the oppressed and the outsiders of his time. Kieran had preached a good deal more in that vein.

He hadn't given a homily in some time. Maybe his delivery was off. A fair number of parishioners looked uncomfortable with his suggestions. The connection he yearned to feel with the congregation was not there. These were early days, of course. They'd have to warm up to him and him to them.

In reflecting on more of yesterday's events, Kieran remembered the woman he had met when he arrived early at the church. She had been in the kitchen with a broom held like a weapon in her hand as she smashed it into the corner and said, "Oh, you sneaky dirty thing, I'll get you this time."

A girl of about ten or eleven who appeared to be the woman's daughter, stood on a chair, jumping up and down and chanting, "Kill it, kill it."

The woman had turned in surprise when he started to laugh. She leaned the broom against the wall and came over to shake his hand. Introducing herself and her daughter, Tabby, she added, "This isn't exactly how I thought I'd meet the new priest. But you'd have discovered the mouse problem on your own, anyway."

During the Mass and later at coffee, he'd enjoyed glimpses of Brigit's wide brow, visible up to her hairline where her blacker-than-black, cork-screw curls stood back from her face. Her large eyes were dark pools of the deepest chocolate. And he noticed that she had this quirky thing that happened when she smiled. Her lip turned up more on one side than the other. It made him want to grin right back at her. At least her looks of encouragement during his homily indicated that she understood the message he was trying to convey.

Later that evening, he had pulled her card from Father Mysner's box. Because so many parishioners were clamouring to meet the new priest, he hadn't had time to talk with her after Mass. Brigit Lafitte and under her name, her daughter's, Tabby. No other name. Cook – Micah Camp – lives in. Refugee committee rep, catechist. Originally from Toronto.

As he cut around the church and covered the last few yards to the rectory, he also recalled how Helen had avoided talking to him at coffee time. He could understand why. Neither of their first two encounters had ended well. Craig's cryptic reference to dead kids came back to him and he reminded himself to follow up on that.

He pushed through the gate and glanced inside the greenhouse to the trays of brightly coloured bedding plants that now nearly overflowed the small structure. At the end of yesterday's Mass, during announcement time, he had asked if any of the parishioners had spare garden tools. He was in the market for a few things. To his surprise, several of the men had shown up at the trailer later that afternoon with truck beds loaded. He was now in the possession of a slightly dented but perfectly serviceable wheel barrow, a couple of shovels, a rake, a hoe, pruners, clippers and an assortment of hand tools. What had surprised him more were the flats of bedding plants that the men hauled out of their trucks. He had argued that he hadn't wanted anyone to go out and buy anything. The parish council chairman told him they always budgeted for repairs and upkeep of the rectory yard. He was told to make sure he presented receipts for any out-of-pocket expenses he incurred. The men had asked if he was sure he didn't want a hand with things around the yard. He told them he thought of the work as a hobby and was looking forward to it.

"And you'll cut the grass yourself?" one had asked. His emphatic nod had met with approval. He was then invited by a couple of the older, retired men to go fishing with them. He'd explained that he had never been good with boats and would have to pass. Fishing, for him, had always meant being with Sean and kicking back afterwards with a half-sac of cold beer. Best to avoid the whole scene. The approval he had gained for cutting his own grass lessened somewhat in his refusal to fish.

✸✸✸✸

"When Weg come, Mama?" Sophie climbed on a chair at the dining room table and peered inside the leather computer bag her mom was packing.

Lisa-Marie glanced at the clock. "Soon, baby."

Liam told Sophie, "You can watch for him from the desk in the library." As the child headed in that direction, Liam glanced at Lisa. "She can't wait for a ride in the bobcat."

"I'll bring my suitcase down and then I can watch him get started on the clearing before I go."

From his chair, Liam had a good view through to the library and he kept one eye on Sophie as she played with some of her toys on the top of the desk. A lively conversation went on between her and the little people in her hands. The desk chair swiveled to and fro every time she got up on her knees to look out the window.

The entry door on the garden side of the cabin opened and Alexander's voice called out, "Anybody home?"

Sophie hopped off the chair and ran back into the living room. "Gandpa." She held her arms out.

Picking her up, Alex kissed the top of her head and said, "How's my favourite little girl?"

Sophie played with the feather hanging down from his hair. "Good." Then she told him firmly, "You no like Aidan, Gandpa."

Alex laughed, "Don't you worry about Aidan. He's little now, but someday he's going to be a great friend. You wait and see." Sophie looked skeptical as she slithered down and ran back to her vigil at the desk in the library.

Liam asked his dad, "How is everything over at the Saltbox?"

"Loud. Do you want to move the baby furniture today?"

"I've got Reg coming with the bobcat to clear a spot for Sophie's play structure. What about tomorrow?"

"No problem."

"Are you all packed for the trip?" Liam had watched his dad's plans for the upcoming trip come together over the last few months. They had all thought Cynthia intended to head off on her own somewhere, but she had decided to go with Alexander. The proposal of an oil pipeline project up the coast meant Alex was invited to meet with native leaders and help organize and integrate a protest strategy. No one knew if the pipeline would even be approved, and if it was, whether it could survive the inevitable court challenges. In Alexander's work, early preparation was imperative.

Alex sat down on the sofa. "Almost ready. Something's come up and we've put a new stop at the top of our itinerary ... the *Chain of Hope Blockade*." Liam raised an eyebrow of inquiry and his father went on. "A group of native women has taken the opposition of this pipeline to heart. They've been crocheting. Canoes are going to cross the channel unfurling spools of these wool chains." Alex's eyes gleamed. "It's a symbolic gesture but a powerful one. They're fighting for the health of the coast, for the whales, for their traditions. If this pipeline were to go through, that channel would see traffic from over two hundred supertankers a year. A spill from one of those tankers would spell the end of the Gitga'at's food supply and their way of life. It's a damn serious situation." Sitting forward, Alex said, "You and Robbie should come with us for this first stop."

Liam shook his head, "I can't leave here right now. Izzy's only just back to work. I've got the play structure to get started on and I think I should hang around in case Fiona needs a hand. Talk to Robbie about it."

Alexander glanced up the stairs to the library. "What about if we take Sophie with us? It's not too early for her to understand what she's been born into. We can boat back to Cedar Falls when the blockade is done and you can pick her up there."

Lisa-Marie had walked into the living room carrying her overnight bag in time to hear Alexander's words ... *take Sophie* and *blockade*. She stared from Liam to his father.

Liam frowned at his dad and told him, "It's up to Lisa."

Alexander stood up and his dark, piercing eyes seemed to look right through her. He was wearing black jeans with a hunting knife at his belt. His steel-grey warrior hair was shaved close to his head on the sides and top, and a long braid hung over his shoulder. Although he was intimidating, Lisa-Marie reminded herself of the love he had for her daughter. She took confidence from Liam's assurance that the decision was up to her. Shaking her head, she looked at Alexander and said, "I don't want Sophie going away now. I just got home."

"Looks as if you're heading out again." Alex spoke softly, laying down a challenge in his statement.

The back door opened and Fiona walked into the room. She glanced from her father, to Liam, to Lisa-Marie. "You guys look like you're re-enacting the stand-off at the OK Corral. What's up?"

Alex continued to look at Lisa as he said, "I suggested taking Sophie with us for our first stop on the trip, *The Chain of Hope Blockade* I was telling you about. Lisa-Marie doesn't like the idea."

Fiona walked straight over to Alex and poked him in the chest. "Old man ... you never learn, do you? Don't you remember how my mom almost went after you with a hatchet for taking me into Oka with you. And I was eight years old." She glanced over at Lisa-Marie, "You keep right on standing up to him." Turning back to Alex, she emphasized each word with another poke, "Sophie's a little kid." She turned, walked a few steps, plopped down on the sofa and folded her arms over her chest.

As if on cue, Sophie ran into the living room yelling, "Weg coming now, Mama. I see him. Let's go."

Grabbing her bags, Lisa-Marie walked past Alex to take Sophie's hand. "Okay ... I'll throw my stuff in the Jeep and we'll go and see Reg." She left without a backward glance.

As the door closed behind them, Alex frowned at his son, "You can't shield that little girl from the struggle forever, Liam."

"The decision isn't yours to make and shielding Sophie isn't what this is about. And as for the struggle ... it's written in her DNA."

Turning his attention to Fiona, Alex gave her a stern look. "I would have expected more support from you. I'm not talking armed warriors at the barricades. These are grannies crocheting chains and drinking tea."

Fiona's shoulders slumped. She got up and gave Alex a hug. "Next time you're going somewhere nearby, let me know. I'll get some time off and go with you. I'll even bring Aidan."

Alex smiled at this victory. Glancing at Liam, he said, "That DNA remark ... good point. I might have to borrow that." He turned for the door. "I better get back to the Saltbox. Fi, how was Aidan doing?"

"Sleeping when I left," she replied.

After Alexander had gone and the cabin was quiet, Fiona let out a whoosh of air. "He drives me nuts. How come you get the praise and I end up being chastised like a kid? I am a doctor, you know."

Liam chuckled. "No idea. We've got some strange dynamics in this family." Comfortable in his chair, he looked at his sister and said, "Tell me about Oka."

Fiona took a few moments to gather her thoughts. Her face held a faraway look as she remembered. When she began to speak, an uncharacteristic tremor was in her voice. "We were all holed up in the Treatment Center making a final stand. When we had to walk out, I was separated from Alex. He got dragged away right in front of me. The soldiers told us to get on this bus. I saw a girl ... she was older ... I'd chummed around with her and her baby sister now and then. She was kneeling on the ground begging her sister to move. The kid was terrified. When she stood up, dragging her sister behind her, one of the soldiers pulled a knife and stabbed her in the chest. It happened so fast, but lots of us saw it. The wounded girl kept on walking though. Somehow, she managed to drag her sister onto the bus. They took us to a military base where we sat in that bus for almost twelve hours. Everyone tried to get help for the stabbed girl. The guards kept pushing people back, telling them to sit down and shut up."

A tear slid out of Fiona's eye. "When my mom finally picked me up she was over-the-top raging about Alex and I made her even angrier by sticking up for him. I told her I couldn't wait for the next protest. Don't get me wrong, Liam ... I was terrified on that bus thinking that girl would bleed to death right in front of us. She didn't. She survived. The way Alex hunkered down to the ground and looked at me, in the Treatment Center before things got out of control ... he was serious, like a grown-up talking to another grown-up. He told me what would happen ... how they would come for the warriors first, and he would be taken. I would have to be brave and do my best to get through. My mom would be waiting for me on the other side. The intensity of that moment and the strength that flowed from him to me was exhilarating. I felt like I was bigger than myself. When he looks at me sometimes, I still feel that – his confidence in me and his belief that I can do anything. I feel bad if I can't meet his expectations."

After a moment to let the story Fiona had told settle in the space between them, Liam asked, "Why didn't you tell us about Aidan?"

Her mouth turned down with discomfort. "I didn't want Nick to know and I convinced myself that I would be putting all of you in a difficult position if I told you. Izzy works with him. Everyone likes him." She bit her lip. "That was all bullshit. I had promised myself that my kid wouldn't end up being raised in two worlds. I thought I could leave him on the reserve with my mom and get through things ... like a warrior, you know. Tough it out." She laughed but it wasn't a happy sound. "Well, I became a doctor right on schedule, but my own baby didn't know me and my mom almost had a breakdown. Looking after a baby at her age and doing her job was way too hard. She misses Aidan now like I cut her arm off and I wouldn't be surprised if she showed up on my doorstep any day, but caring for him full-time was too much for her. Once I realized how off-base I was about everything, I was ashamed of myself." She shrugged. "You once told me, Liam, that when I had a child of my own, I would make the best decision I could for that child. I don't think you were right."

Liam gazed at her for a moment before he said, "You did the best job you could, Fi. When things needed to be changed, you made a new choice. I think that qualifies."

A small grin turned up the corners of her mouth. "With that philosophy, I could do no wrong. When Rosemary contacted me about the locum, I had to say yes. A great career opportunity doesn't come up every day and I knew I would bring Aidan here. It seemed best, at that point, to show up and let the chips fall where they may.

Liam smiled over at his sister. "There's a lot of the old man in you, Fiona. You know that, right? He's harder on you because the two of you are the same. I'm something he can't quite figure out." He clunked the recliner down and got up from the chair, "I better get outside and supervise Reg with that bobcat. He's liable to clear half the property if I don't keep an eye on him. And Lisa is heading into Dearborn overnight for work, so I've got to watch Sophie."

✢ ✢ ✢ ✢

After putting a call through to Roland's office to ask for a couple of days off to deal with personal issues, Nick spent the morning lying on his sofa staring at the cedar ceiling. He hadn't slept and he was in a state of rattled shock. His thoughts were bombarded with memories of his year with Fiona – from the moment she told him, outside Izzy and Liam's guest cabin, that she didn't date white guys and then kissed him in a way that made his pulse beat like a drum, to the moment he came out of the men's room at the Vancouver pub and saw her note. *There is no you and me. It's over.*

He had returned to Micah Camp and had thrown himself into his work. He got his book deal and made plans for further research and his PhD. He spent more than a few difficult nights getting over Fiona. In the end, he chalked her rejection up to experience. With two failed marriages behind him already, he was no stranger to picking up the pieces and moving on.

But his relationship with Fiona wasn't over and he hadn't moved on at all. The moment he saw her again, he knew that. Realizing that she was already carrying his child that evening in Vancouver, he felt a stab of guilt followed by anger. What the hell had he to be guilty about? The whole relationship, from beginning to end, had been Fiona calling the shots. He knew he had pushed her that day. As the time for her to leave for Toronto had approached, he had become more and more frustrated with the nature of their relationship. How might things have been different if he hadn't put pressure on her to make him part of her life? Maybe she wouldn't have run. Maybe she would have told him about the baby.

He thought about Aidan and the child's head of fine, dark hair, the smooth brown skin and the tiny hands. For some reason, the baby's hands kept coming back to him. They reminded him of his father's hands - piano-player hands with long fingers. Aidan, his son. He practiced saying the baby's name out loud. Then the words – *my son*. The experience was disorienting.

The sleepless night caught up with him and he dozed off to dream of Fiona. Her long, black braid was flung over her naked shoulder and she was making love to him. When he reached for her, she wasn't there. He woke up with a hollowness in his gut.

Feeling grungy and unkempt, he had a shower, shaved and got dressed. He was coming out of his bedroom tucking a T-shirt into his jeans when he heard a knock on the door accompanied by a voice calling out, "Hey, Nick. It's Paula."

He crossed the room and opened the door. Paula stood on the top step with a lunch tray balanced on her arm. She was the perky type. He wondered why he'd never noticed.

"I heard you booked off for a couple of days." She looked at the tray, "I brought you some lunch."

Nick stood back from the door. Paula practically skipped into the room and set the tray on the coffee table. Her bright, sunny smile was firmly in place as she straightened and turned to him. "Are you sick?" She looked at him closely, "You look ... good."

The admiration in her tone, impelled Nick to action. "Listen, Paula ... I'm glad you stopped by." Before her pleasure at that remark could ramp up, he continued, "Sit down for a moment. I've been wanting to talk to you about something."

"Should I set out the lunch? You don't want it to get cold."

Nick shook his head, "I'm not up to eating right now."

"Oh ... well then ... I'll put it in the fridge for later. How about that?"

"No ... leave it." Her eyes narrowed slightly at his tone, but she perched on the edge of the chair that Fiona had occupied the previous night. Nick flinched and resisted the urge to ask her not to sit there. She was looking up at him expectantly. He sat down on the sofa across from her, exactly where he had sat last night. An eerie feeling washed over him – as if he were going to redo a bad scene. He was getting a second take and he better get it right this time.

He was not going to mention Fiona for the simple reason that this wasn't about her or the baby. He had planned to have this talk with Paula before Fiona had reappeared and dropped a megaton bomb in the middle of his life. This was pre-explosion stuff and he had to clear it up.

Nick took a deep breath and said, "I guess you know that I'm wrapped up in my research these days and thinking about my time at UCLA." She continued to smile and nod and her huge capacity to be understanding urged him on. "I'm going to have to step back from seeing you, Paula." He ignored the way her smile jittered. "Please, don't take it personally. I enjoyed our two dates. I want to be fair ... to you ... and I know I'm not going to be able to dedicate the attention or time to a relationship right now."

As her face settled into a look of resignation, Nick thought that he'd done a relatively good job of exiting stage left without further drama. She stood up and he followed suit.

"I'll go now and let you get some rest."

At the door, he said, "Thanks so much for understanding."

At the bottom of the steps, she turned and smiled back at him. "Summer is a busy time for everyone. I'm sure we can reconnect in the fall." She waved and headed back along the trail towards the main building.

❦❦❦❦

Ethan pushed through the glass doors of the office only to be greeted by Roland's impatient voice, "Ah, Mr. Black. I'm glad you could find time in your busy day to see me."

Still in his work clothes and leaving a trail of sawdust on the carpet, Ethan plopped down in the chair Roland pointed to. "I hope this won't take long. I'm starving and I want to be out of the dining room early so I can hit the gym for a couple of hours before it gets too crowded." He pulled the ball cap from his head and more sawdust fell as he drew his hand through his hair. In response to Roland's frown, he simply shrugged.

"I'll try not to throw your schedule into disarray. Are you making any progress with your ongoing search for a dance school?"

"If that's what you called me in here to talk about, this is going to be the quickest meeting on record." Ethan picked at a hangnail as he said, "My search, as you call it, continues to suck. Of my last three applications, one was passed over unread, one was rejected with a form letter and the third – well, for me, getting into that school is a long shot at best."

"As the saying goes, nothing worth having is gained easily." Roland pulled a sheet of paper from a file on his desk. "You have been in a three-bedroom cabin on your own for a couple of weeks."

Ethan clasped his hands in front of him and bowed his head. "All I can tell you, Roland, is that it has been a slice of heaven."

"Enjoy the last few days of your solitude. I am assigning two of the new residents to room with you. They will arrive next week." Roland studied Ethan for a moment before he said, "One of the new residents' parents are coming to the camp for a meeting tomorrow afternoon. I'd like you to make yourself available to give them a tour. They want their son to be comfortable here at Micah Camp and I'm sure meeting one of his new roommates will put them at ease."

"When did meeting me ever put anyone's parents at ease?" Ethan asked. "I'm working full time at the sawmill. Reg will chew my butt right off if I try to leave early."

"I'll clear things with Reg." Roland folded his hands on the expansive surface of his desk and returned to their previous topic of conversation. "We need to get you moving along with your life, don't we, Mr. Black? What more can we possibly do for you?"

Ethan smacked the ball cap against his leg as he spoke, "It's not like I want to be here, Roland." He thought for a moment and added, "Tell the new career counsellor that helping me get into a dance school should be one of her top priorities. She sounds like a bit of a nutcase, but still ... like you say, I've got to get moving along. I'm desperate."

"I would appreciate, as I'm sure Ms. Kirk would, that you not repeat your assessment of her. As to special treatment, you are one of thirty-six residents. We can only do so much. I will speak to Ms. Kirk on your behalf."

THIRTEEN

As Beulah's truck rounded a bend in the road, Arianna sat up straighter and craned her neck to get her first view of Crater Lake. "I've missed this so much," she kept her gaze trained on the landscape unfolding before her – the wide expanse of glistening water disappearing into row upon row of mountains far away.

Beulah tapped the brakes lightly as she approached the next curve. Glancing over at Arianna, she said, "I hope you didn't mind eating at the *Beach Road Café*. Bethany wanted to do a big dinner, but she got tied up with a project today."

"I'd never pass up fish and chips in Dearborn. You know that."

Beulah smiled. "Glad to hear that school went so well this year. It seems like you've got all your ducks in a row."

Arianna nodded slowly; she was thankful for the solid footing on which she now found herself. "The first year was really hard. But you knew that. I thought I'd be ready for living in the dorms after Micah Camp, but my floor was like the wild west. Some kids pay a lot of money to go to university and do nothing but party. Keeping up with all my classes was crazy. During the first semester, I gained about ten stress-related pounds and some days I was so tired, I could barely get out of bed."

Arianna knew that she could never tell anyone, not even Beulah, how much she had missed Dylan. She'd had a constant ache in her chest and the times between their phone calls had seemed like not living at all. She stopped herself from sighing – she was doing better now. Time and keeping busy had made a difference.

She smiled at Beulah. "When you and Bethany showed up for that surprise visit, I wanted to beg you to take me back here with you." Arianna was warmed by the memory of how good it had felt to see familiar faces when she was so lonely and lost. "Then one day Fiona and I were having a Skype video chat and she blasted me. She ordered me to get to the gym every day, to eat properly and to focus – or she'd come right to UBC and kick my butt." Arianna grinned, "You can bet I did what I was told. And I applied to live out of the dorm in the cluster housing. Things were way better after that."

"Nothing like the threat of a kick in the butt for motivating someone. Do you keep in touch with that Dylan guy? How is he doing?"

"Oh, he's good. We talk on the phone and text."

Beulah briefly glanced her way. "He was going to cooking school, right?"

"Yup, he's a starting-out chef now."

"Well, good for him. Tell me about this job you've got at the addiction center."

"It's a co-op placement so I'll be doing a bunch of different things ... mostly shadowing the experienced workers. I'll do intake interviews, participate in group work, keep the patients company and fill in wherever someone is needed. It's such a great learning opportunity for me."

"It's a union job, right? I hope they're paying you the proper rate – co-op or not."

"Oh ya, they have to, it's a real job. The money is a major plus. Fiona wrote me a great reference letter and because she's taking on the locum for Dr. Rosemary, I'm sure her recommendations helped me get the job."

"Speaking of Fiona ... she showed up here at the lake the other day with her four-month-old son. Did you know she'd had a baby?"

"Fiona has a baby?"

"I see you're as shocked as everyone here was."

"I haven't seen her in person forever. We mostly email or text. Wow." Arianna was stunned. A mentor relationship wasn't the same as a friendship and she certainly hadn't ever expected Fiona to let her in on the details of her personal life. But having a baby was a big thing to keep quiet about. And she'd never thought of Fiona as the motherly type.

"Fiona's baby has thrown a wrench into your accommodations plans."

"How come?" A sudden concern for her own welfare drove out any surprise about Fiona's life.

"Don't worry ... backup plans are in place." Beulah swerved to avoid a large pothole and got the truck situated back on her side of the road before going on. "Alex and Cynthia are letting Fiona stay at the Saltbox. They think it's a good spot for the baby – close to family and to Nick."

"Nick is the father?" Arianna was having a hard time keeping up. "And what is the Saltbox?"

"The look on Nick's face when Fiona walked in with the baby makes him my choice. The Saltbox is what Cynthia and Alex call their cabin. Something about the shape of it."

"So, where am I supposed to go?" She had been thrilled when Alex had asked if she would cabin-sit their place while they were away.

"Two choices ... you're free to stay with Bethany and me. The whole upper floor of the A-Frame could be yours." Arianna smiled at the offer but her heart sank. She had been looking forward to staying in a place on her own. Beulah continued, "Or ... Alex has this renovated bus you could stay in. It's set up on a site between his place and the A-Frame."

Beulah braked to swing the truck sharply down the drive to her and Bethany's home. Pulling up near the bakery building, she switched off the engine and said, "Alex will be over to show you the bus. No need to decide now." As they got out of the truck, Beulah pointed to the bakery, "I've got something new to show you in there. Come inside to say hi to Bethany first."

Inside the A-Frame, Arianna and Beulah found Bethany sitting in the middle of the living room floor surrounded by stacks of books, papers, and folders spread over the coffee table, the sofa and the armchair. Startled by their arrival, Bethany jumped up from the floor sending the folders in her lap flying all around her. She was wearing an odd-looking, old dress – a bit shapeless and long with a faded flower pattern. She had her hair pinned carelessly up on her head.

Studying the mess of paper, Beulah said, "Still at it, hey?"

Bethany looked around her, "I keep getting distracted." She walked over to Arianna and pulled her close in a tight hug. Backing up, she held the young woman by the shoulders and said, "It's so wonderful to see you. You look beautiful. Are you good?" Glancing at Beulah, Bethany added, "You guys got something to eat, right? Did you tell her about the change of plans?"

Beulah went to the kitchen. "Yes on both counts. I'll make some coffee."

Bethany knelt to pick up the papers from the floor. "I've been trying to sort out all this school stuff."

Arianna scrunched down and began to help. She felt a warning flutter of anxiety in her stomach. She'd had this experience around Bethany before. During Arianna's time at Micah Camp she'd done her work placement at the bakery. She'd been around when Bethany and Beulah had gone through a major relationship blowup. Bethany had left for a time to stay over at Micah

Camp and Beulah had holed herself up in the A-Frame, leaving the bakery unattended. It had all worked out in the end.

Back then Arianna's anxiety about Bethany had been generated by the anger that simmered under the surface of the woman's polite words. This time, things were different. Bethany wasn't angry. She was needy. Arianna was expert at picking up such vibes and she faced an ongoing challenge to resist rushing to help others. Needy people were like sponges – taking all that others could give. She had no time to fall into the helper trap.

As she got up and handed her stack of papers to Bethany, she knew she didn't want to stay here. After a coffee and visit around the kitchen table, Beulah stood up and said, "Come on, like I said ... I've got something to show you in the bakery."

Bethany remained seated with her hands wrapped tightly around her mug. She looked up at Arianna, "You know we'd be more than happy to have you stay here. The bus is quite nice. Alex showed me around it the other day. But it could be lonely for you."

Beulah was headed for the door, "She can check it out and decide for herself."

Bethany nodded but her eyes were already far away as she stared out the window. Arianna gave her a quick wave then she followed Beulah out to the bakery.

Once through the doors and into the bright space, Arianna noted with pleasure the way the various machines gleamed silver in the light. The warm tones of the butcher-block kneading table which dominated the space drew her gaze the way they always had. Something was different. A new piece of equipment stood in a corner near the large mixing vats. "Hey, what's that?"

Walking over, Beulah patted the silver side of a large hopper sitting atop a metal stand. Attached to the side was a round chamber that narrowed to a funnel where a clamp held in place a cotton, flour bag. "This is our brand-new mill. It stone grinds wheat into flour."

Arianna walked over to get a closer look. "You grind your own flour now?"

Beulah grinned widely, "Do we ever. We're giving it a try with a couple of new products. I know this fella down in New Mexico. He runs a bakery/breakfast place with his wife and four kids. Great guy if you don't mind a dose of his religious convictions along with your food. He put me onto this machine and a whole new way of baking bread." She shook her head for a minute. "Never say you can't teach an old dog new tricks because I am sold on freshly milled, stone ground flour. We've got a deal with a farmer in

Colorado who plants a field of non-GMO golden spring wheat for us. It's grown without chemicals and has a higher protein than other wheats." Warming to the topic, Beulah continued as she crossed the floor to pull a cooling loaf off the shelf. "The secret is in the wheat and grinding right before you bake ... there are no preservatives and not a single vitamin or mineral is stripped away." She tore off a small chunk of the bread and held it out to Arianna, "Give it a try. Tell me what you think."

Arianna walked back over to the kneading table and leaned into its comfortable bulk. She studied the golden texture of the bread, the brightly coloured fragments of cranberry and the light brown pieces of walnut. She took a bite and savoured the burst of flavour in her mouth. It was quite simply the tastiest piece of bread she had ever eaten.

"The look on your face says it all, kid." Beulah grinned as Arianna chewed. "Eventually, we'll switch over all our breads to this new method. The end product is costlier because we have to ship the wheat up here. We charge more per loaf but, after one taste, people are willing to pay."

Holding her hand out for another chunk of bread, Arianna asked, "Is Bethany okay? She seems a bit -,"

"Out of it?"

Arianna nodded, "I couldn't help noticing. Sorry."

"No kidding. She's been wearing that weird dress for a couple of days now. Says it's comfortable." Beulah stared out the bakery window. "She's going through some stuff. She found a lump in her breast a couple of months ago, went through a biopsy and all of that." Looking over and seeing the sudden concern on Arianna's face, Beulah said, "She's fine. We got the results a while ago. I thought she'd pick up after that. But she hasn't. The waiting was brutal."

"Hmmm ... seems like staying with you guys right now isn't the best timing."

"Bethany might pull up her socks if you're around. I don't want to put that on you. The offer stays open. But she's right ... wait until you see the bus. It's something."

Arianna and Beulah heard Alex's voice before they saw him. "Lobo, stay." A moment later he pushed open the door of the bakery. "Cynthia wants me to pick up a loaf of that new bread for our trip. The cranberry, walnut stuff. Have you got any left?"

Beulah pointed to a rack of bagged loaves. "And hello to you, too, Alex."

He grabbed a bag and threw a five-dollar bill and a toonie on the counter before turning to Arianna and Beulah. "I had to take care of that order right away or I'd forget and then there'd be hell to pay." He pointed at the bread, "This stuff is addictive." He walked over and leaned a hip against the large table in the center of the bakery. Running a hand over the grey stubble on his face, he said. "I couldn't even get into the bathroom to shave this morning. It's a bit of a zoo over at the Saltbox what with Aidan settling in. Kid has a good set of lungs. He does a lot of crying. And Cynthia is turning the place upside down with her packing. Like I said, a zoo." He looked at Arianna, "Great to see you. And hello, Beulah. Have you given Arianna the news about the bus?"

Arianna walked around the table to give Alex a hug. "She has. No worries. I'm happy to have a free place to stay be it Saltbox or bus."

"Well, let's get you over there and set up. I've got to get back. Where is your stuff?"

"Out in Beulah's truck."

A moment later, hefting her bag, Alex groaned. "I guess I'll have to forgive you for not travelling light. After all, you thought you'd be staying in a cabin and now you're stuck in a bus."

Beulah called out to Arianna, "Don't be a stranger. I mean it."

Up on the trail with Johnny Lobo trotting along beside them, Alex said, "The library bus is great. Imagine the positive energy in that vehicle ... gained by driving around from town to town full of books ... having kids running in and out, serving old people waiting for the bus to stop so they could pick up their month's supply of books."

Struggling to keep up with Alex's long-legged stride, Arianna hefted her pack further on her shoulder and huffed a bit as she said, "My auntie's friend Muriel told me to say hi to you."

Alex smiled, "How is she? When did you see her?"

"She's great. She'll be running all the tribal economic development from Osoyoos to Oliver if no one gets in her way." Arianna took a deep breath and enjoyed the experience – the smell of wood smoke, the earthy odor of decomposing things, the fresh scent of the trees. "I just came from there. I had a week between finishing up at UBC and coming here to start my job."

"Has the band gotten used to the idea that you won't be running that big winery for them?"

"Oh ya ... they like the idea of me becoming a doctor. People are already hitting me up for medical advice and I've only finished my second year of undergrad."

"I believe it and I bet you'd do a better job in your own community than most of the doctors who parachute in there." Arianna was sure that wasn't true, but she let it slide. The more she realized how much she had to learn, the more determined she became. The road to becoming a doctor was a long one and she was going to make it all the way to the finish line, just like Fiona. She had been telling herself that for two years now. But having a baby right at the finish line wasn't Arianna's idea of how she would want to celebrate a win.

A few minutes later, about halfway between the A-Frame and the Saltbox, they came to a trail that branched toward the lake. Two thick gnarled branches were stuck in the ground and between them, a wood sign in the shape of an arrow pointed the way. Block letters read – OLD LIBRARY BUS STOP. Alex pointed to the double-sided, red reflector glued to the top of the sign, "If you come down this path at night your flashlight will pick up that reflector from either side. Wouldn't want you to miss the turn."

Under the canopy of trees the light filtered through in slanted bands. A portion of the way was flanked by a fallen tree now turned into a nursery log and thickly covered in emerald green moss. Spruce, hemlock and cedar seedlings jutted up along the entire length. Further down the path, fern fronds leaped from the ground in double and triple star shapes. And then quite suddenly, the trail spilled out into a wide clearing bordered on two sides by the trees. There the lake spread out before them.

Arianna stopped and Lobo sped past her in a streak of black and grey. The dog seemed pulled forward by the numerous new smells the site had to offer. The old green bus was parked lengthwise along the edge of the slope. A whole side of square windows looked out over the lake. A brightly striped awning spanned the length of the bus and flapped pleasantly in the breeze. Beneath the awning, on a square of patio bricks sat two lawn chairs separated by a small table. The clearing was half-circled by five plywood rectangles that appeared to rise from the cleared ground – they were tent platforms. A large picnic table sat nearby. It was made of new wood and Arianna could smell the pungent tang of yellow cedar as she passed by. Across the clearing was a lean-to shed which contained a pile of firewood. A small red-handled hatchet rested against a wall and a stack of green lawn chairs sheltered in one corner. An outhouse, with a crescent moon cut-out on its door squatted beside the lean-to. In the middle of the clearing was a large fire pit.

Arianna's gaze returned to the bus. A brightly coloured bookworm coiled and stretched along the entire side of the bus. The huge creature had its head reared up and black-framed spectacles were perched on its nose. Small hands held an open book. The mural was quite a sight and all Arianna could do was grin.

Alex beamed as he watched her reactions. "Come on and see the inside." He led her to the back of the bus where steps and a small porch had been installed. He waved for her to go ahead. "Get your first impressions of the place on your own. I'll be right here."

She went through the green bus door and into a narrow, short hallway with thick curtains on each side. She pushed one open and found a toilet and a small pedestal sink; on the other side, she discovered a shower. Leaving the hall, she entered the main area of the bus. Everywhere she looked was pine – the ceiling, the walls and the floor. Light streamed in from the windows facing the lake. She was standing on a small rug – twisted braids of greens. A kitchenette ran along one side of the bus and across from it was a table with a bench on either side. A vase of sunshine yellow daffodils sat on the table.

Walking a few more steps down the length of the bus, she noticed that behind the bench seat was a raised dais surrounded by a mosaic of glossy green tiles on which sat the smallest wood stove she'd ever seen. To her left was a comfy futon, thickly stuffed and covered in a mossy corded fabric. Next to that, was a low bookshelf. She sat down on the futon for a moment and enjoyed the view which included the built-in desk and chair across from her.

This was going to be perfect. She'd be wonderfully and completely alone. She felt as though she hadn't had a moment on her own for two years. Here, she could think. She could sit at that desk and write the journal and paper that would go along with her co-op job to give her a class credit. She couldn't wait to call Dylan and tell him all about this place.

She got up and a few steps on an oriental rug took her to the louvered doors that led to what had been the cab of the bus. It now contained a double bed with a wide, rounded, pine shelf built over the dashboard. Forest-print curtains circled the windshield window. She lay down on the bed and felt instant comfort. After a moment, she spotted, right next to her head on the window side, the crank that operated the folding bus door that was at the foot of the bed. "Oh, Alex ... this is so cool," she shouted out as she reached up and pulled the lever and watched the door fly open.

Alex was through the back door of the bus and across to her in a moment, chuckling all the way. "That's one of the best features. You can crank that door open first thing in the morning and listen to the birds."

Getting off the bed, she was grinning ear-to-ear. "I didn't know what to expect. I had no idea it would be so perfect."

For the next thirty minutes, Alex went over the finer points of the systems that made the bus an independent oasis. An array of solar electric panels was down the slope and unshaded by any trees. This provided electricity via a battery bank and something called an inverter. All Arianna had to do was monitor the meters, watch that she didn't leave lights on unnecessarily and turn on the backup generator for an hour or two if cloudy days meant the batteries were starting to get low. She should let Liam know if the gas tank on the generator needed to be filled and he'd come over and take care of that. She had a composting toilet that did its own thing and outside, next to the solar array, was a solar hot water tank. If that didn't do the job, a propane demand water heater would kick in automatically. The kitchen stove was propane and the tank was full. The energy efficient fridge was electric, so she should make sure the door didn't accidentally get left open. Cynthia had done a duo-tang with colour-coded tabs that contained a write up on all the things he was telling her. She had also been responsible for some of the finer decorating touches in the bus. Alex explained that Arianna wouldn't get a cell phone signal here but if she walked over near the Saltbox, she could pick up the internet. She could also do her laundry there. Wood and kindling for the woodstove were stored in a bin under the bus. She probably wouldn't need a fire very often. Summer was coming and the bus was snug. She could get Liam or Robbie over if anything went wrong, but he assured her that it wouldn't.

Back outside, Alex pointed to the lean-to, "Lots of wood there for a camp fire in the pit. If you have a bunch of people over, make them use the outhouse. Too much action all at once in the composting toilet inside the bus is a bad idea." Looking around with pride, he said, "If you want to invite people here for a camp out, I've stored the tents over at the Saltbox."

Arianna laughed, "I don't think I'm going to be having time to party out here, Alex. I have a full-time job at the addiction center."

"Right ... feel free to use my truck to get there and back. Cynthia and I are taking her RAV4 on our trip."

Arianna breathed a sigh of relief at that offer. Getting to and from Dearborn was the one downside to staying out here at Crater Lake. Lisa-Marie had offered to share her Jeep, but having the use of her own vehicle would certainly make things easier for Arianna. She could have hugged him. They were standing near the fire pit and Arianna did another slow turn, taking it all in. "Why did you build all of this?

Alex followed her gaze around his encampment. "I have a friend ... we go back a ways ... he's coming out here to stay for a few months in the fall. He's the type of guy who needs his own space. So, it all started with needing a decent spot for him. Then I saw the bus for sale - picked it up for a song - and I decided to renovate it." He laughed and the movement made the feathers woven into his hair dance. "Once I got started on the renovation, I realized I'd need some help. I know some fellas up in Cedar Falls who have skills and these guys happened to need a few weekends of good hard work out in the fresh air. So, I built the tent platforms. By then the site was growing. Things evolved. I guess I needed a project."

Looking over at the dog where it was rooting around near the bottom of the wood pile, Alex raised his voice, "Johnny Lobo, don't dig there. Come." The dog trotted over wagging his tail. Alex hunched down to pet him. He looked up Arianna and said, "I've got a favour to ask."

"Sure ... I owe you."

"Can you keep Johnny Lobo for us? I can't see Fiona being able to look after him. Doctoring and mothering are going to have her hopping."

"Sure, I'd love to and a dog would be good company here. But I'm wondering what to do with him when I'm away at work."

"Oh, he's fine outside on his own. He'll hunker down by the bus." He stood up. "Cynthia asked if you would water her plants. She says Fiona doesn't seem like the type to have a green thumb." Alex laughed. "I think she's right about that."

FOURTEEN

Helen entered the kitchen in time to see Mike juggling his lunch kit and thermos while trying to grab his truck keys from the hook by the door. "Michael Allen Sampson, you stop right there. I know you don't have to be at work for another hour. I need to talk to you." Cinching the tie of her terrycloth robe tighter, she took a mug from the clean ones on the top rack of the open dishwasher, filled it with coffee and sat down.

Mike returned to the table. He was a wise enough son to know that when his mother chose to utter his full name, he would be foolish to ignore what he was being asked to do. She was thankful for small mercies but he was obviously not pleased.

He glared across at her, "You have to lay off butting your nose into my life, Mom. If you don't, Wynter and I will move out."

Helen took a quick drink of her coffee. Except for the tick, tick of the yellow daisy wall clock above the pantry door, the kitchen was quiet. She'd always had a hard time connecting with her oldest son. Mike was quiet, somewhat broody like his dad and always quick to take offence at the slightest thing. Things weren't out on the surface with him the way they were with his brother. Even when Mike was a small child, she'd seldom known what he was thinking and she couldn't read his moods. He was closer to his dad and over the years, Helen had fallen into the habit of letting Craig deal with Mike. That wasn't going to do this time. Craig had brushed off her concerns. He'd echoed Mike's words – told her to mind her own business. But she couldn't shake the feeling that her son was making a big mistake and she would not be silent about that. What happened to Mike was her business.

She took a deep breath. "I am sorry, Mike. No excuses ... it was the

111

shock ... hearing about the Lady Brit like that. But I had no right to say the things I said. At least, Wynter was kind enough to accept my apology right away and not make me wait three days."

Besides feeling guilty about her oldest son dodging her for three days, she'd had to contend with the mortification of what had happened at the dinner the other night. "I can't believe I dumped that whole cake on the table then ran out of the room the way I did. Father Galloway must think I'm a raving maniac."

The look on Mike's face said clearly that he could not have cared less what Father Galloway thought. "I'm sure he's seen worse."

Helen reached over and placed a hand on her son's. "Mike, I need to talk to you and I need you to hear me."

Frustration edged his voice, "That's all I've been doing for weeks and I'm sick of what you're saying."

"No ... you haven't been listening. You shush me up or you storm out. Once you've really heard me, I promise ... no more."

Mike sat back in his chair with his arms folded over his chest. "Okay, I'm all ears. But I'm going to hold you to that promise."

She took her time to gather her thoughts. If this was going to be her one chance to get through to him, she wanted it to count. "Wynter is your first girlfriend. I'm afraid that you're rushing into marriage and I don't want you to end up divorced or see your children ... my grandchildren ... shuffled back and forth between bitter parents. I want you to have the kind of marriage your dad and I have."

"Nothing like the doom and gloom crystal ball. Thanks for having so much faith in me. Dad was your first boyfriend and things turned out okay for you guys."

"Times were different then, Mike. I didn't have the same expectations for my life that a modern young woman like Wynter must have. She has a promising and glamorous career in front of her." Helen could tell she wasn't make a dent in Mike's conviction that he and Wynter were going to walk off hand-in-hand into the sunset of life.

She took a different tack. "It's easy to be fooled about love ... I don't want to seem crude, but sex gets in the way of wise decision making and sex alone isn't enough of a foundation on which to build a long-term relationship." Mike squirmed in his seat but she went on, anyway. "I don't see that you and Wynter have common interests – the type of interests that the two of you can build on. She was brought up so differently than you were and she must have had scads of boyfriends. Then that year in Europe ...," her words trailed off.

112

She wasn't sure what she meant by that. Wynter was so beautiful. No ... she was more than that. The word beautiful didn't do her justice. She was striking. She was the type of young woman that stopped traffic. You couldn't help staring at her. Helen had seen Zach and even Craig caught up in the power of Wynter's allure. She wasn't jealous ... not at all. She understood. Sometimes she caught herself struggling to turn her gaze from such perfection.

Mike's face turned red with the effort he was expending to keep from blowing his lid completely with his mother. If he did that, his dad would be out here in a flash. Although his father clearly agreed with him in this case, he would not tolerate his son mouthing off. But Mike had heard enough. He lowered his voice to be on the safe side. "If you are trying to imply Wynter slept around when she was in Europe, you are wrong and you have no right to think of her that way."

Mike seethed inside with the injustice of his mother's insinuations. Wynter hadn't had scads of boyfriends before Mike. He knew and cherished the fact that on that night in the tent on the west coast, with the waves caressing the stones on the beach and the full moon tracing a path across the water, making love had been as new an experience for her as it had been for him. But that was none of his mother's business.

She reached over and touched his arm. "All I know is that you're my son and I'm worried for you. How is such a beautiful girl with so much of her own money," she held up her hand to stop his words. "There's no use denying that it's her money buying the Lady Brit. You could never afford a place like that. How is she going to be satisfied married to a mill worker in a little town like Dearborn? She's going to want more and she's going to make a life for the two of you that you won't feel comfortable in. How can something like that last?"

Inevitability settled down on Mike like a shroud. His mother's discomfort wasn't about Wynter. She always disapproved of his choices. Nothing he did would ever be good enough. Mike was convinced that his mother's feelings about him were rooted in the underlying tension in her own marriage. His dad managed a lumber yard and hardware store in a small town and tinkered with cars in his spare time. He didn't want to do anything else. Though Mike didn't doubt his parents were happy together, he could tell that his mom was irritated by his dad's limited ambitions. Many times, she had been after her husband to open his own business, to consider running for president of the local Chamber of Commerce, to contribute more, to better himself somehow.

Mike was like his dad. He'd never be the apple of his mom's eye the way Zach was – off at BCIT first and now headed for UBC with boundless ambition and drive. He got up. "I don't suppose you'd be saying any of this if it were Zach getting ready to marry Wynter." He saw his mother flinch slightly at that remark. "How we pay for our home is none of your business. If you want to know how Wynter sees her future here in this town with a lowly mill worker, then ask her."

As he tucked his lunch kit under his arm and headed for the door, he heard his mother's tone become desperate. "What about getting married in the church? They offer marriage preparation courses and I'm sure something like that would help the two of you understand that marriage is a serious thing."

"I've told you a hundred times. No church wedding, it isn't what we want."

His mom got up from the table and followed him to the door. She passed him his thermos. "Here, don't forget this. Will you at least talk to Father Galloway?"

Wrestling his keys from the hook, Mike knew when he was beaten. His mom had a way of wearing him down. He remembered the time Zach and his mom had badgered him into accepting a blind date for prom night. The blind part was that they wouldn't tell him who the girl was because, of course, no one could have a blind date in Dearborn. He'd gone to school with the same kids since kindergarten. Zach set up the date because the girl he wanted to take wouldn't go unless Zach found a date for her friend. The all night, dry grad – two aspects of the event that contributed to its nightmare quality – had not gone well for Mike. He had been paired up with Monica Baker. She was short, he wouldn't say dwarfish because that would be crossing a line, but close enough. An unfortunate genetic shuffle had dealt Monica a head of afro-like, black fuzz for hair. She wore thick braces and even thicker glasses. And what she lacked in height, she made up for in volume. Within his hearing, people remarked he was the beauty to her beast and the word troll was tossed about. He wanted to be the guy who rose above it all and looked beyond mere appearances, but he wasn't that guy. At that time in his life, he didn't have a lot of confidence and all he wanted to do was blend in and get by.

He turned to face his mother. Hoping to wrestle at least a guarantee of peace from her at a future date, he said, "I'll drag Wynter with me to see the priest on one condition. You need to promise to mind your own business from now on. And our going to see Father Galloway doesn't mean we are getting married in the church or sitting through any course. Geez, Mom ... is it too much to ask you to be happy for me?"

❧ ❧ ❧ ❧

Wynter sat near one of the large glass windows at the *Kitty Kat Café*. She stroked the fur of the cat that sprawled on the window sill. She wanted to acknowledge the waitress who set two cups down on the table and filled them with coffee from the pot in her hand. But she couldn't. All her attention was riveted to the show that was happening near the white van parked outside.

Tyler had both his hands up on the van on either side of Lisa-Marie. The roped muscles on his arms rippled under his tight T-shirt. His faded jeans rode his hips, snuggled his butt and stove-piped down to tuck into a pair of dusty-black work boots. He leaned in and his lips began a slow trek from the collar of Lisa's shirt, up her neck to her face. When his full lips reached their destination, he slid them onto her mouth and kissed her for what seemed, to Wynter, like forever. She fanned herself with her free hand.

Lisa-Marie slid away from the kiss before Tyler moved his body up against hers. She ducked quickly under his arm and stepped back onto the safety of the sidewalk. Tyler shrugged, flashed her a smile that was drop-dead gorgeous and waved as he strode over to the driver's side of the van. He backed out of the parking spot and was gone by the time Lisa came into the restaurant. She threw her purse onto the bench seat and slid into the booth across from Wynter.

"Oh, great ... you ordered coffee." Lisa-Marie reached for the cream and poured some into the black brew. When she raised the cup to her lips to take a sip she noticed that Wynter was staring at her. "What?" she asked.

"What do you mean what? That kiss is what."

Lisa-Marie sipped her coffee and asked, "Aren't you going to drink yours?"

Wynter stopped petting the cat and picked up her cup with both hands. "Tyler is as hot as I remember him from Rome. Tell me everything."

"Not much to tell." Lisa picked up the menu and flipped it open. "I wonder if they serve eggs benedict. I'm starving."

Wynter reached across the table and covered the menu with her hands. "There must be something to tell when a guy kisses you like that right out in the street."

"Oh, that's just how Tyler is. He rises for a public performance. He likes it when people stare at him."

"I guess he's used to it." Wynter decided to change the subject. In her friendship with Lisa, she had learned the wisdom of digging for information at an angle. "How is the job going?"

"We were out scouting all day yesterday. He's heading up to Cedar Falls now to check out a few sites. I'll come back to town later in the week. We have four days of work filming up on Mount Cain and on some of the islands up the coast."

"How long will he be staying in Dearborn?"

"He'll be going back to Vancouver to edit his film as soon as we finish up with the islands. I might have to fly down in June to help pull our whole submission together. Then we'll have to wait to see if the film people like what they see or if they want more footage."

"Where did you guys stay last night?" Wynter slipped the question into the conversation. A look of casual curiosity appeared on her face.

"At the hotel. Tyler's got a room there." Closing the menu, Lisa-Marie caught the waitress's eye and ordered her breakfast – eggs benedict, sourdough toast and a side of bacon. Wynter asked for a raspberry cream muffin.

The orange tabby cat that had backed away when Lisa-Marie joined Wynter in the booth, crept closer along the window sill. Wynter reached out to scratch it behind the ear. "You seem to have quite an appetite. Must be all that public kissing." She ignored the face Lisa made. "Do you and Tyler want to get together with me and Mike one night? Maybe go for a drink or dinner?"

"No ... that would be awkward. He's not my boyfriend." Lisa-Marie's phone chirped and she glanced down at the screen. "I better answer this. Tyler wants to know if we should fly up to the islands or get a boat charter." She grabbed her phone and texted rapidly. After a moment and a few more chirps, she put the phone in her purse.

"About Tyler," Wynter paused before she said, "I'm just going to ask. Are you sleeping with him?"

"Oh, my God ... you make it sound so cheap." Lisa grinned as the waitress floated by the table and refilled their coffees.

Wynter's frown became a grin. "I know ... right? I can't believe I just said that. I'm trying so hard to get Mike's mom to like me that I'm starting to sound like her. I'll mind my own business. Sorry."

"No worries. I can't imagine why Mike's mom wouldn't love you. What's up?"

"She doesn't think I'm cut out for small town life and she doesn't want Mike to get hurt. I can't blame her for that."

Lisa-Marie raised an eyebrow at her friend, "I know you are over the moon in love with Mike but you have to admit, you could have moved in a different world."

Wynter shook her head, "You know better than most, Leez ... all the glamour is ninety-nine percent hype. I'm not cut out for that world."

Nodding, Lisa-Marie asked, "What's it like living with Mike's parents, besides the part about how his mom thinks you are not good enough for her baby boy?"

"Well, at least Mike's dad wouldn't let his mom force me to sleep upstairs in Hannah's room. That's a good thing." They both laughed. "And Helen's a great cook. I feel like I've gained ten pounds since I moved in there."

"Well, you don't look it."

"We'll only be living there for a few months." Wynter's expression brightened, "We found an apartment. I can't wait to show it to you. It's in the Lady Brit."

Lisa-Marie's eyebrows lifted, "Wow. That must be pricey."

"These are so good." Wynter pointed at the last bite of muffin on her plate. "I have enough money from the sale of my grandmother's house in Victoria to buy it outright with some left over."

"Your grandmother is still alive, right?"

"Yes ... all the rest of her money is going to keep her in that fancy clinic in Europe. I visited her before I came back to Canada and she didn't know me at all." Wynter brushed her thick hair out of her face. "Anyway, I'm glad I have the money to buy the apartment, but even better, I have all this furniture that has been in storage for three years. I can't wait to get it here and into that apartment. My grandmother had some gorgeous stuff." Wynter's eyes shone. "Oh Lisa, I'm so happy. All of this is like a dream come true for me. I can't wait to be Mike's wife and for us to have our own place and I want to get pregnant right away. I want lots of kids ... enough kids to fill that beautiful Lady Brit right up to the crown molding."

"Wait until you go through one pregnancy and delivery before you decide you want to do it over and over." Lisa smiled as she pushed her plate away. "Having a baby is a great way to lose that fashion model figure."

"Like I told you, I cannot wait. How was Sophie's party?" Wynter asked.

"Great. There were some family fireworks at the end but it didn't affect Sophie's day. The cake Helen made was amazing. I know she had something more girly in mind, but her snake cake was a big hit. Make sure you tell her, okay? And you didn't need to send a gift, but Sophie loved the dishes ... a real china tea set. She insisted on setting it up right away in her playroom so she could give her stuffed animals tea." Lisa looked at her watch. "I've got to get back out to Crater Lake but I wanted to let you know that I'm putting the finishing touches on my plans for your bachelorette party. Be prepared to be away for the entire long weekend in August."

Wynter's eyes went round, "We're going somewhere? Tell me. Where?"

"Nope, it's a surprise. But I will say this. Lady Gaga is involved."

Wynter let out a squeal of delight and then clapped her hand over her mouth, giggling as the other customers in the café stared at her. Sliding out of the booth, she asked, "You invited Arianna to come with us, right?" Lisa-Marie nodded and as they walked up to the front to pay, Wynter touched her friend's arm. "Do you feel okay about Justin being Mike's best man? The two of you are bound to be thrown together a bunch of times. I don't want anything to be awkward for you."

"Brides shouldn't worry about stuff like that. I'm fine. Justin and I have had our ups and downs but we're friends. We'll always be friends."

⚜⚜⚜⚜

Izzy stood back from the crib and give her handiwork an admiring look. "I loved this owl quilt when Sophie had it." She turned in a half-circle to study the room that had been Cynthia's writing office up until a couple of hours ago. The room was now transformed with a crib, matching dresser and change table. She bent down and opened one of the large plastic bins labelled four to six months. "Even skipping over all the pink stuff, there's still plenty of clothes here with lots of use left in them."

Cynthia was filling the change table with baby supplies taken from the two large drugstore bags that sat on one of the shelves – diapers, wipes, lotions, shampoo, soft face clothes, a packaged set of tiny nail clippers and a blue hair brush. She straightened the two stacks of diapers one last time and turned to lean against the solid piece of furniture. "I'm going to get this off my chest, Iz. The way Fiona showed up with Aidan in her arms ... without ever saying one word about being pregnant ... I have never in my life known anyone to do such a selfish thing. Poor Nick. I didn't realize a person's face could go that white, that fast. What is wrong with her?"

Sitting cross-legged on the floor sorting the baby clothes into neutral-coloured piles of undershirts, T-shirts, pants and sweaters, Izzy shrugged helplessly. She remembered the way Liam had thrown up in the flower bed when he heard about Lisa-Marie's pregnancy. Fatherhood did odd things to men. "She probably didn't expect Nick to be at Sophie's party." Seeing the look of exasperation on Cynthia's face, she added, "I do hear what you're saying."

"And not telling Alex ... he's been worried about her for months." She slapped her hand against the side of her leg. "If we had known about Aidan, we wouldn't be going on this trip now. Alex told Fiona we could cancel and she said she didn't want to put us out." She glanced around the room. "Like arriving with a four-month-old you haven't told anyone about isn't going to put people out. Alex even offered to take Aidan with us on our trip; the suggestion was ridiculous, but I know him. He'd have done it and managed fine." Cynthia shook her head and her silver hair swayed around her face. "I can picture him standing at the head of a war canoe with the kid in a snuggly." She and Izzy exchanged a smile at the thought of the things Alexander could do. "Fiona can barely look after her own child. How she got all the way here from Toronto with Aidan still in one piece is a mystery to me."

"No doubt the flight attendants gave her a hand. They're usually good about that sort of thing." Passing up piles of clothes for Cynthia to arrange in the dresser drawers, Izzy said, "We'll all pitch in to help her out. At least she's had a few months of hit-and-miss mothering experience. I'm sure Nick doesn't have a clue what to do with a baby."

"How is he? Have you seen him since Fiona dropped her bombshell?"

"He booked off a couple of days." Izzy got up from the floor and rested a hand on Cynthia's arm. "Let's grab a coffee and sit out on your beautiful deck. They'll probably be back from Dearborn in an hour or so. We can enjoy the peace while it lasts." After helping his dad unload the furniture, Liam had shown Alexander how to secure Aidan's car seat into Cynthia's RAV4. Alexander drove with Aidan while Fiona followed in the rental car. After she returned it, they were going to check in at the clinic and see Dr. Rosemary's apartment in the Lady Brit. Fiona would be staying there three nights a week when she was on call.

The two women settled out on the deck overlooking the wide expanse of grass that sloped down to a hedge of bushy, waist-high japonicas. Beyond that, the ground dropped away to the wavering blue of the lake. Cynthia savoured a drink of coffee before she asked, "How does Fiona expect to get to and from Dearborn?"

"I suppose she'll use Liam's truck. He hardly ever drives it." Izzy glanced at her friend for a moment. "I think you've already fallen in love with Aidan. I bet you had so much fun picking out all that baby stuff. Now you're worried about him and Fiona and Nick and you don't want to go on the trip but Alex has made all the plans, so you have to." With a triumphant flourish of her hand, Izzy added, "And that's why you're all worked up about Fiona and her unbelievably selfish behaviour."

Cynthia drank her coffee in silence. Finally, she said, "Okay ... you're on to me. When I picked that little guy up the other night and he stopped crying and fussing and fell asleep in my arms, I admit it, I got all gooey like a marshmallow. When I was a nurse, I looked after lots of babies. But something about holding Aidan was different." Cynthia gave Izzy a stern look. "That doesn't mean what I said about Fiona isn't still my opinion."

"Fair enough." Izzy stared out to the lake and watched a lone duck trace a V in the rippling water as it sedately paddled by. "You are generous to offer her the use of the house while you're gone, Cynthia. It's the best solution under the circumstances. It will be interesting to see how she and Nick work things out with shared child care." She paused, "Well, that's assuming he wants anything to do with Aidan."

"Oh, of course he will ... when he gets over the shock. He's a responsible man. And Aidan is the sweetest baby. Nick won't be able to resist for long. Mark my words ... I give him twenty-four more hours at the most before he shows up here begging to see his son."

FIFTEEN

N ick walked down the hall of the camp's main building shaking his head. He'd just come from Alison's office where he had managed to send the woman into a tizzy simply by knocking on her door and poking his head into the room. To streamline his work schedule, he'd asked the career counsellor to take responsibility for the new resident orientation session later in the week. With meetings eating into the bulk of this day, he needed to focus on catching up with the appointments he'd missed. Doing the orientation would be good experience for Alison.

He left the camp and headed out on the trail that would take him to Fiona and his son. He'd made up his mind. The truth had come to him yesterday afternoon on the back nine of the golf course. After extricating himself from the Paula situation, he had begun to go stir crazy in his cabin. He packed an overnight bag, put his golf clubs in the trunk of his car and headed down Island. Booking a hotel room with a great view of Departure Bay, he hit the green for an early evening nine holes followed by a beer and a burger at the clubhouse. The next morning, he'd enjoyed a leisurely coffee and breakfast out on the small deck of his room. From there he watched the boats in the harbour zip up and down, a couple of float planes take off and a long, sleek BC Ferry glide into port. Hitting the road, he managed another eighteen holes at Crown Royal, a nice lunch and then an uneventful drive back to Micah Camp.

Pushing all personal issues from his thoughts and focusing on his golf swing had allowed everything to fall into place. He had a son. He needed to face that reality and step up to the plate, whatever that meant. Fatherhood was going to be a learning process for him, of that much he was sure. He had no idea when he'd get a chance to swing a golf club again.

He passed the A-Frame and organic bakery and waved to Beulah who was leaning against the outdoor oven. A few more minutes down the path, he came to Alex and Cynthia's. He stopped at the top of the drive to admire the lines of their cabin and the way the cleared space in front seemed to sweep down to the lake. The view was different than the one he enjoyed from his deck. The cove's uneven shoreline jutted in and out. In some places, tall trees came right down to the water; in others, cliffs butted up against the lake and gentle slopes formed sandy beaches. The view altered every few minutes along the trail that wound from one end of the cove at Micah Camp, past the various dwellings and on to the far side.

The place was quiet as Nick climbed the steps to the porch and knocked on the door. A few moments later it opened. Fiona stood there giving him a look that was a cross between frustration and relief. In their time together, he'd become adept at reading her moods. He hadn't lost the ability. Keep it simple, he told himself. "I'm here to talk."

She stepped back and waved him into the house. "Do you want coffee," she asked.

He nodded and walked through the entry to the open dining room off the kitchen. "Where is ... Aidan?" The pause made it sound like he couldn't remember the kid's name but that wasn't true. He'd been going to say – *my son* – but that had a ring of possession which didn't seem to strike the right tone. The words – *the boy* – seemed archaic and cold. In the end, he'd decide to use the child's name.

Fiona raised an eyebrow in his direction before putting two cups of coffee on the table and sitting down across from him. "He's napping ... upstairs." She noticed him looking around and added, "Cynthia and Alex have gone to town."

He relaxed slightly and reached for his coffee. Alex could be intimidating. He had no desire to have this conversation with Fiona's father lurking in the wings. He cleared his throat. "We have a son. Let's figure out how we're going to make this work."

As she slid down in her chair and stretched her legs out under the table, a smile touched the corners of her mouth. She reached for her coffee. "So, that's it. No resentful recriminations. Just where is my schedule and when do I start?"

"If you mean do I want to go chapter and verse over how we ended up here ... what's the point? Let's move forward."

"Okay ... Cynthia and Alex have offered me this place while they're away. I'm thinking that it's best, for the most part, to have Aidan here. You're right next door and so are Izzy and Liam. They're going to help us out for the first couple of weeks. I know you have a job and so do I. We're going to need daycare. There's a place in Dearborn that takes drop-ins."

Nick held his hand up, "Hold on a minute. You and Aidan are going to be staying here? I assumed you'd be in Dearborn."

"I have to stay in town three nights a week when I'm on call but because I'm on call, I can't have Aidan with me. I'll be staying at Rosemary's apartment in the Lady Brit."

"I'll have to stay here those three nights and be with Aidan."

This time Fiona's relief was obvious. "Yes ... I'll grab my clinic schedule and we can at least figure out the next week."

When the details had been hammered out to ensure the most basic requirement – that there would be an adult available to care for Aidan twenty-four-seven – Nick drained the last of his coffee and said, "There's still a major problem ... for me, at least." Fiona narrowed her eyes slightly as she stared at him. "I have zero experience in parenting and no knowledge of how to care for a baby." She laughed. "Hey," he said, "I'm serious."

"Nick, I'm not far ahead of you on that score." For the first time since seeing this woman standing in Izzy's kitchen with his baby in her arms, he felt like smiling. Because, of course, from the moment he saw her, he knew Aidan was his. He'd experienced a visceral reaction that couldn't be denied. "At least we're truly in this together." He stood up. "Can I see him?"

Fiona led the way up the stairs to the second floor. Across the open loft, she gently pushed open a door and Nick was amazed by what appeared to be a ready-made nursery. Through the wooden slats of the crib against the far wall, he could see his son lying on his back, arms flung out, fast asleep. Together, he and Fiona tiptoed into the room to stand beside the crib. He watched as Aidan's tiny mouth sucked quickly on a soother. The room was so quiet Nick could hear the baby's slow, steady breaths. He felt a strange ache take up residence in his chest.

Out on the porch a few moments later, Nick looked at Fiona and asked, "Are you at least sorry for not telling me?"

She met his gaze. When she looked him in the eye the way she was doing now, he knew that whatever she said would be the truth. When she finally spoke, her voice had a tone of sincere regret. "Yes, Nick. I am sorry. I know I made a mistake."

Izzy rapped lightly on Alison's open office door and stepped in to find her friend carefully arranging a vase of lilacs. "Those smell divine." Alison glanced up. Smiling and moving closer together, the two women shared a quick tentative hug. Izzy stepped back. "It's been a while, hasn't it? You look well. I'm sorry I wasn't here when you arrived but I only work a couple of days a week now and we had a family celebration on the weekend." Izzy paused for a moment before she added, "I thought you might like to settle in before catching up with an old friend."

Alison nodded. She pointed to a chair for Izzy to take and sat down herself. She arranged her hands in her lap. She was neatly attired in slacks and a short-sleeved blouse with a peter pan collar that sat pertly over a string of pearls. "I suppose you heard about my arrival?" Izzy sat down and nodded. "I had no reason to panic the way I did. I was overtired and stressed about the move and ... other things." Her colour was rising.

Izzy felt sorry for Alison. "Maybe the best thing to do is move forward. I hope the incident hasn't put you off staying in the trailer. I've heard it's quite nice."

"No, of course not. The trailer is very comfortable."

"I was trying to figure out how long it's been since we saw each other."

Alison gazed out the window to the lake for a moment before she said, "I think our last meeting must have been at the counselling conference ... the one in Montreal."

Izzy took a deep breath. "Yes, of course, right before Caleb died. No wonder I couldn't remember. I felt as though the whole world stopped."

"Things do change." Alison looked down at her folded hands. "Now Bradley is not in my life, I've left the prairies for the mountains, traded my beautiful home for a trailer and abandoned old comforts for a new job.

"Do you want to talk about it?" When Alison had inquired about the career counsellor job at Micah Camp, Izzy had asked around and learned from a couple of mutual friends that Alison had gone from being happily married for twenty-two years to being single and looking for a new job.

"Not yet ... not here at work."

Izzy changed the subject, "I've been lobbying the Board for years to get a full-time career counsellor. I know the hiring process was a bit rushed but I've had lots of time to consider how Micah Camp can benefit from your expertise."

Alison appeared to relax slightly as they embarked on a conversation related to the job. "I've made a start by going over the intake files on each of the residents. And I've looked at the files kept by your previous career person, but as to specifics ... I don't have a full picture yet."

"I can tell you how I see the job." Alison got up to grab a notepad from her desk and waved a hand for Izzy to go on. "The residents need one person to oversee their programs. Your job would include agreeing on their initial plan for the year, recommending the courses that will help maximize their chances for post-secondary opportunities or employment, identifying the pre-requisites they must meet, knowing when they need to be applying for various programs or scholarships and making sure that their work placements help them toward their goals."

"Yes ... I anticipated most of that. I think I should meet with the teachers on a regular basis. It's important to keep the lines of communication open. I'd like to try skills groups to maximize my time with the residents."

"I like the group idea. As you get to know the kids, you will see who needs what and you'll be able to decide for yourself how you want to spend your time."

A frown creased Alison's brow. "I'm assuming I report to Roland but he hasn't asked to meet with me."

Izzy smiled. "Roland is usually up to his ears in administration matters. He always attends the direct client meetings. Those sessions include you and me and Nick and Roland. Most issues get ironed out during those meetings." Izzy glanced up at the clock, "The time is flying by today. I have a client session in fifteen minutes and then we have the meeting with Charlie Sutherland's parents." In response to Alison's look of confusion, she added, "One of the new residents."

"Am I to attend?" Alison asked, reaching for her calendar

"Yes. Roland wants all the counselling staff there. And then we have the full staff meeting this afternoon."

Glancing up from her calendar, Alison said, "Nick asked me to do the orientation session but he didn't bring me any information on how to do it or provide me with the files for the new residents."

Izzy wasn't surprised to learn that Nick was clearing his work schedule. The man had to be reeling. "Come along to my office now and I'll give you my orientation file. I have a checklist of things that need to be covered and some handouts."

Gordon placed their math tests face down on the table in front of Robbie and Tabby before he left the classroom, saying as he went, "Good job, the both of you."

Robbie turned his paper over slowly and checked his score. Tabby was already smiling broadly and smirking at him as she gestured for him to let her see his mark. He pushed his paper across the table towards her. By the sudden spike in her shifting light, he knew that he had finally managed to beat her at math.

"Only by two percent. That's nothing." Tabby tried to sound okay about Robbie's slight edge but she was upset. He could tell. She stared at the two papers side-by-side. He watched as she dashed a tear from her eye. She stood up quickly, "The cookies are probably ready. Let's get out of here."

In tense silence, he followed her down the hallway and across Micah Camp's vast living room, through the dining room lined with tables and chairs and into the kitchen. She took two chocolate chip cookies from the rows cooling on the rack and scooted up onto one of the chairs by the counter. He slid in beside her. She shoved a cookie at him and he picked it up and bit into the gooey goodness.

Brigit walked into the room from the pantry and smiled at them. "Hey, you two. Finished math? Did you get your tests back? How did you do?"

Robbie saw Izzy coming into the kitchen with her coffee cup. She walked over and stood close to him, resting her hand on his shoulder as she said, "Hey, Robbie, Robbie, McBobby ... what's up?"

He tried to grin at the old nickname but his mouth was full of cookie and his senses overridden by the fact that the girl next to him was going to explode.

Tabby slammed her cookie on the counter and crumbs went flying. She jumped off her stool with such a jerk that the thing fell over with a loud clang. Her face was a dark, ruddy tone of red. "Math is stupid. Who cares about a score in a stupid subject? Not me." She turned and ran out of the room.

Izzy's eyebrows rose and Brigit stared after her daughter in surprise. She gave Robbie an inquiring look. He shrugged, got up, grabbed another cookie for good measure and said, "She probably went home. I'll wait over on your porch until she cools off." He strolled out of the room.

Brigit leaned into the counter and watched Izzy pour her coffee. "I'm worried about Tabby," she said.

Going to the fridge for cream, Izzy gave Brigit a sympathetic look. "Well ... she's at that age, right? Moody."

Brigit frowned, "I suppose. But Izzy, it's odd ... you know ... that she has no girlfriends. She's growing up and I'm starting to think something like that might matter ... having another girl to talk things over with."

Izzy glanced at her watch. She had the meeting with Charlie Sutherland's parents in ten minutes. But she could tell Tabby's behaviour seemed more serious to Brigit than the tantrums of a kid acting out. "Is this about going to school in Dearborn?"

"I don't want to sound ungrateful for everything Liam's done with the homeschooling but I do wonder if it's time for Tabby to start interacting with more kids. She should have girlfriends to chum around with. Don't you think?"

Brigit's question left Izzy in a difficult position. If she agreed, she would be adding weight to Brigit's concern and perhaps precipitate a harder stand on Brigit's part. If she disagreed, her opinion could be interpreted as defensive – as if she believed Brigit's uncertainty about Tabby's social life somehow meant that Robbie's friendship wasn't enough. She reached over and patted Brigit's arm, "I hear that you're concerned about her. What I think doesn't matter. You'll have to talk it out with Tabby."

⚜ ⚜ ⚜ ⚜

Izzy pushed through the door to the small meeting room with her black leather day planner in hand. Roland was already in the room. He waved her over to the table. "Before everyone else gets here, I've a favour to ask." Izzy sat down and gestured for him to go on. "I'd like you to talk to Jeremy about the whole trailer incident. I think a reprimand would be better coming from you. You have a rapport with him. I'd be liable to strike the wrong tone and I don't want Darlene Evans parking the loss of our volunteer computer tech teacher on my doorstep."

"Yes, okay," she said as the door opened and Nick came in.

Izzy gave him an inquiring look. He said, "I'm good. Working things out."

Roland flipped through some papers on the table. "I'm hoping your two days off have done the trick. I rescheduled all your clients."

Alison came into the room and banged her hip against the table as she tried to edge past Nick. He frowned and she grimaced as she pulled out a chair. A moment later, one of the residents who worked at the front desk appeared in the doorway. She waved two people into the room, "Mr. and

127

Mrs. Sutherland are here, Roland. I'll bring the coffee cart. Brigit has it all ready."

Roland moved forward to shake hands, introductions were made and soon, with cups of the steaming beverage poured and chocolate chip cookies passed around, everyone was seated at the table.

Roland looked at the Sutherlands, "I think the best way for us to proceed is for you to tell us about Charlie."

Warren Sutherland spoke up first, "We love our child. I don't have much more to add. Bev usually does most of the talking at times like this. And believe you me, we've attended our share of meetings."

Bev smiled at him, took a drink of coffee and placed the cup down on the table. "I think the best thing I can do is tell you how we learned about Charlie." She took a deep breath. "Maybe we would have noticed earlier that Carlie was in distress," she paused and scanned the faces around the table. "I call her Carlie only because at that time, in her early years, that is how we knew her … as our daughter."

She glanced quickly at her husband who reached out and patted her arm. "We might have noticed earlier but we were the type of parents who had this bug-a-bear about gender specific clothes and toys and attitudes. We provided dresses and pants, dolls and trucks. Most activities for toddlers are not particularly gender based. We kept our daughter's hair short in a kind of pixie cut because she fussed so much over hair brushing." She smiled sadly at the memory.

"The first real problem came up when we began taking Carlie to the family swim at our local pool. She was about three. Every time we went, she made a huge production about wanting to go to the men's dressing room with her dad and not to the woman's dressing room with me. No amount of explaining the difference got through to her. She would try to pull the top of her bathing suit off and kept insisting she wanted a bathing suit like her dad's. She had always had a stubborn streak but, somehow, her genuine distress struck us as odd."

Bev stopped to take another drink of coffee and let what she had said so far sink in. "Soon after that, she began to talk about being a boy. And that got our attention. We took her to our family doctor and then later to a child psychologist. The evaluation was thorough and the report came as no surprise to us – Carlie was convinced that she was a boy not a girl."

Making eye contact with each one of them and glancing to her husband before continuing, Bev added, "As Warren said, we love our child. We looked around until we found a kindergarten that would allow our son,

Charlie, to attend as the gender he identified with. The journey has been difficult from the start and we've had to fight at every stage of Charlie's education to find places that will accept him and adapt for him when necessary. We did a lot of research on Micah Camp before deciding that this could be a good next step for Charlie. He's a young eighteen and there are so many things he's working out for himself. He wants to be out on his own, going away to school like the other kids from his grad class, but we think he needs more support than a typical university campus is likely to provide.

Warren leaned forward, "By support we don't mean special treatment. He's not disabled or unstable. He's lived as a boy and then a young man for his whole life. When you meet him next week, I think you'll agree - he blends in."

Bev nodded at her husband's insistence on the need to treat Charlie like any other young man. "We've been to the clinic in town and Charlie has met Dr. Wells. We were so impressed to find a young doctor who is knowledgeable about the medical issues Charlie faces now and may face in the future. Dearborn is fortunate to have Fiona."

Nick's coffee cup came down on the table with a small thud and Bev lost her train of thought for a moment as she looked over at him with a quizzical glance. "Sorry about that," he said.

She smiled and went on, "Fiona and Charlie hit it off right away. And that is such a relief for us. He needs to see her every two weeks and we are confident that he feels comfortable to discuss any medical issues with her."

Bev reached down into the large bag she had toted in with her and pulled out four copies of a book. She placed the stack on the table and the words – *Trans Bodies, Trans Selves* – were visible. "I believe in people having useful resources. This book is like the classic – *Our Bodies, Ourselves*. It you make the effort, it can become your bible on transgendered issues."

Bev smiled as Alison immediately reached for the top book from the pile and put it down on the table in front of her. Looking at Izzy, Bev said, "Without ruffling anyone's feathers," she glanced quickly from Nick to Roland, "we want Ms. Montgomery to work with Charlie." Reaching again into the large bag, Bev pulled out two stapled sheaves of paper. Holding up one, she said, "Warren and I were impressed by this article by Ms. Montgomery about kids falling through the cracks of the medical system ..." picking up the other, she continued, "... and this one about approaches to trauma work with young people." She gave Izzy a searching look. "It's not as important to us that you have specific skills related to transgender issues as it is that you recognize the importance of letting Charlie take the lead. He's

129

always been our main instructor. If you listen to him, he's going to let you know the kind of help he needs."

Izzy glanced over at Roland and he nodded his approval. She smiled at Bev, "I'm looking forward to meeting Charlie. And please ... both of you ... call me, Izzy."

Bev encouraged them to ask questions. She emphasized that they should not feel stupid about anything they wanted to know, however simple it might sound to others. She was an experienced advocate for her child and it showed. When things wound down, Roland said, "You wanted to have a tour of the camp. I've lined up a young man who will be one of Charlie's roommates to show you around."

Roland slipped out of the room and soon returned with Ethan right behind him. He gestured for Izzy, Nick and Alison to follow him back to his office. Once inside with the door shut, he said, "I want to stress again the confidential nature of Charlie's situation. No matter what any of us may feel about the wisdom of secrecy, allowing Charlie to take the lead is what his parents want and they are paying a substantial amount of money to send their son here."

He walked over to his desk, opened a drawer and pulled out three brown envelopes. "These are the new residents' personal essays from their application packages. The board has decided that these are not to be placed in the resident's general file. They think it more appropriate to consider the essay on the same level as counselling case notes." He frowned and addressed Alison. "I should have gone over the file system with you before now. Each resident has a general file ... colour-coded blue and residing in a locked cabinet in the file room. You have free access to those files. Your career counselling case notes will go in those blue files. Residents also have a red file where confidential counselling notes are kept. These red files are stored in a locked cabinet in the counsellor's office. You do not have access to the red files." Alison coloured slightly at that remark. If ever a firm divide was drawn between her role as a career counsellor and the roles of Izzy and Nick as trauma counsellors, access to the red files was that line. Roland glanced at the locked file cabinet in his own office. "A third set of files is kept here in my office. These are yellow files and, like the counsellors, you will make a copy of all your notes to go into these files. They also contain medical information, correspondence with social services or parents, and various other information that can be made available on a need-to-know basis." He gave her a searching look, "Understood?"

For Alison, Roland's question represented an adjustment. In the private school where she had worked, she had been the one to keep the confidential files that were available to the teachers on a need-to-know basis.

Roland turned to Izzy, "Here's Charlie's essay." He passed the other two envelopes to Nick, "You'll have these two. I've checked your case load and you have room for two more clients." They all nodded their agreement.

Roland gestured for Alison to stay behind a moment as Izzy and Nick left the room. "I'd like you to make Ethan Black's career goals one of your first priorities, Alison. He's coming up on two years here at Micah Camp and it is far past time for him to be moving on."

SIXTEEN

Jeremy slumped in the chair across from Izzy who was seated at her desk. All she could see was the shadow of the nineteen-year-old boy who had sat in her office with a load of emotional crap weighing down his thin frame. She had cut her counsellor teeth on his problems as surely as she had helped him work his way through them.

She resisted the urge to ask – *well, what do you have to say for yourself* – as if he were Robbie's age. Instead she simply stared at him and waited for him to speak.

Shifting uneasily, Jeremy finally met her gaze. "Look, I'm sorry. But seriously, if the woman hadn't shown up a day early we wouldn't even be having this conversation."

"That's hardly the point, is it?"

"No real harm's been done, though, right?"

She gave him a stern look. "Alison was shaken up by the shock of finding you and your yoga mom in her trailer. Everyone is talking about how she ran across the camp looking like she'd witnessed a murder. She did not exactly make a great first impression. I do think all of that constitutes harm."

Jeremy's left knee, hidden under his baggy shorts, hammered up and down. "She didn't need to run off in such a huff. It wasn't as if she'd walked in on Caligula in full-scale orgy mode. I may have practiced poor judgement in my choice of a love nest but I wasn't committing a crime." He grinned, "And remember, I don't technically work at Micah Camp. I'm a volunteer."

"You are seriously irritating me, Jeremy." She gave him a frosty look. "You're fortunate Roland decided that dealing with you was beneath his dignity. I'm not happy to be here either. No one appreciates having to referee antics more suited to a college frat house than a facility that deals with the educational and emotional needs of vulnerable young people. And the fact that you are a volunteer has no bearing on anything. Altruism does not trump idiocy."

Jeremy straightened in his chair. "I am sorry, Izzy. I messed up but please don't think I lack respect for the work we do here. I'll make it up to Alison. I promise. And I'll do everything I can to squelch the gossip."

"It won't be easy to put that cat back in the bag. But I can't imagine what else I'm supposed to say to you." As Jeremy rose from his chair, she held up her hand. "I can't let you leave the office after less than ten minutes. Can you give me a hand with the screen resolution on my laptop? All my icons are bigger than they're supposed to be. I can't figure out how to shrink them and they are driving me crazy."

❧❧❧❧

Paula left the Micah Camp's teacher's office on the upper floor, came down the main staircase and out the door onto the breezeway. She watched the clouds scud across the sky as a sudden rain drenched down and pinged off the surface of the water. She carried on and pushed her way through the double doors to the paper and soap shop. The large, brightly lit work space bustled as it always did. Kids were sorting flowers into the drying trays, her mom was supervising at the soap vats, and someone was wrapping bars of soap and packing them into boxes for shipping. She smiled seeing the corner of the shop that was taken up with Noah's toys and a comfy sofa. Her mom often kept an eye on Paula's busy two-year-old when she was teaching.

Josie saw her and came across the shop, stopping on the way to give instructions to a couple of kids. She waved a hand at her office door and called out, "I'll be right there."

Paula was hardly through the door of the closet-size office, when Josie came in behind her. She turned in time to see the top of her mother's high ponytail bouncing as she leaned over to gather up a pile of invoices off the only chair, "Sit. Who's looking after Noah?"

"I left him at the drop-in daycare in town."

Josie sniffed, "I don't like it. He'll pick up something there. I heard that last month someone dropped a kid off who had hoof and mouth disease."

"It's hand, foot and mouth disease, Mom. And they closed the place for three days to do a total disinfecting. What choice did I have? We both have to go to the staff meeting this afternoon."

Josie had been rooting through the invoices as she spoke. She stopped now and gave her daughter a searching look, "What's wrong with you? You look mopey."

"I'm not mopey." Paula frowned at her mother's accurate description as she said, "I heard Nick went down Island. I wonder if he'll be back for the staff meeting." She watched as her mom made a face and the telltale *humph* sound was a definite tip off, "What?" she demanded. "I told you ... we're taking a break until after the summer. I still like him. He's a great guy."

Josie leaned into the file cabinet. "I've heard a thing or two about Nick Anderson ... things you need to know." Though Paula held up her hand to stop her mother's gossiping, her gesture was of no use. "Reg told me he heard Justin talking to Mike in the lunchroom at the sawmill."

"Mom ... stop. I don't want to hear such third-hand stuff."

"Trust me, you want to hear this. Nick was over at Izzy and Liam's on Sunday and out of the blue, Liam's sister, Fiona, showed up with a baby in her arms. Take a guess who the father is."

Paula sat back in her chair and stared at her mother. Shocked, she asked in a low voice, "Not Nick?"

"No other ... I told you he was involved with Fiona a couple of years ago when she was around here working with Dr. Rosemary. She's back now and she's got Nick's baby with her."

"Why would she come back?"

"She's taking over Dr. Rosemary's practice for the next four months."

"She's our new doctor?" That was a shock, too. Paula had an appointment the next week. She slumped in the chair and folded her arms over her chest, holding her body tightly. Her foot began to tap up and down. She realized now that Nick hadn't been saying they should take a break. He had dumped her and she'd been too stupid to get it. She stood up, "I'll see you at the staff meeting. I've got stuff to do."

Heading back into the main building she almost ran into Jeremy. Since they were standing in the same spot where she had passed him a few days before when he was running out of the building wearing that ridiculous pink T-shirt, the whole gossipy story of his behaviour came back to her.

He stopped and smiled at her, "Hey, Paula ... want to grab a coffee before the staff meeting?"

Her eyes shot sparks. "I'm not your type. I don't do yoga." She walked away telling herself that she was done with men – period.

* * *

Carrying his mug of coffee, Reg walked through the paper and soap shop and into Josie's office. She was jotting notes down on a piece of paper. "I saw Paula over in the main building," he told her. "She looked to have a real head of steam on. I'm guessing you repeated what I told you about Nick."

She looked up, "You shouldn't have told me if you didn't want it repeated. I'm not going to keep something like that from her. She comes in here mooning over how she hopes to see Nick at the staff meeting. He's been leading her a fine dance. She has a right to know."

Reg shook his head as he sat down in the only chair. "You don't know what's gone on between the two of them."

"I could tell by the look on her face that he hadn't said a word to her about his old girlfriend or a baby. That tells me all I need to know."

"It's none of our business, Josie."

She put her hands on her hips and stared him down, "I'll tell you this, Reg Compton. Paula's welfare is damn well my business. I won't let anyone take advantage of her."

He held his hand up, "Okay, okay ... your daughter, your business. Enough said."

She took a deep breath and studied him closely. "You look tense. You're working too hard." She came around the edge of her desk and slipped behind his chair to rub his shoulders. "I was looking online the other day at cruise packages. We should go on a holiday. I might be able to get Lisa-Marie to take over running the shop for a couple of weeks. It would be good to kick back and live a bit." She continued kneading with her thumbs. "Geez, Reg ... your muscles are bunched up in a knot."

He forced himself to relax. Take a holiday, kick back, go on a fucken cruise. He didn't think so. "Things are busy at the sawmill right now."

"Oh, you always say that." She patted his shoulder. "Maybe you need to see a doctor, Reg. Your colour isn't good and I hear you wheezing when you aren't even doing anything. You might be getting that bronchitis back again."

❧❧❧❧

Alison pushed aside Izzy's orientation file. Lunch had come and gone and she had ignored the smell of food coming from the dining room. She didn't have much of an appetite. She swiveled her chair around and let her mind wander as she watched Jim, the maintenance guy, walk across the lawn on his way towards the large greenhouse. She had met most of the staff and people seemed friendly. Penny had offered to clean the trailer once a week and she had smiled broadly when Alison said that wouldn't be necessary. That smile had given Alison the courage to ask if Penny could see about having the bedspread cleaned. The woman had given her a knowing look before taking the bundle and walking away.

The teachers, Gordon, Maryanne and Paula were all approachable and seemed to want to work with her. She hadn't had to face Jeremy yet. Gordon said Jeremy's schedule was erratic. Brigit was a friendly, no-nonsense, energetic type and her daughter seemed to be cut from the same cloth. Alison had thoroughly enjoyed the tour Josie gave her of the paper and soap workshop. She was scheduled to visit the sawmill the next morning and the organic bakery in the afternoon.

Roland struck her as the type of boss who was distant and demanding all at the same time. In her opinion, that was not the best combination. She hadn't known how to take his admonition to make Ethan a top priority. Naturally, she would do her best work with every resident. And the way he had emphasized the confidential nature of their meeting with the Sutherlands had made her feel like he was talking for her benefit. Did her ridiculous entrance to his office the other day in a state of hysteria convince him she hadn't a clue how to act professionally?

Izzy was a friend ... they did go way back. Still, Alison hadn't deceived herself into thinking that being a friend of Izzy's would make working with her any easier. Even back in grad school, Izzy's confidence and her competence were intimidating.

Nick was the exception to Alison's conclusion that she could, one way or the other, get along with her coworkers and the staff at Micah Camp. She wasn't convinced he should be dumping his work on her as he had done with the new resident orientation. And she hadn't appreciated the way he had banged on the door of her trailer first thing Sunday morning and said they needed to discuss the overnight supervision rotation. There didn't seem to be much to discuss. She had told him to pencil her into the schedule wherever she was needed. She would certainly take responsibility for anything that was part of her duties. The job of night supervisor entailed clearing out the main building and locking it up at ten p.m. and being available as first responder for any problems. Nick had stared at her with a raised eyebrow when he said those words. Was he trying to remind her of her inability to deal with a simple problem like finding a naked couple engaged in a sexual act in her bed?

The sun broke through a patch of clouds, interrupting all unpleasant thoughts. Alison stood up and rested her hand on the back of her chair as her breath caught at the sight of the rainbow arching over the lake toward the mountains. She stared at the colour shimmering on the water. This was a beautiful place.

A loud knock on her door startled her to the point that she stumbled against her chair and sent it sliding away from her. The force of the movement tipped the chair over backwards onto the floor. She felt completely disoriented as she stared from the chair wheels spinning in the air to the open door and Nick's head appearing around the corner.

"I've got these files for you." He waved three blue folders in the air. "Are you planning to attend the staff meeting?" Nick glanced from the tipped chair to Alison and added, "Rearranging your furniture?"

Alison ignored the question. She bent over and righted the chair as she said, "Of course I'm going to attend the staff meeting. Why do you ask?"

Glancing at his watch, Nick said, "It's starting in a few minutes."

Alison looked to the clock on the wall and realized how the time had slipped by. She felt her face flush as she hastily gathered her notebook and day planner. "I'm coming right now. There's no need for you to wait." The last thing she wanted was to be shepherded like an errant child into the meeting by Nick Anderson.

✄✄✄✄

The dining room was crowded with people milling around and helping themselves to coffee and doughnuts from the table near the kitchen. Jim and Penny joked to one another as they took seats at one end of the table. Brigit set a cup of tea in front of Alison. Waving away Alison's words of thanks as unnecessary, the cook smiled and took a chair near Penny.

The spots around the table were rapidly filling. Jeremy entered the meeting room and looked around for a moment. He slouched into a chair at the far side of the table next to Nick who said something to him. They both laughed.

Josie touched Alison's shoulder and she jumped slightly as she looked around. "Alison, I want you to meet my partner, Reg. He manages the sawmill up the hill." Josie hooked an arm through Reg's and tilted her head towards Alison, "Our new career counsellor. She's the one who'll be deciding work placements."

Alison smiled and reached out to shake the hand of the man who stood beside her chair chewing on a toothpick. He was dressed in jeans, suspenders and a grey Stanfield shirt. Reg spoke around the toothpick, "I hear you're coming up to see the sawmill. I'll be looking forward to giving you the grand tour."

Josie gave Alison a quick wave as she grabbed Reg's arm and headed for two empty chairs on the other side of the table. Izzy walked in with a tall, thin

137

woman. They were deep in conversation. Izzy laid her hand on the woman's arm for a moment and then they parted. The woman took a seat by Reg. Izzy made her way to the head of the table where Roland sat. She took the chair to his right.

Gordon slid into the empty seat next to Alison, placing a plate overflowing with pastries on the table. He smiled at her while pointing to the plate, "Dig in Alison. Don't make me eat all of this by myself." He patted his rounded stomach. Maryanne and Paula walked into the room together and took seats down from Gordon.

A loud voice came from the direction of the dining room, "I'm coming, I'm coming. Don't start without me." A large woman glided into the room wearing a fire engine red dress and a matching fedora that sat at a jaunty angle on her head of salt and pepper curls.

Gordon leaned close to Alison to tell her, "That's Darlene Evans. She's on the Micah Camp Board of Directors. If you think she just made an entrance, you should see her and her husband on the Legion dance floor when a polka number starts."

Roland glanced at his watch, stood and did up the button on his suit jacket. He shuffled the papers in front of him as he said, "Let's get started. In honour of our new staff member, we'll begin with a round of introductions. Alison, you go first."

As everyone stared at her, a blotchy red colour crept up her face. "Alison Kirk," she said. "Lately from career counselling in Saskatoon. I'm pleased to be here and I'm looking forward to working with each of you."

After a round of name giving and various comments related to how nice it was to meet Alison, to welcome a new staff member, to have a career counsellor, to meet another person who hailed from Saskatchewan and, in Jeremy's words, to have Alison on board, Roland cleared his throat and invited Darlene to speak.

With a flourish of the red dress, she rose from her chair. Her voice rang out, "Expansion -," the word hung in the air like a balloon threatening to explode. Darlene laughed and banged her fist on the table. In no time, the infectious sound of the woman's laugh had everyone at least smiling. "I have started my report at so many of these meetings with that word, I couldn't resist one more crack at it." She looked over at Roland. "You will all be relieved to know that, for the present, expansion is done. I'll never say it's over, but you can breathe easy for now."

Glancing at her notes, she went on, "Fundraising is going to be low-keyed this year. I've signed Micah Camp up to run the Big Jackpot Bingo that will kick off Dipsy-Doodle Days. You'll be working with St. Bertha's." She grinned, "Those Catholics know everything about Bingo, so you're in good hands." Checking her notes again, she added, "Oh … I've also put you down for the food wagon on the midway."

She stared down the table. "Jeremy," when he looked her way, she said, "I'm counting on *Mad Man Computers* to run the sound system for the Karaoke stage." Jeremy pulled his laptop forward to enter the information.

Darlene sat down and reached for a doughnut as Jim got up to give his health and safety report. It included several references to what the boat shed should be used for as opposed to his broad hints at what it was being used for. Alison looked confused. The committee reports continued.

While Alison struggled to keep up, Paula's glance flicked often to Nick and then away. Jeremy spent most of his time texting on his phone and everyone ignored his lack of participation. Josie glared over in Nick's direction. Her body posture was one of stern disapproval. Gordon kept his head down as he flipped the page of his Sudoku book and started a new puzzle.

When the floor was opened for new business, Maryanne gave a presentation on grade twelve English requirements and Alison took careful note of the dates for the Dearborn high school career fair. Jim extolled the features of his new ride-a-mower and said he could use a couple of kids to work in the greenhouse. Beulah talked about the organic bakery and Alison scribbled yet another note in her book.

When Reg was given the floor, he jammed his ball cap up and down on his head before he started to talk. "Just want to say, for the record, that Ethan has been one of the best goddamned workers I've had at the mill in a hell of a long time. The kid can put in a back bustin' day of work and dance out the door at the end of his shift like he could do the whole bloody thing again." He leaned forward, "I've got some big orders coming up. I'm gonna need a couple more kids if you have them to spare. If not, I'll look in town."

Roland glanced down the table at Alison then over to Reg. "Let's give Alison a chance to get up to speed on each of the residents. Then, I'm sure she'll get back to you on this, Reg." Turning to Josie, Roland said, "I've a note here that you had something you wanted to say."

Josie folded her arms on the table. "All the kids in the paper and soap shop are doing great." She looked around as she spoke, "Some of you will remember back to the beginning of Micah Camp when the paper and soap shop first got started. Besides jobs like helping in the kitchen, cleaning rooms and taking care of the gardens, the only other work available to residents was in my shop. But now we have the sawmill and the bakery. I'm sure we'll be reaching further and further afield for our kids in the future." She took a deep breath, "I'm thinking of slowing down. The soap has always done better than the paper. I'm going to concentrate on that and run the shop only three days a week."

Reg had tuned out what Josie was saying. His mind was busy calculating the profit margin on an order for beveled cedar siding he had finalized that morning. She turned to smile at him and he wondered what the hell was going on. He had bit into a large bear claw doughnut when he heard her say, "... no time like the present to be cutting back with an eye to retirement, right Reg?"

He sucked in his breath and began to choke on the doughnut in his mouth. Jesus, Mary and Joseph, what the bloody hell was she talking about? His face turned red as he gasped and spewed bits of pastry on the table in front of him. Josie jumped out of her chair and began to thump him on the back, all the while saying, "Reg, are you okay? Come on, baby, breathe."

He finally managed to stop coughing and reached for the glass of water that Brigit had run to the kitchen to get him. He took a drink and waved Josie away. She sat down with a mixed look of hurt and concern on her face.

Roland stood up. "Well, on that note ... meeting adjourned."

SEVENTEEN

Coming across the bridge to the small hill that led to Justin's cabin, Lisa-Marie concluded that it was no wonder Sophie and Pearl were such great pals – they moved at the same pace. Resisting the urge to rush them, she strolled along behind them with a small rhubarb pie in her hand. Truth be told, she wasn't anxious to reach their destination. Being friends with Justin was complicated. They'd tried before and failed – most episodes had ended with her humiliation. She knew she had to walk a fine line but her feelings for Tyler were already shifting. She was not looking forward to the next few days of working closely with him. She didn't want to admit that the change in her attitude was because of Justin, but nothing else in her life was different enough to have caused her shifting affections.

Nearing the steps to Justin's deck, Lisa-Marie had taken the lead. Pearl and Sophie were peering with great interest into the bushes at the side of the trail. She was about to call out hello when she heard Justin's voice rising as he spoke, "Oh, sure, right ... go ahead and be a total bitch about everything. Nothing new there." Lisa-Marie froze, casting a quick glance back to Sophie who, having plucked a salmonberry from a low-hanging branch, was oblivious.

Sophie called out, "Mama, look, look. I see a geen bug." The child was staring intently at the berry in the palm of her hand.

At the same moment, Lisa-Marie raised her voice and said, "Hey, Justin. Anybody home? You've got guests carrying pie." She beckoned to Sophie and the two of them were looking at the bug when Justin stepped forward onto the edge of the deck.

He shoved his cell phone in his pocket as he smiled at them, "Is it pie and Sophie or Sophie pie?"

Sophie giggled and ran up the stairs. Lisa-Marie stooped to give Pearl a boost before she followed up the steps. The dog's tail wagged wildly. She handed Justin the pie. "It's rhubarb. We were going for a walk, so we came by to drop it off. I should have texted you to say that we were coming but I forgot I could." She glanced at the satellite dish.

Ignoring any reference to his phone service, Justin said, "That's okay ... you know you're always welcome here. Especially when you bring pie." He smiled. "I just got home. I was in town this afternoon for my Western Forest interview. I had fish and chips for dinner at the *Beach Road Café*. This pie is going to be great for dessert."

Sophie had pulled her Belle and the Beast plastic figures out of her pocket and was walking them along the railing. Lisa-Marie smiled when Sophie had Belle say, "No Beast, you walk behind me."

She turned back to Justin, "How did it go?"

"They did a group interview. To answer most of the questions, I drew way more on experience from working at the sawmill than I did on my engineering degree. It's a waiting game now to see if I'll get called back for a one-on-one interview."

Having walked Belle and the Beast all around the deck, Sophie looked from Justin to her mom before she said, "Justin have cookies, Mama."

"Just one," Lisa-Marie told her daughter as she followed Justin and the child into the small cabin. Sophie went with confidence to a lower cupboard, opened it and pulled out a bag of Oreos. Pearl went to another cupboard, sniffed, and stared at Justin with a begging look. Justin walked over to grab the bright red Milk Bone box. Sophie settled cross-legged on the floor with Pearl beside her and they both munched on their cookies. Lisa-Marie told Justin, "Those two sure know their way around here."

"You all do. Stay for a coffee?"

"No ... I've got to get that one home for a bath." Lisa-Marie pointed at Sophie. "Do you want to come over to the Old Library Bus tonight to welcome Arianna? Mike and Wynter are coming."

"Ya, sure. Sounds like fun. I'll bring my guitar." He paused for a moment before asking, "How is your job going?"

"I'm heading out tomorrow for four days of shooting."

"I heard from Zach that you're working with a guy named Tyler." The comment was so casual but so loaded with implication that Lisa-Marie had a difficult time hiding her sharp intake of breath.

"Come on, Sophie. We've got to go." She told Justin, "Tyler does the filming and I do the photos." Shooing Sophie and Pearl in front of her, Lisa-Marie headed for the door.

"I'll come by Liam and Izzy's and get you around nine. How does that sound?" Justin asked.

"Great. That will give me time to get Sophie settled." Going down the stairs, she called out, "See you, later."

❧❧❧❧

Brigit tucked herself into the chair across from Alison and blew across the surface of the hot tea in her cup. She sipped and let out a satisfied sigh before saying, "This is nice. I'm glad you stopped by. It gets quiet here in the evenings after Tabby goes to sleep."

"Thanks for inviting me." Alison glanced around the cabin and played the fingers of her free hand in and out of the chain that held her glasses around her neck. "Have you been working here at Micah Camp for long? You seem so settled ... part of the place ... I envy your easy rapport with the residents."

"I've been here almost two years. It's hard to believe how fast the time goes by." Brigit chuckled. "Being a chef certainly wasn't my first career choice, but cooking and running the kitchen have become enjoyable jobs." Brigit thought that the best way to put Alison at ease would be to do most of the talking. "I was a police officer in Toronto before I came here." She noted the surprise on Alison's face. "I know, I know ... it's a long way from law enforcement to food preparation."

"And a long way from Toronto to Micah Camp," Alison added as she relaxed slightly in her chair.

"You can say that again. I needed a change, for a bunch of reasons, then the opportunity for this job came up ... it has turned out to be a marriage made in heaven." Brigit saw Alison give a nod of understanding and she suspected that this woman's journey to Micah Camp might also have been a matter of good timing. "The place has been good for Tabby. I sure don't regret taking a chance and coming here."

Alison set her tea cup down. "It's isolated though, isn't it? What do you do with yourself when you're not working?"

Brigit's mouth turned up in a small grin. "The work is far more demanding than I thought it would be, so I don't have a lot of free time. When I first came here, Izzy was doing Roland's job as director. She told me that if I did my job well, people would feel so at home in the kitchen that it would become the heart of Micah Camp. I guess I'm doing okay because the place is always packed with kids. And, of course, Tabby keeps me hopping. I do get out now and then. Soon after I came here, I volunteered to do a few things at St. Bertha's in Dearborn. I teach religious education and I represent the parish on a regional refugee committee."

"Is that the Catholic church I passed when I first drove into Dearborn?" Brigit nodded and Alison went on, "I never missed church back home but lately, with travelling and other things, I've gotten out of the habit of attending services."

"Well, if you ever change your mind, you're more than welcome to come with Tabby and me. Mass is at 10:00 a.m. every Sunday." Brigit stretched her arms over her head for a moment before she said, "There's a movie theatre in Dearborn and I take Tabby to a show now and then. Over the fall and winter, we went into town for skating most Saturdays. I suppose it's like living in any small place ... you have to make your own entertainment." With a small shrug, Brigit said, "That's enough about me. How are things going for you?"

"I've been hoping to make up for lost ground after my disastrous arrival but I don't see how it's possible." Colour crept up Alison's neck as she said, "I know everyone is still talking about me and every time I see Jeremy, I wish I could drop through the floor."

"No one is saying much of anything anymore and I actually heard Jeremy ream out a couple of residents who brought it up the other day. Gordon says Izzy told Jeremy to make it up to you and I think he's trying."

"Thanks for telling me that. It helps to know Jeremy isn't laughing at me all the time."

Brigit grinned, "It should be you laughing at him. He was the naked one. I don't know what you saw, but even with his clothes on he's not exactly my idea of Mr. Hot and Handsome."

Alison blushed at the memory of what she had seen but in the face of Brigit's impish smile, she had to grin. She relaxed and before she had a chance to censor herself, she blurted out, "I can't stand Nick." When she realized the implications of her remark, Alison clapped her hand over her mouth then dropped it to add, "Please, forget I said that. It's unprofessional of me to speak that way about a colleague."

"I won't tell on you, Alison. Relax. He wasn't on my list of favourites when I first arrived here either. What's he done to upset you?"

"He obviously isn't going to let me live this thing down. He barged into my office –," Alison made a face. "I suppose that isn't fair. He did knock, but then he walked right in without a by-your-leave. He dropped the new resident orientation on me like he's my boss." She shook her head, "He takes up way too much space. And he's always asking me if I can handle things. He makes it seem like he's being helpful but he sounds condescending to me. When he's around, I feel like screaming and stamping my feet. Why is it that we tend to act down to the expectations of others?"

"I'm not sure about that ... sounds pretty philosophical. But listen ... I'm going to tell you about something that happened over at Izzy's on Sunday. Keep it under your hat but I think it will help you understand why Nick's being so pushy." Brigit described Fiona and Aidan's arrival at Sophie's birthday party. "Nick went white, I thought he might keel over from the shock. And there was Fiona, calm as a cucumber, walking up to him and saying, meet your son."

Alison held her hand up for Brigit to stop speaking, "Whoa ... who is Fiona?"

"Have you met Izzy's husband, Liam?" Alison shook her head. "Fiona is Liam's sister. She's a doctor. She came here a couple of summers ago to work with Dearborn's Dr. Rosemary and she stayed in Izzy and Liam's guest cabin. She and Nick were an item but she left first to go to Vancouver and then back east. She dropped off the radar. I assumed she and Nick had split up. Lately, he's been dating Paula."

"The French teacher ... Josie's daughter?"

"Yes ... you're starting to get all the connections." Brigit smiled. "Anyway, Nick obviously had no idea about the baby and I can only imagine that having fatherhood thrust at him the way Fiona tried to drop that cute-as-a-button baby in his arms, has thrown him for a loop." Brigit started to laugh, "Don't get me wrong – I feel for the man – but if you could have seen his face. It was like Fiona was offering him a grenade with the pin unplugged."

⁕⁕⁕⁕

Arianna was coming out of the library bus with Mike, Wynter and Zach at her heels when she heard Lisa-Marie call out a greeting from the edge of the clearing. With Justin beside her, she was heading towards the group. Mike waved to Justin and turned to Zach, "Let's get the fire going. It'll be dark soon."

Lisa-Marie gave Zach a quick hug before greeting Arianna and begging for a tour of the bus. "I've heard from Izzy and Liam that the place is unbelievable."

Arianna grinned, "It's so cool. You won't believe it." She hugged Justin and said, "Come on, both of you, I'll show you everything." Waving hello to Wynter, Justin followed Arianna.

145

Lisa-Marie grabbed Wynter's arm before she could move further away. She leaned close, "Not a word about, Tyler, okay?"

Wynter's eyebrow rose as she said, "Sure, no problem."

After the tour of the bus that concluded with Lisa-Marie lying on the bed and cranking open the bus door, they assembled outside. Wynter had stacked all the fixings for Smores on the picnic table. The chairs had been pulled out of the lean-to and set up around the crackling fire. The large cooler that Zach had carried in from the trail was open and he was handing out beer and cider. Justin unsnapped his guitar case, got out the instrument and sat on a chair to tune it up. Lisa-Marie sat down beside him. Mike and Wynter were cuddled close together. Zach took the chair by Arianna. He looked around the clearing in the fading light. "I guess you don't get a cell phone signal out here, hey?"

"No ... I have to walk over close to Alex and Cynthia's place to pick up their internet." Arianna frowned as she said, "The addiction center wasn't too happy when I told them they wouldn't be able to get ahold of me. I didn't think that would be an issue but they were worried about emergencies and things like that."

"They're right," Zach said. "Why don't you let me put a dish up for you? You've got a good sightline here and I can get you satellite cell service and internet. Cable TV, too, if you want it."

"Alex might not like that. Besides, it's probably too expensive." Arianna smiled, "And I definitely don't have time for TV."

"Minor details. I'll get you a deal. Some used equipment came back to the shop the other day. It's just lying around and we can't sell it. I can set that up for you on a temporary basis ... like you're trying it out. Then I'll take it all away before Alex comes home."

Mike looked skeptical, "Wouldn't you have to run wires into the bus."

Zach grinned, "Give me some credit, bro. I've got my ways. I could put a whole system in here and take it out again and no one would be the wiser."

Justin was strumming his guitar, so Arianna told Zach, "Let me think about it, okay?"

Settling around the fire and shifting about to avoid the periodic billows of wood smoke, they listened, now and then singing along with Justin's tunes. When he put his guitar down for a break, Wynter got the Smore supplies out and the sticky snacks were soon making the rounds. She nudged Mike, "Go ahead and have another beer if you like. I'll be the designated driver." She got up, pulled a flashlight from her pocket and headed to the outhouse.

Zach laughed, "I don't know if Mike trusts his truck on that road to anyone else."

"I trust Wynter," Mike told him. "It's you I wouldn't let behind the wheel."

Justin passed Lisa-Marie another cider. "Lucky for us we don't have to worry about anything but the dark trail and I brought along two flashlights."

"Hey, Justin," Zach glanced across the flames, "you've been on that hike up to the Cat's Cradle, right?"

"If you can call being skunked twice by the weather and not making it to the main summit, I have."

"I'd like to tackle it this summer. Maybe we can get a group together and make it an overnighter." Zach smiled at Arianna, "You should come with us."

Justin took a drink of his beer before he said, "We'd have to watch the weather and coordinate schedules but it's definitely doable."

When Wynter came back, Arianna asked, "How are the wedding plans going?"

Wynter made a face as she sat down. Mike put his arm around her. "Wynter's way too polite to say so, but my mom is making things difficult. I don't think she got the memo saying she can't be a mean mother-in-law until after the wedding."

"She's not mean, Mike. Exaggerating the whole thing won't help."

"We're stuck having to go talk to the priest even though I told my mom a hundred times we don't want a church wedding. I said I would do it on one condition – that she stop sticking her nose into things."

Wynter sighed, "And that backfired because when I asked her the other day about hall rental stuff, she said she didn't want to interfere. That Mike wouldn't like it."

"She knows that isn't what I meant when I told her to stop interfering all the time," Mike told them.

Zach drained his beer and reached for another from the cooler, "Maybe you guys should elope."

"No way. I want a wedding with family and friends and all the trimmings." Wynter looked over at Lisa-Marie, "Remember when Izzy and Liam got married? I want a big deal like that."

Mike pulled Wynter close to him. "I remember watching you dance the tango with Ethan and thinking you were the sexiest girl I had ever seen in my life."

"Ethan's dance moves would make any girl look good," she told him.

Lisa-Marie nudged Justin as she looked at Mike, "I thought you got your ideas about how sexy Wynter is from that time you busted our nude photo shoot down on the beach."

Mike laughed, "Ya, that would have helped for sure but I didn't see much. I seem to remember Dylan having the best view." He looked over at Arianna, "Do you keep in touch with him? How is he?"

"Good. Finished at culinary school. He's coming back out to BC for work."

"I follow him on Twitter," Wynter told them. "Did you see that photo of him with that hockey player from Ottawa?" She looked at Mike, "Didn't you say he was looking like a top draft choice?"

"Dylan is a hell of a ball player." Zach looked around the circle, "Has anyone heard from Beulah about getting together a team this year." He smiled at Arianna, "You were pretty smoking out on the field, too."

Lisa-Marie picked at the label on her cider as she said, "They've had a lot on their plate over at the A-Frame. Auntie Beth had a cancer scare."

Wynter leaned forward, "Oh, no."

Justin touched Lisa-Marie's arm, "I never heard anything about that."

"They kept it quiet, I guess. She's going to be fine but I think it's taken a lot out of them."

Arianna looked over at Lisa-Marie, "When I talked to Beulah she seemed worried about your aunt."

The silence stretched out for a moment. Justin cracked open a beer and asked Arianna, "What's your new job like?"

"Today was my first shift but I think it's going to be good. Not easy, though. I sat in on a family meeting that was heartbreaking and a couple of intake interviews where the patients shared things that were hard to hear. People's rock bottoms can be awfully low. But that's why I wanted this job. I'm thinking of down the road. Doctors don't get nearly enough training in addiction treatment. Although most of them don't let themselves get close to all the messy emotional stuff, it is important. I'm probably being idealistic and naïve but I want to be a doctor who looks at the whole patient."

Zach laid a hand on her arm as he stared over at his brother, "You see, Mike. I'm not the only one planning for future employment."

Wynter snuggled closer to Mike and reached down to slide his hand up her thigh under the blanket she had thrown over them. He grinned at her and whispered, "I know you're only trying to distract me from wanting to punch Zach out but keep it up, okay?" They both started to laugh.

Arianna reached down to pet Johnny Lobo. The dog had taken up residence right by her chair. They had become quite inseparable the last few days. Johnny Lobo had given her a confused look when she left so early that morning. The dog had greeted her on her return like a long-lost friend. She spoke up, "I think I've made a miscalculation about being able to manage the drive out here ..."

Lisa-Marie poked at the fire with a stick, "I wondered what you'd think of travelling back and forth to Dearborn."

"Alex's truck is ... challenging. I had to crank the steering wheel like I was driving a semi to get around the corners and I felt like my foot was going through the floor boards, I had to jam on the brakes so hard. I've never driven a truck before and it's harder than I thought it would be."

Mike let out a snort, "No power anything, for sure. I'm surprised he would offer you that old beater."

"You're welcome to use my Jeep when I'm not in Dearborn," Lisa-Marie said.

Arianna shrugged, patted Lobo one more time and sat back up in her chair. "The road makes me nervous. I can drive but I have very few hours of driving experience and none of them on a twisting, narrow gravel road. I came up on a big truck near one of the corners and I thought I'd have a heart attack. When I got back here tonight, I was a wreck. I had been holding the steering wheel so tightly my arms felt like spaghetti noodles." She sighed. "I guess I should have found a place in town to stay but now that I've seen the bus, I really want to be here. And, of course, the price is right."

Zach, who had steadily edged his chair closer to Arianna's with every chance he got, said, "I can drive you back out here after work, if that would help. I'm always off by six. And I could give you a few driving lessons." He smiled his most winning smile at her, "You probably just need to build some confidence in a vehicle that isn't ready for the scrap pile."

Wynter nudged Mike and leaned close to his ear to whisper, "Way to make a move, Zach."

Mike whispered back, "Typical."

Arianna looked doubtful. She smiled at Zach, "Thanks, but I'd still have to get to work and the way I felt when I got back here today, I'm not sure I can face that drive again."

"No problem," Zach said, "I'll pick you up, too."

"That's way too much. I couldn't ask you to do something like that for me."

Justin got up to throw another log on the fire. As he rubbed his hands free of dirt, he said, "I'm already out here, Zach. I'll drive Arianna into work. It's only three days a week. I'm always up early, anyway."

Arianna ran her hands through her long, dark hair, "Oh, you guys ... I feel like I should say no, no, don't worry about me but I want the job and I love living here," she waved her hand in the direction of the bus. "So, I'm going to take your help. Zach, the driving lessons would be great. Hopefully, I won't have to be a pain for too long."

Later, Zach took his time putting the last of the chairs away as Lisa-Marie and Justin headed off and Arianna said goodbye to Mike and Wynter. Waving to Mike, he called out, "I'll be right with you guys." He walked Arianna to the door of the bus. "So, I'll pick you up at the addiction center tomorrow, okay?"

She smiled at him, "I'm grateful for the help, Zach."

He leaned into the edge of the bus near her, "We can set up a time for a driving lesson then." He reached over and pushed a strand of her hair back from her face. "And you'll think about the satellite dish? It would be nice to text back and forth and you shouldn't be out here all on your own and not able to call anyone."

The moment stretched out and Arianna felt a funny little thump in her chest. She stared at Zach and wondered. He leaned close and kissed her – just a brush of his lips against hers. Backing up a step, he said, "I wanted to do that all night." He grinned, "I better go. Don't want them to leave without me." He turned and began to walk away. The sudden glare from his mag flashlight flooded the area in front of him. He glanced back, waved and was gone.

Arianna stood by the bus with her hand on the porch railing. She had not been expecting the kiss. Two summers ago, she'd chummed around with Zach when they played together on the same baseball team. He'd been going with Lisa-Marie then and she'd been head over heels stuck on Dylan. Well, Lisa-Marie and Zach were a thing of the past and though she still felt stuck on Dylan, that little kiss had snuck through her body right down to her toes with a couple of delicious stops on the way. She smiled, called Johnny Lobo who came running from the edge of the clearing where he had seen Zach down the trail. She went inside the bus feeling infinitely better than she had before her friends had arrived.

❦❦❦❦

Out on the trail, Lisa-Marie shone her flashlight onto the path ahead as she and Justin walked back towards Izzy and Liam's place. The twin beams of light, his and hers, crossed and intertwined as they made their way around corners, through the trees and into the spaces where the trail opened to the black expanse of lake beyond the cove. The night was clear with no moon to light the way. Pinprick stars sprinkled the velvet background of the night sky and reflected like dots dancing on the dark mirror of the water.

"I wrote to my mom," Justin told her as they passed the Saltbox.

She could hear the confusion in his voice and that was an odd experience. From the time she had met Justin, he had always been sure of himself. "Now what happens?" she asked him.

"Izzy talked to the psychiatrist. They gave the letter to my mom and the doctor says it meant a lot to her. She reads it over and over."

"Do you think she'll write back?"

His arm brushed hers and she felt a familiar tingling, making her want to move closer but she stopped herself. He reached up to brush a low-hanging branch out of the way as he said, "I want her to. But everyone is telling me to be patient ... let her make the first move. It's so hard, Leez." She felt him looking towards her. "I thought losing her when I was kid was bad but this waiting and wondering if she'll get better ... it's worse. Before the letter, it felt like she had died. Now, I'm thinking about her all the time."

They had come down through the apple trees to Liam and Izzy's. Lisa-Marie sat down on the bench near the end of the long planter that ran the length of the deck. Justin sat beside her, leaning forward to stare at his feet. She watched his knee pump up and down. "I want to see her." He glanced at her, "Is that so wrong?"

Lisa-Marie wrapped his hand in hers, "No, of course it isn't."

Reaching his arm around her shoulders, Justin pulled her close beside him, "I've been dreaming about Angie. That hasn't happened for a long time." She held his hand and leaned into him. The silence lengthened between them until he said, "I know you heard me on the phone with Lauren earlier." His shoulder slumped. "We don't want the same things ... she won't leave the city, I won't go back there. It all seems to be falling apart."

Lisa tensed up and thoughts skittled through her head like a dog scratching at the door to come in. Why doesn't he end it? He must not want to. He must still love her. She was surprised, after all this time, how much that realization hurt. She let go of his hand and moved slowly away. "I better go in. I'm leaving early tomorrow. I'll see you when I come back."

EIGHTEEN

A lison shrugged into her sweater and left her office. She walked out to the grounds behind the building and followed a path that meandered along the lake shore. She tried to slow her breathing and think.

Not one to shield herself, Alison readily admitted that she was off her game. Her first career counselling session had been a disaster. She had let Ethan's prancing, preening behaviour rattle her. The pressure she'd placed on herself to make the young man's career goals a priority had caused her to overreact to his work placement. Even now she felt justified in questioning how his assignment at the sawmill could further his goal of getting into a prestigious dance school. But all she'd done was raise an eyebrow and Ethan had misread her thoughts. He had folded his arms across his chest and spaced his words out like he was speaking to someone who was mentally challenged. "Do you have a problem with me working at the sawmill?"

Not expecting his sudden animosity, she had scrambled for a response. "I ... well ... do you think it's a good fit with your career aspirations?" Desperately searching the papers on her desk, Alison said, "I see you've applied to several dance schools."

She had obviously hit a nerve because Ethan was off his chair in a flash. He leaned over the desk to glare at her, "Applied and been turned down ... right? I don't need you rubbing my nose in that. Do you think I can't handle working at the sawmill because I'm queer? Maybe a girly-boy like me can't handle working with the *real men*. Is that what you think? Get this straight, Ms. Kirk ... I've worked at the sawmill for almost two year and nobody's complained about my performance yet. Why don't you write that in your file? Right next to *loser kid can't dance.*"

152

Alison broke eye contact first. She had fumbled her hand across her desk to gather up the pages from his file and had knocked the small, covered dish that held one of her favourite rosaries to the ground. Ethan had jumped back as if he had been scalded and gawked at the simple prayer beads like he was staring at a poisonous serpent. With a performance that could have won him an Oscar, he had thrown his hands up in the air and gasped out the words, "Did you think flinging your rosary at me would do you any good? I'm not a frigging werewolf. How about I leave you alone to pray that God will change my evil ways?"

Alison had stood up, "Ethan, wait –," but the young man had flounced out the door. She heard him laughing as he headed down the hall. She had been seriously shaken by the way the session had concluded.

She strolled along the path, oblivious to the panorama of lake, mountains and trees around her. This was all Bradley's fault. He had managed to devastate their marriage and her entire personal life and now, the shock of all that she had lost was affecting her work. She brushed tears of self-pity from her face and took a deep breath. She had to get ahold of herself.

Alison bent down and reached for a smooth stone from the path at her feet. Throwing it out towards the calm water, she watched as it splashed against the surface, causing ripples to move out rapidly in concentric circles. She resolved to pay attention to every word that came out of her mouth in the upcoming orientation session for the new residents. She could not afford another misstep.

An hour later, Alison walked into one of Micah Camp's small meeting rooms feeling ready to tackle the orientation session. She had the resident contracts in hand and she had gone over all three case files. The two boys were already in the room. Charlie Sutherland was seated in the middle of the small arc of three chairs. She noted that he was on the slim side. He wore jeans and an untucked, button-down shirt. If she hadn't been told anything about him, she would have taken him for exactly what he appeared to be. The other young man, David Ralston, looked like many of the boys she'd worked with while career counselling at the private school – clean-cut, wholesome, wearing a polo shirt tucked into chinos. His blond hair was cut in a fashionable style – short on the sides and back with a longish mop of curls on top. He was standing over by the windows looking a bit jumpy.

Alison chose a chair for herself from the front of the room and pulled it closer to the row where the three residents would soon be seated. She checked over the papers one more time and was about to sit down when the last new resident breezed into the room. Sadie Hart was dressed in a long, embroidered dress. Calf-high, laced boots were visible beneath the swaying hemline. She was what Alison would have described as quirky. She had a head of wild auburn hair with bits of coloured thread woven in here and there. Her nose was pierced on both sides, she had a smattering of freckles across her face and startling green eyes. Multiple bangles jingled on her wrists and silver rings adorned every finger. She looked like a cross between a 70s hippie strolling towards Woodstock and a Shahrazad-type belly dancer.

Sadie looked around the room, acknowledged Alison with a small nod and took the chair on one side of Charlie. Alison sat down, cleared her throat and said, "It looks like we're all here so, let's get started." She watched as David walked a wide circle around Sadie to get to his chair. He greeted her friendly smile with what was close to a sneer. "I'm Alison Kirk ... the career counsellor here at Micah Camp."

Izzy's file contained a couple of ice-breakers for small groups but Alison rejected those and decided to go with an activity she had always enjoyed. She smiled at the three, young people in front of her. "To get things started, I thought we could each answer this question. If you were a colour, what colour would you be? I'll start. If I were a colour, I'd be green. I guess that makes sense with my red hair."

Sadie's face wore a look that could only be described as scathing. She had been scowling ever since David had snubbed her smile. Charlie had one eyebrow raised in quizzical fashion and David looked positively hostile. Although things weren't going as Alison had hoped, she didn't feel she could switch gears partway through. So, she said, "Why don't you start, Sadie."

"This is lame ... and I can't choose one colour." She waved her arms out, almost knocking Charlie on the head. He ducked to the side as she said, "Put me down as a rainbow. Rainbow bright." Laced with contempt, her words sent a cold shiver up Alison's spine.

Charlie said, "Brown."

When it became obvious that he had no intention of elaborating, Alison turned to David. There were splotches of red on his neck and he was almost vibrating on his chair. She felt slightly alarmed even before he started to speak. "I am not participating in this activity. Pretending isn't my thing." His voice took on a droning quality as he said, "Flee from all forms of idolatry – first Corinthians 10:14."

Rattled by his response, Alison tried to hide her reaction. She was as well versed in the Bible as any Catholic, but she adhered to a different way of expressing her faith. For her, Bible quoting was kept to church on Sunday. She had prepared a list of items for the icebreaker – if you were an animal, if you were a vegetable. The activity was meant to be funny in a slightly revelatory way. She knew when she was beaten and scratched the rest of the activity.

Explaining that she wanted to switch over to the business at hand, Alison got up to give each of the new residents a general information sheet. To save paper, she had printed the Micah Camp Contract on the other side of the page. First, Alison drew their attention to the list of rights and responsibilities. Beginning with their rights, she emphasized that residents could expect to be treated with respect regardless of race, creed, culture, sexual orientation or disability.

Sadie raised her hand and when Alison pointed to her, she said, "I'm vegetarian. It doesn't say anything here about respect for a person's food choices. That's pretty basic don't you think? Food – the stuff we consume to keep us alive."

"Freak." David said the word under his breath as he crossed his arms over his chest and stared straight ahead. Sadie leaned back in her chair so she could see David past Charlie's head. She glared at him with cat-like eyes that looked as though they might bore holes through his ear and start a fire in his brain. Alison had a hard time dragging her attention away from such a laser beam stare.

She forced herself to focus as she opened her notebook. "I'll set up an appointment for you to discuss your dietary requirements with our cook, Brigit. I'm quite sure she will be able to accommodate you, Sadie." She returned to the paper in her hand. "On to responsibilities," she said.

Alison stressed the importance of treating cabins and common spaces with respect. She told the new residents that they were expected to engage in appropriate educational tasks, take advantage of counselling opportunities, agree to work placements and participate in fund-raising activities. She underlined the fact that there could be no use of drugs or alcohol on the premises and that they would be agreeing to all of these conditions in the contract they were about to sign. She stumbled only slightly when she explained that sexual relationships between residents were discouraged. The last item she covered was that condoms could be found in the second-floor bathrooms.

She asked if anyone had any questions but didn't wait to see if anyone did. Referring to the contract, she said, "After you've signed these and I've collected them, I'll tell you which cabins you're assigned to and you can get settled in before lunch."

Charlie pulled a pen from the side pocket of his pack and quickly signed his contract. Sadie was clearly looking around for a pen and Charlie passed her the one he was still holding. David was staring at the paper in his hand. He looked across at Alison. "I'm not signing this."

Taken aback, she asked, "Why not? Do you have a question? I did ask for questions."

"This part," David pointed down to the paper, "that tells residents where to find condoms ... I don't agree with that."

Charlie was studying his sneakered feet and Sadie was frowning. Alison said, "That section of the page is for resident information only. It has nothing to do with the contract of rights and responsibilities."

David flipped the page back and forth. "It's all on the same paper, isn't it?" A small grin played around the corners of Charlie's mouth and Sadie began to bang her foot up and down impatiently. David sat back in his chair and said, "Even making condoms available is promoting sexual behaviour. That isn't right."

This was not a reaction that Alison was at all prepared for and her silence only egged David on. He told them, "I've signed a covenant. It's between me and God. I won't have sex until I'm married to a woman." David stressed the word *woman*.

"Did God sign, too?" Charlie asked quietly.

His remark was lost on David as Sadie leaned forward and blasted out her words, "Are you for real?"

David tensed as he said, "It's the will of God ... abstain from immorality, control your body, do not give into the passion of lust – that's from the book of Thessalonians. The Bible ... you've heard of the Bible ... right?" To make his point, he leaned forward in his chair as well.

"That's crap." Sadie pointed a finger with its black-painted nail at him, "Sounds to me like you could use some lust. Maybe then you wouldn't be such an uptight asshat."

The meeting was getting out of control and Alison was letting it happen. She held up her hand to get everyone's attention but Sadie was on her feet. She took an aggressive stance in front of David and pulled her lower lip down to expose the inside of her mouth.

David's face twisted with a look of disgust. "Having the inside of your mouth tattooed is gross and it only shows you have no respect for the temple of God that your body should be. And the lettering doesn't even make sense ... it isn't even a word."

"Ceridwen is the name of the Welsh goddess of poetry and inspiration ... it means SheKnows ... it means I am a white witch." She pushed her hair back from her face. "So, how about you keep your snotty attitude and your Bible quoting bullshit and your covenant crap to yourself?"

Not only had she let the meeting get out of control, Alison now wondered if she was even qualified for this job. And that meant she was treading on ethically serious ground – taking this on when she couldn't handle it. First her ridiculous arrival, then Ethan and now this. If she didn't get control, the orientation meeting was in danger of dissolving into a brawl. "Sadie, take your seat."

The girl turned to look at her. "Would you like me to cast a circle to clear this room of bad energy?" She looked over her shoulder at David.

"I'm out of here right now if you let her start casting devil spells." David was on his feet and his breath was coming fast.

Sadie turned around with her hands on her hips as she raised her voice, "White witch, you idiot. I'm not a Satanist – I'm a pagan, I believe in nature."

David's fists clenched at his side. "I'll tell you what you are ... a nut job, that's what. You aren't a Christian. You'll only get to heaven through Jesus. He's the way, the truth and the light. And if you aren't getting to heaven, I guess we all know where you're going." He paused to make his point. "Hell." He sat back in his chair with a thud and looked over at Charlie. "What do you think? Are you born again? Do you believe that Jesus Christ is your Lord and Savior? Do you think we should be sitting here with a devil worshipper?"

That small grin played again around Charlie's mouth. "I'm more like an agnostic when it comes to religion." When David looked at him blankly, Charlie added, "I'm not sure if there is a God or if there isn't. And to be fair, she says she's a pagan."

David directed his attention to Charlie like he was a challenge to be met. "You can't stay on the fence that way. God needs you to commit."

"Everyone ... quiet." Alison recognized her voice sounded overly shrill and a tad hysterical. But she had their attention. She took a deep breath. "We aren't here to discuss religious beliefs. We are here to get this contract signed." She looked at David. "If you are not comfortable signing, you can take it up in a meeting with our director. I'm sure the two of you will be able to work out something that respects your beliefs."

Sadie got up and passed her signed contract to Alison. As she turned she said, "The circle would have been a good idea." Charlie handed Alison his contract as well. Everyone was standing now. Alison quickly gave out the cabin assignments and watched as the three young people left the room. She slumped in her chair and held her hand up to her chest. For the love of God, all other deities, nature, believers, unbelievers and the unsure ... what had she got herself into?

Before dinner, she caught up to Roland outside the dining room. "Did you have a chance to see David this afternoon?" To her boss's nod, she added, "Were you able to find a compromise so he would sign the contract?"

"I simply gave him the contract with nothing printed on the reverse side. That seemed to satisfy his conscience." Roland met her eye and added, "Double-sided photocopying is not always the most efficient strategy, Alison. Perhaps you can keep that in mind for the future." Her shoulders slumped as she watched him walk into the dining room. Alison's appetite disappeared and she headed to her trailer for a quiet evening of self-recrimination.

❧❧❧❧

David came back to his cabin from checking out the gym to find a guy dressed in a dance leotard doing a weird stretching thing on the middle of the living room rug. His butt was up in the air and the rest of his body was laid out flat like a snake. The kid he had met at orientation, Charlie, was sitting on the sofa with his laptop open. He was talking to the guy on the floor about something on the screen. "I found a YouTube video of this work out with weights to build upper body strength. It says you can increase the size of your biceps by like as much as three inches or something in a few weeks."

Hopping up to a crouch and then landing back on his butt, the guy on the floor noticed David staring. He batted his lashes and blew him a kiss before he said, "I am loud and proud, brother. Gay as gay can be. There, it's been said. You can put your eyes back in your head, okay." He twisted his legs into a pretzel shape and glanced over at Charlie. "Most of that stuff about increase in size is bullshit."

Charlie looked from Ethan's kissing gesture to David's face and grinned. He quickly switched to a neutral expression, "Sorry, man." He pointed to Ethan who had moved his body over onto his bent arms and was raising himself up into a handstand. "That's Ethan. He's our roommate." Pointing to his computer, Charlie added, "Do you know anything about weight training? I'm trying to figure out a good routine." When David didn't move, Charlie said, "You could come all the way in and sit down. You live here."

David tried to concentrate on what Charlie was saying but he could not drag his open-mouthed stare from Ethan. He had never even spoken with a gay guy before and now he was sharing a cabin with one. That alone was shocking enough without considering the possibility of sitting in the same

158

room with a self-expressed homosexual prancing around in a skin-hugging leotard with his package outlined like an advertisement for men's underwear.

David opened his mouth to speak and his voice choked out in a strange gasp. He cleared his voice, pointed at Ethan and said, "Your blood is on your own head, man ... it says so right in Leviticus, 20:13." He looked toward Charlie to add, "And you can get behind me Satan."

As he walked quickly to his own room, David heard Charlie saying, "He's right, Ethan ... your blood is certainly on your head since you're standing on it." Then Charlie started to laugh. The last thing David saw before he slammed his door was Ethan collapsing to the ground. His hysterical laughter could be heard despite the barrier now between them.

David lay on his bed and raked his hands through his hair. He felt as though he had entered some alternative universe. Ever since he was eight years old and was first placed in foster care, he had been raised to believe certain things. He'd had those things drilled into him in years of homeschooling, twice weekly Bible studies, Sunday church services, nightly prayer and summer Bible camps. The only way to heaven was through Jesus Christ, Catholics were in league with the devil, homosexuals were evil, abortion was like taking a meat hook and pulling apart a real baby, sex was something dirty that could be made right only in marriage, adultery was wrong and on and on it went. He rubbed his hand over his forehead. It gave him a headache to think of all the things that were dirty, evil and corrupt in the world.

He had been taught to be grateful for having been taken in by the foster families that all attended the Spirit Lives Fellowship. When he was younger, he truly was grateful. What if he had been taken in by evil people? What if he had never had a chance to learn how to live his life as God meant people to live? Those thoughts had tortured him and he remembered offering fervent prayers, on his knees by his bed, night after night, for having been so lucky to have the foster parents he had. Of course, those parents kept changing but they were always people from the community, so he never had to adjust too much or even change those nightly prayers.

When he got older, he began to rail against some of the teachings, even if only to himself. After all, they weren't Amish or anything like that. They had TV and internet and cell phones. He heard things and he wasn't an idiot. And he saw that many of the adults in the fellowship didn't practice what they preached. There were sinners amongst them.

He turned nineteen and had to leave the foster care system. He was given a new social worker and the guy asked him what he wanted to do with his life.

That was a novel experience. The community expected him to get a job; more than a few employment options were already on the table. Leaders in the fellowship made it clear that there would always be a place for him, but that now he had to pay his own way. They told him he was good with his hands and they could find work for a guy like him. But David thought he might like to attend the local college. Expressing that idea within the community only led to suggestions that he go to Bible college and think about becoming a minister. He knew for sure he didn't want to do that.

He shared some of his doubts with the social worker and the guy suggested David fill out an application for Micah Camp. Part of what he had to do was write an essay that answered the questions – Who are you and who do you want to become? He bared his soul in that essay. He poured out his cloudy memories of the night his father had shot his mother and then come after David only to change his mind in favour of locking himself in the bathroom and blowing his own brains out. He described the years with his foster families, what he had been taught, what he had come to doubt. He ended with a statement – *I don't know who I am or who I want to become. All I do know, is that I want a chance to find out.* The experience of writing had been freeing and terrifying all at the same time.

He was accepted to Micah Camp and he told members of the Spirit Lives community that the facility provided educational upgrading at the province's expense. They liked that idea. All the families he had lived with had been generous with the kids they fostered. At the same time, they never missed a chance to see if they could access more funds. He was warned over and over to beware of the influences of the world. Evil apparently lurked around every corner and temptation was in the unlikeliest of places. People would try to turn him away from the truth. He would have to be strong.

He'd walked away with a lilt in his step and got on the bus that would bring him to Dearborn. He was free. It didn't take him long, though, to discover that freedom was scary. All he had wanted to do was question a few things, explore what more there might be out in the world. He hadn't wanted his entire belief system to be trampled. But that's what had happened since the moment he arrived at Micah Camp. His thinking had been challenged by the way people dressed, the way they talked, condoms in the bathrooms and a devil-worshipper casting spells. And now an actual homo-in-the-flesh was sharing the same cabin with him.

He understood that every single word he had uttered today was channeled by his upbringing. The way he was acting even surprised him. But he was so freaked out, he was falling back on what was familiar and he didn't know how to stop himself.

He groaned and looked at the clock. How long were those guys going to stay out there? He had to use the can. He rolled onto his side and fought off the urge to pray. He had to move forward and that would be going back. But he couldn't remember being this scared since he was a kid, hiding under his bed and hearing the echoing sound of the gunshot from the bathroom down the hall.

⚜ ⚜ ⚜ ⚜

Ethan stood by the open window of his bedroom and listened to the waves snug gently up against the rocks on the beach. He was considering his options. When he had first arrived at Micah Camp, he would have completely ignored a guy like David, either that or punched him in the nose. The reaction would have depended on Ethan's mood. But after almost two years here, he understood more about the code of conduct that governed this place. David had missed the part about respect for diversity. Ethan knew he was well within his rights to waltz straight into Roland's office and lodge a complaint. But David had just arrived and he was totally green.

He made up his mind to avoid the guy for now. It wouldn't be that hard. Ethan didn't spend a ton of time around his cabin – he had a full-time job and when he wasn't at the sawmill, he was working out in the gym. He had his poker nights at Justin's and the occasional trip to Dearborn with a few of the other residents. Any other free time he had, he usually spent in his room watching movies or TV shows on his iPad.

There were strict limits set on the amount of content residents could download from the internet. If Jeremy had wanted to, he could have gotten rich by selling black market flash drives filled with all the latest shows and movies. But the guy just handed it all out like candy and Ethan was one of the lucky recipients. He was currently working his way through several seasons of *Breaking Bad*.

As he got comfortable on his bed and waited for the next episode to load up, he thought about Charlie. The new guy had coppery brown hair and almond-shaped eyes like Ethan's own. But Charlie's eyes were a bright blue rimmed by a darker shade and framed by thick sweeping lashes. He had an amazing mouth with a lush bottom lip. Ethan felt a familiar breathlessness as blood rushed to various parts of his body in a way that thrilled him. This kid was totally his type and he hadn't met anyone he could say that about for so long.

And Charlie was funny, too. He had a witty kind of sarcastic humour that Ethan found irresistible because they had that quick way of thinking in common. Ethan would go slowly, see how things developed. What had Nick always told him when he was in counselling? Be authentic, be a friend first.

NINETEEN

Fiona shrugged into her white coat and lifted her stethoscope from the desk. She had wanted to get here earlier but she'd had to take Aidan to the drop-in daycare for the first time and he'd cried when she left. His tears tugged at her emotions and surprised her all at the same time. She'd left Aidan in the care of her family since she'd arrived. They all seemed happy to look after him, especially Cynthia. Then Alex and Cynthia had left on their trip and she'd had only a day alone at the Saltbox with Aidan. She hadn't expected the baby to bond with her in that short time.

She had driven Liam's GM Sierra into Dearborn this morning. Nick had arranged to come to the clinic and get the car seat so he could pick Aidan up from daycare and drive him back to the Saltbox. She was looking forward to the possibility of peace and quiet over the next three nights during which she'd be on call, staying here in town on her own.

As she turned to leave her office, the receptionist met her at the door with a medication vial. "Charlie Sutherland's meds, Dr. Wells," she said. Fiona thanked her, dropped the vial in the pocket of her white coat and carried on to the examining room. She retrieved the file from the slot in the door and went into the room. "Hi, Charlie," she said, flipping open his chart and glancing down at the top page. "You're here for your shot, right?"

"You bet ... top me up with the testosterone, Doc." He grinned at her.

"Have you settled in at Micah Camp?" she asked him as she assembled syringe, needle, alcohol and cotton ball.

"It's slow getting into everything there but it's good. I'm working out a lot in the gym." He grinned, "Have to ... the food's so good I've been eating like crazy."

"Ya, tell me about it. I love dropping in there at meal time." Doing a double check of the dosage written in the chart, she filled the syringe from the vial in her pocket. Turning back to Charlie, she said, "Okay, kid, drop your drawers for me."

A few moments later as Charlie reached back to hold a cotton ball on the injection site, Fiona deposited the used needle in the bin and asked, "Are you feeling okay with this dosage? Go ahead and pull your pants up now, you're good."

While he zipped up his jeans, Charlie said, "My other doctor told me it would take time. I won't turn into the Incredible Hulk overnight or anything like that." He buckled his belt and winced a bit as he sat down in the chair. "I hate all the back acne. On the up side, my voice is way deeper and I've got this great Adam's apple coming along." He stroked his fingers over his throat for emphasis. "I'm getting hairy legs and some hair on my chest to go with the tits." He shrugged, "It's good I've always been flat-chested. I can keep everything in place with a tight undershirt." He pointed to his upper lip, "Peach fuzz here but my dad says he couldn't grow a decent moustache until he was in his thirties. I get some of that from him."

Fiona smiled as she pulled the blood pressure cuff from the holder on the wall. "I'll prescribe you something for the acne. But keep an eye on what you eat. Stay away from greasy food as much as you can." She pumped up the cuff, slipped her stethoscope into her ears, pressed the end against Charlie's arm and tilted her head to one side as she listened. The only sound in the room was the air whooshing out of the cuff like wind from a depleted balloon. "Okay, your blood pressure is good." She sat down on her rolling stool and flipped through his file. "I see your last Pap test was two years ago. We should schedule you in for one."

"Ya, I guess."

Fiona studied the young man sitting in front of her. "How do you handle that type of exam?"

"I've only had one. It sucked but I know I don't have much choice." He met Fiona's glance. "I've never gone through any of the nightmares some kids have ... you know ... being examined over and over, poked and prodded and stared at by five or six doctors at a time. But what I have down south isn't deformed or anything. It's just girl stuff."

She listened for a tone of disgust and didn't pick it up. The kid seemed to have a positive attitude. She explored a bit more. "It can be hard to accept a disconnection between what your brain says you are and what your body looks like. A pelvic exam can intensify such feelings. Has the testosterone therapy held off your periods?"

"Except for some pink pee now and then."

Fiona closed the file and rolled her chair a bit closer. "Are you sexually active ... or planning to be?"

Charlie blushed slightly and asked, "You mean with someone else?"

Fiona smiled, "Yes." When he shook his head, she added, "Okay ... if you decide to get involved, please come and talk to me first. Even though you don't have a period, you can get pregnant."

Charlie sat up straight in his chair with a look of shock on his face. "If I was with someone, it wouldn't be a guy. I'm not gay."

Holding up her hand, Fiona said, "I'm not saying you are. I need to consider all possibilities and you should, too. What if you hooked up with another transgendered person ... a male to female who identified and appeared as a girl but had a guy's genitals? What then?"

As his shoulders slumped slightly, Charlie muttered, "I wish my life wasn't so frigging complicated."

Fiona stood up. "Don't we all. I'll see you again in two weeks and we'll schedule the Pap smear then. But feel free to make an appointment any time, if you have any questions or concerns, okay?"

⚓⚓⚓⚓

"It's not fair. I have no idea why this is happening to me again. I've worked so hard. I don't deserve this ... not now." Bethany got up from the chair in the counselling space. She walked over to the window and stood there staring out to the garden.

Izzy had struggled over the last twenty minutes to redirect Bethany's tirade about life being unfair to her. They had agreed that unfortunate circumstances did sometimes make a person feel like a victim and that talking about those feelings was important. But Izzy had emphasized that making hardships the primary focus of one's thoughts was not an effective coping strategy. She'd done all she could to help Bethany see that even though things had gone off the rails, that wasn't the whole story of her life.

She watched as her friend of many years straightened her back and turned around. "This isn't going to work, Izzy. I don't want to be here and I don't want to do this."

"My job is to help and if being here won't help, then what else can you do, Beth? You came here because you know there's a problem."

Bethany returned to the chair and sat on the edge of it as if ready to make a break for the door. "Beulah wanted me to come and talk to you."

Izzy tilted her head to the side as she looked at Bethany, "You didn't come because Beulah told you to. You aren't that person anymore."

"Well, that's true." Bethany stared down at the floor. "I know I have to do something. I thought this might work but it feels all wrong ... like going back in time. Every moment I sit here, I feel more and more like a failure."

"Do you think meeting with a counsellor in Dearborn would help?"

"No, I'm not ready to talk to a stranger." She glanced out the window and her eyes lingered on the movement of the water that rippled like plastic wrap, shaken over and over. "I wish I could go out fishing. But I can't even get close to the boat." She shook her head. "That was so unfair, how Dan stole fishing from me."

Izzy held up a hand and spoke gently, "Let's stay focused, Beth. What happened with Dan was a long time ago and you've dealt with that."

Bethany sat silent for a moment. Her voice was tentative when she said, "I wondered about journaling. I feel like I need a way to get some of these thoughts out of my head."

Being careful not to sigh with relief at this first positive step, Izzy said, "Okay." She got up and went to the book shelf. She found the journals with the leather covers that Liam had made. She chose the robin-egg blue one that matched Beth's eyes. Then she ran her finger along the titles of the books on the shelf until she found what she was looking for. Sitting back down, Izzy handed the journal and the book to Beth. "The book has a few tips on journaling and some exercises. Use the ideas if they appeal to you. The main thing is to write and make the whole process work for you."

Bethany traced her finger around the design on the edge of the journal. "Does Liam still do this kind of work? It's beautiful."

Izzy smiled, "Not as much as he used to."

⁂⁂⁂⁂

Robbie sat cross-legged on the playroom carpet glancing from his small sketch book to the picture on the page of a larger pad on his knees. He had drawn a mother bear and two cubs walking towards a thick bank of trees. He frowned. The cubs were waddling along okay but he would need to work on the mother bear. He reached over and flipped a page to see the drawing he had done of the eagle up on the Cat's Cradle. He began to sketch the bird into the sky of the larger picture.

He glanced up at Tabby where she sat on one of Sophie's small chairs. "How come you're staying over on a week night?" he asked her.

"My mom's going to some church meeting in town."

Sophie came to the table with a book in her hand. She looked at Tabby and said, "What you like today, Tabby?"

Tabby slammed a hand on the table. "Waitress, it's about time. I will have a bowl of soup. And fast. I'm in a hurry."

Sophie giggled as she pretended to write down Tabby's order. She walked over to her toy kitchen, opened a bin and began to throw things into a small pot. Tabby and Robbie could hear her talking to herself, "Chicken leg? Ya ... potato, cawwot ... stwabewwy? Ya."

Tabby called out, "No strawberry. I'm allergic." Sophie threw the strawberry back in the bin. Glancing over at Robbie, Tabby told him, "My mom's taking me for a tour of the school in Dearborn. She says I can't decide if I've never even been in the building but why should I even go in the building when I am not going to school there."

Robbie shrugged as he smudged at some pencil lines on the eagle's wing, "Maybe your mom won't like it when she sees it."

Tabby raised her eyes to the ceiling, "She's going to love it because of all the girls. She keeps going on about me needing girlfriends. That is such a load of crap."

Sophie walked carefully to the table balancing the toy pot overflowing with play food. The chicken leg stuck out over the top. She put the pot down in front of Tabby. "You no say cwap, Tabby. Izzy say that a bad wowd."

Robbie grinned over at her as Tabby said, "Izzy's right, Sophie, I'm sorry. I won't say it again."

Sophie asked, "You like milk?" Tabby nodded.

Robbie watched Tabby's light shift. She pretended to eat her soup even though she was confused, sad and anxious. While Sophie was busy at her fridge getting the glass of milk, Robbie spoke low enough so that only his friend could hear, "You belong here, Tabby. Don't worry. Nothing will change that." He watched as she looked away. In a moment, he saw her wipe a tear from her face.

Izzy's voice drifted down to the playroom, "Come on you guys, dinner's almost ready. I need someone to set the table."

Sophie whooped and ran ahead of them. She was already kneeling on her chair at the table by the time Tabby and Robbie got to the kitchen. Lifting the stack of plates from the counter, Robbie asked, "Where's Liam."

Izzy pulled a chafing dish from the oven. "He's watching Aidan until Nick finishes work. He should be here any minute."

Tabby sniffed the air as she laid out forks, knives and spoons, "Is that teriyaki chicken I smell?"

Sophie leaned over the table to see out the window and down the trail. She called out, "Liam coming." Then she sat back on her knees, "I see Uncle Nick and Aidan." She drew out Aidan's name and a frown settled between her dark brows.

Passing glasses to Tabby from the cupboard, Izzy gave Sophie a look. "Be nice," she told the child. "Aidan is a baby." She turned to Robbie, "Set another place for Nick, okay?"

Sophie picked up her fork and poked it in the air as she said, "Him not a baby ... him a load of cwap."

Robbie and Tabby stared from Sophie to Izzy to each other. Their eyes locked in shocked glee and they both choked with laughter which they tried to smother by clamping their hands over their mouths. Izzy turned a hard stare from Sophie to them and pointed at Robbie, "Go and get another chair. And Tabby help me put this food out." As she brought the dish of chicken to the table, Izzy looked at Sophie and said, "Watch yourself if you want dessert tonight. I told you that's not a nice word to say and you know better than to call people names."

✄✄✄✄✄

Brigit walked into the kitchen area of the church and her heart sank. The room was set up for a meeting of at least a dozen people; the chairs were placed in an inviting semi-circle. She could see that the coffee urn had been plugged in - it held thirty cups. Two dozen cupcakes sat on the counter still in their grocery wrap. A printed sheet of paper lay on each chair. She stepped closer to stare down at the page - an agenda for the ministry meeting.

On the previous Sunday, Father Kieran had announced that tonight at seven they would have a ministry meeting. He wanted the people who headed up each ministry to attend. That would include representatives for children and adult religious education, youth group, liturgy, social justice, social activities, fundraising, parish council and preparation for the sacraments. He also invited any parishioners who thought they'd like to get involved in a leadership role. Brigit's cell phone had chirped steadily at her all week. One question was asked again and again - *what does he want from us?* There were variations on the theme of - *I'm not in charge of anything and I don't want to be.* As well as - *Where does Father get off thinking that he's not in charge?*

168

One after another, the parishioners said – *you go, Brigit, then let us know what he wants.*

She turned at the sound of the door and watched the new priest stride into the room with a wide smile on his face. "I saw you drive up." He glanced at his watch, "Hmmm ... it's seven now. People never do show up on time for things like this, do they? Can I get you a coffee?"

Not knowing how to break the news to him in a nice way, she simply said, "No one else is coming, Father."

He frowned, glanced from the arc of chairs to the coffee pot to the cupcakes, "Are you sure?" he asked her.

"Positive."

"Was it something I said?" A moment of silence preceded the grin that brightened Brigit's face. Soon they were both laughing. Finally, he said, "Help me clear this up and then come over to the rectory. We'll have a coffee together and you can tell me why no one but you had the courage to show up for my meeting."

Later, curled into the corner of Father Kieran's sofa with a cup of coffee in hand and a plate of cupcakes on the table in front of her, Brigit glanced around the trailer and thought that the space was nice – peaceful with lots of books crammed onto shelves, plants in the corners, a Lauren Harris print on the wall. Several gardening books were stacked on the floor by the chair that the priest obviously favoured. A framed photo of two young men sat on the top of a cabinet. When it caught her eye, Father Kieran said, "My brother, Sean, and me." The tone in his voice indicated far more than he was going to say.

Sitting down in his chair, he asked, "Okay, come clean. Why are you the only one who showed up for the meeting?"

"I was delegated to find out what you want from people."

"I suppose they expect me to be responsible for everything. I am the priest after all."

Brigit reached for a cupcake, "Yes, you are," she agreed.

"That doesn't make it my parish. St. Bertha's belongs to the parishioners. They have to take responsibility for what happens here."

Sipping her coffee, Brigit pointed at the cupcakes, "You should have one, Father, they're quite good." She chose her next words carefully. "People do take responsibility. They fundraised to get that church building, they got this trailer for the rectory, they keep things going, they make sure St. Bertha's is part of the Dearborn community. But when it comes to being in charge of liturgy or religious education or things like that, well ... they don't want to overstep themselves." He was quiet, listening, so she went on. "They've gotten used to the priest running the show. You'll have to lead them along a bit more gently if you want them taking charge of a ministry. Even the word is frightening for most of them."

Kieran took a deep breath and reached for a cupcake. "Okay ... fill me in on how things currently get done around St. Bertha's." He held up a hand, "No wait ... let me guess. Helen Sampson takes care of everything to do with social activities and fundraising; the woman who plays the piano picks all the music; the men who did readings on the last two Sundays do them every week; the altar servers weren't out sick or missing in action, there aren't any altar servers; a few moms teach catechism; and when it comes to sacraments, the priest does it all." He bit into the cupcake and raised an eyebrow at her.

"By George, I think he's got it." Brigit whistled softly before she said, "You really have your finger on the pulse of this parish, Father."

"If you're going to be sarcastic in a witty way, then you must call me, Kieran. It's only fair. Tell me about your refugee work."

Brigit described her involvement with a group based out of Campbell River. She spoke of the two refugee families already sponsored, thanks to the work of the group, and she assured him that she got lots of support from St. Bertha's parishioners. They donated money and whatever else she asked for and they were always eager to hear about how things were going.

She and Kieran moved effortlessly from talking about refugees to gardening and cooking and books and music. After a second cup of coffee and another cupcake, Brigit looked at her watch. She hastily got up from the sofa. "I had no idea it was so late, Kieran. I better get going."

He walked her to the door. As she turned to say goodbye, he said, "Thank you for not letting me sit over in that empty church wondering if I had gotten the meeting night wrong."

She smiled and leaned over to pat his arm, "They don't know what they missed. I'm the lucky one. Take care, Kieran. I'll see you on Sunday."

TWENTY

Nick strapped Aidan into the child's lounging chair on the floor of the spacious bathroom in the Saltbox. He dropped his boxers, stepped into the shower and turned on the water. Pulling back the curtain to check on the baby every few minutes, Nick managed to get through his first challenge of the day. He even amazed himself with how quickly he could now handle the basics of personal cleanliness. In his first week of caring for Aidan, he had been hard-pressed to get his teeth brushed. The baby chewed quietly on the ear of a plastic giraffe as Nick stood in front of the sink to shave. He caught himself making faces at his son in the mirror.

Carting the child with him into the kitchen, Nick laid Aidan in the playpen. The baby worked at rolling over while his father made coffee and fixed himself some breakfast.

Nick had reached the end of his second week of staying at the Saltbox while Fiona was working and on call in Dearborn. Izzy and Liam had helped him a lot during the first week. When he'd arrived at the Saltbox after work each day, they had Aidan bathed and fed and his bottles ready in the fridge. They had even invited Nick over to their house for dinner and sent him away with leftovers. Despite all the help, that first night alone with Aidan had given Nick a new definition for the word anxiety. He'd hardly slept, starting awake at the least sound and tiptoeing across from the guest room to his son's room over and over to make sure the child was still breathing. Aidan had slept much better than his father, right through the night, and he was wide awake at five a.m. Nick quickly learned that was the baby's regular routine.

Not quite equal to his anxiety about caring for Aidan was the discomfort Nick felt about sleeping in the bed Fiona had recently vacated. When he had lain down that first night, though she'd stripped the bed and left out clean sheets for him, he could feel her presence. She had left a shirt draped carelessly over a chair, her things were in the bathroom. Being plunged back into such proximity with a past lover was disconcerting.

That first week, he had looked forward to the Friday when Fiona would return and he could go back to his own place and regroup. It hadn't worked out that way. Fiona had texted to say she was running late, so he had trekked back to the Saltbox after work, relieved Liam and waited for Fiona to show up.

Nick had been walking the floor with Aidan draped over his shoulder. He was getting ready to sit down and burp the child when Fiona came in. One quick glance at her told Nick she was exhausted. She reached for Aidan and said, "Wow, he looks bigger than he did when I dropped him at daycare on Tuesday. How has everything been going?" She tried to smile but the expression required too much energy to reach her eyes.

As Aidan fussed in Fiona's arms, Nick smiled back. "I'm started to get the hang of things." He gestured toward his son. "I fed him. I was about to burp him." As he said those words, Aidan spewed formula all over Fiona's black shirt.

She held the baby away from her. "Yuck ... should have expected that, I guess." Nick took Aidan while she used her sleeve to mop the front of her shirt. "I know you're probably anxious to get going, Nick. I'll get changed first, okay?"

Staring into eyes that pleaded for a few moments of reprieve, Nick had found himself saying, "Have you eaten?" When she shook her head, he said, "I'm not in a rush. Grab a hot bath. I'll get Aidan settled and make us a couple of omelets." He was shocked to see quick tears come to Fiona's eyes. She stared at Aidan in Nick's arms and then massaging the back of her neck, she headed to the bathroom.

Later, as she brushed out and braided her long black hair, Nick had whipped up the omelets and they sat down to eat. He found a good bottle of red wine in the cupboard and poured them both large glasses. They carried the wine with them to the living room when they were finished eating.

Fiona had looked at him from over the rim of her wine glass. "I don't know how to thank you, Nick. I dreaded coming into the house, I was so tired." She frowned, "I had a call out to the hospital in Cedar Falls one night because they had an overflowing emergency room. I only got back in time to shower and head right to the clinic. Then I had to go to the addiction center the next night to deal with a guy who was having serious DTs and needed extra meds." She sighed, "I'm used to functioning with little sleep, but Rosemary's practice is much more demanding than I remember from my internship with her. Even with Gary's help –" To satisfy Nick's questioning look she added, "He's a doctor from Cedar Falls who comes down to Dearborn to work with me on Saturday. He covers the clinic on Monday when I'm off and he's on-call for Dearborn the days I'm not around." She had finished her wine and held her glass out for more. "I'm going non-stop and using the evenings to study charts and try to get up to speed."

He had offered to stay over that night, sleep in the upstairs room and listen for Aidan. She could take Alex and Cynthia's room. She smiled her gratitude. She had worked at the clinic all day Saturday, too, and they fell into a similar routine that night – only deviating to walk over to Micah Camp so he could pick up a few more clothes and stay there for dinner. Sunday, the one day off they shared, slipped away while they did various chores. They went to Dearborn together to buy groceries and diapers. Fiona had invited Liam, Izzy, Robbie and Sophie for supper and she and Nick decided to prepare and host the meal together since they both wanted to thank them.

The evening had ended well and Aidan had been asleep before Nick made a move to leave. He'd had to get back to the camp because he was scheduled for overnight supervision Sunday and Monday. He had looked in one last time on his son, told Fiona he would see her at the clinic on Tuesday to pick up the car seat and get Aidan from daycare, and he had left. At the end of that first week, he had missed the baby. He'd thought he would sleep better back in his own bed but he hadn't. He'd wakened a few times thinking he could hear Aidan crying.

When he returned for his second week of staying at the Saltbox, he had brought a large white board from the camp and leaned the thing against the wall on top of a cabinet in the living room. Fiona had laughed when she saw it but she agreed that they had to get themselves organized. During the first week, way too much time had been taken up texting back and forth about who was looking after the baby each day. Now, at the end of the second week, Nick's plan was taking shape.

Having finished up his breakfast, he leaned over the playpen to pick Aidan up. He carried the baby to the living room and studied the chart he had drawn on the white board. He pointed at a calendar square and told Aidan, "You'll be with Arianna this morning. She's taking you to Liam after lunch. And I'll pick you up after work." He stared into the baby's dark eyes and asked, "Are you looking forward to seeing Mom, tonight?" Aidan gurgled a response that could have meant anything. As for Nick, he was certainly looking forward to seeing Fiona. He decided not to plunge too deeply into analyzing that feeling.

He stared back at his chart. It contained several blanks. He had an idea that he thought might simplify their daycare issues. He planned to present his proposal at the direct client meeting today over at the camp. But even getting a firmer grip on daycare wouldn't change the fact that Nick's summer plans were in disarray. The month at UCLA was not going to happen. He had phoned his supervisor after the first days at the Saltbox. The PhD, the research, the next book were all on hold for the moment. He wasn't sure how he felt about any of it. He was too busy keeping up at Micah Camp and looking after his son.

❧❧❧❧

Justin went straight to the lunchroom fridge. He dug around, moving things aside so he could get out a large pizza box and a cold pop. Sitting down at the table, he flipped open the box and pulled out a cold slice. As he bit into it, he glanced at Reg who sat across from him scowling as he flipped through *The Used-Equipment Journal*.

Justin swallowed a bite of pizza, took a swig from his pop and asked, "Wow, Reg ... what's up? You look like you're about to blow."

Flipping the paper over to wave a page in Justin's direction, Reg said, "Fucken unbelievable. You can't even get a used CAT for under a couple of grand." He closed the paper, rolled it up and slammed it against the side of the table. "Did you get through that list of cold calls?"

Starting on another slice of pizza, Justin said, "I did. I've got a couple of people calling back this afternoon and two guys are coming by to see you tomorrow."

A small grin replaced Reg's scowl. The sound of work boots stomping on the stairs preceded Mike into the room. He made a beeline for the pizza on the table, veered to the fridge for a pop and then sat down. He took a bite and pointed at the box, "Gotta love this *Dearborn Pizza Pie Man* special, two for the price of one." To Justin's nod, Mike added, "Have you heard anything back from Western Forest yet?"

Justin shook his head. Reg's scowl was back in place. "I got one goddamned word to say to you," he pointed the rolled paper at Justin, "loyalty." He smacked the paper against Mike's back, "This guy here, look at him."

174

Justin grinned at Mike who was bent over the table trying not to choke on the pizza in his mouth. "I'm looking at him, Reg and it think he might need some first aid."

Reg crossed his arms over his chest. "He'll survive. Mike's been here at *Crater Lake Timber* since he was sixteen fucken years old. Still here ... still loyal. You think about that, boyo, before you get too big for your britches with a Western Forest job."

Justin drained his coke. "What about more money, Reg? I've got my future to think of."

"More to life than goddamned money." Reg looked at Mike who was reaching for another slice of pizza. "I got a new guy coming later today and I need you to start training him on the saw."

Mike stared at Reg, "That's going to be impossible the way you have me running the thing full tilt. No can do, boss."

"You could stay late. It's a bitch to keep that pretty fiancé of yours waiting, but it's what a loyal employee would do."

"Are we talking overtime, here?" Mike asked.

"Not damn likely," Reg barked.

Mike rolled his shoulders and said, "Ditto that on my end."

Ethan strolled into the lunchroom knocking his work gloves against his leg. He looked at the last slice of pizza in the box. "Why the hell are you guys eating that cold. There's a microwave right there." He waved towards the small kitchen as he claimed the last slice and walked over to get a plate.

Reg stood up and said, "Ethan, I hope to hell you're up here because that order is ready to leave the yard after lunch."

Ethan stared into the spinning microwave. "Ya, ya ... boss man ... all stacked at the edge of the yard and waiting to be loaded."

Reg started to smile but a sudden grimace ripped across his face as he leaned forward to grip the edge of the table. He straightened up quickly as he rubbed his chest. When he noticed all three of his employees staring at him, he dropped his hand to his side. "Damn, fucken indigestion."

Justin frowned, "You sure, Reg. Maybe you should sit down for a minute."

Reg brushed off that suggestion with a wave of his hand, "Nothing a couple of Rolaids won't fix. Don't you worry about old Reg." He left the room.

Mike looked over at Justin. They both shrugged. Mike said, "Wynter wants you and Lisa to come to dinner with us at *The Sea Shed* on Saturday night."

"What are we celebrating?" Justin asked.

"We just took possession of our apartment in the Lady Brit. We'll meet you guys down there before we go out. Wynter wants to show it off."

Ethan sat down in the chair Reg had vacated. "What about me? Are you going to invite me?"

Mike shook his head, "Couples only, Ethan. If you have a date, you can come."

"Ya, right ... screw you, Mike. Nothing like kicking a guy when he's down." Ethan chewed slowly on his slice of pizza as he said, "Lisa-Marie is hardly Justin's date, is she?" He stared at Justin, "Or is she?"

Ignoring Ethan, Mike scowled, "My mom is driving me crazy."

Ethan made a pouty face, "Oh, poor Mikey. You are such a bellyacher. Grow a pair, man. Try standing up to your mother."

Mike frowned, "Easy for you to say."

Ethan shook his head, "If you want to hear about a real problem, listen to this. My new roommate is some kind of Bible thumping freak who told me to my face that I'm devil spawn."

Heading for the door, Justin stopped. He looked at Ethan. "Go talk to Roland. You don't have to put up with that."

"Sticks and stones, man. We're avoiding each other by a mutual, unspoken agreement. On the up side," Ethan told them, "I think I might be in love."

Mike got up hastily and joined Justin by the door, "Not interested," he said as he pushed Justin to hurry him out of the room.

Ethan called out, "I'd tell you all about him, Mike, if you weren't such a mama's boy, homophobe." Ethan laughed as he pushed back his chair and made his way over to the old sofa jammed against the wall. He lay down with his hands behind his head and thought about kissing Charlie's pouty lips.

⁂

Izzy settled into the chair behind the desk of her new office at Micah Camp. She had left Nick with the larger room she had used before taking time off. She was here only two days a week, so taking the smaller office was fair. Still, she found it hard to get used to counselling in this room. Though the scenic expanse of trees past the camp's circular drive was nice to look at, she'd lost her view of the lake. She swung her chair towards the door at the sound of a quick knock.

"Hey, Charlie," she said, "Come in. I'm Izzy." She walked forward to shake the hand of the slim, young man who stood in the doorway of her office. Once they settled in chairs across from one another, Izzy went over issues associated with confidentiality. Charlie was relaxed in his chair as he listened.

Izzy began, "When we met with your parents, your mom requested that I be your counsellor. She suggested that I let you instruct me on the kind of help you need." She smiled, "It seems like great advice. In our counselling sessions, we'll talk about what you want to talk about."

Charlie nodded slowly. He sat quietly and was obviously considering her words. Izzy had worked with many clients at Micah Camp but she'd seldom had one who was so calm. He didn't tap his fingers, jerk his knee up and down, pick at his face or nails. He didn't seem likely to jump up and wander around the room or to burst into tears or to hit the wall with his fist. She and Charlie might have been getting ready to play a game of chess on the small table between them. His composure and concentration would have suited such a situation.

He met her gaze. "I'll probably want to talk about being a guy who can't stand up in the bathroom to take a leak." He gave her a bit of a grin, testing the boundaries. She smiled back and he went on, "I don't get messed up about who I am because I've always been like this. But the changes from the testosterone mean I'll be thinking about the possibility of other changes and that's big for me."

She watched his forehead wrinkle with a frown. She led him gently, "Say some more about that, Charlie."

"It's the whole idea of the future ... things changing, decisions, choices. Even coming here to Micah Camp. I'm sort of confused by all of that." He shrugged, "I know it's normal but I think it would be good to work on that ... the confusion," he added for her clarification.

"Are you up for doing an activity?"

"Like an ink blot test or something?" He raised an eyebrow at her.

"Not quite." Izzy went to the file cabinet in the corner and opened the bottom drawer to riffle through the folders. Finding what she was looking for, she pulled out a sheet of paper and then went to her desk drawer to find a pen and two pads of post-it-notes. She came back to her chair and placed the materials on the table.

"This activity can help you zero in on the things about the future that are confusing you." She pointed to the sheet of paper that had a drawing of an open suitcase on one side and a trash can on the other. "Imagine you're going to carry that suitcase into the future. Take the green post-it-notes and jot down things you need to pack. Like any trip, you can only pack so much. The yellow notes are for the things you need to get rid of ... you don't want them with you in the future. Jot those down and stick them in the trash can."

Sitting back in her chair, Izzy stared out the window as Charlie worked. From the corner of her eye she could see him carefully consider each note before sticking it in the suitcase or the trash can. After about ten minutes, he said, "I'm done."

Together they looked down at the paper, now covered with a smattering of green and yellow notes. Charlie pointed to the suitcase, "I put down university because I'm interested in the law or maybe being a teacher." He pointed to another note, "Definitely a car. I'd like to drive into the future." He looked down again. "I want some friends that I can be myself with, the kind of friends who don't judge." He paused before he reached out to smooth one of the sticky notes down. "This one ... chest reconstruction. I want that but it means surgery and that's scary." He moved the last note to the edge of the suitcase's lid. The word - *penis* - was written on the note. He looked up at her. "I think about it but I don't know. That's a thing that confuses me."

Izzy listened while the young man across from her laid out a road map of the work they might do together. She said, "What about the things that need to go in the trash."

Charlie pointed to a sticky note that was right down at the bottom of the can, "Tits ... I definitely think about trashing those." Pointing to another note, he said, "Back acne. I sure don't want that in the future." He looked at the trash can for a moment and finally touched another note. "This is another big thing. My parents aren't always going to be able to make everything right for me. They always have, and even sending me here is their idea of making things easier for me. But the day is coming when they can't protect me." Resting his hands on the arms of the chair, Charlie sat back and said, "The last one says sex and that means I don't want to take fears about having sex into the future. But since I don't even know what having sex is going to mean ... with this body ... that one is confusing."

Izzy let them sit in silence for a couple of moments before she said, "Let's not do anything else to unpack the suitcase or deal with the trash right now. I think these will all be good points for us to come back to as we work together." She pointed to the paper on the table, "If you're okay with the idea, I'd like to photocopy your work for my own reference. Then you can take the original and think about where we should start in our next session."

"Ya ... sure, no problem."

As she was walking him to the door a few minutes later, she asked, "Would you consider a work placement at the organic bakery next door. I know they need someone and it might be a good fit for you."

"Sounds okay. Can I meet the people there first before I decide?"

"Definitely," Izzy assured him.

❧❧❧❧

Roland pulled a pile of files toward him. "That leaves the new residents. Go ahead, Alison." He tapped his thumb against the edge of a file folder as the woman shuffled through her notes, cleared her throat and shuffled some more. He wondered if she was waiting for divine inspiration.

"I've started things in motion for David's upgrading –,"

Nick sat forward and leaned across the table, "Can you speak up? It's hard to hear you."

As her face reddened at the interruption, Alison raised her voice and continued, "I think the kitchen will be a good work placement for David." She opened another file and frowned. "Sadie is proving to be a challenge. She's all over the map. One minute she says she'll work at the sawmill and the next she thinks she'd like to try the library. For the moment, I think we've settled on the greenhouse."

Izzy scribbled a note in her black journal and pushed her glasses up into her hair. "Nothing like gardening to settle someone down. It always works for me."

Nick sat forward again. Roland stared at him. The man kept billowing across the table like a wind sock in a gale. "Hold on a second," Nick told Alison. "I have an idea for Sadie's placement. She's interested in becoming an early childhood educator."

"News to me." Alison spoke under her breath as she closed Sadie's file.

"Fiona and I are having trouble finding daycare for Aidan. I thought that Sadie could take it on as her work placement."

Roland stared at Nick in disbelief but before he could set the man straight, Alison's voice came out breathy and sharp, "I understood that finding work placements for the residents is my job."

Nick's idea was absurd and Roland could only conclude that the burdens of fatherhood were affecting his better judgement. Even so, Alison was overstepping. Roland told her, "I'd like to think we all work together." He turned his gaze to Nick. "Are you suggesting you would leave your infant son in the care of a resident who has been here only a couple of weeks?"

"I've checked her out. I'm not a fool. I spoke to her social worker and the foster family she was with for the past few years. They all assure me she is a well-adjusted, responsible young woman."

Opening a file in front of him, Roland traced his finger along a line of text. "A vegetarian, white witch." He looked up. "I'm reading your own file notes here, Nick. And that's just what she shared with you in the first session." He riffled through the file and extracted another page. "This is a note Brigit left me. *Observed Sadie harassing David in the dining room on two occasions. I've spoken with her about her behaviour.*"

"She's trying to stand out by being different. It's an attention-getting thing. Common for young people." Nick pointed to the paper in Roland's hand, "And she believes she has good reasons for feeling negative towards David. Her behaviour with him is not the norm. We're working on that. She's getting along fine with the other residents."

Roland replaced Brigit's note and closed the file. "Did she tell you that before or after her white witch revelations?"

Nick crossed his arms over his chest, "I live here, Roland. I see her with her roommates and the other residents."

Roland raised an eyebrow before he said, "I couldn't approve childcare as a work placement unless the resident was supervised. There are liability issues to consider." Roland folded his hands on the table in front of him. "You needn't thank me, Nick, but I am doing you a service by saving you the trouble of worrying that your infant son is eating tofu and being turned into a druid."

He watched Izzy cover a quick smile, as she said, "I have a suggestion. I know that Paula struggles to find daycare for her little guy and often brings Noah to work with her. Josie watches him in the paper and soap shop. She's got a regular jungle gym set up in one corner. Sadie could do some hours there, caring for the kids under Josie's supervision, and then make up the rest of her hours in the greenhouse. What do you think, Alison?"

Roland sat back and tapped his fingers together. Having Izzy back was a treat. She was as beautiful as always in her designer heels, tight-fitting skirt and cotton shirt, smooth to a glow and open two buttons down the front. Of course, she could be a major pain in her own way but after her brief sojourn spent filling in for him, she knew the challenges of administration.

Alison swallowed frustration and no doubt a dose of professional jealousy as she said, "Yes, I could see an arrangement like that working out."

Izzy turned to Nick, "What do you think?"

"I need daycare. If anyone had told me a few weeks ago that I would be sitting at a meeting saying those words, I'd have said that person was nuts."

Roland gave him a sympathetic look. Nick had gone from book deal to diaper bag in no time flat.

Izzy flipped a page in her day book and said, "Speaking of work placements. I'm wondering if Charlie would be a good fit for work at the bakery. He seems interested and Beulah's been asking for someone for a couple of months." She glanced Alison's way, "What do you think?"

Alison had now been thwarted two times in a row in what she saw as her work placement responsibility. Roland was curious if she would stand up to Izzy.

Their new career counsellor took her time responding. "I had thought he might work in the paper and soap shop." She coloured before adding, "His parents were clear when they told us they did not think Charlie needed or would benefit from special treatment."

A slight frown furrowed Izzy's brow. "How is working in the bakery special treatment?"

Taking a deep breath, Alison said, "First Charlie is roomed in with Ethan and now we are considering a work assignment at the bakery. Is he being marginalized by living and working with a specific group of people?" Alison's face got redder as her words were met with silence.

Roland found himself admiring the woman's nerve. Even though he considered her concern a red herring, he wouldn't have thought she would dare to raise such a challenge. He could see by the look on Izzy's face that she was taking Alison's remark personally. And like clockwork, Nick billowed forward in another gust. "Alison, are you suggesting that there's some ghettoizing LGBTQ conspiracy happening here?" Nick stared up to the ceiling and shook his head.

Alison was obviously defensive now. "Certainly not. I've been reading the book Charlie's parents left us and from what I understand, we shouldn't think Charlie will do better rooming or working with people who identify on the LGBTQ spectrum. That was all I meant."

In a neutral, deescalating tone, Izzy said, "I thought of the bakery not because of anything to do with Beulah and Bethany other than that they run a business right next door, they need a helper and Charlie seemed interested in the work."

Looking slowly around the table, Roland decided the time had come to bring a halt to this conversation. "I agree with Izzy. In terms of work placement, the most important consideration is whether a resident and the site will be a good fit. Let's move on."

Alison fiddled with her paperwork and gratefully changed the subject. "Charlie is strong on the academic front – his marks are excellent. I'm going to find a couple of first year university courses for him."

Roland stared down at his agenda for a moment then said, "Okay ... I think we can wrap this meeting up if no one has anything else to add." He was already stacking files and ready to stand when, to his astonishment, Nick folded his arms on the table and leaned forward yet again, addressing Alison. "I understand you're not making much progress with Ethan. Is there anything I can do to help?"

Alison's colour deepened to a blotchy red creeping over her skin. She gripped her pen and stared at Nick as she said, "Dance schools are highly competitive and Ethan has set his sights high."

Nick pulled a sheet from a file in front of him. "Ethan says you keep a rosary on your desk. Your office might not be the best place for religious trinkets."

Roland held up his hand, "I've read Alison's notes. I think we can all agree that Ethan's dramatic flair puts a spin on the way he reports things. Meeting adjourned."

TWENTY-ONE

"This is nice, isn't it?" Out in the grocery store parking lot, Izzy passed Liam the last bag from the cart.

He swung it into the back of the Highlander beside several others. "Grocery shopping?" he asked her with a frown.

She smiled, "Well, not necessarily grocery shopping but getting out, just the two of us. It's great having Lisa home and knowing she and Sophie are together."

Closing the back of the vehicle, Liam dusted his hands off. "Shopping is definitely more low-key without Sophie. Do we have everything for tonight?"

"Yes, we're good. I feel bad that it's taken this long to get Alison over for dinner. Do you want to have some lunch down at the *Beach Road Café* before we head back?"

"Sounds good but don't breathe a word of it to Sophie or Robbie. If they find out they missed fish and chips, they will never let us hear the end of it."

Carrying the teapot and mugs, Izzy followed Liam out to the deck of the café. He was loaded down with the fish and chips. The sun reflected off the glossy white of the picnic tables whenever the breeze lifted the corners of the flowered plastic tablecloths. That same breeze off the water, sweeping the billowy white clouds across the sky, was chilly. Izzy was glad she had brought her sweater from the car. She spotted Kieran sitting at a table near the deck railing. His gaze was turned towards the harbour. She touched Liam's arm, "Let's sit with Kieran."

She veered toward his table and said, "Hi, Kieran. Can we join you?"

The priest got up and smiled. As Liam set his tray down, Kieran reached over to shake his hand. "Good to see you again, Liam."

183

They ate their lunch amid talk of the weather, the activity in the harbour and gardening. As Izzy sipped her tea, she asked Kieran, "How is your settling in going?"

"It's good. I called a ministry meeting that no one attended." He shrugged as he added, "Seems my invitation was intimidating. But I'm catching on. Tonight, I have my regular Saturday dinner at the home of a parishioner. There's a sign-up sheet in the church. It's a *get-to-know-the-new-priest* strategy." A frown tracked across his face. "I've been surprised by the number of parishioners who offer me booze and how disappointed they seem when I say, no thanks."

Encouraged by Izzy's look of sympathy, Kieran turned to Liam and said, "I've got a problem when it comes to alcohol." Liam inclined his head slightly and Kieran changed the subject. "I'm actually glad we ran into each other today, Izzy. I have an idea I want to run by you." He got up from the picnic table and swung his leg over the bench. "I'll get some more hot water in these teapots first."

As Kieran disappeared inside the café, Liam looked at Izzy and said, "Seems he and I have more in common that I thought we would." Izzy nodded.

Setting the steaming teapots on the table, Kieran sat back down. He poured hot water into his cup and reached for a new teabag. He dipped it in and out of the mug as he spoke, "I'd like to start a grief and loss support group ... have it run weekly for about six sessions. I've put out a few feelers in the parish and there's interest. It would be open to the whole community." He smiled at Izzy as he added, "I will need an experienced person to act as co-facilitator and I wondered if you'd be interested." He discarded the teabag to the edge of the saucer, opened a creamer and dumped it into his cup.

"I am interested. Definitely. I have a client who might benefit from a group experience."

"Great ... I'll get back to you on dates and put some notices up around town."

They spent some time discussing the proper timing for moving various plants from greenhouse to garden before Izzy glanced at her watch and said, "We better get going, Liam. That roast for tonight's dinner isn't going to cook itself." They all got up.

Standing by the table, Liam looked at Kieran and said, "I attend a men's group at the reserve in Cedar Falls ... it's not AA or any type of step thing and we don't tell our addiction stories. It's a few men who sit together. Mostly in silence ... though words of pain do get spoken. A couple of guys drum now and then. But like I said, mostly silence. You'd be welcome to join us."

Kieran seemed taken aback for a moment. He rubbed his temple as he said, "I'd have to be just another man with an issue. I don't want to be the priest in the group."

"You're safe on that count, padre. These men aren't after that brand of absolution."

Kieran nodded his understanding. "I am interested."

"I'll give you a call the next time I'm headed up that way." Liam paused for a moment then said, "And tonight, when those drink offers come pouring in, you could try saying – I don't drink." Liam patted Kieran on the arm, "I find that cuts down on the repeat propositions."

As they walked back to the Highlander, Izzy linked her arm through Liam's. She smiled over at him as she asked, "Are you trying to steal one of my few clients?"

Liam smiled back, "If it weren't for you, he'd never have the strength for silence."

❧❧❧❧

Brigit stood by the kitchen's bank of ovens and watched as David scooped Caesar salad dressing into the large bowls of romaine lettuce lined up on the counter. He had been with her in the kitchen all week. She always asked for full immersion when she was starting to train a new resident. She liked him. He was a hard worker and he took instruction well. She was glad to see that after a few days of sprinkling Bible quotes around the kitchen like pixie dust, that he seemed to be relaxing. He hadn't quoted scripture even once today. She turned to check the turkey burgers and called over her shoulder, "When you're done mixing up that salad, you can start taking everything out. I'm going to put some cheese on these and then they'll be ready."

She kept an eye on the grill in the upper oven as she checked on Sadie's veggie burger patties in the lower one and slapped a slice of soya cheese on each. Pulling everything out, she reached for a separate plate for Sadie's lunch. David returned to the kitchen and she told him, "Ring the bell. We're ready to rock-and-roll."

Brigit placed the burgers into a stainless-steel pan which she passed to David. She walked to the door of the dining room herself with Sadie's burger patties. She saw the girl come into the room. Sadie was hard to miss with her wrist-to-elbow bangles and that head of hair. Brigit had to smile as she handed her the plate. "Two veggie burgers with soya jalapeno cheese. Enjoy."

"Thanks, Brigit. They smell yummy." Sadie waltzed away, hips swinging and bangles clashing.

Back in the kitchen, Brigit removed from the cooler two heavy trays of glass dishes filled with chocolate pudding. David topped each dish with whipped cream. Brigit gave him a thumbs up for presentation. "At the end of the month we're going to have a girl from Dearborn working in the kitchen full-time for the summer. You should be up to speed by then and you can help me train her. I plan to have her work the weekends with you."

He grinned, "You mean I'm going to be the boss of somebody?"

Brigit was looking forward to having two weekend workers she could count on. She had been without good help for the last couple of months. She'd still have to do extra cooking on Thursday and Friday to make sure dinner entrees were ready in the cooler for the weekends, but the kids would take care of side dishes, serving and clean-up. With the dessert ready to go, Brigit looked around the kitchen and told David, "You go ahead and grab your lunch now. Things look good here. You can handle the rest of the cleanup when you're done eating and I'll check in with you in plenty of time before dinner."

David untied his apron and hung it on the hook near the panty. He headed into the busy dining room. He fixed himself a turkey burger fully loaded and heaped Caesar salad onto his plate. He turned to scan the room. None of the tables was empty but he saw Charlie sitting on his own near the wall. David walked over and sat down across from him.

Pointing to the burger in his own hand, Charlie said, "Good stuff." He took a big bite, chewed, swallowed and asked, "Is the kitchen job working out okay?"

"Ya, I like it. Brigit's cool to work with. She used to be a cop, you know."

"No kidding. I wouldn't have guessed that." He stabbed some salad and said, "I checked out the bakery the other day. I'm going to work there. They made that bun you're eating."

David was about to take a bite of his burger when Sadie walked by and stopped to lean across the edge of the table so the low-cut front of her flowing dress was almost in David's face. He couldn't stop himself. He stared ... he could see the outline of her nipple through the lace of her bra. His mouth went dry and he dropped his burger on his plate. Out of the corner of his eye, he saw Charlie craning to get a look, too.

Sadie jiggled her body as she said, "Better go and check the fine print in that covenant of yours, David." She stood up and sniffed loudly. "I definitely smell lust in the air." She laughed as she walked away.

Charlie grinned and said, "Wow ... that was one nice view." He took another bite of his burger and added, "Don't let her bug you. She's like one of those bees that flies around at a picnic. The more you swat at it, the worse off you are." David nodded as he returned his attention to his lunch.

Ethan turned from the food counter and scanned the dining room. He spotted Charlie right away, over by the wall, sitting with David. He weighed the cost of avoiding David with the advantage of sitting beside Charlie. Coming down on the side of Charlie, he headed for the table. Pulling up a chair, he sat down and said, "Hey, roomies. How's it going?"

David stood and picked up his unfinished plate of food from the table. The burger was now a spilled mess. Charlie looked at him, "You don't have to go."

"I've got cleanup to do and I've lost my appetite." He walked away towards the kitchen.

❧❧❧❧

Kieran greeted Mike and Wynter at the rectory door. He led them through the office and into his living room. "I thought we'd meet here. It's more comfortable. Have a seat. Can I get you guys coffee or tea?"

Wynter smiled as she sat on the sofa, "Don't go to any extra work, but if the coffee is made, I'd love a cup."

Sitting down beside her, Mike said, "Nothing for me, Father. I'm jumpy enough about being here without adding a shot of caffeine."

"I promise not to preach or bite. I hope that helps," Kieran said as he went to the kitchen to pour a coffee for himself and Wynter. Moments later, seated in his chair, he said, "Okay, what can I do for the two of you?"

Mike glanced at Wynter then said, "We aren't getting married in the church no matter what my mother says. Wynter isn't even Catholic and I haven't been through the church doors since I was a teenager."

"That isn't a problem for me," Kieran said. "And where you get married would have to be your decision, not your mother's."

"How about you tell her that?" Mike shook his head, "She insisted we come and talk to you. But, seriously, we're wasting your time."

"Let me be the judge of that, okay Mike?" He put his cup down and sat forward. "Why do you think she would insist that you two come here if you've made your wishes clear?"

When Mike didn't say anything, Wynter answered, "Maybe she thinks you'll change our minds."

Mike added, "She wants you to tell me I'm rushing into this. Marriage is a serious business." He imitated his mother's voice.

Wynter held Mike's hand tightly. She assured him, "No one is going to stop me marrying you."

Kieran thought it best to deescalate the tension – banish the ghost of Helen Sampson from the room, for the moment anyway. "Let's change the subject. Tell me how the two of you met."

Mike frowned, "Why would you want to know that?"

"I'm a sucker for a good love story. And you two are the most in-love couple I've run across in a while."

Wynter nudged Mike with her elbow, "See, Father Kieran gets us."

Not able to resist her smile, Mike's relaxed as he looked at Wynter and said, "You start."

"I was a resident at Micah Camp –,"

"She was helping on this ridiculous committee to arrange a beauty pageant for Dipsy-Doodle Days." Mike took up the tale, "My sister Hannah was in the pageant –,"

"But remember, Mike," Wynter slapped at his arm, "We weren't allowed to call it a beauty pageant. We had to say the *Young Women of Dearborn Shine* or something ridiculous like that."

Mike chuckled before going on, "She was sitting at the dining room table of my house for a meeting. I took one look at her and almost had a heart attack. I guess you could call that love at first sight."

Excited to carry on the story, Wynter broke in, "I wanted him to ask me out –,"

"She wanted *me* to ask *her* out. How was I to know that? I was so tongue-tied around her, I was practically a mute. I had to drive her home to Micah Camp after practically every pageant rehearsal with Hannah cramming Wynter in right beside me."

Kieran smiled as Wynter interrupted again, "I felt like the Dipsy-Doodle Days dance was my last chance. I was wearing the most gorgeous dress. If only he would ask me to dance ... and he did." She clapped her hands with glee. Then her face fell, "But when the music stopped, he walked away and left me standing all by myself in the middle of the dance floor and he didn't ask me out or even kiss me."

Mike gave a hoot of laughter laced with disbelief, "She wanted *me* to kiss *her*. I was in a state of shock after one dance ... like I was having an out-of-body experience. I don't even know how I got home." Wynter giggled. Mike went on, "I was running in the half marathon the next day so I had twenty-one miles of pounding the pavement to regret my ineptitude. Wynter was there at the finish line giving out the medals and -,"

Mike and Wynter said the words at the same time, "We kissed." They grinned at each other and then at Kieran.

He smiled back at them. "Hey, thanks. I like that story. You made my day." He let them all bask in the aura of love for a moment before he said, "When I came to your house for dinner, I could tell there were some tensions between your mom and the two of you."

"I guess that flying cake gave things away, hey?" Mike crossed his arms over his chest as he spoke.

"That was a memorable moment. The tension is obviously being caused by more than whether or not there will be a church wedding." He looked levelly at the young man sitting relaxed now on the sofa. "It might help to talk about what's going wrong."

Wynter spoke up, "Mike's mom is worried about him. She's not sure I'm the right girl for him and I get that. Moms worry. I'm determined to show her she's wrong.

"Why the disapproval and, Mike, why does your mom's opinion matter so much?"

Mike's anger had disappeared. He was resigned. "My mother thinks I'm playing out of my league wanting to marry a girl like Wynter. She thinks I'm not good enough. I don't have enough ambition. I'm not like Zach. I'm content to live in Dearborn and work at the sawmill. She thinks I'll end up divorced and bitter and she'll never get to see her grandchildren."

Shaking her head, Wynter said, "I hate it when you say that. *A girl like Wynter.*"

Mike pulled her hand up to his face and laid it against his cheek, "It's what my mom thinks. I know exactly what kind of a girl you are." He looked over at Kieran. "It matters what my mother thinks because, whether it seems like it or not, we're a close family. I take after my dad. He's the one I go to when I need to talk to one of my parents. But my mom is my mom. She doesn't get me. She never has, but I love her."

Wynter said, "It might be my upbringing that makes Helen feel uneasy about me marrying Mike." With a nod of his head, Kieran encouraged her to go on. "I grew up in a place called the Peach Valley Commune in the Niagara region of Ontario." She held her hand up, "I see it in your face. The minute I say the word commune people jump to all kinds of crazy conclusions."

Kieran smiled, "The only thing I was thinking is that I'm from Ontario, too, and my mouth is suddenly watering for a Niagara peach."

Grinning, Wynter said, "I've never had a better one from anywhere else." She went on, "The commune was just a bunch of people who wanted to live on the land, grow organic food and raise their kids like one big family. Growing up in that community was wonderful."

"How long did you stay there?"

"My mom died when I was eleven and then I went to live with my grandmother. None of the modeling stuff would ever have happened if I hadn't gone to live with my grandmother. I would have been an ordinary kid, like all the other kids."

Mike shook his head, "I doubt that, Wynter. Your grandma didn't make you beautiful."

"You'd be surprised. If you saw my before picture," she poked him in the side, "which you never will ... you'd know what I mean. My grandmother had been a model and she knew how to shape someone else for the business. She insisted on braces, ballet and discipline. A few years of that can turn any old sow's ear into a silk purse." Kieran laughed and Wynter joined him. "She always used to tell me that."

Kieran asked, "Where is your grandma now?"

"She's in Europe, in a facility." Wynter sighed, "She has Alzheimer's."

Watching the young couple on his sofa, Kieran felt a weight of sadness burrow in to sit with the joy of new beginnings. Here was a girl who wanted to belong, to recreate the cohesion of her earlier life. And Helen Sampson, from all accounts a woman devoted to family and community, was apparently doing all she could to drive Wynter away and alienate her own son.

He sat back in his chair and cleared his throat. "I'd like to give the two of you a piece of advice," he waited to see them nod. "It's your wedding and you have your own lives to live. Make your own decisions. Trust your gut, Mike. You said your family is close. Your mother may hold certain opinions now that are hard to understand but I doubt she's going cling to those and risk losing that closeness." He paused for a moment to let that sink in. "I'm only starting to know St. Bertha's, but if there comes a time when you change your mind about church, the community will be here to welcome you with open arms and they won't care about where or how you got married. And that goes for me as well. Feel free to drop by and chat any time."

As he walked them to the door, Wynter said, "Would you come and have dinner with us one day at the Lady Brit, Father Kieran?"

"I'd love to. But no flying cakes, okay." While they laughed, he decided to heed Liam's advice. "And one other thing," he told Wynter and Mike. "I don't drink."

TWENTY-TWO

Brigit glared at her daughter. "I am already angry enough at you for that stunt you pulled yesterday." Tabby gave her an innocent stare. "Don't look at me like that. You know what I'm talking about." She watched Tabby scuff her running shoe against the edge of the doorjamb of their cabin. "You are not taking off again when Father Kieran is coming here for dinner."

"Oh, mother ... please. He isn't coming to visit with me. It's you he likes to talk to. And I hate Chinese food. You know that. Alison is going to Izzy's for dinner and Robbie says they're having baron of beef. It's my favourite."

As a whining plea crept into Tabby's voice, Brigit gave up. "Go, then. But don't think I won't reschedule that school tour because I plan to do just that. And your allowance for the next two weeks ... consider it gone." She slapped her hands together as if she was dusting Tabby's allowance into nothing.

Tabby made a face as she grabbed her packsack and scampered out of the cabin. That kid was getting on every single one of Brigit's nerves. She knew she was taking the easy way out by not insisting Tabby stay home for dinner, but the last thing she wanted was a pouting tweener hanging around making the dinner with Kieran miserable. Brigit loved Chinese food and appreciated Kieran's thoughtfulness in offering to bring something for them to eat so that she wouldn't have to cook.

She went to shower and change hoping that dinner over at the camp would go smoothly. She was looking forward to a quiet evening without having to run back and forth from her place to the camp's kitchen. Later, as she smoothed the yellow fabric of her dress down over her hips and pulled a comb through her curls, the doorbell rang. She went to greet the priest.

He came in bearing two large brown bags; the smell of food wafted ahead of him. "The food should be hot. I picked it up right before I left town and I had them double wrap everything."

She took the bags from him as he looked around and said, "This place is nice. The whole camp is impressive." He glanced around again, "Where's Tabby?"

Brigit carried the food to the kitchen counter. Looking over her shoulder, she said, "She's gone next door for dinner. She hates Chinese food and if it doesn't sound too unmotherly of me to say, she's not the best company."

Kieran laughed, "If anyone has the right to make an assessment, I'd say you're the one."

Brigit glanced over at the table as she pulled cartons from the bags. She had a sudden thought. "I can't offer you anything to drink, Kieran. Sorry. I never keep liquor in the house unless there's a reason and I totally forgot to pick up anything."

Kieran pulled out a chair, sat down and stretched his legs under the table. "You have no idea what a relief that is." He saw her inquisitive look and said, "Go ahead with the food. I'm starving. I'll tell you as we eat."

As they dished up portions of rice, noodles, vegetables and meat, Kieran smiled across the table at Brigit. "I don't drink."

"Okay ... I love the way they do the chow mien at the *Won Ton Bowl*. I don't like the kind that's runny."

Kieran shook his head, "No, no, no ... you don't get to talk about chow mien when I've just bared my soul." He began to eat, raising an eyebrow at her.

With a fork full of noodles halfway to her mouth, Brigit asked, "You telling me you don't drink is baring your soul?"

"I don't drink because, in the not-that-distant past, I had a serious problem with drinking."

"Oh ...," Brigit stared across the table as she asked, "Could you pass that Kung Pow chicken?"

Kieran laughed as he passed the carton. "You are a woman of focus when it comes to Chinese food."

Shrugging, Brigit said, "I don't mean to minimize your drinking problem, Kieran. But everyone's got issues and a past. I'm not surprised that you do, too." She grinned, "And I do really like Chinese food."

As they ate, Brigit listened with empathy to Kieran's story of how he came to realize he needed help after he fell down the stairs from the pulpit and hit his head on a pew. He told her about the treatment center and coming to see

Izzy for counselling. As she pushed her plate away, she said, "It sounds like you're doing everything you need to stay on top of things."

Brigit fixed tea and brought a tray to the living room. She sat in her chair and Kieran settled on the sofa. As she poured the beverage into stoneware mugs, she said, "I joked about Tabby but the truth is, she's is seriously stretching my patience."

He reached for his mug. "More than her age?"

"Who knows? I want her to consider going to school in Dearborn in the fall. I set up an appointment with the principal of the school for the two of us to have a tour. Tabby disappeared right before we were supposed to leave. I had to cancel."

"Where has she been going to school?"

"Liam has homeschooled Tabby and Robbie for the last two years. Have you met everyone over at Izzy's?"

Kieran shook his head, "Only Izzy and Liam. Is Robbie their son?"

"He's Liam's younger brother. Robbie and Tabby are practically the same age and they're inseparable. Robbie doesn't want to go to school in Dearborn, so Tabby won't even consider it."

"What's your investment in the matter?" She stared at him and he added, "Why does it matter so much to you? Is she not doing well with the homeschooling?"

"She's doing excellent ... working a grade above her age."

"That's confusing. I would imagine that for most parents, how well their children are doing at whatever school they go to is the priority. Why do you want to rock a boat that's floating along just fine?"

"I don't think it's right that a girl her age has only one friend and that her only friend is a boy." Kieran raised that eyebrow again and Brigit whooshed out her breath. She was getting used to that look. It indicated, as clearly as if he'd spoken the words – *come on, I know there's more you're not saying.* "Okay ... okay ... when I first came here, to Micah Camp, two years ago, I wanted desperately for Tabby to fit in, to be happy. I'd had a hard struggle in Toronto. I felt as though I'd neglected her. We both needed a new start."

Kieran watched her as he said, "What happened? In Toronto, I mean."

"I was a police officer and that didn't work out. But having to leave was a real struggle. Being a cop meant a lot to me. From when I was a little girl, it's all I wanted to do." She waved her hand to indicate the cabin and beyond, "Micah Camp is great. I'm grateful for this job and this beautiful cabin. The whole area is a treat. I make good money and I'm able to save a lot of it. And Tabby has thrived." Her face held a rueful look. "Be careful what you ask for in life, Kieran. I wanted her to fit in and boy oh boy, does she ever." She stopped talking and stared at the twisting flower pattern in the carpet at her feet. When she looked up at Kieran, she said, "I never planned that I would be a cook here for the rest of my life. I still want to be a cop. I still want to get back to that someday."

"Okay ... how does that relate to Tabby?"

"She loves this place. She doesn't want anything but Micah Camp and Robbie. It's a tight knit community here and these are good people. I couldn't ask for a better group of people to surround my child with." She paused before she said, "But if I don't do something to broaden Tabby's world soon, she'll never want to go with me when I'm ready to leave." She looked across at Kieran as she said, "And I do not plan on losing my daughter."

❧ ❧ ❧ ❧

"This wine is nice ... smooth without being boring." Alison had refused the swing bench and taken the chair in the corner of the cliff deck. She sat up straight and her eyes were on the fire glowing warmly in the outdoor chimney stove. Izzy couldn't help but notice that Alison was still as tense as she had been when she first arrived for dinner. Even outside on the deck, her quiet tension showed in the tightness around her mouth, in the firm set of her shoulders and in the slight jiggle of her foot.

"I'm glad you could come to dinner and that we finally have a chance to talk. I wanted to do this sooner but the time flies by – you've been at the camp three weeks now, right?" Alison nodded. "You are right about this wine," Izzy leaned forward in her chair to touch her glass lightly to Alison's.

Alison stared at the light from the fire glinting off the edge of her wine glass. "Do you remember the apartment we had in Kits and how we jogged the sea wall to deal with all the grad school anxiety. It seems like a lifetime ago but I often think about it."

Izzy laughed at the memory. "I certainly remember the thin walls in that apartment with Marlene and Tim in the next bedroom – if they weren't having sex they were fighting like cats and dogs and we heard every bit of it." With her eye on the crackling sparks flying up the chimney of the stove, Izzy added, "Tim and Marlene are coming up this summer for a few days to stay in the guest cabin. It will be a real reunion now that you're here."

Alison, Izzy and Tim had met the first day of grad school, drawn together by their mutual need to find a place to live. Alison and Izzy had no idea Tim would be moving in with a wife until the day they all gathered at the two-bedroom apartment in the colourful neighbourhood near Stanley Park.

Alison nodded, "I'd like to see them again. For all the drama, I remember the whole grad school experience as good ... all of us living together and going through the program." Looking out over the water, Alison's voice wavered as she said, "I never would have finished if it hadn't been for you guys."

Izzy had to agree with Alison's assessment – she wouldn't have made it without sympathetic classmates like Izzy and Tim to ease her through the endless rounds of self-doubt she had experienced about her ability to be a counsellor and the overscrupulous way she examined each and everything she said and did. They had discovered that Alison had a core of stubbornness that ran like an iron rod through her being. Once she had made up her mind, they were challenged to help her see alternatives. Living with the ambiguity of the learning process and the shades of grey present when it came to the profession of counselling had been difficult for all of them. Alison could never have negotiated that steep learning curve on her own.

Alison spoke quietly, "I've been thinking that I might not be a good fit for the job at Micah Camp."

Izzy shook her head vigorously, "No, don't say that Alison. One of the reasons I'm so glad we have time to talk now is that I wanted to apologize for what happened at the meeting the other day. Nick and I did interfere in the work placements. We're used to operating that way but we gave no thought to how our meddling would make you feel. And I've been reading the book Charlie's parents left us, too. I overreacted to your comment at the meeting on a personal level. I've been friends with Beulah and Bethany for years. But you had a good point – we do need to examine our choices to be sure we aren't providing a type of special treatment Charlie doesn't need. I don't think assigning him to room with Ethan or arranging for him to work at the bakery were conscious moves to single him out or treat him differently but the caution you raised was important. I'm sorry I didn't realize that at the time and help facilitate an open discussion on the subject."

Alison's shoulders slumped ever-so-slightly as she stared at Izzy. "You can't imagine how much I appreciate your saying that." She took a small sip of her wine. "I have no backup plan if this job doesn't work out and with one thing after another going wrong for me, I admit ... I've felt a bit desperate. The meeting the other day seemed like the last straw." She ran a finger around the rim of her glass and the silence between them lengthened.

Deciding to change the subject, Izzy said, "I'm glad you got to meet Liam."

"He's quiet. I like that in a man. Quiet men don't convict themselves out of their own mouth every two minutes by saying something you wish they hadn't."

"True, Liam is quiet. Caleb always stood up to me and I could say whatever came into my head because he could take it. Liam's different. He goes silent and withdraws to consider things. All I can do is wait him out. He won't say a single word until he's good and ready."

They sat quietly and enjoyed the view of the lake and the moon tracing a ripple pattern along the water. Alison smiled, showing what Izzy judged to be the first genuine expression of pleasure she'd seen on the woman's face. She said, "It's wonderful to see you amid such an extended family. Sophie is adorable and Robbie is a nice boy. And of course, Tabby is a card."

Izzy rose from her chair to stir the fire before she added a log from the small stack by the railing. She refilled the wine glasses. She knew Alison was far too polite to ask any probing questions. She trod carefully. "Sophie is the daughter of a young woman named Lisa-Marie. You would have met her; she lives with us, but she's out for dinner with friends tonight. We've looked after Sophie since she was born and her mother, too. Lisa first came here the summer she turned sixteen. She was visiting her Aunt Bethany. When Sophie came along, Lisa was so young and she had to finish high school. After she graduated, she had the opportunity to do a photography internship in London. That led to a year of travelling and freelance work. She's home now for the first time in a long while." Izzy gazed out at the water for a moment. "And Robbie is Liam's younger brother," she added.

Alison was wide-eyed at Izzy's explanation. "Goes to show how far off-base a person can be. I assumed you inherited a ready-made family when you married Liam."

Izzy shrugged, "I suppose I did, in a way."

As the silence lengthened, Alison sighed. "You must be curious about what happened with Bradley." Alison began to speak, slowly at first, then the momentum of her story took over and everything spilled out.

Finally, her words slowed and stopped. She slumped in her chair. Izzy leaned forward and touched Alison's hand. "Getting a shock like that, when your life seemed so settled, had to be devastating. I'm so sorry. Hearing your story made me think of the way I felt when Caleb died. Some things send your life spinning down another road." They both sat quietly for a moment before Izzy went on, "I understand why you wanted to get away. As soon as I could, after the immediate things were done concerning Caleb, I bolted. I had to go down to California and settle some legal stuff. After that I headed for the desert outside of Tucson. I just wanted the sun. I rented a place with a private pool and hot tub right out on the edge of the desert. I stayed there for a whole month. I never left the place at all. I ordered in what little I ate. Every single day, I would get up at around ten and buy a coffee and a paper from a little place around the corner. I'd make myself do the crossword and then I'd lie in the sun by the pool watching the clock until two p.m. Then I would drink until I was ready to pass out around two am. It was all I could manage."

⁂

Mike and Justin headed out to the lawn of the Lady Brit to check on a couple of trees by the edge of the beach. Mike was sure they needed to be topped but wanted Justin's opinion. Lisa-Marie leaned against the kitchen counter and sipped from a plastic glass of champagne. Mike had popped the cork from the bottle before the grand tour to help them celebrate his and Wynter's new home. She looked at the array of dresses on the screen of Wynter's iPad. "I like this one," she said.

Wynter stared at the screen, "It's nice. And you can each choose what type of neckline, sleeves and length you want." She pushed the machine away. "I'll send you the link then you can let me know. I should order them by the end of the week. We'll still be able to get your Aunt Beth to do any alterations, right?" She sighed, "Another thing off the list." She reached for the bottle of champagne, "You want more?"

Lisa-Marie nodded and held out her glass as she looked around the large kitchen, "This place is something, Wynter."

"I know. I'm so in love with it and wait until we get the furniture in here." Wynter sighed and got that dreamy look on her face that Lisa-Marie was getting used to. She changed the subject, "How was your meeting with the priest?"

"Good. He was so nice. He almost made me want to start going to church. How were your four days working with Tyler?"

Lisa-Marie looked over her shoulder to check that Mike and Justin were still out by the trees. She scooted up to sit on the counter as she said, "Tense. I had decided to cool things with him and I was going to tell him that, but it never came up."

Wynter hoisted herself up beside Lisa-Marie and asked, "For four days it never came up? How is that possible? He was so hot for you the last time I saw you guys together, I thought he might rip your clothes off right on the street."

197

"The first night we had to sleep on the floor of a boat galley. The next, we were put up in two separate houses on one of the islands. Then up at Mt. Cain we had this cabin that was so filthy we wouldn't even take our hiking boots off." She paused to sip her drink. "The last night, back at the hotel, I told him I had to talk to him. Before I could say anything, he started going on about having to go out and get something. Then he was gone."

Wynter's eyes widened over the top of her glass. "Talk about being on the wrong track. What happened then?"

"He texted me about five minutes later to say he had run into a few guys from the band that was playing at the hotel and he'd be about fifteen minutes. He never showed up back in the room at all."

Wynter frowned, "Sounds as if you're not the only one who cooled off. Did you hear from him again?"

"He texted me later the next day to say he was sorry but something had come up."

"Will you see him again?"

"I have to go down to Vancouver next week ... we'll be working on the submission stuff. But I'll be staying at Maddy's."

Mike opened the side door from the gallery and called out, "Come on you two. We're starving. There's a thick steak smothered in crab waiting for me at *The Sea Shed*."

By the time the two couples had finished dinner, Justin realized what was wrong with him. He was as jealous as hell of Mike. He and Wynter were so happy, Justin could almost see a glow around the pair of them. It made his back teeth hurt. And that was a shitty way to feel about the great fortune of a guy who had become his best friend. Hands down, no bullshitting himself any more, he knew he and Lauren had never been in love the way Mike and Wynter were. And on top of that dose of reality, Leez was right across from him, looking so sexy in her sleeveless, short dress with her pearls glistening warmly against her throat. He swallowed hard every time their eyes met.

As they left the restaurant, Justin drew Wynter to one side. He leaned close to ask her, "What's up with Leez and that Tyler guy?"

Wynter met his gaze with sincerity, "She works with him. Why?"

Later, as Justin parked his truck in Izzy and Liam's driveway, Lisa-Marie got out of the passenger side and met him near the back of the vehicle. She meant to say a quick goodnight and head inside. He reached out and gently held her arm. "Hey ... don't go in yet. Come over to my place for a drink. It's early still."

A funny stutter started up at the base of her throat. Justin had been looking at her so intently the whole night. At first, she thought it was because they shared a good-natured joke about how Mike and Wynter were creating a new definition for the concept of being sappy in love. But as she had smiled at him and he held her gaze a moment too long, over and over, the connection changed. "I better not."

He kept pace with her as she walked, still holding her arm. "We could sit out on the cliff deck for a bit."

She glanced up at the cloudy sky, "I think it's probably going to rain."

"Come on, Leez," He chuckled as he gently pulled her closer, "Let's go to the garden house. I don't want to be alone."

She felt something inside shattering. One part of her mind – an Emma-like voice – told her, that's your resolve, stupid. But she couldn't stop herself. She let him guide her to the small building. Once inside the dark, glass enclosure, he pulled her close and ran his hand over her hair and down her neck. His fingers rested right on the pulse that was hammering in her throat. He traced a finger around her lips and his body vibrated now with something she couldn't fail to recognize. Something she wanted. He said, "Let me kiss you, okay?"

A howling – no – that lived deep in the hurt of the last time this had happened between them tried to make its way up through her being, but the part of her that wanted his kiss, that had never stopped wanting him, acted first. She looked up and her stare locked on his face. Then his lips were on hers and she was held tightly against him. His desire for her came close to melting away every doubt she had. But close was only good in horseshoes, as Maddy would say.

She stepped back, wiping her hand across her mouth. "What about Lauren?" The words practically choked her.

Justin stared down at the floor. The only sound in the garden house was Lisa-Marie's harsh breathing and finally, his sigh before he said, "It's the right question for you to ask, Leez." The silence between them stretched out until she thought she might scream. Finally, he said, "The problem is, I don't have an answer."

She stood still for a moment because, after that kiss, she couldn't believe he wasn't going to say the words she wanted to hear. She backed up toward the door. With her fingers circling the handle, she said, "I won't do this with you again. I won't let you hurt me again." She turned and left the garden house.

TWENTY-THREE

Izzy relaxed into her chair as Kieran got up to turn on the music. She glanced at a few familiar faces in the group around her – Gordon, who probably saw a notice about the grief group in town; Alison, who must have seen one of the flyers Izzy had handed out at Micah Camp; Helen, who had no doubt heard about the group at church; and Bethany, reluctant at first to take up Izzy's suggestion of attending but agreeing to come along at the last moment.

Considering the meshing of her and Kieran's facilitating styles, Izzy thought the session was going well. She was enjoying the experience of leading a group with him. Before people arrived, she and Kieran had set up a flip chart on a stand in the corner and had prepared five large circles of poster board each with one of Kubler-Ross' stages of grief written on it in large block letters – denial, anger, bargaining, depression and acceptance. These had been tacked onto the floor randomly inside the circle of chairs.

Kieran had started the session off by welcoming people to St. Bertha's and stressing that the group was not a Catholic one. He explained that St. Bertha's worship space was available and that's the reason they were meeting in this place. He went over a few housekeeping details including the location of the washrooms. He made it clear that each session would run for two hours, that meetings would start on time and that on this first evening, coffee and the lovely cake Helen had provided would be served at the halfway point.

Izzy had then stood up to discuss what could and could not be expected from a group experience. She emphasized that while respect for one another was a given, no one could expect total confidentiality in a group situation. She invited all members to consider that reality when sharing personal information. At the same time, Izzy reminded them that hearing other people's stories was a great honour. She urged them to treat anything another person shared with the group as a piece of that person's soul to be held in absolute trust.

Next, she had led the group in a brainstorming activity, asking them to call out reasons for attending a grief and loss group. Using the flip chart, she jotted down their ideas – a safe place to share, to find acceptance, to learn, to understand the grieving process, to stop feeling so alone. She pointed out to the group that no one had mentioned coming here to give or receive advice. She urged members to resist the natural temptation to tell another what to do or feel. In Izzy's experience, most people were quite capable of finding their own solutions if they were given the opportunity to do so.

Kieran had taken over then. He spoke of the seminal book on the grieving process by Elisabeth Kubler-Ross and David Kessler. He pointed to the circles on the floor and explained that the process was not linear and that no one should expect to move through grief in a lock-step plan laid out in a book.

Finally, Izzy had handed out an article on ways to build a meaningful life and the concept was discussed in smaller groups. At that point, they had taken their break which Izzy and Kieran deliberately let stretch longer than the fifteen minutes they had originally planned. The group was relaxed and interacting and that was good. When they reconvened, members would be called upon to dig deeper emotionally.

The instrumental music filled the room and Izzy closed her eyes. She focused on her breathing. When Kieran rose to turn off the sound system, she sat up straight and took a quick reading of the group's mood. People seemed comfortable, curious as to what was coming next. Kieran sat forward and said, "We're going to go around the circle and each of you will have an opportunity to say something about the grief that has brought you here. You don't need to say everything tonight." He smiled, "I know that once you get a chance to talk, you might find it hard to yield the floor." Izzy watched him make friendly eye contact with everyone in the circle. He went on, gesturing towards her, "Izzy and I are the facilitators of this group but we are also participants. So, we will start." He paused for a moment, then his voice got deeper, as if his throat had tightened up with emotion. "My younger brother, Sean, died almost ten years ago. We were close, he was my only brother. I still think of him and dream of him. Losing him still hurts."

The room was silent but there were a few nods around the group. Izzy noticed that Helen had seemed uncomfortable as Kieran talked. She was staring at the ceiling and crossing and re-crossing her legs. She might be finding it hard to hear the priest speak on such a personal level. Izzy put that on her mental clipboard to mention to Kieran later when they debriefed the session.

When Kieran looked to her, Izzy said, "Two years ago, my father died. He had cancer. I think one of the things that makes accepting his death difficult is that he didn't die of that cancer. He was shot and the violence around that event makes it harder for me to accept his death."

Again, the group listened to the sharing with quiet attentiveness. Gordon spoke next. His head tilted in Kieran's direction as he said, "It has been a few years since I lost my wife." His gaze found Izzy in the circle because he knew she'd had a similar experience; Gordon's wife had died the same year Izzy had lost Caleb. With his hands folded neatly below his round belly, Gordon tapped his fingers together lightly as he spoke, "Like Kieran and his brother, Sean, I dream of my Susan. I don't want to forget her. I go out of my way to keep her memory alive." His face wore a rueful expression, "I'm still driving the same car we had when she was alive and it was old then."

The group took a moment to digest Gordon's last comment. When the silence was broken, Alison's voice revealed her bitterness. "My husband, Bradley, didn't die. He's still alive and well but as far as my life goes, he may as well have died. The day he said he was leaving me was as much like a death as anything I can imagine." Izzy could see a few group members cringe at Alison's tone but she was glad of the woman's presence in the circle and the rawness of her emotion. Alison's sharing could lead others to the realization that grieving happens for several reasons and it evokes various strong emotions.

Allowing her long-time friend, Bethany, to find her own time and space in the group was one of Izzy's challenges. She was relieved when her friend sat forward to speak. "A year ago, my mother died." Bethany's voice was quiet. Izzy saw group members straining to hear her. "I felt bad that she had died but going home to Kingston was very hard for me. I think I was so overwhelmed by my own sadness that I forgot to feel anything for my mother. The trip triggered all these thoughts about how unfair my life has been and how, no matter what I do, I can't put things in my past to rest." She had visibly gained strength and volume as she spoke. Bethany scanned the group with an expression of surprise and gratitude on her face for their acceptance of her truth.

Helen was the last to speak and Izzy could see Kieran's eagerness to know what this woman might have to share. Helen made a choked sound somewhere between a laugh and a moan of disgust before she said, "I feel like an imposter sitting here in this group." Izzy was proud of the group for not responding with any words. If Helen was looking for permission to be here, she'd have to find it in their silent attention. Helen shifted in her chair, folded and unfolded her hands in her lap. "Everyone knows about the three young people who were killed in the car crash right before Christmas." Izzy did know of the accident, a real tragedy for a community as small as Dearborn. She was unsure of Helen's connection.

Scanning the people in the group, with tears glistening close to the edges of her eyes, Helen said, "If one of the family members of those poor kids had been in this room tonight, I would have walked right out the door." Tears began to run down her face. "One of the girls was my daughter's best friend. I'd known Shawna Donovan since she was in preschool. I knew them all." She paused and dug a Kleenex out of her pocket. After wiping her nose, she said, "The fourth person who would have been in that car on that night ... if I hadn't kept her home because she was getting over a cold," Helen choked out the last words, "was Hannah."

Izzy noticed that Helen's emotion was contagious. Most people in Dearborn were connected in one way or another to the families of the dead kids. There were tears in a few people's eyes. Helen took a deep breath. "Life sure doesn't come with a guarantee that it will treat any of us fairly. My heart breaks for those young people cut off before their lives could even begin, and for their parents and families. Did they get a fair shake?" She paused and stared at the floor. "But what I felt more than anything else, something that haunts me ... what I felt was relief ... relief that I didn't lose Hannah."

The room was quiet. People seemed to be feeling the weight of pain in Helen's admission. Izzy noted a few looks between members that seemed to be asking – *what are we supposed to do?* She looked at Kieran. He nodded and said, "Let's take a few moments of silence now."

❧ ❧ ❧ ❧

Bethany had been quiet in Izzy's Highlander all the way back to Crater Lake. Her mind was full of thoughts and Izzy seemed to understand her need for silence. Saying a quick goodbye in the drive near the bakery, Bethany practically ran into the A-Frame. Beulah was sitting in her chair. Having heard the vehicle pull up, she had clearly set down the open book in her lap and was ready to greet her wife. Bethany went by Beulah with only a quick wave, telling her, "I have to write something down."

She pulled her journal from the cabinet drawer, sat down at the kitchen table, flipped to an empty page and began to write. *Life doesn't come with a guarantee that it will treat any of us fairly.* These words, spoken earlier tonight in the group, had caught Bethany's attention to such a degree that she had forced herself to remember them.

Now, as she considered this idea about fairness, together with the article on living a meaningful life that the group had read and discussed, Bethany felt as though a light bulb had flashed on in her head. The part of the article she had summarized for her small group had mentioned transcendence. She understood the theory to mean that because you can't ever go back and you can't change what has been, the important life question becomes – *What can I do, given what has been, to give myself purpose, to rise above?* Transcendence is about rising to meet the challenges life throws at us and understanding that in that rising, there is reward.

She tapped her pen against her journal and considered what she had written. She realized now that she had never risen above the belief that life had dealt her a crappy hand. Through all the adversity life had thrown at her, she had never considered transcending the feelings of outrage that accompanied that one gut-wrenching, plaintive wail – *it isn't fair.*

She stared at the words hastily scrawled at the top of the journal page in front of her. What would her life look like if she gave up on the expectation of fairness? She could certainly save herself a lot of bellyaching. She slammed her hand on the table and said, "Exactly." Her voice echoed in the quiet cabin.

Beulah jumped and her book fell into her lap. "What the hell, Beth."

Bethany chuckled as she stared around her kitchen. The coffee canister was out of place – Beulah's doing. She got up and pushed the canister a few inches over to the right spot. Then she opened a cupboard and began to pull things out.

The footrest on the recliner chair thumped loudly and a moment later Beulah walked into the kitchen. "What are you doing?" she asked.

"These cupboards are driving me crazy. Everything is out of place. I'm putting things right is what I'm doing."

With a shrug, Beulah leaned against the counter, "How was the group?"

Bethany turned to her. "The group was good. I felt way better there than I did in Izzy's office." She shortened the space between them and put her arms around Beulah, resting her head against her chest. "And I was grateful to sit in that circle and not have to say that the woman I love is dead."

Beulah's arms tightened around her, "Me, too," she said.

Opening the workshop door, Izzy groped for the light switch in the dark. She crossed to the old desk in the corner and pulled open the lower drawer. There, just as Liam had told her, was the pile of Caleb's journals – brightly-coloured exercise books, a large stack of them all tied together with a string. She lifted the whole pile to the desk. Undoing the knot, she examined the date on the first book – 1971 – the year Caleb arrived at Crater Lake. She ran her finger across the numbers; he would have been just twenty-one years old.

Removing the top book, she laid it on the desk in front of her and weighed her options. There were risks. She didn't want to open old wounds. Two years ago, when Liam had first discovered these journals, he had invited her to read them. She had declined. But the words she had spoken tonight in the grief group, about giving meaning to life events, meant first knowing about them. As she opened the book, the words of Anais Nin ran through her mind – *the day came when the risk to remain tight in the bud was more painful than the risk it took to blossom.*

She opened the first journal. Across the top of the page, in Caleb's slanted handwriting, were the words – *Caleb Jenkin – Landowner.* Below this was taped an aerial surveillance map of Crater Lake. In faded, fluorescent yellow highlighter their property was marked out. Above the road, the woodlot, below, the land stretching to the lake. Under the map, he had written – *I'm going to put some roots down in this place. I find I don't like the experience of being a wanderer.*

She took in the rest of the page – a cut-out from a flyer with a chainsaw circled in red. Scrawled across the top was the name and model and date of purchase and the words – *lumberjack Caleb is born.* Near the bottom, a date and the words – *Camped out last night in the spot cleared for the shop. Wind came up and lifted the tent out of the ground. Rained so hard, I thought I might end up washed right into the lake. This land is demanding – it will not suffer a fool gladly.*

She flipped quickly through a few more pages. She wasn't sure what she had been expecting but this was a surprise. Settling in the chair she began to browse. A half-hour later, when Liam came into the shop, he found her sitting in the chair bent over the book in front of her. She turned at the sound of him and pointed down, "I'm reading a letter Caleb's grandmother sent him. She's telling him how to grow tomatoes."

Swinging the chair to face him, she smiled as she pointed to the pile of exercise books, "These are amazing. I've always been curious about Caleb's first years here at the lake. When you said journals, I was nervous. But these are more like scrapbooks – totally fascinating. I feel like I could sit here all night." Rising, she rubbed her shoulder, "I won't though. I want to savour the experience not gobble it all up."

Liam smiled as he crossed the shop floor to put his arms around his wife. He pulled her close as he said, "I felt the same way."

TWENTY-FOUR

Paula stood by the three-foot-high picket fence that Reg had put up to enclose a whole corner of the paper and soap shop. The low barrier was painted in alternating slats of red, blue and yellow and it had a small gate for easy access. Sadie, in her long dress and boots, set out crayons, glue and paper on the round table in the middle of the enclosure. Noah's little daycare corner had been transformed. There were colourful posters on the wall. A dollhouse that Josie had found at the recycling center sat bright and inviting next to the table. A comfy futon on a small rug had a stack of kid's books nearby. Sophie latched onto Noah's hand and practically dragged him over to the small slide which was always a hit with the kids. There were more toys scattered about and a playpen in the corner for Aidan's use.

Only Noah's look of joy as he ran after Sophie could lift Paula's mood. Seeing Nick by his office door smiling and taking Aidan out of Fiona's arms had dampened her spirits. She felt so far out of Fiona's league that she was surprised Nick could ever have spent a moment with her. The way he had taken to fatherhood made the loss of him as a potential partner even harder for her to accept. It would be different if she could comfort herself with the thought that he hated kids. No such luck. And now, like the icing on the cake of her misery, she had to book appointments at the clinic only on Mondays when Fiona wouldn't be there. Though self-imposed, the choice to do so still felt inconvenient.

Paula walked over to join her mom and Izzy. Josie was smiling as she told Izzy, "Sophie is so cute with Noah. I love the way she rushes up to hug him."

Izzy grimaced, "More like bowls him over. She does love coming here to play with him."

Josie turned to Paula, "Hey, honey. How are you doing this morning?"

"Good. Hi, Izzy. I didn't know you'd have Sophie here today."

"Lisa's still in Vancouver and Liam has taken Robbie and Tabby up to Cedar Falls for the morning." Izzy gestured to the fenced area. "This mini daycare has turned out great."

Josie laughed, "I wasn't sure I could sell Reg on the fence idea but he came through. He was cursing a blue streak, popping Rolaids and telling me I'd have to pay full price ... but he got it done."

Paula edged closer to her mom as Nick came through the doors carrying Aidan in his arms. Sadie placed a tray covered in piles of dried herbs and flowers in the middle of the small table and came to the fence with a smile on her face. She held out her arms for Aidan, "Hey, little guy," she said as Nick handed his son over, "How is my favourite baby today?"

Nick smiled, "He seems good. Happy not to be going too far from home." He glanced back at the gathering of women and waved a hello. Including them all in his comment, he said, "He hates being in the car seat."

"Noah was the same," Josie told him.

Izzy nodded, "Sophie, too."

With a smiling Aidan on her hip, Sadie called out, "Hey, Sophie. Don't push. Let Noah go down the slide on his own." Izzy smiled as Sophie narrowed her eyes but did what she was told. Sadie turned back to the adults with a grin. "I've got a cool activity for them this morning. And when Aidan naps, Josie is going to keep an eye on him while Sophie and Noah learn how to wrap soap."

Nick chuckled, "Sounds like fun. I might come back early." He waved casually at Paula as he strolled out of the room, calling to Sadie, "Text me if you have any problems. I'll be in the building all morning."

As Nick disappeared around the corner, Paula's shoulders slumped. Her mom came up to her and put an arm around her waist, squeezing her close. Izzy turned and said, "I've got to get going, too." She called out to Sadie who was busy strapping Aidan into a small chair near the table, "I'll be back for Sophie at lunch time."

Paula moved away as her mom asked, "Do you want to stop for a coffee?"

Shaking her head, she said, "I'm going to the teaching office. I've got some prep to do before I see a few kids and I have an assessment test to do later." The last thing she wanted or needed was her mom feeling sorry for her.

As she left the paper and soap shop and walked around the corner to the breezeway, she saw Jeremy strolling along like he didn't have a care in the world. He stopped and grinned, "Hey, Paula ... what's new?" He leaned against the wall and looked at her with real pleasure.

She could see Nick ahead by the main building holding the door for Izzy. She looked at Jeremy and shrugged, "Oh, you know, same old, same old ... work, a busy toddler to look after. Nothing too exciting." Without considering her motives, she asked, "Do you want to grab a coffee?" The way his head swayed back in surprise was almost comical. But right now she needed to spend some time with a guy who liked her, even if that guy was Jeremy who always seemed way too far along the geek scale for her tastes.

"Ya, sure. I'd love to," he said as they fell into step together.

When Paula realized that thirty minutes had gone by in pleasant conversation with Jeremy, she was more than surprised. She hadn't expected to enjoy soothing her bruised ego quite so much. She glanced at her watch and made a face, "I've got a student appointment in ten minutes."

Leveling a sort of goofy looking grin at her, he said, "I can't wait to try out your strategy on my girls. When they hear they aren't getting the Wi-Fi password unless daily chores are done, they are going to freak out ... and get to work."

Paula laughed, "Don't forget to make sure they send you a time-stamped photo of the completed work before you release the info."

Getting up, Jeremy said, "Right ... I want to start things off on the right foot because I'll have them the whole summer and our time together will be a drag if I have to nag about chores every day."

Paula waved and headed out of the dining room. Until today, she had never thought of Jeremy as a single dad struggling with how to manage visiting time with his daughters. She had rarely considered Jeremy at all and when she had, she thought of him as a former resident at the camp who somehow managed not to grow up at all. He didn't even look all that different. But he did run his own computer store. And though she had judged him harshly for the failure of his marriage, she was hardly one to talk.

⁂⁂⁂

Nick watched David slump in the chair across from him for their second counselling session. At the end of the first, Nick had challenged David to get beyond his rote Bible quoting. He suggested David come to the next session prepared to tie any scripture he might feel the need to share to concrete details of his own life.

Nick had no problem with the Bible but he wasn't interested in wasting valuable counselling time with someone who, as far as he was concerned, was using religion as a crutch. Since David seemed to be struck mute without his recourse to Bible passages, Nick decided he would take a different tack.

He got up and walked over to his desk to pull a sheaf of paper from the drawer. Sitting back down, he held up the papers, "This is the essay you wrote to get into Micah Camp. How would you feel about discussing parts of it with me?"

David sat up somewhat straighter. "You've read it?"

Nick nodded and passed the stapled pages to David. "Pick something you'd like to talk about. Take your time."

While Nick waited, David flipped through his essay. At one point, he said, "I forgot how much I wanted to come here." He looked down and read some more. He marked a section with his finger. "You told me not to come to this session and throw around scripture. Believe me, I don't want to. Part of the reason I left the community was that people quoted the Bible too much. They were doing it so they didn't have to give a straight answer to a question or deal with a problem." David ran his free hand through his hair. "Now I can't stop doing the exact same thing."

"What are you not dealing with?"

"A girl who shakes her tits in my face ... my faggot roommate. Take your pick." David had gone quickly from confused to angry.

Nick shook his head, "You can't talk like that in here or anywhere else at Micah Camp."

"Tits or faggot?"

"Both."

David dropped the sheaf of paper and got up to walk over to the window. He shoved his hands in his pocket and stared out at the lake. After a few moments, he came back and sat down. "I feel like I've been dumped into some kind of nightmare world."

Nick tried to keep a look of skepticism off his face as he said, "I'm sure you've noticed before that girls have breasts and I can't believe you aren't aware that there are people in the world who identify as gay."

"Ya, I've heard of ... homosexuals," he looked at Nick. "Is that better?" Nick waved a hand for David to go on. "I never thought I'd be sharing a cabin with one."

"Fair enough," Nick said. "How does sharing a cabin with Ethan change anything for you."

"It doesn't. I hardly see him."

"Then I guess we've covered that issue. As to a girl getting in your face with her breasts, tell me about that."

David opened his mouth to say something, checked himself and slumped in his chair, "I don't know what to say."

"Were you aroused by her behaviour?"

"What do you think? I'm not a fag ... sorry ... I'm straight. But I wasn't brought up to stare at girls that way. Girls are off limits until marriage."

"Okay ... you could look away. Staring is a choice."

Frustration edged his voice as David said, "A bunch of the people in the community said I'd have to watch out for temptation but I didn't think it would be like this. I'm more confused than I've ever been."

Nick made the decision to go deeper, "Have you ever been to a counsellor to talk about what happened before you went into foster care?"

David shook his head slowly, "No. My foster parents thought prayer was the best form of healing."

"Do you think you can talk about it now, with me?" Nick watched carefully for David's reaction. If anything, the young man seemed relieved. His anger, frustration and confusion seemed to fall away and his face slackened. He was going back to another time.

He began to talk, slowly at first, "It's always been like disjointed images, sounds and then nothing." He was silent for a few moments and then the tempo of his words sped up, "I remember jumping out of my bed. Then I'm in the hall in my pajamas and I've wet myself. I'm scared about getting in trouble for that. It's dark. I see someone at the end of the hall where my parents' bedroom is. Nothing is clear, but I know it's my dad. He's waving something in his hand. I call out – words, I don't know what I'm saying. Then I'm on the ground and scrambling under my bed." David looked up at Nick. "It's all black after that. I've never been able to remember anything else."

"How are you feeling right now, as you tell me these things?"

"Shaky. But I'm glad to say it out loud. I've gone over those fragments of memory in my head about a million times."

"As you got older, did anyone ever talk to you about what had happened to your parents?"

"No ... a couple of social workers thought I should hear about that but I always gave them the community line – *Jesus is my Savior. That's all I need to know.*" He stopped and stared down at his hands. "But I went online as soon as I could manage that without anyone else finding out. I read about what happened." He spoke slowly, "I know my dad killed my mother, I know it was him in the hall with the rifle. I know he went in the bathroom and shot himself."

Nick watched as David's hands tightened on the arms of his chair.

"David ... look at me." When David raised his head, Nick said, "You're safe here. What you're telling me is scaring you, the way it scared you when you were eight years old. That's normal. Take a deep breath. Look around. No matter what you feel now, remember, the events you are recalling happened a long time ago."

David nodded. "The newspapers said I was found curled up next to my mom's body. I don't remember any of that. For me it all ended under the bed."

Nick let the silence build. David needed to know he could talk about these memories out loud and the walls wouldn't come tumbling down. Feeling the time was right, Nick brought David back to the present. He pointed to the papers on the floor, "It's clear from the essay you wrote that you have questions about your upbringing in foster care and your future and that you wanted a chance to discover your own answers. But since coming here, you've had a hard time controlling the power of the community's teaching." He paused to let that sink in before he asked, "What do you think is going on?"

"I know what's going on. I'm rattled and I'm spouting all the things pumped into my head for years."

"You were young and scared when you first went into care. Is it reasonable to think your situation made you open to the teaching you received and it caused it to sink in at a deeper level than you realized?"

"Now you're doing what my foster parents said counsellors do." David glared at Nick, "Blaming the foster parents for everything. You guys are always looking for a boogie man in the closet. Foster parents step up and do the best job they can but do they get any thanks? No ... there's always some nosy social worker or counsellor trying to pin something on them when all they did was have the guts to look after screwed up kids."

Nick held up a hand, "I'm trying to explore why you are struggling to question teachings that you say you want to question." He waited for David to calm down so they could end the session on a better note. Not sure that was going to happen, Nick finally said, "Let's leave it at that for now. As a question, something to think about."

❧ ❧ ❧ ❧

Jeremy knocked on Alison's door and went in when he heard her call out, "Yes." She was obviously taken aback to see him and he tried to reassure her with a slight smile. "I come in peace," he said as he held up two fingers in the universal sign. When she didn't freak out or throw anything at him, he took a couple more steps into the room and said, "Can I talk to you for a moment?"

"Yes, of course."

He smiled and placed an electronic notebook, slim and shiny white, on her desk. "This is for you ... my way of saying sorry."

She stared for a moment at the fancy gadgetry. "I can't take something like this from you. It looks brand new. You certainly don't need to give me anything this expensive as a way of saying you're sorry. Besides, I shouldn't have overreacted the way I did."

"I messed up your arrival." Jeremy pointed to the machine, "It's brand new. I won it in a promotional thing at the store." Alison looked confused so he added, "I own and operate *Mad Man Computers* in Dearborn." He glanced down at his black AC/DC T-shirt and baggy shorts. "I may not look it, but I am a respected member of the Dearborn Chamber of Commerce."

"But why on earth give it away? Seriously, this is unnecessary."

"It may be new but it doesn't have half the capability of my own laptop. I wanted to find a way to apologize that had some punch and this seems perfect."

Alison took a deep breath. "Okay ... I'll accept your apology and this unnecessary gift under one condition."

He wasn't expecting conditions. He was giving her a brand new, expensive notebook. He fidgeted with his ponytail for a moment before he said, "Such as?"

"I want you to start participating at the staff meetings. I'm going to be presenting a proposal for setting up career skills groups and I'd like you to provide input on how those groups could be supported with video link classes or internet resources."

Jeremy raised an eyebrow, "You drive a hard bargain." He gave it a moment. It wouldn't pay to let her think he was too eager. "I'll see what I can come up with. Now, can I ask you for a small favour, too?" When Alison nodded, he said, "I'm trying to get Paula to notice me in a good way. If it's possible, when she's around, could you mention how I gave you this notebook and tell her that I'm sure a generous guy."

Alison raised an eyebrow, "You want me to vouch for your character?"

Jeremy laughed, "Why not?" His hand waved to indicate the pair of them, "You and I ... we're on a whole new footing. We do each other favours." He headed for the door as he said, "It's all good, Alison."

❧❧❧❧

Alison tapped the glossy flyer she had received in yesterday afternoon's mail against the edge of her desk as she waited for Ethan to show up for his appointment. When he appeared in her doorway, Alison waved him in. He plunked himself down in a chair and folded his arms across his chest. She passed him the brochure and said, "Do you know anything about this dance school?"

Ethan took the brochure, glanced at the front and shook his head. "Is this your idea of being funny? Are you trying to get back at me for telling Nick about that rosary thing?" He pointed to the file on her desk with his name on it. "That file is filled with rejection letters from schools not even close to being as good as this one or as hard to get into." He tossed the flyer on her desk and said, "It's all about who you know or who you can screw and since I'm stuck here at Micah Camp, I can't accomplish either."

"I don't care about the places that have said no." Alison waited for the young man across from her to meet her gaze. "We need to focus on a place that will say yes. All I need to know is one thing, Ethan." She had his attention as she pointed at the flyer. "Are you good enough for that school?"

Ethan smacked his hands down on the arms of the chair, "Hell, yes. I'm more than good enough but I'll never get in there. It's not as simple as being good enough. It's about more than talent."

"You're getting ahead of yourself. The application says you need a dance demo tape and three letters of reference. Let's get started putting those things together."

Ethan frowned, "I'd need to do a new demo."

"Okay ... how will you make that happen?"

He sat up a bit straighter in his chair. "There's equipment here at the camp and I can book the gym. But I need new moves and music."

"I'll leave that part to you. What about the reference letters?"

"I've got two dance instructors from before I came here." Ethan tapped his fingers together, "I'm not sure about the third."

Looking at the brochure cover, Alison said, "I think you want someone who can speak about more than your dancing. Someone who knows you're a hard worker, someone who can attest to the fact that you are up to a challenge. What about Reg? He spoke highly of you at our last staff meeting."

Ethan appeared somewhat stunned by her suggestion but he said, "I can ask him."

After he had left her office, she picked up the brochure and turned her chair to the view of the lake. Ethan had said getting into a good school was all about who you knew. Well, he was probably right about that and she hoped that knowing someone who knew someone could get the job done. Her brother was acquainted with a woman who served on the board of the dance school advertised in the glossy flyer. He had told Alison he would be willing to speak to this woman. He thought she might be able to pull some strings and move an application from his sister's client up the line. After that, it would be up to Ethan to show he had the right stuff. Hopefully, he was as good as he thought he was.

❦❦❦❦

Nick poked his head into Izzy's office, "Do you have a minute?" he asked her.

"I've got about ten minutes before I leave to get Sophie for lunch. What can I do for you?"

He shut the door and paced a circuit of the small room. She waved to the chair by her desk. "Sit ... you look like a caged tiger."

"I'm mad as hell."

"What's up?"

"I had a session with a client earlier who has serious trauma issues ... eight years old, in the house when his father shot his mother and then the old man went into the bathroom and killed himself. My client has never had one session of counselling to deal with that ... grew up in some Christian community that thought prayer was the best answer."

Izzy raised an eyebrow, "Don't pull any punches, Nick. Tell me how you really feel."

"I guess I'm easy to read on this one. I think the *Jesus is all you need* attitude is bullshit. He's trying to question some of the stuff this community drilled into him but he can't. I feel like I'm deprogramming a cult kid."

Izzy got up and moved around to perch on the corner of her desk closer to Nick's chair. "What did you do in your session?"

"I got him talking about what had happened when he was a kid. Tried to link how scared he must have been when he went into foster care to the power of the indoctrination. Instead, I triggered a bunch of stuff he'd been told about how social workers and counsellors always try to blame foster parents for everything."

"What will you try next?"

Nick expelled his breath in a whoosh. "Keeping quiet about my opinions on belief in Jesus as a form of therapy."

"Good idea. What else?"

"I think I need to keep coming back to the idea that he was the one who wanted to question."

"Okay ... it sounds like he might need tools to be able to do that questioning. I'd keep him rooted in the here and now with carefully titrated trips back into the early trauma. Help him feel safe enough to ask his questions."

"I was worried after he left the session that I had moved too quickly but he seemed relieved to be able to talk about his memories of what happened."

"If he's not had a place to do that for all these years, that's a distinct possibility. I think he trusts you on some level or he wouldn't have talked about it at all. Now you can leave the ball in his court. My bet is he'll be the one to take subsequent sessions in that direction."

TWENTY-FIVE

Ethan came into the office of *Crater Lake Timber* and spotted Reg. "Can I talk to you for a minute?" he asked.

Pulling open the top drawer of his desk, Reg grasped his bottle of Rolaids in what looked like a death grip. He shook a couple out and palmed them into his mouth. He waved Ethan over, "Make it fast. I've got to be on one of the saws all morning." Ethan shifted his weight from one booted foot to the other. Now that it came to making his request, he couldn't think of the right words.

"Jesus H Christ, Ethan ... I said I was in a hurry. What part of that don't you get?" Reg's voice barked out as he rubbed his jaw. His face took on a sheen of sweat. "As if I don't have enough fucken problems. Now I've got a goddamned bad tooth. I feel like someone socked me in the mouth."

Ethan held up his hands in a gesture of surrender, "Sorry, man. Take it easy." He took a deep breath. "I'm applying to a dance school in Toronto and I need a letter of recommendation. Ms. Kirk thought I should ask you."

Reg stood up and laid his hands flat on the surface of the desk as he leaned forward. "That's a bloody ridiculous idea. I don't know a fucken thing about your dancing and it would be a frosty day in hell before I wanted to."

"Geez ... Reg, you don't have to get nasty." Ethan rolled his shoulders as he spoke, "She says that I need a letter that talks about different things."

Reg waved his hand wildly, "What different things. If you don't hurry this up, the only fucken letter I'll be writing will be to Roland to tell him why I kicked your ass right up the mountain."

"Okay, okay .... things like how hard I work, what a fast learner I am, how I don't give up when faced with a challenge."

"The not giving up part is sure as shit true." Reg narrowed his eyes, "You think me writing crap like that will help you get into this dance school?"

Looking miserable, Ethan said, "Probably not but Ms. Kirk is not letting me off the hook on this application and she says I've got to ask you for a letter. So here I am."

"What the fuck next." He pointed to Justin's empty desk. "Go sit over there and write me a bullet list of your points. I'll see what I can do."

⚜ ⚜ ⚜ ⚜

Fiona came through the foyer and into the living room of Izzy and Liam's cabin, carrying Aidan and calling out, "Hey, Liam. We're here." Liam walked down from the kitchen, wiping his hands on a tea-towel. Fiona held out Aidan, "It should only be for a couple of hours. They wouldn't call me in if it weren't important. I texted Nick and he'll go over to the Saltbox as soon as he finishes up at the camp."

Liam took the baby from her. "No problem, Fi. We're here to help. Get going. You have doctoring to do." He gave her a one arm hug as he bounced Aidan up and down with the other.

Sophie came up the stairs from the playroom. Taking one look at Aidan, she made a face, left the room and headed for her bedroom. Liam watched her go; Aidan was certainly not growing on her. A few moments later, she returned with her bunny tucked under her arm. Liam was in his chair with Aidan on his knee. Sophie stood in front of them like a boxer about to deliver a one-two punch. She stared at the baby. "I don't like Aidan. Him smelly and him always cwys." Her lip came out, "When Mama be home?"

Hooking one arm tightly around Aidan, Liam pulled Sophie close to his knee with the other. "Your mom will back tomorrow. You can come with me to the airport to get her. You miss her, hey?"

Sophie nodded, "That's why I don't like him cwying. He make me cwy, too."

Aidan reached out his chubby arms towards Sophie, waving them and smiling as he chortled. Liam pointed at the baby. "Aidan doesn't cry all the time. And he likes you."

As they both looked at Aidan, the baby's face screwed up with intense concentration and then his small body emitted a series of sounds that widened Sophie's eyes. Liam made several loud sniffing noises that brought a grin to Sophie's face. She tried to hide it but she couldn't. Soon she was laughing and plugging her nose. Liam told her, "You're right about one thing. He does smell sometimes." They spent a moment making faces at each other while

218

Aidan looked between the two of them. A broad smile revealed his toothless gums.

Liam stood up and told Sophie, "I'll change his diaper then we can take Aidan for a walk. You can tell him about all your favourite spots."

Sophie followed Liam down to the sun porch where they kept Aidan's supplies. She asked, "We go all the way to the camp and see Izzy?"

As Liam dug in a cupboard for a diaper, wipes and a change pad, he said, "Yup ... as far as you want. And we'll finish up over at Grandpa Alex and Cynthia's place in time to visit Uncle Nick and drop Aidan off."

"Aidan's a baby, he can't walk like me. I'm big."

Liam smiled as he changed the baby's diaper, "Yes, you sure are." He smiled down at her, "No more dirty diapers for you." Sophie put her hand over her mouth and giggled. The expression on her face said she could not imagine that there had ever been a time when she had been a baby like Aidan in need of a diaper change.

⚜⚜⚜⚜

Mike pointed to the loaded dolly and imitated Reg's toothpick chawing as he said, "Good goddamned practice for the new kid, cutting those boards for you."

Justin laughed, "Ya ... but seriously, thanks. I need to get that boardwalk fixed before someone goes right through and breaks an ankle. Probably me. And then where the hell would you guys be?"

"Up the goddamned creek without a fucken paddle and a shit storm coming down on us."

Shaking his head, Justin said, "It's like Reg has gotten in our brains."

Beulah's truck swung into the yard of the sawmill. She rolled the window down and held out a stack of mail wrapped with a thick rubber band. Justin walked over to the truck. "Just sawmill stuff. Nothing for you."

He had reconciled himself to the fact that all he could do was wait for his mother to write to him. Accepting that didn't make the waiting any easier. He went inside and dropped the mail on Reg's desk. Their illustrious boss had decided to spend the afternoon up on the woodlot operating one of the machines and harassing the fallers. Getting a break from Reg was a nice change.

Justin crossed the yard, dragging the dolly behind him. Moving into the thick trees, he alternated between pushing and pulling to get the load down the narrow, twisting trail that was bordered by salmonberry bushes run amok. Watching that he didn't get whipped by the thorns, Justin realized that

219

trimming those bushes was another task that needed his attention. Living here wasn't a picnic and it would be less so when he had to drive out for work, if he ended up getting the job with Western Forest.

After a particularly steep section, he stopped for a moment with the dolly lodged at his back. He relaxed the muscles in his legs and took a deep breath. The air was heavy with the scent of the nearby lake and the trees. Life at Crater Lake might not be a picnic but he wasn't going to trade it for anything else.

He left the dolly at the far end of the boardwalk and moved carefully over the number of punky spots where the wood gave with stomach-dropping dips. Stopping at his cabin, he picked up his tool belt, nails, a hammer and pry bar. He pulled a pair of work gloves out of a box on the porch and retraced his steps to the spot where he'd left the new boards.

The work was mindless, identifying the boards to replace, cracking them with a good stomp, using his hammer and the pry bar to pull out the rotten wood, clearing away the debris with his gloved hand and hammering in the new board. A good-weather wind out over the water had the tall trees around him creaking as he knelt on the boardwalk and worked. A squirrel chattered from high up on a branch and the sound of the stellar jays squawking kept him company.

Conscious of being an easy target crouched low to the ground, Justin reminded himself to stand up, windmill his arms and turn a full circle in between clearing one board and banging in another. If he happened to be on the route of a passing cougar, he hoped to send the message that he was a bigger threat than he seemed. He got into a routine and his mind wandered. He had some cold beer in the fridge that would go down great after this job. He'd throw a steak onto the gas barbecue Mike's dad had picked up for him at the recycling yard. Like new, he had told Justin. Well, it was not exactly like new. The lid was dented up but it worked fine. He had a good-sized portion of a leftover potato and cheese dish that Izzy had sent home with him after he had stayed for dinner over the weekend. That would go well with the steak.

What had happened with Leez, before she left for Vancouver, bothered him. The situation would have been bad enough if his motives for wanting to kiss her had been purely physical. She looked hot and he was turned on. But with Leez, the way he felt was always more complicated than that. He should stop bullshitting himself. He had been using her. If he could have convinced Leez to sleep with him like she did two summers ago, then this time when she begged him to choose her, he wouldn't have hesitated. And that would mean the whole Lauren situation would disappear.

He was being a jerk. He had asked Leez to be his friend. Sleeping with her so he could end things with Lauren qualified as a definite friendship betrayal. He wondered why he couldn't just make a clean break from Lauren. They had run out of any common interests and what they were doing now – picking apart the whole relationship like a pair of snakes devouring each other – served no purpose at all.

He knew he had to go to Vancouver and deal with the situation. He couldn't just end a three year relationship on the phone or by text. He would need to see her but he hated the thought of another confrontation. Even though he knew the end had come, the thought of pulling the plug made him feel hollow inside.

※ ※ ※ ※

Lisa-Marie stood by the door of the upscale restaurant and read Maddy's text – *I'm in the cab. Find us a table.* Moments later, she followed the hostess to a table for two in the center of the busy room that was alive with the sound of cutlery clinking, dishes rattling and numerous conversations rising and falling. Lisa-Marie shook her head, "We'd rather have a booth, thanks."

A micro look of displeasure flitted across the woman's face before she smiled and said, "Of course." She led the way to a booth. "Should I send your server over?" Lisa-Marie nodded as she shrugged out of the thin sweater she had thrown on over her dress.

Before the drinks arrived, Maddy crossed the restaurant, weaving her way between the tables and pulling a small travel bag behind her. Her short, dyed blacker-than-black hair with its skunk wave of white near her face acted like a beacon, drawing people's attention. Her dress clung to her tall body like a second skin. Most of the looks she got were admiring ones. She slid into the booth as the drinks arrived.

"First things first," she told Lisa-Marie. After a sip, she sat back against the smooth upholstery and sighed, "That's good. You've been in town for almost a week. We've been staying in the same apartment and I've hardly seen you. We haven't had a chance to talk until your last night here. How crazy is that?"

Pointing at the suitcase, Lisa-Marie said, "Seems like your last night in town, too."

Maddy scanned the menu, "My flight to Palo Alto is at eleven. I'll get a cab to the airport from here." A bad-girl-Maddy expression lit her eyes. "I haven't seen Jesse for about two weeks and I can't wait to get naked with him." She dropped the menu on the table and said, "Do you want to split a few appetizers. The crab and artichoke dip is delicious and I have to have the garlic fries." She laughed, "To heck with how the other passengers on the plane feel about that."

After they had placed their order, Lisa-Marie said, "I saw your note about being at the studio. What are you working on?"

"Getting ready for our show at the end of August."

The waitress set the hot dip and a large bowl of oven-crisp tortilla chips on the table between them. Reaching for a chip, Lisa-Marie asked, "Our show?"

"You'd be surprised and probably shocked. It's all part of our business venture with your photos. This part focuses on my dark side of things."

A passing waitress pointed to their nearly empty drink glasses and mouthed the words – *two more?* Lisa-Marie nodded at her, turned back to Maddy and said, "How is the business going? I feel bad for not taking much interest."

"You do your part by sending along the photos." Maddy dabbed at her mouth with the thick, linen napkin. "The business is doing so well I can hardly keep up with the book covers and art cards and still have time in the studio."

"Tell me about this show."

"It's at a cool little gallery on Granville Island." Maddy flicked back the white chunk of hair from her face, "I take one of your photos that hooks me emotionally ... like the one of the little girl on the street in Rome. Remember that one?" Lisa-Marie nodded. "Then I start to play around with it on the computer ... layering on some things, stripping out others – doodling – that's what Jesse calls it. After a while, I have something I want to take to the studio. Then comes the 3-D work with fabric and texturing and adding an artifact or two.

Maddy grinned, "The woman at the gallery says our works of art look intriguing at first glance, enough to draw a person in and then something – an open safety pin or a drop of what looks like blood – jolts the viewer to a closer inspection." The waitress slid the metal baskets of garlic fries onto the table and Maddy gave her a broad smile. Looking back at Lisa, she said, "The frames are layered, so it's like you see the work down a tunnel."

"Wow ... now I'm really curious."

"You should come to the show." Maddy sipped her drink and changed the subject. "How did things go with you and Tyler this week?"

"Fine. We work well together. We've sent everything off to the movie people."

"Come on, Leez. I thought you two were more than work buddies."

Tilting her head to one side, Lisa-Marie said, "For a while we were, then we weren't. The minute I saw Justin again, I couldn't get in bed with Tyler. It's stupid."

"Man, oh man ... I'm starting to think you are not ever going to get over Justin."

"You and me both. I don't want to talk about that until we are on our third appetizer. Do you think we should order wings? Are they good here?" As Maddy nodded, Lisa-Marie asked, "How are things with you and Jesse?"

Finishing the last fry, Maddy said, "Good ... but the relationship is a lot of work and that part doesn't seem to get any easier. Every day I kind of wonder how he puts up with me." Her shoulder lifted in a half shrug, "I need to stay on my meds and see my own counsellor on a regular basis. Down in Palo Alto, we go to a counsellor for couples ... costs a fortune but it's worth every penny." She looked thoughtful for a moment. "We have these lines we don't cross. I never cut and he works hard at trying not to trigger my anxieties. Having separate places is good for us. We both like our own space."

Maddy signaled to the waitress and placed the order for the wings. Returning to the subject of her relationship with Jesse, she said, "You'll never guess what Jesse and I are thinking about."

"With you two, nothing would surprise me."

"A baby." She held up her hands, "Not right away ... but we want to decide yes or no and do it before we're much older than twenty-five."

Trying not to frown, Lisa-Marie said, "That's a big step. First Wynter and now you. Everyone I know is talking about babies."

"I'm letting myself get used to the idea." Maddy sat back in the booth and asked, "Speaking of Wynter, is her bride's night out all planned?"

Lisa-Marie nodded, "Flights to Vegas arranged, rooms booked ... we're staying at the Mirage. The tickets to the Lady GaGa concert are purchased." She glanced across the table, "I wish you were coming."

"Ya ... me, too. But Jesse and I have had this trip planned for a while – three weeks camping and hiking in Yosemite, the Grand Canyon and Yellowstone. That's why I've been working so hard to have everything ready for the show. I'll get back here only a week or so before it starts."

The chicken wings arrived and Maddy gave her friend a penetrating look. "Okay, Leez ... we are now officially on the third appetizer. Did something happen with Justin?"

"The night before I left to come to Vancouver, we went out for dinner with Mike and Wynter. When we got back to Izzy and Liam's, Justin invited me over to his cabin."

Maddy leaned forward, "Did you go?"

"No way. You know what would have happened if I had. I did go to the garden house with him and he kissed me. It was a close call ... too close. I can't go through that with Justin again."

"What does he say about him and Lauren?"

"He says it's impossible. She won't come here and he won't go back to the city ... but he doesn't end it. He must still love her."

Frowning, Maddy said, "I think he thought he loved her once. But he's like the rest of us screwed-up twenty-somethings, playing at being grownup but staying the same abandoned little kids we always were. Scared shitless. We go after all the wrong things and when we latch onto them we can't let go, even when we know we should."

They were quiet for a few minutes, finishing the wings and draining their drinks. Finally, Lisa-Marie asked, "Why does he have to act like I'm this puppet he can jerk around whenever he feels like it?"

Maddy laughed, "You're sort of dumb for such a smart girl. You two have a truckload of unfinished business. He can't stop himself. You're no different. Can't even get naked with a hot guy like Tyler if Justin is in a fifty-kilometer radius."

A bitterness crept into Lisa-Marie's voice, "Tyler's a bit more flash than substance. And Justin could have chosen me instead of Lauren. He had his chance."

Maddy asked for the bill before she said, "If by substance you mean size," she grinned, "all the internet articles say that doesn't matter." Lisa-Marie made a face and Maddy went on, "I'm betting Justin's scared. He knows if he ever lets himself get attached to you, he'll never be able to let go and what if something goes wrong? Fears, Leez ... think about it. You're the same way." She glanced at her watch and then pulled her cell phone from her bag. "I better call the cab. I'll get it to drop you at the apartment, if you like."

At Maddy's apartment, Lisa-Marie spent some time getting her things together for her own early morning flight up to Cedar Falls the next day. Tucked into the bed in the spare room, she opened her journal.

Dear Emma:

Why is it that I'm always out of step with my friends? I was the freak when I was as big as a house pregnant with Sophie and now, Sophie's a toddler and being pregnant seems like it happened to someone else ... and having babies is all my closest friends are talking about. I feel on the outside of everything ... as usual. There's Jesse and Maddy trying so hard to make their relationship work ... you heard me right, Emma ... Jesse, of all people, busting his butt to go to couple's counselling so Maddy can keep from cutting herself. And Wynter and Mike are so happy together it's like watching an ice cream sundae with chocolate sauce running right out of the dish into my lap. What about me? Having meaningless sex with Tyler ... okay but not great and now, not even doing that. That's what about me. And don't even mention horseshoes. You can't believe how jealous I felt of Maddy bragging about how she couldn't wait to get naked with Jesse. I'm sitting on this bed feeling like I'm going to jump right out of my own skin every time I think of how Justin kissed me. You said it, Emma ... pathetic.

TWENTY-SIX

Charlie smacked a chunk of dough on the surface of the large table in the center of the bakery and began to shape a loaf of bread just as Beulah had taught him to do. He was getting fast at this job and today that was a good thing because his attention was being seriously diverted by the girl who was over by the mixing vat yacking with Beulah. Earlier, when he had watched her stroll into the bakery, the top of his mouth went dry. She had tossed her long, dark hair over her shoulder and smiled at him when Beulah introduced her – Arianna – even her named sounded hot.

She had said something to him – a joke about having Beulah for a boss. He'd laughed on cue but couldn't remember her exact words. His entire focus had been on her large, dark eyes and the way she smiled – her full lips and her flashing white teeth.

Continuing his loaf shaping, Charlie snuck looks across the bakery whenever he could. Now she was leaning against the wall watching Beulah pour ingredients into the mixing vat. He heard her say, "It's about time you arranged for a ball team meeting. The tournament is in a few weeks."

"Couldn't get to it until now. A bunch of young people shouldn't need too much practice." Reaching for the salt, Beulah asked, "How are you finding the old bus and the job?"

"Both are good. I've been getting some driving lessons and hope to be able to handle the road on my own soon." Charlie watched as she stretched an arm behind her head and arched her body to the side. She kept on talking, "I love the bus. It's so quiet over there and I need that after a day on the job." She reversed arms and stretched the other way. Her shirt rode up on the side to reveal smooth, brown skin. "The work is intense. It can easily overwhelm a

226

person." She frowned, "I don't want to see my mom in every single woman that comes through the door."

Beulah patted her on the shoulder, "Look after yourself first or you won't be much good to anyone else." Beulah flicked the switch on the mixer and said, "I've got to check the oven. Keep an eye on that guy for me," she pointed at Charlie.

Arianna walked to the table and stood beside Charlie as she reached for a piece of dough and began to shape a loaf. He slanted a look to the side at her and asked, "What's this about living in a bus?" He thought about the sound of his voice as the words hung out there. It seemed okay.

Arianna worked as she talked, "It's in a small campsite about five minutes down the trail. And once you're in it, it doesn't seem like a bus at all. It's awesome. You're over at Micah Camp, right?"

"Ya," he wasn't sure if that was a plus or a minus. "You work in Dearborn?"

"I have a summer co-op job at the addiction center. I'll go back to UBC in the fall." They reached for the same last chunk of dough and their hands met for a second. Arianna smiled and straightened up, "You take it." As Charlie formed the last loaf and put it on the tray, Arianna leaned a hip against the table and asked, "Do you have any school plans?"

"Well, astronaut is off the list because I've had this thing about heights ever since my parents took me up the CN Tower. Same for fighter pilot. This baking thing is cool," he stopped to smack flour out of his apron. "But I'm not sure about the long-term effects of all this flour inhalation." He smiled at her before he added, "I'm thinking of law school. My dad's a lawyer; he has a practice in Vancouver. If that doesn't work out, maybe teaching."

Arianna looked at him closely for a moment. "You're not a foster kid, right?"

Charlie shook his head. Wondering at the question, he asked, "Why?"

Beulah came through the door waving a hand, "Come on, both of you. Help me get this bread inside."

Arianna pushed away from the table, "I'll tell you another time."

She hung around the bakery helping out and talking to Beulah until they had finished up the baking and the trays were loaded for delivery to Dearborn. Beulah took her apron and cap off and said, "Join us for lunch," she looked over at Charlie and added, "You, too."

Inside the A-Frame, Beulah called out to Bethany who was standing by the kitchen counter, typing quickly on a laptop, "Do we have enough for two more?"

Bethany continued to type as she said, "It's leftover chili and cheese and bread. Add another scoop to the pot. I'm trying to finish this application."

Later, seated around the small table, Arianna dished chili into her bowl and smiled over at Bethany. "What are you applying for?"

"You remember Jillian?"

Arianna nodded and touched Charlie's foot with her own to get his attention, "She's Roland's partner."

Charlie raised an eyebrow, "Roland has a partner? That's hard to picture."

Beulah chuckled, "If you met her, you'd find it even stranger."

Picking at her food, Bethany said, "I'm applying for a research assistant position with her when she comes back in the fall."

Buttering a slice of sourdough bread, Beulah said, "I think you can do better."

"It's not my only iron in the fire. I've applied for a job at the high school but I wouldn't like to drive into Dearborn all the time. I'm not in a big hurry to find anything," Bethany said. "I need time to figure out a few things before I start working."

Beulah changed the subject, "So, Charlie ... are you interested in coming out for the ball team?"

Each time Beulah had brought up the idea up with him, Charlie had remained noncommittal. He was ho-hum on team sports. Having seen Arianna's enthusiasm, his perspective had radically changed. "Ya, sure," he said, "I'll give it a go."

Beulah glanced from Arianna to Charlie with a knowing wink before she said, "Good. I always like to see a kid who's interested in baseball." She spoke to Arianna, "Want to come into town with me to deliver the bread?"

Arianna shook her head, "I'm taking it easy this afternoon. I'm going to see if I can scrounge some supper over at the camp then visit with Fiona."

After waving Beulah off as she drove up the driveway, Charlie said, "What about a tour of your bus?"

Arianna smiled, "Sure, follow me."

Sitting inside the bus after the short tour, Charlie felt like they were travelling somewhere together in a motor home all close and cozy. Arianna was in her desk chair with her long legs stretched out and crossed at the ankle and he was on the futon with his feet not far from hers. The dog, Johnny Lobo, took up what was left of the floor space. He looked around, "You were right ... definitely awesome."

She grinned, "I know, I love it."

Charlie took a pull from the cold coke she had given him, "What did you mean earlier, when you guessed I wasn't a foster kid?"

Tipping her head to one side, Arianna studied him, "You're a well-adjusted kid who wants to be a lawyer and work with his dad. That's not the profile of a foster kid." Charlie was still confused and he supposed it showed because she went on, "When I first arrived at Micah Camp, all the residents were foster kids and all of us were screwed up in one way or another."

Charlie frowned, "I didn't know that."

"Did you think everyone's parents anted up the big bucks for them to be there?"

"I haven't gotten to know a lot of the kids. Though, come to think of it, the two who arrived with me are sort of out there." He frowned again, "But I know Ethan's parents pay for him to be at the camp."

Arianna's foot stroked the dog's fur and her toes dug into the ruff at Lobo's neck. "Ethan was one of the first kids to come to the camp who hadn't been in foster care." She folded her arms around her body, "You rich kids are changing things."

"What do you mean?" He wanted her to keep talking and he was also curious. "And by the way, my parents aren't rich."

"It's all a matter of degrees, Charlie." She sighed, "Imagine a whole camp full of foster kids ... all of us in the system because we didn't come from great family environments to start with ... getting here at the age of nineteen, most of us had spent years being bounced around from place to place. Now, throw in a few rich kids with supportive parents. Everyone isn't on a level playing field anymore." Arianna shook her head, "Geez, us foster kids are not even in the same ball park."

He thought about what she was saying for a moment. "But lots of kids have problems, even kids who grow up in a home with their own parents."

She nodded, "Ya, I know. But foster kids leaving the system don't have many choices. There's no daddy with the big bucks to fall back on and there aren't many foster parents keen on paying for college or anything like that. They collect their money for a kid every month and when the well runs dry, it's bye-bye and who's next on the list. It's a job to a lot of them."

"And us paying kids take up space," he said as he watched the play of emotion on her face.

"It's not that simple." She rested both feet on the dog, using him for a footstool. "I know that the government was cutting back on funding and I bet they charge you guys enough to subsidize other kids. And Micah Camp is way bigger now than when I was there, so there are more available spots." She smiled at him, "I'm probably telling you all of this because I'm jealous of a kid who feels like being a lawyer is possible."

"You want to be a doctor."

"Ya, but I spent a whole year of upgrading and working my tail off in counselling with Izzy before I could even say the idea out loud without almost puking. How long have you been at the camp? A month?"

"Ya, about that long." Charlie stared down at his feet for a moment. "But, like I said, Arianna, everyone has problems."

She answered him in a playful tone, "Right ... your parents wouldn't be dumping you at Micah Camp for a year if you were Mr. Perfect son on his way to law school, would they?" She touched his foot with her own, "Us Micah Camp kids got to stick together."

He hung out with her the whole afternoon. When she discovered that he had spent his first month mostly at the camp or being driven into Dearborn, Arianna decided Charlie should see more of the area. Together they walked the entire length of the trail around the cove. Along the way, they stopped to water Cynthia's plants in a house Arianna referred to as the Saltbox and cut through the garden at a large residence that she described as Izzy and Liam's home. They continued on until they crossed a bridge to a small cabin she called Justin's place. From there they walked along a boardwalk striped with recently replaced planks and up a steep trail to the logging road above the camp. Arianna pointed out a large lumber yard and several buildings as she said, "*Crater Lake Timber.*"

"Hey," he commented, "That's where Ethan works."

She nodded, "Justin, too."

Back at the old library bus, Charlie helped her restack a bunch of firewood that she explained had somehow been all knocked over when she got up that morning. At quarter to five, they both talked of feeling starved so they walked over to Micah Camp together. Arianna nudged him with her arm, "You have to vouch for me, okay."

Charlie grinned. This was turning out to be the best afternoon of his life.

✻✻✻✻

Ethan walked from the gym down the wooded path towards his cabin. He'd made up his mind partway through his weight routine. Tonight's the night. He hummed a few bars of the old Rod Stewart tune. He was going to tell Charlie straight-out how he felt. He'd just say it – *I'm going crazy knowing you're in the bedroom next door to me. If you feel the same, come into my room right now.* The direct approach was the right way to go.

He glanced at his watch as he came into the cabin. It was dinner time, so he'd have the place and the bathroom to himself. An hour later, coming out of his room fresh and ready, Ethan saw Charlie sitting on the sofa reaching for his laptop. Looking up at the sound of Ethan's door, the kid smiled and Ethan's heart stuttered. "Where were you at dinner?" Charlie asked him.

"Working out." Ethan walked into the living room and flopped into a chair. He cast a quick look at Charlie and his mouth went dry. For some reason, the kid was vibrating. Ethan hoped Charlie's excitement might have the same root cause as his own.

Raking his hand through his hair, Charlie said, "I had the best day ever."

Ethan smiled, "Do tell."

"If you'd been at dinner, you would have seen me sitting with a gorgeous girl." As Ethan tried to control his facial features, Charlie talked on. "I met her over at the bakery. Her name's Arianna. She's living in this old bus past the A-Frame. She gave me a tour of the place after I got off work."

When Charlie finally paused for a moment in his reverie about Arianna's charms, Ethan said, "I know Arianna. She was getting ready to leave the camp when I got here. I seem to remember her having a thing for a guy I roomed with."

Charlie frowned, "But that was ages ago, right? She didn't talk about having a boyfriend now." Incapable of curbing his enthusiasm, Charlie went on, "She told me she used to be a resident here. She's going to be on this baseball team Beulah's putting together. I said I'd play, too." Charlie grinned over at Ethan, "She's only a year or two older than me. Stranger things have happened, right? Over at the old bus, we talked and talked. I mean, like really connected."

While Charlie droned on in a similar vein, Ethan worked hard to hide his disappointment. He'd been in this position before. And though he thought that Charlie had as much of a chance with Arianna as he might have of flying to the moon, it didn't matter. Charlie liked girls – end of story – and it wouldn't be Ethan's job to tell him that Zach could talk of nothing but Arianna at their last poker night.

Ethan knew that a lot of gays found dating hard because they had the added pressure of determining the sexual orientation of a person they found attractive. But he'd always been good at telling that kind of thing. Shit, he'd known Dylan was gay when no one else at the camp suspected he could be. Well, Ethan had clearly been off base about Charlie and now he'd pay the price for getting his hopes up.

He rose from the chair when Charlie's story wound down and the kid started to talk about work at the bakery. Ethan took that as a signal to excuse himself. "I've got stuff to do. Talk to you later," he said as he left the living room and headed to the sanctuary of his own four walls.

He lay down on the bed, clasped his hands behind his head and closed his eyes. He'd been pushing himself hard this past week since Ms. Kirk had suggested the dance school application. With his job at the sawmill, the regime in the gym, a new routine on the dance floor and dreams of romance, he'd had very little time for things like eating and sleeping. Sharing a cabin with Charlie was hard enough when Ethan was obsessed with the hope of success. Now it would be torture. Ethan sighed. He did feel crushed. But he knew he wasn't going to stop thinking about Charlie.

He felt this delicious shroud of hopelessness slide over him like a cozy blanket. He was in love with Charlie and Charlie was never going to love him. That was truly tragic. Ethan was right in the middle of a genuine tragedy and he never performed better than when he was hyped up to the max on the drama of unrequited love. Thinking about it, he actually felt tears in his eyes. Then he saw the opening moves of his dance as if he were watching a video on the dark side of his wet eyelids. He was up off the bed in a moment knowing he had to get back to the gym.

※ ※ ※ ※

When Arianna knocked on the door of the Saltbox, she heard Nick call out, "Come in." Johnny Lobo bounded through the door ahead of her like it was homecoming week. Nick was in the kitchen drying dishes. She pointed at him, "This whole domestic thing, Nick ... I've got to say, you wear it well."

He laughed as he waved the tea towel in his hand, "You think kitchen duty suits me better than a set of golf clubs slung over my shoulder? Wait until you see me change a diaper. I'm heading for the pages of *Parenting* as we speak."

Fiona came into the room carrying Aidan in her arms. The baby was fresh from a bath with his dark hair combed back from his round face. He was wearing a white sleeper covered in bright yellow ducks. Fiona pointed her free hand at Nick, "He's only heard of *Parenting* because he saw a copy at the clinic when he was there. Don't let him fool you." Arianna reached out to take Aidan as Fiona smiled and said, "He is fast on the diaper changing. That part is true."

Nick leaned over to kiss Aidan's head. He glanced at Fiona, "I'm off, then. I'll be back by eleven or so. That should give you two a chance for a bunch of mentoring." He turned to Arianna, "I can walk you back to the bus then, if you like."

"You don't need to do that. I've got this huge flashlight Zach gave me ... I bet I can see the bus from here if I turn it on." She laughed as she pointed to the counter where she had laid the long black object. "And I'll have Johnny Lobo. The drive to Dearborn still freaks me out but I'm not afraid of a stroll on the trail at night. Go figure."

After Nick left, they played with Aidan on the floor of the living room for a while, passing him toys and watching him roll from his stomach to his back. When he got fussy, Fiona said, "Bedtime, for you kid." She picked him up and pointed to a magazine article on the coffee table. "I printed that out for you, today. It's about a research study that looks at an inverse correlation between youth suicide rates and aboriginal communities that have embraced self-government. You should have time to read the whole thing ... this bedtime routine usually takes me about half an hour."

When Fiona came downstairs, Arianna had just finished the article. "Interesting," she said.

"Take it with you. I'm going to pour some wine. Do you want a glass?"

"I don't drink much at the best of times but since I've been working at the addiction center, I've decided to go without." She shrugged, "I know it can't make a difference but it's a solidarity thing."

"Okay ... I'll make tea for both of us. I like your full immersion attitude." Arianna wandered around the living room and dining room as Fiona made tea and set some butter tarts on a plate. Looking across the open concept lower floor to the kitchen counter, she joked to Fiona, "Did Nick bake those for you?"

Fiona laughed, "No ... people bring baking to the clinic all the time. It's crazy. A woman gave us two dozen of these the other day. The girls at the desk begged me to take some home."

Settled back in the living room, Arianna had the chair with the best view of the weaving over the sofa. She pointed at the wall hanging, "I love that. The colours are so vibrant ... it's like looking out a window."

Curled up on the sofa, Fiona sipped her tea, "One thing I have to say for Cynthia ... she knows how to decorate. The whole place is amazing. I never thought I'd see my dad settled down anywhere but he sure is comfortable here." She laughed, "I always pictured him perpetually driving around in that old truck of his and sleeping in his beat-up camper."

Arianna relaxed into her chair. With the reality of their proximity here at Crater Lake, her mentoring relationship with Fiona had moved quickly from short email contacts to more intimate chats. They usually covered all the *path-to-becoming-a-doctor* stuff first and were then able to enjoy each other's company. In that vein, Fiona asked her what she was learning at the addiction center and how she was handling the emotional impact of the work. She checked in with Arianna on the progress of the paper she had to write. Finishing up, she said, "I'll forward you the email address of one of the researchers who wrote that paper. He's based out of the university in Victoria, Nuu-chah-nulth from a place called Friendly Cove. He might have some on-site research you'd be interested in for next summer."

"Wow ... you don't plan to go easy on me, do you? Addictions this summer, suicide next summer. I'm scared to ask what I'll be doing the summer after that."

"You'll be finished your undergrad degree and you'll be wanting to do something impressive to lead into your Masters."

Arianna held up her hand, "Enough. I'm close to being overwhelmed on a good day."

Sipping her tea, Fiona nodded, "I'd like to say it gets better but it doesn't." She smiled, "Let's talk about other things. I see that Zach kid around now and then. How is that going?"

"He's driving me back from the clinic three days a week and giving me driving lessons, so I owe him, big time. He's nice." She ran a finger around the rim of her mug, "I like him. He asked me to have dinner at his parents' house next week."

"Whew ... meet the family? That sounds serious."

"I think it's the type of family he has. They seem close and he's comfortable in his own home."

Fiona cocked her head to one side, "I don't want to say be careful but considering the position I am in now -," she waved her hand back towards the staircase in the foyer that led upstairs to Aidan's bedroom, "I am not one to talk. But having a baby while finishing up my residency year was a brutal experience. I wouldn't wish it on my worst enemy."

Arianna shook her head, "I'm not sleeping with Zach."

Fiona gave a rueful, little laugh, "You say that now." She sipped her tea, "Just make sure you carry condoms with you at all times. And I mean all times no matter how sure you are that you aren't going to have sex with him."

"Yes, Dr. Wells," Arianna told Fiona, dipping her head like a supplicant. "You and Nick look pretty comfortable here," she said as she raised her eyes to meet Fiona's.

"I'm not sleeping with Nick," Fiona echoed Arianna's words and they both smiled. "Like we would have time." The corners of her mouth twitched in a rueful smile, "Aidan would be a full-time job all on his own. Between him and the clinic and the travelling back and forth, this is every bit as demanding as med school ever was." She refilled their mugs with tea. Sitting back, Fiona said, "Nick has been great. He stepped up to the plate big time. We had this whole schedule worked out where he would stay here when I was in Dearborn and go back to his place when I came home. But he mostly stays. I don't think he wants to be away from Aidan."

Arianna grinned, "So, like I said ... pretty cozy in this house."

"He takes the bedroom upstairs close to Aidan and I sleep down here." She shook her head slowly, "It is a bit of a waste ... but anyway, moving on." Talk ranged from the workload at the clinic to the possibility of Arianna co-facilitating a group at the addiction center before she finished work there. At one point, Fiona said, "Oh, before I forget ... do you want to do a talk with me over at Micah Camp – Sexual Health in Your Twenties. I've done it once before." She laughed. "That's how I met Nick ... though we are not in our twenties and we obviously didn't take my advice."

Arianna nodded, "As long as I don't have to be the one who puts the condom on the banana."

Fiona laughed, "No, I better do that. It's always good to refresh my memory."

"I met a kid today named Charlie. He's from over at the camp. He works in the bakery with Beulah."

"Oh, ya," Fiona said.

"He seems like a nice guy. Wants to be a lawyer." Arianna glanced at her watch as she yawned. "Think I'm going to call it a day." She pulled Lobo up by his collar, "Come on lazy dog, let's head out."

TWENTY-SEVEN

L iam was sitting at the kitchen table sipping his tea and thinking about how he would go out to the workshop soon and take care of the sawmill payroll. Having Lisa home was a big help. When he was the only adult in charge of looking after Sophie, the hours in a day simply melted away and his to-do list never got shorter.

After doing the payroll, he might walk over to the bakery and have a cup of coffee with Bethany. He hadn't done that in a while. It used to be a daily ritual when he'd drop off the eggs on his way to Micah Camp to deliver their standing order. Between the bakery and the camp, the egg business had done well. But when all his chickens had been taken out by a cougar, he hadn't thought about replacing them. With Sophie around, he wanted nothing to draw cougars down onto the property. They'd be around anyway, but hopefully just passing through. It was dangerous to offer any incentive that would tempt them to stay.

He heard Sophie's small steps running up the stairs from the playroom. She called out, "Liam ... Pewl not get up. I call and call her." He felt his heart sink. He had known this moment was coming but like all things of such magnitude, he hadn't wanted to believe it would. He walked down to the living room. Sophie was standing by the railing to the playroom. "Her make a funny noise, too."

Lisa-Marie had been working in the sunroom on her laptop. She met Liam in the living room and followed him down to Sophie's room. The child stood over the dog who lay on the rug by the bed struggling to get her breath. Lisa dropped to her knees by Pearl and touched her gently below the ear. The dog turned drooping eyes to her and whined a pitiful, low sound in her

236

throat. Pearl tried to move and her whole body shook with the effort.

Lisa-Marie's face wore an expression of dismay. "Oh my God, Liam, what do we do? It looks like something's really wrong with her." She leaned closer to Pearl, "No, no, stay still. It's okay."

Liam knelt by Sophie and spoke to the child, "You and your mom stay here with Pearl while I go and get the dog cage. I have to take her to the animal doctor, okay?"

Sophie frowned, "Pewl is sick?"

Liam looked over at Lisa-Marie. She said, "We'll stay with her. Go."

Liam headed out to the workshop to find the dog kennel and a few old blankets. He took them inside and down to the playroom. He called Lisa out of Sophie's room. They stood together for a moment and watched their daughter where she sat cross-legged by the dog gently touching the animal's head and whispering to her, "You be bettew soon, Pewl. You a good dog."

Liam told Lisa-Marie, "Take Sophie out through the kitchen, okay? Go for a walk to the beach or something. I don't want her to see me move Pearl. She might be in pain and howl or something like that. And could you text Izzy and tell her where I've gone."

Lisa-Marie nodded, "Ya, sure. Call us as soon as you know something. Pearl's going to be okay, right?"

Liam took a deep breath. "Let's wait and see what the vet has to say."

When he was alone in the cabin, he carefully moved the dog from the rug in Sophie's room to the kennel. He worked slowly and tried to be as gentle as he could but she suffered. Her whimpers cut through him like a knife. Outside, he slid the kennel into the far back of Izzy's Highlander and secured it so it wouldn't rock or slide. Grabbing his keys from the workshop, he started the vehicle and drove up the driveway.

Out on the gravel road, Liam remembered the day Caleb had come strolling up the trail to Liam's cabin with Pearl by his side. Liam had just started doing the chickens and Caleb had arrived on the doorstep, ushering Pearl in ahead of him, asking for a coffee and saying that a dog would be a good thing for Liam to have. They had sat at the table while Caleb pulled out his flask and poured a shot into his coffee. Pearl had been sniffing and had decided to settle on the rug in front of the stove. Caleb had pointed at her while he took a slug of the coffee, "She's a year old. A guy in town had her but he does shift work and he was leaving her outside in the yard for days." Caleb rubbed his bearded jaw as he said, "Didn't seem like he deserved such a good dog."

✄✄✄✄

Out in the choppy water up to her thighs, Tabby pushed her wet hair back from her face and looked over at Robbie, "Go." She dove under and swam as hard as she could for the raft. Moments later, standing on the wood deck as Robbie pulled himself up, she put her hands on her hips, "There's no use racing if you aren't even going to try."

He sat down and drew his knees up to his chest, "I got a stitch in my side."

Tabby plunked her body down and stretched her legs out in front of her. She smoothed the flounce attached to her bathing suit bottom as she stared at him. "That's not true. I know when you're fibbing. You were letting me win." She shook her head, "That doesn't count." Robbie's head was down and his dark, dripping hair hung in his face. "Hey," she asked, "What's wrong?"

"Liam had to take Pearl to the vet. She couldn't even get up anymore." Tabby's shoulder's slumped as Robbie went on, "Pearl won't be coming home."

Tears came into Tabby's eyes, "No ... don't say that."

"Sorry," Robbie told her, "I could see for a long time she was getting worse."

She brushed the tears away and sniffed, "It's so sad."

Nodding, Robbie spoke quietly, "She was suffering. Everything dies. Like a big circle. Animals and people ... nothing lives forever."

Tabby's body stiffened and she jumped to her feet. "I hate it when you talk like a know-it-all. Pearl isn't everything ... she's Pearl. Don't you care if she dies?" She glared at him and then turned and walked to the edge of the raft. She dove into the water. Surfacing further out, Tabby turned and swam slowly towards the raft with the waves slapping at her face.

She climbed back up on the wooden deck shivering. She sat beside Robbie and drew her knees to herself in an imitation of his posture. "I'm sorry," she told him. "I know you must be sad about Pearl, too." She wrapped her arms around her bent knees and laid her head against them. "I don't know why I said that."

Robbie nudged her with his shoulder, "You felt too sad. When people feel too much, they say things they know aren't true. It's okay."

Tabby sighed. "Do you always have to be nice to me when I'm mean to you?" She glanced at him, "It makes me feel like I'm a rotten friend."

"I don't know how to be mean to you." Robbie shrugged. "And you're not a rotten friend. You're my best friend in the whole world."

Liam came into the cabin through the door from the garden. He held Pearl's faded red collar in his hand as he stood quietly in the foyer and tuned into the pulse of the family that lived in this house. He smelled dinner cooking in the kitchen; heard water running and dishes rattling. He listened for the familiar sounds of Robbie's music, Sophie's laugh and Lisa's voice.

He walked slowly into the living room and stood watching Sophie build a puzzle at her small table in the playroom. Lisa knelt on the floor helping her daughter find the next piece. Sophie looked up and saw him. She jumped off her chair and ran towards him, "Liam ... you bing Pewl." She looked behind him and kept running to the back door calling the dog's name.

Lisa-Marie came up the stairs at a slower pace. "How is Pearl?" Her voice was edged with concern. She caught sight of the collar swinging in his hand and she glanced up at him, her eyes widening.

Sophie came back into the room with a frown on her face, "Pewl not hewe."

Picking her up, Lisa-Marie said, "I told you that Pearl might have to stay at the vet clinic for a few days." She looked to Liam for assurance.

He met her gaze and held it until he saw a dawning realization in her eyes. "Let's sit down for a minute," he said. Sitting in his recliner, he watched as Izzy came into the dining room. He looked up and saw Robbie by the railing. Lisa-Marie perched on the edge of the sofa with Sophie on her knee.

Liam cleared his throat as he stared into the child's round, dark eyes. "Pearl won't be coming home, Sophie. She was sick and the vet couldn't make her better."

Sophie took a moment to process his words. Then she shook her head, "No ... Pewl come home."

Tears brimmed over Lisa-Marie's eyes. Liam took a deep breath, "Pearl is dead. She can't come home ever again."

Sophie jerked away from her mother and stood up. She slapped Liam's leg, "No, that not twue." She ran out to the foyer and came back with her shoes, "We go get Pewl ... we get Pewl now." She sat on the ground and tried to pull her shoes on.

Izzy and Robbie had come down to the dining room and Izzy walked forward to put an arm around Robbie's shoulder. She met Liam's look of anguish with her own gaze of empathy. Liam got up and went to Sophie. He scooped the child into his arms and took her with him back to the chair. "Shush ... shush, Sophie. I want to tell you something."

"No ...," The child pushed at his chest with her hands and turned her head to see her mother. One look at the tears running down Lisa-Marie's face made Sophie go still in Liam's arms. Her bunched up fists suddenly dug into her eyes and she wailed, "I need bunny."

Izzy went to the Sophie's room and returned a moment later with the stuffed animal. She passed it to Sophie, sat down on the sofa beside Lisa-Marie and hugged the young woman close to her side. Robbie had sat down on the floor near Liam's chair.

Liam cleared his throat again. He stroked Sophie's hair as he spoke. "When I was a little boy, my grandma died." Sophie's breath hitched loudly. "I was sad because I loved her so much. I couldn't believe she was gone and I wouldn't see her anymore."

Sophie looked up at him. Now tears were streaming down her face, "Like I neva see Pewl again?"

Liam nodded. "I didn't want to eat or play or do anything." He glanced at Izzy and saw her eyes bright with tears. "Grandpa took me out on the land and he talked to me."

"Gandpa?" Sophie asked.

Liam smiled at her, "Yes, your grandpa. My dad." Reaching to touch Robbie's shoulder, he added, "Robbie's dad, too. He's a smart man ... he knows a lot of things. He told me that I missed my grandma so much because I had loved her so much. Loving is good. But when you love, it will always be like this ... you'll be sad when that special someone has to go." He tipped Sophie's chin up to tell her, "I know you loved Pearl a lot and you miss her and you feel sad."

Sophie looked away and tears choked her voice, "How I sleep without Pewl?" She got off Liam's knee and ran into her mother's open arms.

Lisa-Marie cuddled Sophie close, rocking her back and forth as the child sobbed. She whispered, "I know, baby, I know. It hurts."

TWENTY-EIGHT

Helen was filling the decorator bag with a bright shade of yellow icing when she heard the kitchen screen door open. Craig banged his feet on the mat and came into the room. He grabbed the coffeepot and went to the tap to fill it with water. "I thought you'd be at the church for your dose of forgiveness."

She deftly twisted the loose fabric at the top the bag. "I don't go to confession anymore and I have to have this cake ready for pickup later this afternoon."

Scooping coffee into the white paper filter, Craig chuckled, "I couldn't imagine what a good woman like you would have had to confess all these years, anyway."

Glancing over her shoulder at him, Helen said, "You know what, Craig? That just isn't very funny." He made the low whistling sound under his breath that meant he thought she was in a mood. She hated that noise.

"What's that," he asked pointing at the long, white box on the table.

Holding the full decorating bag, Helen began to maneuver it with quick deft movements of her hands – one guiding the decorative tip and one squeezing exactly the right amount of icing onto the cake. Flowers began to appear on the white fondant surface as if by magic. "It's Hannah's grad dress. I found it squished up under her bed. I thought if I could find the box I might be able to return it."

Craig leaned into the counter and she could imagine his face wearing an *I-told-you-so* look. His words accompanied the sound of the coffee dripping into the glass carafe. "She told you a hundred times that she wouldn't go to the grad dance. Staying away from all of that was her way of dealing with

241

things. Her decision. You shouldn't have got the dress in the first place. You should have listened to her." Her silence didn't stop him. "What matters is that she graduated. A lot of kids in that class didn't manage half as well as she has."

Dropping the bag of yellow icing, Helen selected the one she had filled with green. She piped stems and leaves as she spoke. "It must be nice to be right all the time." She put the bag down on the counter and turned to face him. "We're losing them ... all of them."

Craig gave her a puzzled look, "If you mean the kids, the house is as full of them as it's always been. You know how I know that?" Without waiting for an answer, he said, "Because I see the grocery bills and there's never any hot water when I want a shower."

"Go ahead and make jokes. But you're wrong. They may be here now to eat and shower but nothing is the same. Hannah's never home. Since you gave her that car, I don't have a clue where she's going or who she's with."

"She's eighteen and you're exaggerating, she's home lots of times and she needs a vehicle."

Helen brushed away his response with a wave of her hand, "She's taken a job at Micah Camp when she could have found a summer job right here in town."

"She wanted something different ... to see different people. There's nothing wrong with that."

"I'm worried about her on that gravel road. Arianna's scared stiff to drive out there. She's got Zach barreling back and forth to taxi her around whenever she twitches a finger at him."

Craig made a humph sound before he said, "City girl ... I like her better than I've liked a lot of Zach's hit parade of girlfriends. But he's met his match with that one. Arianna's not Hannah. Our daughter's been driving on logging roads since she was fourteen." Helen's eyes widened. He held up a hand, "You know she'd beg every chance she got to be able to drive ... first with me and then with the boys once they had trucks of their own." He turned to get a mug from the cupboard as he added, "And she's driving the road in broad daylight."

Helen watched the coffee slop onto the counter as he poured. Why did he always have to pour it so fast? As Craig pulled a dish cloth from the sink to clean up the mess, Helen said, "Zach doesn't seem like himself when he's with Arianna. Next thing we know, he'll be throwing away his educational plans for her."

Swallowing a mouthful of coffee, Craig snorted, "I doubt that. He'll be more set on going to UBC because she's there and I don't think I've ever met a girl who is more serious about her own plans. If anyone is going to get thrown over, it's likely to be Zach. Do him good, if you ask me."

As she watched Craig dig a couple of cookies out of the jar on the counter, Helen knew he was getting ready to make his escape from the kitchen and the conversation. She asked him, "What about Mike?"

"What about him?" Impatience ringed the edges of Craig's voice. "He's happy. Wynter is good for him. Why are you making something that's good into a problem?"

She leveled a hard stare at him, "You don't get it. Sure, Mike's happy now but how long will it be before she breaks his heart? Look me in the eye, Craig, and tell me you see a girl like her settling down as just a regular Dearborn housewife."

"I might be an old dinosaur, but even I know there's no such thing as a regular housewife anymore, if there ever was. You're sure as hell not regular. Wynter will find her own way in Dearborn."

Craig set his coffee cup and cookies down on the counter and walked over to her. He placed his hands on her shoulders. "Helen, listen to me." She crossed her arms tightly over her body and didn't meet his eyes. "It's like you've put on a pair of dark glasses and now they're stuck on your face and you can't get them off."

She knew what was coming next. Twisting away from him, she turned her back and busied herself with the decorating bag. He kept on talking. "You can turn away all you want but ever since those kids died, you're not seeing things right. You need to snap out of this, Helen. Our kids are alive and well. They need a mother, not a harpy of doom."

Tears came to her eyes as she whipped back around to face him. "Alive and well ... I'm sure Casey Donovan and his wife thought that once, too. I'm sure they thought they had all the time in the world. And now their daughter is dead."

As she left the room she heard him say, "If you keep this up, you'll only drive them away."

⚜⚜⚜⚜

David stood at the kitchen sink and scrubbed potatoes while stealing glances at Hannah as she loaded the large dishwasher. She had been working in the kitchen for days now and he still wasn't close to being used to the sight of her. He didn't know where to start. Everything about her was perfect ... the tumble of long blonde hair that she wound up on her head when she arrived each day and let cascade down again before she left ... her eyes, so blue they seemed lit from behind like coloured pegs in the sky part of a picture on a Lite-Brite screen ... her cute little nose with freckles splashed across the bridge ... the serious look on her face whenever Brigit was telling her how to do things ... and the slight tilt of her head when she nodded and said, "Okay ... okay ... I get it."

He washed another potato and thought about Nick's words – *I guess it isn't the first time you realized girls have breasts.* No ... it wasn't the first time but the shape hinted at by Hannah's low cut T-shirt gave a whole new meaning to the concept. And he could hardly keep his eyes off her tanned skin and her long legs. When Brigit was around and he wasn't required to say much, he could handle things. But today he and Hannah were on their own in the kitchen. He was supposed to be in charge.

Flipping the switch that started the dishwasher, she turned to him, "What do you want me to do now, David?" She smiled at him as she did that cute head tipping thing.

He kept working as if the task of scrubbing potatoes required the skill of a brain surgeon. "You can bring the foil and the box of kosher salt from the pantry and give me a hand with these." When she was standing beside him, he forced himself to be cool. "Dry each one, rub it down with butter, roll it in the salt, sprinkle it with pepper and wrap it in the foil."

She laughed, "Okay ... I got it ... dry, rub, roll, sprinkle and wrap." As they worked, she said, "It's sort of fun ... just you and me in here today." She twisted the foil around a potato and set it on the tray. "Brigit's great but I'm always nervous I'm going to mess up when she's watching me."

Desperate to say something, David asked, "What's it like to live in Dearborn?"

Hannah shrugged, "I've never lived anywhere else. It's a small town but people can always go down Island if they want to shop." She grinned, "There's a good fish and chip place right on the water and a movie theatre and bowling alley." She glanced across at him, "Where did you grow up?"

"Outside of Abbotsford. Over on the mainland."

"What was that like?"

She had leaned her hip into the counter and when he looked to the side, his eyes were drawn to the smooth line of her neck. "Good, I guess," he replied and she grinned at him. It made those eyes of hers crinkle at the corners and he found himself staring at the dimple in her cheek. "Why did you want to work out here?"

As she set the last potato on the tray, the look on her face changed. "I didn't want to run into any kids from school."

"How come?"

"At Christmas, my best friend died in a car crash. Two other kids from our grad class died, too." She fiddled with the knot in the string that wrapped her apron around her waist. "No one from school talks about it anymore but I know everyone is still thinking about it and I can't stand to be around them. I didn't go to any of the grad parties or anything. It's all too hard."

David was stunned. He was desperately afraid she might start to cry. He didn't have a clue what to say, so he kept it simple. "I'm sorry."

With a small shake of her head, she continued, "Life goes on, right. What next?" She glanced around the kitchen.

He pointed to the sink, "We'll prep the vegetables for roasting in the upper oven while we do those potatoes in the lower."

As they chopped the vegetables, Hannah said, "When I'm off at seven, I'm going over to the organic bakery next door for a baseball meeting. Do you play baseball?"

David nodded, "Ya, sure."

"Beulah runs the bakery ... she's putting together a team for the Dipsy-Doodle Days tournament. Both of my brothers will be there. Why don't you come with me to the meeting?"

"Okay ... my roommate, Charlie, works at the bakery. He told me he was going to be on some ball team. He must have been talking about the same thing."

"Cool."

Later, as David stroked marinade over the steaks, he thought about being the luckiest guy in the world to be walking with Hannah over to the bakery next door when they finished up after dinner. He decided to push his luck and ask her if she wanted to take a coffee break together. If he timed things right, she would be finished unloading the dishwasher as he was putting the steaks away.

He looked up and spotted Ethan at the kitchen door. Striking a dramatic pose, his roommate stretched out a hand to Hannah and wiggled his fingers, "Hey, girlfriend, get your pretty self over here."

Hannah turned and squealed with delight as she ran across the room and threw herself into Ethan's arms. David watched as she hugged Ethan for what seemed like forever before she backed up and said, "I've been looking for you every day since I started. Where have you been?"

Ethan moved his feet in a few quick steps as he twirled Hannah around,

"Busy with work and choreographing a new number for a video I'm doing. I'm applying to a dance school in Toronto."

Ethan's presence in the kitchen doorway was bad enough but Sadie's sudden arrival made the situation even worse. Making her way over to Ethan, she nudged his arm and said, "Those moves you were doing in the gym were amazing."

Ethan swung one arm around Sadie's waist and the other around Hannah's. He looked at David and grinned, "Some guys have all the luck, hey? Gay little me with these two hotties." He bumped hips with both girls and then backed up a step. "You can both come and keep me company. I'll tell you all about my new dance demo."

Hannah glanced back at David and asked, "Is it okay if I take a short break now?"

"Ya, sure," David told her, "Be back in about fifteen minutes so we can get started on the garlic bread."

"Okay, boss." She grinned and walked away. He watched as Sadie stared over her shoulder at him and then leaned close to Hannah to say something.

David scowled at the steaks. Sadie was bound to tell Hannah all about his covenant speech. He felt like squirming with embarrassment when he recalled how he had spouted off during the first couple of weeks at Micah Camp. Sadie wasn't the type to let him live it down either.

Fifteen minutes later, when he thought he might have the awkward task of going to tell Hannah her break was up, he saw her and Sadie walking toward the kitchen. They both came through the door. Sadie walked over to him and stopped to put her hands on her hips like she was going to ream him out. David backed up a step.

Then several things happened at once. Nick came into the kitchen from the hall by the pantry. He was carrying Aidan in his arms. A man David had never met appeared in the doorway to the dining room. He wore a short-sleeved, light grey shirt and a clerical collar. Sadie's voice rang out loud and clear, "You're right, Hannah, he is cute. But don't waste your time. Before you know it, you'll be wanting to get naked with him down at the boat shed but he won't want anything to do with you. He signed a covenant and he won't have sex until he's married." She reached out a hand and tousled David's curls. "He's all about avoiding lust."

Hannah spotted Father Kieran in the doorway and the blush that had started on her cheeks at Sadie's words flowed the rest of the way up to the roots of her hair. David who had backed away from Sadie until he was up against the counter, looked desperately to Nick for rescue.

Nick walked into the room and pointed at Sadie, "As far as I know, you have no business in the kitchen."

Sadie looked somewhat chagrined as she reached out and tickled Aidan, "Hey, baby Aidan. How's it going?"

Nick shook his head, "Buttering up to the baby will get you nowhere. Move along." He pointed to the door. "Harassing the kitchen staff does nothing to increase my confidence in you as a child care provider."

Sadie looked over at Hannah, "It was cool meeting you."

As she flounced past the stranger in the doorway, Nick walked over to the priest and said, "My name is Nick Anderson. I'm a counsellor here." He pointed to the baby in his arms, "This is my son, Aidan. How can we help you?"

"Kieran Galloway. I'm looking for Brigit. I thought I'd find her here."

Still shaken, Hannah said, "No ... I'm sorry, Father Kieran. Brigit has today off. She's probably at her cabin."

Nick looked back at David, "Everything under control here?" David nodded. Nick turned to Kieran, "I'll walk over that way with you. I was on the way back to my own place."

When she and David were alone in the kitchen, Hannah sat down on a stool by the counter. She regretted having told Sadie she thought David was cute. How was she supposed to know the girl would stomp into the kitchen and say such rude, embarrassing things? David had his back turned to her and was throwing loaves of French bread onto the cutting board. When he finally looked her way, she said, "I'm sorry. I had no idea she was going to say anything like that to you." She waited a moment before asking, "What did she mean about signing a covenant?"

"When I first came to the camp, I blabbed about a few things I should have kept to myself. Can we leave it at that?" When Hannah lifted a shoulder in agreement, he changed the subject, "That man who was at the dining room doorway ... he's a priest, right?"

She nodded, "Father Kieran. He's the new priest at St. Bertha's."

"How do you know him?"

"He was at our house for dinner not that long ago."

"Are you Catholic?"

"Ya ... why?"

David stared at her for a moment. She was looking back at him with those baby blue, innocent eyes and doing that thing again, tipping her head so her hair, loose now, slipped over her shoulder and spilled down her side. "No reason."

She got up from the stool and walked over to stand beside him. "When Sadie asked me what I thought of you, I did tell her I think you're cute."

David blushed and said, "You, too."

Hannah laughed as she twisted her hair up on her head and said, "Okay ... what are we going to do with all this bread?"

¥¤¥¤¥¤¥¤

Kieran waved to Nick and veered off the path to come up the steps of Brigit's cabin. Tabby and a slim native boy walked out the door and onto the porch. They wore matching soccer T-shirts – red with a large, black, stylized killer whale on the front. They were pulled over what he assumed were bathing suits because the kids had beach towels rolled up under their arms. Tabby called over her shoulder, "Mom, Father Kieran's here." She smiled at him and said, "Hi. Mom's inside." She pointed to the boy beside her who was looking closely at Kieran. "This is Robbie."

"Hi to both of you," Kieran said, "Swimming? Isn't this lake really cold?" He pointed through the trees to the sparkling waters of Crater Lake.

Robbie grinned, "Not for kids."

Tabby skipped down the stairs, "See you," she called out as they strolled away side by side.

As he walked into the cabin, Kieran saw Brigit working in one of the bedrooms. She briskly shook a patchwork quilt and let it go so it wafted down towards the bed. She smiled at him, "Make yourself at home. I put the coffee on. I'll be out in a minute."

He was settled at the table with two coffees poured when she came out. "There must have been a pound of popcorn in that bed." She laughed at the look on Kieran's face, "Robbie stayed over and they were watching a movie in my bed."

Kieran pointed to the coffee, "You were expecting me?" he asked.

Brigit nodded, "Roland told me he was dumping the Big Jackpot Bingo fundraiser on me and that you were coming out this afternoon to talk about it." Her eyebrows rose as she said, "He seems to think that because there's a concession involved the whole thing is right up my alley."

Kieran chuckled, "It works out well. We can pull it together ourselves. I'm happy to be working with you."

Brigit sat down and sipped her coffee, "What about Helen? She always runs fundraisers for the parish."

"I've left her three messages and she hasn't answered one."

Brigit frowned, "That doesn't sound like Helen."

248

Kieran paused before he said, "I haven't got off to the best start with a couple of parishioners. It's something I have to work on."

Brigit nodded as she got up and brought a plate of lemon squares to the table. Kieran took one and bit into it with appreciation. "How are things going with the school in Dearborn issue?" he asked.

"We're having an uneasy truce. I haven't given up, mind you, but with school out now for the summer, the tour is not going to happen."

He took a drink of his coffee and stared at the mug before he asked, "Where did the kids get those soccer T-shirts they were wearing? These cups must have come from the same place. I like the design."

"Up at Cedar Falls. A woman has a studio there where she makes a bunch of stuff with that design."

"Looks like she's quite an artist. That reminds me, I was at the reserve the other day with Liam. We went to a men's group together."

"Oh, ya. How was that?"

"Mostly silent," he paused before adding, "I liked it." He finished off his square and asked, "When did Hannah Sampson start working here? I went looking for you in the kitchen and ran into her instead."

"A week ago. She's great. A quick learner. I have her five days a week from eleven to seven. Today is her and David's first day on their own. How was it going?" she asked as she bit into a square.

Kieran made a face, "A girl named Sadie was giving David a hard time. A counsellor who introduced himself as Nick sent her packing."

"I'm glad of that. I've been working with David for a month now and he's settled into the routine. He must have grown up in some kind of Christian community because he was quoting scripture left and right at the beginning. He rubbed Sadie the wrong way and she's a bit of a handful."

"Your job seems more challenging than simply training a kitchen assistant."

"You've got that right. There is one thing all the kids here have in common," she paused before she added, "problems."

He reached for another square as she refilled their coffees. "I guess that's where Izzy and Nick come in," he said.

Brigit nodded, "But we're all expected to do what we can. I keep a close eye on the ones who sit alone or hang around the kitchen door wanting a cookie. And of course, when I have a kid working with me, I have lots of opportunities to lend a sympathetic ear."

Pulling a notepad from the drawer, Brigit said, "Okay ... let's get on with organizing this Bingo."

Kieran held his hands palm up, "I hope you know more about what's involved than I do."

Brigit laughed, "A walk in the park. St. Bertha's does it every year. The Lions take care of all the cash and giving out the prize money. There's only one thing you have to worry about." She grinned at him and asked, "How good of a Bingo caller are you?"

Kieran frowned, "I've never done it in my life."

"Well ... it's tradition. St. Bertha's always offers up the priest as the caller for the Big Jackpot Bingo."

"What exactly do you mean by ... offers up?"

Brigit raised her eyebrows, "Just what it sounds like. It's always a brutal crowd. They don't respect collar or creed. I'd prepare for a few hours of roasting if I were you."

Later, right before dinner, Brigit stopped in at the kitchen. She waved to David and Hannah, "Ignore me. I'm not here. Is that Sadie's pasta sauce?" She pointed to a small pot on the stove. When David nodded, Brigit served up a plate of pasta and ladled on sauce from the pot. She stood at the dining room door and looked around until she spotted Sadie dumping her bag on a table near the wall.

Walking over to the table, Brigit passed the plate across to the young woman. Making eye contact, she said, "I hear you've been giving David a hard time again. I don't appreciate having to speak to you about this for a second time, Sadie. Stay out of my kitchen unless you can conduct yourself in an appropriate manner. Do you understand me?" Brigit watched as a few expressions flitted across the girl's face – defiance, anger, shame and finally, acceptance. Sadie nodded silently and Brigit added, "That's good. Bad vibes in the kitchen really play havoc with food preparation." She gave Sadie a sharper look. "If necessary, the next one talking to you about this will be Roland and I have to tell you, he just doesn't have my charm."

❧❧❧❧

Leaving Micah Camp by the main doors, David walked beside Hannah towards the trail that wound its way along the cove to the organic bakery. She pointed to a black Suzuki four-by-four in the parking lot, "That's my car. It's not new or anything. My dad fixed it up for me."

"Cool," David told her, openly admiring the vehicle.

Charlie called out from the path that ran down to a row of resident cabins, "Hey, wait up, you guys." He jogged over to them as Sadie strolled casually along behind him. He pointed back at her, "I told her about the

250

baseball meeting and she wanted to come along."

David made a face and Hannah elbowed him gently as she said, "It's no big deal."

He stared at Sadie's long dress, boots and flashing jewelry as the four of them stood at the opening of the trail into the trees. "I don't think your regular outfit is going to work on the ball field."

She gave him a withering stare as she pushed her wild hair back from her face, "I'm sure they'll have uniforms."

※·※·※·※

Lisa-Marie ran back across the deck to give Sophie one more hug and kiss. She turned a couple of times to wave at the little face pressed against the kitchen window before she and Justin reached the trail that disappeared into the trees. "I wasn't even going to go to this meeting. Sophie woke up about twenty times last night crying about Pearl. She's taking it hard." Lisa-Marie kept to her side of the trail. She and Justin were back to being awkward in one another's company because the night in the garden house was still unresolved. "It's the first time she's ever lost anything."

She heard him say, "I don't blame her ... first time, hundredth time ... I don't think people ever get used to losing things." They walked along in silence for a few moments until Justin took her arm to slow her down. He turned her towards him, "I know you're as sad about Pearl as Sophie is. Go ahead and say it."

A quick tear came to her eye and she dashed it away with the back of her hand. "I'm not three."

She tried to pull away but he held her elbow firmly. After a moment, he let go and opened his arms to her. She stepped into them and the hug felt good. When she moved away, he said, "About the other night ... I'm sorry." She began to walk and he kept pace with her. They were coming within sight of the Saltbox and she could see Zach's truck pulling up near the back of the house. Justin slowed her down again with his hand on her elbow, "Wait, Leez ... I've been thinking a lot about things. Lauren and I are done but I have to go to Vancouver to end it."

She waited a moment but he didn't say anything else. "Well ... it's hardly the moon. I was just there and now I'm back." She pulled her arm away. "This is none of my business, Justin. It's your life."

Zach waved to them and called out, "Hey ... Arianna texted that she'll meet us on the trail. Let's go."

A few minutes later, Justin, Lisa-Marie, Zach and Arianna clattered up the back steps of the A-Frame. Beulah threw open the door, "Sounds like a herd of elephants." She stood back and waved them all into the building, "Get in here."

Mike sat on the sofa with a beer in his hand. He pointed to the stairs, "Wynter's having her first wedding dress fitting. She said to send you two up the second you arrived." He pointed with his can to Arianna and Lisa-Marie.

Beulah went to the fridge and pulled out beers for Justin and Zach. She raised her own can, "We have enough time to enjoy these before the kids from the camp get here."

Justin laughed, "Because we all know the kids from the camp never drink."

"Ya, well, maybe they do," Beulah told him, "but I don't encourage rule breaking. Unless it's in a ball game."

Mike looked at Zach, "Mom was fit to spit at dinner because you didn't come home or even call." He chugged his beer, "She said, and I quote – *I told you that girl was leading our Zach around like a trained pig with a ring in his nose.*"

Zach look surprised, "She said that about me?"

Mike chuckled, "I thought the imagery was good."

"The reason I missed dinner had nothing to do with Arianna. I was installing a system out near Zeballos. I only got to the cut-off to Crater Lake in time to get here and I had no cell phone coverage most of the way."

"It got worse. She practically made Wynter cry."

Zach frowned, "What happened?"

"Wynter asked Mom if she wanted to see the wedding dress before she brought it here for Bethany to alter and Mom said she didn't think she could. She had to load the dishwasher. Dad went into the kitchen and lit into her. Wynter and I made a quick escape."

Zach's shoulders sagged. "I asked Arianna to come to the house for supper next week. Maybe that's not such a great idea. Who knows what Mom's going to say or do these days?"

Mike nodded, "Don't forget Father Kieran and the cake."

A burst of giggles followed by several oohs and aahs drifted down the stairs, lightening the mood that Mike's story had created. Justin smiled at him and asked, "Aren't you even a bit curious about the dress?"

"No way. Wynter takes all the bad luck stuff seriously. I won't get a glimpse of that dress until she walks down the aisle."

The conversation drifted to the topic of trucks. By the time the beers were done and the kids were arriving from Micah Camp, Justin had decided he should have Mike's dad listen to the tick in his truck's engine and Beulah had finally admitted that she needed a new vehicle.

Lisa-Marie came down the stairs to the living room and said to Beulah, "Wow ... Auntie Beth has transformed that upper space. The office and a sewing room look great."

Beulah nodded as she headed for the back door, "After all her courses, she had enough paper for ten offices and the sewing stuff has always been out of hand. She thinks she might set up an alteration business by advertising in Dearborn." She looked at Mike and Zach, "Apparently, your mom has made a good amount of money with her home-based business of decorating cakes."

Charlie walked into the A-Frame in time to watch Arianna making her way downstairs. He grinned and she waved to him. The rest of the kids crowded inside and soon the small living room was overcrowded with bodies.

Beulah called out, "Let's get this meeting started. Gather around the table. We have food." With Bethany's help, they soon had the table heaped with plates of cut up cheese, pepperoni pieces, chunks of sourdough bread, spinach dip and tortilla chips surrounded by bowls of salsa, guacamole and sour cream. Bethany handed out cold soft drinks.

The table and the kitchen counter were soon surrounded by kids eating and chatting. Charlie sidled up close to Arianna. David staked out a spot for himself and Hannah as far from Sadie as possible.

Beulah clapped for everyone's attention. "Keep eating. You can listen while I talk. I know it's late to be getting a team together for a tournament in two weeks. A down Island team scratched and we were first on the waiting list. The question you need to ask yourself is this ... are you coastal wolves material or are you candy-ass crybabies?"

Zach cupped his hands around his mouth, tipped his head back and howled towards the peak of the A-Frame. Beulah said, "There you go. That's what I'm talking about." Counting heads, she added, "Five girls and five guys. Perfect. It's mixed softball."

Raising her hand, Sadie asked, "Are there uniforms?"

Beulah laughed as Bethany held up a baseball jersey – royal blue with a shaggy, grey, wolf head logo on the front. The words – *Crater Lake Coastal Wolves* – ran in a circle around the wolf that howled to the sky. Bethany turned the jersey so they could see the back. White letters above the number read – *Bethany's Alterations* – and beneath was a phone number.

Zach laughed, "Nothing like advertising to get a business going."

Charlie raised his hand and when Beulah pointed at him, he said, "If this is a Crater Lake team, how come people who live in Dearborn are on it?"

"You wouldn't have much of a team without the Sampsons," Zach told Charlie.

Mike threw in his two cents worth, "I work at the sawmill, Hannah works over at Micah Camp." He pointed at Zach, "And what other team would even consider taking a show-boat guy like him."

Wynter nudged Lisa-Marie and pointed to the jersey that was still draped over Bethany's arm, "You and I will look good in those."

Mike whispered in Wynter's ear, "You'd look good in anything. Actually, the less you wear, the better you look." She giggled at the way his lips were tickling her neck. He glanced across the table at Hannah who was standing close to David. Mike leaned over to whisper again, "What's with that?" His chin pointed to his sister.

Wynter watched as Hannah raised a napkin to wipe a drop of sour cream from David's lip. She whispered back to Mike, "She might be your baby sister, but she's no baby."

With the food reduced to crumbs on plates and skiffs of dip in bowls, Beulah waved everyone into the living room. "Find a seat or a place on the floor. Let's discuss the lineup" She pointed at Justin, "You'll be catching. Anyone here ever done any pitching?"

David raised his hand. She looked him over. "Are you any good?"

"Ya ... not bad."

"I'll be the judge of that." Beulah looked around to see if anyone else had a hand up. "You seem to be in a league of your own. I'll give you a try."

Justin gave David a high five, "You and me, kid. We'll go far."

Mike, seated in one of the armchairs, nudged Lisa-Marie with his foot. She was on the floor next to Wynter who was leaning back into Mike's legs. He told her, "You're with me in the field, right?" He glanced at Beulah, "We're not fit for much else."

Beulah lips pursed for a moment before she said, "Glad you said it, Mike." She looked at Wynter. "And what about Miss Universe, there?"

Wynter grinned, "I've never played in a real game before."

Beulah and Zach let out simultaneous moans. Mike patted Wynter on the shoulder, "Come out in the field with the rest of us losers."

"That's no good." Zach shook his head. "What if a ball gets hit past the infield?"

Arianna, who was wedged on the sofa with Zach on one side of her and Charlie on the other, said, "I'll be at shortstop. I'll stop anything that comes my way from leaving the infield."

Nodding his head, Zach said, "I call first base and let's put Hannah on second." He smiled at his sister. "I seem to recall you're pretty good at reaching for the high ones." Turning to Mike, he said, "You'll have to come out of the field and go on third." He looked to Sadie and then past Arianna to Charlie. "Those two can take turns filling out the field."

Charlie leaned forward, "Hey ... you don't even know what I can do."

Zach leaned his head to one side, "So, what can you do?"

Arianna nudged Charlie with her arm and whispered close to his ear, "You tell him."

Grinning, Charlie said, "Not much with hitting, or catching, or throwing but if I get on base, I can run faster than any of you."

Beulah's head tilted to the side as she studied Charlie. "Something to keep in mind." She looked over at Zach, "If we put Charlie up to bat when things are tight, he can bunt and he might be able to run the bases if a good hitter is up after him."

Wynter glanced over at Lisa-Marie, "I thought you guys said this was for fun. Zach and Arianna and Beulah look like they've got money on the game or something."

Beulah laughed, "Don't ever let anyone tell you that baseball is for fun."

Sadie jingled her bracelets up and down her arm to get everyone's attention. "I am a decent ball player ... just saying."

David frowned, "Was that in another life, before you became a white witch and had your inner lip tattooed?"

Hannah looked at David and said, "How do you know what her inner lip looks like?"

And Zach leaned forward to say, "Cool, can I see?"

Sadie pulled down her lip and panned around the room before she looked at David. "You're lucky I like to eat and Brigit says you're off limits."

When the meeting broke up, Mike advised Hannah, "I'll wait with my truck up by the sawmill. You follow us out on the road. Dad's orders." Hannah nodded and edged closer to David for the walk back to Micah Camp.

Charlie was about to offer to walk Arianna to the library bus when he heard Zach say, "My truck's over at the Saltbox." Arianna waved a quick goodbye to Charlie and fell into step beside Zach.

Charlie sighed and joined Hannah, David and Sadie for the walk back to Micah Camp. When they came out of the trees near the path that led down to the water, Sadie did a little dance and shimmied her dress up her legs. "Skinny dipping down at the lake anyone?"

Hannah took hold of David's arm, "I have to go. My brother is waiting for me." She swung around quickly, pulling David with her as they walked toward the parking lot.

Sadie smiled at Charlie. "I hate the water," he told her. He was in a bad mood and he never risked public swimming, not even in the dark. He headed towards his cabin.

David walked with Hannah to her car. When she got to the vehicle and pulled her keys from her bag, she stopped, leaned into the driver's door and looked at him. "Is there something going on between you and Sadie?"

Shaking his head, David said, "No ... we can't stand each other."

"Oh," she said as she reached an arm around his neck and pulled his face gently toward hers. As their lips met, he shuddered and wrapped his arm around her waist to draw her close. Hannah's tongue darted around his mouth and the kiss went on and on. He could feel the length of her body so close to him. His heart was thudding wildly when she pulled back. "I better go." He watched as she slid into the driver's seat of the vehicle and smiled up at him. "I'll see you tomorrow."

He saw her car drive away. He stayed in the same place as she passed the Micah Camp sign. He kept vigil until the red glow of her taillights disappeared around a corner. Nothing like that kiss had ever happened to David before. He was stunned, he was hot and he felt a bit sick to his stomach. He turned and walked slowly back to his cabin. He thought about how he'd told Nick that girls were off limits until marriage. Nick's take on that had been clear - *go ahead and resist if you want, no one is stopping you.* David now knew that in theory, resistance meant making a conscious decision to back away, but in practice, it wasn't what any normal guy would choose to do.

TWENTY-NINE

O n his knees, hammering a board onto the upper platform of the play structure, Justin looked up as the kitchen screen door slammed shut. Lisa-Marie had come outside with Sophie who was wearing a small, brown-leather tool belt. The child began running toward Liam where he was hunched over, measuring for the stairs that would run up to the platform. "Liam," Sophie called, "I help you."

Lisa yelled, "Sophie ... don't run up there." The child had already covered the distance to the clearing for the play structure. Her sneaker caught on the edge of a concrete footing and she sprawled out in the gravel they had spread around the whole area in preparation for the softer bark mulch that would go on top.

In a smooth movement, Justin swung his legs over the edge of the platform and dropped to the ground almost beside the child. Her screams only started when he lifted her up and turned her over. He looked at the blood pouring down her chin and froze. His vision tunneled and he thought he heard sirens in the distance. The next thing he knew, Liam had a hand on his shoulder and he was shaking him, "Justin, give her to me. I think it's just a split lip but I need a closer look."

He jolted back to the here and now. Sophie's lower face was covered in blood and the sound of her choking sobs rang in his ears. He passed her over to Liam who quickly checked the child's lip and wiggled her tooth.

At her desk in her upper counselling room, Izzy jumped up from the chair when she heard Sophie scream. She left the room, ran down the stairs and hurried out to the driveway. She could see Liam passing the crying child into Lisa's arms. He spotted her walking quickly over and called out, "It's okay. Just a lot of blood. She split her lip." He turned to Lisa, "Take her inside and put a cold cloth on her lip. I'll be there in a few minutes to take a closer look."

Justin was leaning into the upright pillar on one side of the structure; his head was bent and he was rubbing his forehead with his hand. Izzy pointed her head in Justin's direction and raised an eyebrow. Liam shrugged as he said, "I've got to clean up these tools."

Izzy walked over to Justin and laid a hand on his arm, "Hey ... are you okay?"

Looking at her with a stunned expression, he said, "I don't feel okay. That was a lot of blood from such a small bottom lip."

Frowning, Izzy said, "Why don't you come over to the office and we can talk?" Waving her hand to indicate the situation in general, she asked Liam, "Have you got this?" He nodded and she turned to walk with Justin back up to her office.

Five minutes later, Izzy glanced at her watch. Justin was sitting in a chair with his shoulders bent, hands folded on his knees and eyes staring at the floor. He was taking an extraordinarily long time to gather his thoughts. She cleared her throat and said, "Come on, Justin. Talk to me."

He looked up with a type of anguish in his eyes that she hadn't seen for a long time. "I froze ... because of the blood." He dropped his head, "I don't freeze in an emergency. You know that. I've taken industrial first aid and even before that, I never froze." He stared at the floor again as he muttered, "Do you think Maddy would be alive today if I was the type to freeze."

Izzy sat back in her chair and took a deep breath. Maddy's suicide attempt was a harsh memory. It still jolted her to be reminded of that night. She composed herself before she said, "Okay ... so, what's changed? Let's figure it out."

His knee started to jerk up and down erratically and his hands clenched tighter. "I jumped down from the upper platform when I saw her fall. When I picked her up out of the gravel and turned her over and saw the blood all over her face ..." Justin got up quickly from the chair and bolted for the door. Izzy could hear his footsteps all the way to the bottom of the stairs. She waited a few moments, then she heard his slow progress back to the office.

He came through the door and sat down. "I needed some air."

She flashed him a look of sympathy. "How about a glass of water?"

"No ... I'm good now." He straightened against the back of the chair. "It wasn't Sophie. I was way back ... holding Angie. All the blood was going out of her body as I stared at her."

"No wonder you froze. That's a terrifying flashback."

"In all these years since it happened ... I don't freeze." Frustration edged his voice.

"How many times since that day have you been first on the scene to hold a bleeding child ... a child you care for deeply ... a child the same age as Angie was when she died?

Justin stared at her as he answered, "Never." He raked his hair back from his face. "It's this thing with my mom and the waiting." He bowed his head, "And the dreams ... like I'm always trying to get somewhere and I never get there in time."

Izzy carefully reviewed the methods Justin had used to deal with flashbacks when she had worked with him years before – focusing in on the present moment through naming what he could see, what he could hear, what he could sense. Justin smiled slightly when he remembered. "I used to lie on my bed in my cabin and do that over and over." Then he frowned, "What if I can't ever trust myself in an emergency again?"

Izzy shook her head, "I think this is a specific situation, Justin. I'm even wondering if, on some level, you knew Sophie wasn't seriously injured and because of that, your brain let you have the flashback and freeze." She paused for a moment. "We are only able to process as much trauma as we can handle at any given time. You came a long way with the memories of Angie's death but the trauma isn't totally resolved. You're still working your way through it. This situation with your mom has simply opened the door for you to do some more of that processing and integration work."

"I can't say I'm grateful for the opportunity," Justin told her.

"Fair enough. But since your brain isn't likely to give you a choice, let's deal with it."

With a coping plan in place, Justin was at the door before he turned back and said, "Things are over with Lauren. I have to go to Vancouver and break up with her."

"That's a big decision."

He nodded. "But I can't seem to book the time off and go."

Izzy had risen from her chair, "Do you want to come back in and talk about it?"

"No ... it's like she's got me hostage somehow."

She frowned, "You're making it sound as if she has a voodoo doll of you bound up somewhere."

Justin's shoulders slumped. "Right ... I'm letting her hold onto me ... I know that. I don't know why."

Izzy pointed to the chair and Justin shook his head. "I'm not ready to talk about it."

She waved him out the door, "Use your grounding strategies," she called as he went down the stairs. She sat back down at her desk knowing that Justin would eventually have to talk to her about why he was not able to break up with Lauren when that was what he wanted to do.

✄ ✄ ✄ ✄

"Do you think we should head in?" Robbie asked Tabby as he stared up at the cloud that had snuck across the sky and hidden the sun.

"No way. We're not going in until my dive is as good as yours."

Robbie sat down on the raft. "Okay ... but let's rest for a minute." When Tabby joined him, he asked, "Is your mom still talking about the school thing?"

"She's not saying anything but I bet she's still thinking about it." Tabby lay down and rolled onto her stomach, "Hey, if you lie like this you can suck up a bit of warmth from the wood," she told Robbie.

He stretched out on his stomach beside her. "Liam buried Pearl out past the garden near the cliff. He's going to make a marker. I want to carve a picture of something on it but I can't figure out what." He laid his cheek against the warm wood.

Tabby did likewise. She looked at him and asked, "Not a dog?"

"It might not turn out looking like Pearl and then it would be weird."

"What about an eagle? You're good at eagles and it could be like Pearl is flying off ... free or something like that."

He smiled at her, "You always have good ideas." He glanced up at the sky. "Five minutes and the sun will peek out and we can try a few more dives."

On the beach, Lisa-Marie stretched out on a lawn chair and watched Sophie playing by the edge of the water. Every time the child touched the lake with her bright pink water shoe, she jumped back, screaming over her shoulder to her mother, "It feezing, Mama." Then she would laugh and wave to Robbie and Tabby out on the raft. Soon, Sophie was busy filling buckets with water and sorting piles of small rocks.

The sun came out from behind the clouds and Lisa-Marie welcomed the warmth. She shaded her eyes when she heard Justin's voice on the far

260

staircase. He was calling to Tabby and Robbie, "I can hear you guys all the way to my cabin. Is the water that cold?"

Tabby jumped up and down and screamed, "Come in and find out for yourself unless you're a chicken."

Justin laughed, "Those are fighting words, kid." He got to the bottom of the stairs and without pausing, tore off his shirt and ran straight into the water, diving under and swimming strongly for the raft.

Lisa-Marie watched his arms plough through the water. Sophie stood up and clapped. She looked back at her mom, "Justin go fast."

Staying put on her lounge chair, Lisa-Marie felt no urge to tear off the T-shirt she wore over her bathing suit and swim for the raft to race with Justin in a reenactment of what they had often done. The reason for her reluctance wasn't only that she could not leave Sophie alone on the beach. Falling into the old patterns with Justin was too easy. They were thrown together all the time. And no matter how hard she tried to resist, she was still attracted to him. And he was still with Lauren. She could not let herself forget that.

When Justin swam back from the raft, he grabbed his towel and made his way over to Lisa-Marie. Pulling up a chair, he sat down and leaned forward to towel dry his hair. She tried to keep her eyes off his body but the view was too tempting. She noticed his broad shoulders, muscled arms and the way the hair near his navel disappeared into the band of his shorts. The sight of him made her breath hitch. She sat up further in her chair and looked away. Justin dropped the towel around his neck and stretched out his legs. He pointed at Sophie, "She seems completely recovered from her fall."

"Her lip is swollen but she's fine."

"I got a letter from my mom. It came in yesterday's mail. I found it on my desk when I got up to the sawmill."

Turning to search his face, she asked, "Is everything okay?"

He nodded, "Her letter was short. She's not ready for a visit yet. She wants me to keep writing and she told me that she's sorry for leaving me the way she did."

"That's good, right?"

"Ya ... I feel easier about waiting now that I've heard from her directly."

Robbie and Tabby swam to the shore. Donning a T-shirt that hung over his wet bathing suit, Robbie told Lisa-Marie, "We're going to take the canoe out." He looked over at Justin. "You guys will be on the beach for a while, right? Liam doesn't want us to take the canoe out if no one's on the beach."

"Don't go out of the cove."

Sophie begged to go in the canoe and stuck her swollen lip out when Lisa-Marie said, "You're too little to go in the canoe with Robbie and Tabby."

She stomped her foot, "Why, Mama? I go with Liam."

"Well, Robbie and Tabby aren't Liam. The answer is no."

Justin pushed the canoe off for the kids and said, "Paddle out and wait. I'm going to get the other canoe." He turned to the angry child. "Sophie," he waited for her to look at him, "I'll take you and your mom for a canoe ride, okay?" He glanced at Lisa-Marie, "Let's paddle down past the camp. I haven't seen it from the water forever."

Lisa-Marie nodded. Resisting Justin's smile or Sophie's pleas was impossible.

¤¤¤¤

Fiona awoke in the downstairs bedroom of the Saltbox to the sounds of Aidan crying. She lay in the bed for a moment, listening to hear if Nick was getting up. The baby's sobs increased. She got out of bed and followed the noise upstairs. In the open loft space between Aidan's nursery and the guest room, the lamp was on and Nick was walking back and forth across the floor holding Aidan.

"What's happening?" she asked as she pushed her hair back from her face.

Nick threw her a baffled look. "I don't know. He's hot and he keeps crying."

Fiona frowned as she laid her hand against Aidan's forehead, "He is hot." She took the baby from Nick's arms and tried to comfort him but Aidan's cries only ramped up into the plaintive range. She stared at Nick, "I knew the wind was too cold down at the lake. I asked you not to dip Aidan's feet in the water."

"I don't see how an *I-told-you-so* lecture is going to help." Nick looked around, "Do we have a thermometer?"

"Not for a baby."

"For a doctor, you're not very prepared, are you?" Nick took Aidan back from her as he asked, "What do we do? We can't let him cry forever." He touched the baby's head again, "It feels like he's getting hotter."

Fiona folded her arms across her body and rested her chin in her hand as she tried to think. An uncharacteristic panic took hold of her. She felt it racing through her body. Her heart started to beat faster. Her palms itched with sweat. Fever – it could be serious. Babies could come down with meningitis in a snap and here they were out in the middle of nowhere. "Where are your car keys? We should get him to the hospital up in Cedar Falls as soon as we can. They can draw some blood and do some tests. He could have a seizure any minute for all we know."

"Whoa," Nick raised his hand. "Don't you think you're overreacting?"

"Well, I don't know, Nick ... you said it, I'm the doctor."

Nick glanced at the clock. "I know it's late but I'm going to call Liam and Izzy and see what they think." Fiona followed him down the stairs to the main floor and after a few moments on the phone, Nick hung up and turned to her. "Liam thinks Aidan is probably teething. He says we should give him some baby Tylenol and a cool bath if his temperature goes up any more."

Fiona sat down on the sofa and crossed her legs. She realized she was somewhat skimpily clad in sweat shorts and a clingy undershirt. She brushed that aside – teething, of course, and probably a better assumption than meningitis. She should have remembered the principle of Occam's Razor and gone with the simplest explanation that fits the circumstances. During her internship, they had talked endlessly about Occam's Razor when learning to make an accurate diagnosis. "We do have baby Tylenol. It's on the shelf in Aidan's room."

Within an hour, Aidan was sleeping soundly. Nick came into the living room and said, "He feels a lot cooler."

Fiona had thrown on a long sweater and had made tea. She poured Nick a cup and he took the mug before sitting down across from her. After a drink, he looked at her. "That was brutal. How are we going to manage if he gets really sick?"

"You are obviously going to be the calm and cool one, while I am going to be the panicky one coming up with the worst-case scenarios." Fiona shook her head, "I didn't feel like myself at all. I wouldn't want anyone at the clinic to have seen me like that ... ready to order a spinal tap for my teething baby."

Nick smiled, "I won't tell a soul." He paused before saying, "Us being parents ... we haven't talked about that at all." He stared at her, "You must have wanted a baby to have gone through with having Aidan at such a difficult time."

"No matter how bad the timing, I did want him from the moment I knew I was pregnant." Fiona expression softened, "I always planned to have a baby one day. I just thought it would be after I had settled into my own practice somewhere." She looked at him, "What about you? Did you want children?"

"The first time I was married, my wife and I were busy getting our teaching careers off the ground; if we thought about it at all, having a family was something in the distant future. The next time ... the marriage didn't last long enough for us to talk of kids."

"Well, we're in it now, for sure." Fiona got up and stretched. "Back to bed, I guess." She left the last two words hanging out there.

Nick got up as well. "Right, see you in the morning." He turned and headed for the staircase and his bedroom on the upper floor.

THIRTY

Helen banged around her kitchen putting the final touches on dinner. She was feeling hard-pressed to recover the Buddha like calm she preferred to have when she was preparing food. She hadn't expected a table of eight for a Monday night dinner. Zack had announced he was bringing Arianna around this evening, and Mike and Wynter were prompt for dinner on most nights. Today was Hannah's day off from Micah Camp and she had invited this David boy to come over since they had a ball practice afterwards.

Her feelings were conflicted because she had always enjoyed having the kids bring their friends home with them for meals. Their presence made her think she and Craig were doing something right. The kids were proud of their home and liked to share their family with others.

She lifted the chicken from the roaster to the platter. David was way too quiet for her taste. Forget the whole still waters run deep saying. He wouldn't be a Micah Camp resident if he didn't have a problem or two. She scraped the mashed potatoes from the pot into a warmed serving bowl. And Hannah was far too familiar with him. Every time she looked, her daughter's hands were on the boy's body. She whisked the gravy over the heat before pouring its flawless smoothness into the gravy boat.

Zach seemed over the moon about Arianna. Helen had never seen him this way with any other girl. She couldn't remember a time when Zach had missed dinner without even calling and yet, he had done that not so long ago.

Draining the broccoli, she dumped it into a bowl and topped it with a dollop of butter. She pulled the Greek Salad from the fridge and began to carry the food out to the table. As she called everyone to dinner, she picked up the silver serving spoons from the sidebar and set them beside the trays and bowls. She glanced into the living room and watched Wynter unwind her body from Mike's and smile as she came towards the dining room. Helen blocked out the thought of Wynter and Mike. Obviously, Father Kieran had not done his job. His meeting with them had achieved nothing. Mike was still marrying the girl and not in the church.

When everyone gathered around the table, both Zach and Hannah insisted that Mike and Wynter didn't have to sit together. Mike sat down on one side of his father and Wynter took the chair on the other. Helen had the pleasure of having David sit to her left. "Hannah," she waited for her daughter to stop nudging David in the side, "Say grace, please."

Hannah made a face and shot her mother a glare that spoke volumes but she lowered her head and quickly recited, "Bless us, O Lord, and these Thy gifts which we are about to receive from Thy bounty. Through Christ, our Lord. Amen."

Raising her eyes as all the Sampsons crossed themselves, Helen caught the shocked expression on David's face. She patted his hand, "No need to panic dear. It's only the sign of the cross not a black magic incantation." She watched as Hannah fumed and turned to her dad with eyes that pleaded – *make her stop, Dad, please.* Craig dutifully locked eyes with his wife and raised an eyebrow.

Helen allowed herself a modicum of pride as praise for the food came her way. Though she tried to make herself not care, she was happy to see all the young people load their plates and pleased that David took seconds of everything except broccoli. When he asked her how she got her gravy so smooth, she almost beamed. She found herself engaging him in conversation, asking questions as she usually did. "Tell us about your family, David. What do your parents do?"

The silence that followed Helen's question was broken only by the clattering sound of cutlery as it fell to Arianna's plate. Her face was filled with sympathy as she looked at David. In that moment, Helen noticed how uncomfortable he was. Getting information out of young people was a struggle and she hadn't thought twice about how David had given one-word answers to her previous three questions.

Arianna spoke softly but her eyes never left Helen's face, "Not all kids want to talk about their parents, or how they grew up." Then she turned to Zach, "I'm sorry. I'm not trying to be rude. You have a wonderful home." She stared down at her plate. "Not everyone is so lucky."

Helen felt her colour rising when even Zach, usually a staunch ally, looked at her in disbelief. She mumbled an apology to David and he looked as uncomfortable as she felt.

As the meal wound down, Hannah asked Wynter, "How is the furniture arranging going?"

Wynter glanced quickly at Helen before she said, "Oh, you know. It's furniture. Just moving it here and there. No big deal."

Mike frowned across the table at his fiancé, "Why are you saying it like that? We've been having a blast down at the Lady Brit every night arranging that furniture. We must have moved that huge bed a dozen times already." Zach choked a wild laugh into his napkin as Mike said, "Arranging furniture. Get your mind out of the gutter." He flinched and stared at Wynter. "Don't kick me and don't pretend you haven't been having the time of your life just because some people might not approve." He stared down the table at his mother.

Craig told Mike, "Okay, that's enough."

Helen got up and dropped her napkin beside her plate. "I'll whip the cream for the gingerbread cake."

She had the table-top mixer out and the cream was whirling in the metal bowl. She reached into the cupboard for the bottle of white vanilla which she had bought at a specialty shop. It was expensive and so strongly flavoured that a quarter of a teaspoon would do wonders for the whipped cream. She tried to concentrate on what she was doing but Hannah's glares, Zach's betrayal and Mike's sarcasm were swooshing around in her head like the waves of cream in the bowl. She had the vanilla bottle poised near the tiny measuring spoon which was over the bowl. At the same time, she was thinking that if she had to hear one more word about the arrangement of the furniture at the Lady Brit, she would probably scream.

Wynter came into the kitchen and said, "Could I give you a hand with something, Helen?"

She slopped more than a quarter teaspoon into the bowl as the guilt of her thoughts caught up with her. "No, that's fine, I wouldn't want you to get anything on that beautiful outfit."

Wynter frowned as she looked down at her casual summer dress, "It's nothing fancy, Helen. I could wear an apron," she offered.

Helen waved her off. She continued to watch the cream spin. The way Arianna had rushed in to defend David made it seem as though Helen had been pulling out his fingernails with a pair of pliers simply because she'd asked him a couple of questions about his upbringing. She had a right to know something about the boy her own daughter couldn't stop touching. Her attention was caught by the measuring spoon in her hand. The cream was getting thick. She had to add the vanilla. She measured and poured.

At that moment, Hannah came in with a stack of dirty plates and froze Helen in place with a single stare. She put the dishes down on the nearby counter then leaned in close to her mother so her voice could be heard above the whirring of the mixer. Helen had the distinctly uncomfortable sense that she was being buzzed by a hornet. "Stop trying to make David uncomfortable or else," her daughter warned her.

As Hannah flounced out of the kitchen, the thought occurred to Helen that she was probably having sex with that boy. She stared at the measuring spoon and couldn't remember if she'd put in the vanilla. She added another spoon. Then she noticed her regular stopping point for whipped cream – touched by a mere hint of yellow – had passed. The mixture in the bowl was on the thick side but she thought it would be okay.

She cut the gingerbread, placed the squares on the dessert plates and dolloped on the cream. Helen carried the large tray out to the dining room and distributed the plates around the table. Craig sniffed with pleasure, "This smells great. I love your gingerbread." He shoved a large bite into his mouth and as he chewed an odd expression came over his face. His jaw stopped moving and he seemed to be rolling the food in his mouth back and forth from one bulging cheek to the other.

Zach had a whole bite swallowed and was going for another before the taste hit him. He frowned as he reached quickly for a napkin.

Hannah spit her cake out onto her plate and reached out to stop David's fork halfway to his mouth. "What is wrong with the whipped cream?" She looked at her mother as she wiped bits of gingerbread from her lips.

Feeling confused and sorely put upon, Helen tested the whipped cream with the edge of her teaspoon. Her face blanched as she realized that she must have used way too much vanilla. The cream had a harsh almost metallic aftertaste.

She put the spoon down carefully, lining it up with the edge of her dessert plate. She got up slowly and with infinite care refolded her napkin and set it down. She looked around the table. "If anyone in this house wants dessert ... ever again ... make it yourself." Seeing the stunned expressions on the faces of her family, she turned and left the room.

❧ ❧ ❧ ❧

Walking along the trail away from Micah Camp with Sadie beside him,

Charlie had a brainstorm. They were headed for the A-Frame to get a ride into Dearborn with Beulah for a baseball practice. Earlier in the day, Beulah had mentioned that Arianna would be catching a ride with them as well.

"Sadie," Charlie clutched at the girl's arm to slow her down, "I need you to do something for me."

Sadie frowned down at Charlie's hand on her arm. "What?"

"When we get to Beulah's truck, say that you have to sit in the front because you get car sick and you'll puke otherwise."

Tipping her head to one side, Sadie considered the request in conjunction with Charlie's desperation. "Why?"

Because time was of the essence, he decided to tell her. "I want to sit in the back with Arianna."

A knowing grin covered Sadie's face. "What's in it for me?" she asked as she stuck her hand out and wiggled her fingers.

Digging in his pocket, Charlie pulled out a five-dollar bill and passed it to her.

She smiled as she took it from him. "It'll cost you another five for the way back."

Arianna and Beulah were coming down the back steps of the A-Frame and heading for the truck when Charlie and Sadie arrived. Arianna actually had her hand on the passenger door of the front seat as Beulah said, "Come on, you two. Let's get a move on. We've only got this one practice, so we better get in every moment we can." She heaved a couple of heavy equipment bags from the ground into the bed of the truck.

Sadie walked forward and stopped near Arianna. "I need to sit in the front seat." She made a face, "Sorry. I get bad car sickness."

Arianna stepped back, "Sure, no worries. We don't want anyone puking out the window of Beulah's truck." She smiled at Charlie who had come up beside her. "I guess it's you and me in the back."

When Arianna turned to climb into the truck, Sadie smiled and gave Charlie an okay sign. He tried to ignore her. He could see Beulah watching as she said, "Hurry up, kiddies, or there won't be any treats after practice." She laughed as she swung into the driver's seat.

Charlie basked in the time it took to drive into Dearborn. He felt the thrill of every corner that brought Arianna's arm a fraction of an inch closer to his own, every shift of her leg, every smile that lit up her face and every single word she spoke. They were in a time warp that held only two. The back seat of Beulah's truck became his universe.

Bumping along the road, Arianna grinned and asked him, "What did you have for dinner over at the camp?"

"It was taco night."

"Darn ... I love tacos." She reached to the front to tap Beulah on the shoulder, "No, offence. Your barbecued pork loin is the best."

He asked her, "How's work going?"

A small frown preceded a shrug, "It's good because I'm learning so much everyday but it's hard, too. Sometimes people's stories remind me of home." She brushed off her momentary sadness. "What kinds of stuff are you doing over at the camp?"

"For school ... two university transfer courses and upgrading in French. And counselling," he paused before saying, "I wasn't sure about that but it's pretty cool." He shifted as if to get more comfortable and brought his body a few inches closer to hers. "I signed up to work at some kind of fundraiser thing ... a Bingo ... and for the food wagon at the midway for the Dipsy-Doodle weekend." Beulah took a sharp corner at a good clip and Arianna slid closer to him until their shoulders were touching. Crossing his fingers that Beulah would keep up the swerving, Charlie added, "Do you think with only one practice, we'll be good enough for the tournament?"

Flipping her glossy hair over her shoulder, Arianna grinned at him as she raised her voice, "One practice with Beulah can achieve wonders, you wait and see."

As they made the turn off the gravel road, Arianna's phone chirped. She pulled it out of her pocket and smiled as she read the text. "Zach's at the ball field already. He's got the key to the equipment room."

Charlie's lips quirked to one side. Zach – even the guy's name was irritating.

⚜ ⚜ ⚜ ⚜

From behind the wheel of her Suzuki, Hannah made a face as she glanced over at David in the passenger seat. "I'm sorry about my mom. She used to be borderline normal but lately ... she's gone off the deep end."

Acutely aware of the way her body moved as she casually turned her head to back the vehicle out of her driveway, he said, "No big deal. That cake smelled great. I wonder if Brigit has the recipe."

"I'll get it from my mom and you and I can make it next time we're working on our own."

Hannah pointed out various Dearborn landmarks as she drove but David was having a hard time concentrating on her words. Being alone with her was a major distraction. Since the kiss after the ball meeting at the A-Frame, he'd seen her every day. Even on the days she didn't need to be at the camp, she'd shown up to work with Ethan on his dance video. One afternoon, when David had walked with her to the greenhouse to pick lettuce, they had made the best use of their time out of sight of the busy camp. Leaning up against a back wall and surrounded by the strong smell of tomato vines, they had kissed and kissed. She broke away from him only when they both heard Jim's telltale whistling as he came down the path from the maintenance shed.

In his last session with Nick, David had considered asking if perhaps everything he had been taught about right and wrong when it came to being with a girl, had been bullshit. But Nick would dig into that like a dog chewing on a bone. Though the counsellor tried to hide his opinions under a thin layer of tolerance, David could tell that the guy was only waiting for such a question so he could go full steam ahead and pry up all of David's beliefs. And David did not want that. Maybe everything he believed might have to go. But if that were true, he wanted to be the one who made that choice.

He agreed with some things Nick had to say. He knew now that not speaking to a counsellor about what had happened to him as a child had been a mistake. The moment he started to talk about the memories and the terror of that night, he realized how much he had wanted to be able to say the words. He also began to understand that the fear he had felt as a child was still part of him. No amount of prayer on its own was going to help him figure out how to make sense of that. He was sticking with Nick for one reason – the guy knew what he was talking about when it came to bad stuff from the past.

He cringed inside when he tried to imagine Hannah's face if she knew about what had happened to his family. She'd be ashamed of making apologies for her alive-and-well mom who had wrecked their dessert.

❧❧❧❧

Beulah swung her truck into the gravel parking lot right behind Hannah's Suzuki. Zach was out in the field tossing down the bases and securing them. Charlie got out of the truck and stood by to have a look as Arianna crawled out behind him. That little thrill was quickly replaced by frustration at the way she waved to Zach with a big smile on her face.

Justin drove up and he and Lisa-Marie got out of his truck. He and Charlie hoisted the equipment bags and together they all made their way to the ball field.

Beulah ordered everyone out to the field. She set up an old-fashioned ghetto blaster and popped a cassette tape into the machine. Within moments,

John Fogerty's voice boomed out over the field – *put me in coach ... I'm ready to play ... today ... look at me ... centerfield.* She swung a bat around her head; then crouching over home plate, she began to hit grounders and pop flies into the field.

Straightening up, she shielded her eyes and watched as Lisa-Marie missed an easy lob to Fogerty's centerfield. She shouted, "What the hell ... that was an easy one. Wake up." Mike came in for a roasting as well when he flubbed a grounder that was making a bee-line for third. Sadie got thumbs up from Beulah when she ran backwards with her gloved hand up in the air to snag a high flyer out in left field.

Waving everyone in after about twenty minutes, Beulah told David, "Let's see what you've got. Warm up with Justin and then we'll check to see if this team can hit."

Justin trotted over to home base with the catcher mask in hand. He banged it down on his head and the cage slipped over his face as he squatted and slammed his fist into his glove. "Let it rip," he called to David.

Lining everyone up for batting practice, Beulah advised David, "Take it easy on them this first round. Throw something they can hit."

Lisa-Marie struck out. "No surprises there, hey," Beulah told her as she observed from the sidelines.

Beulah smiled when Wynter fluked into a base hit and looked stunned before she started jumping up and down and calling to Mike, "I did it, I did it." Mike punched his fists in the air in a congratulatory gesture.

Hannah, Zach and Mike were all solid hitters – there were line drives all the way for the Sampsons. Sadie managed a pop fly and when Charlie picked up a bat, Beulah called out, "Try a bunt and let's see you run those bases." She high-fived him when he rounded third base on the way to home plate. As he caught his breath, she told him, "You said it kid, you can run."

Beulah clapped her hands, "Heads up." She walked over to Justin and gestured for David to come in from the mound. "You two work on some signals and a few more challenging pitches." She turned to Zach, "Throw the ball around the infield. I'm going to work with our outfielders."

Soon, Beulah shouted Mike's name. "Get out here. This Sadie kid can catch. I'm putting her on third."

Mike walked out to left field. "No problem, Beulah. You've only restored the natural order of things. I am outfield through and through." Wynter ran over. Mike swung her over his arm to deliver a Hollywood kiss while the rest of the *Crater Lake Coastal Wolves* howled and hooted.

Kicking back in the dugout at the end of the practice, Beulah passed out soda from a cooler. She popped a can and took a drink. "I've got to say ... I never thought the bunch of you would make even a half-assed team but I'm surprisingly impressed. You won't totally shame the *Crater Lake Coastal Wolves* uniform."

Sadie sat forward, "Speaking of those uniforms ... when do we get them?"

Beulah chuckled, "I'll pass them out before you leave."

Charlie had spent the practice trying to stay close to Arianna but he couldn't compete with Zach whose passion for baseball clearly matched Arianna's. Charlie did manage to sit beside her in the dugout but soon enough Justin was suggesting that everyone over nineteen should head up to the Legion for a drink. As Arianna got up, Beulah said, "I'll be taking the kiddies home to Crater Lake soon. How will you get back?"

Zach was right there, edging up beside Arianna as he said, "I'll drive her."

Arianna shook her head, "You don't need to do that. I'll catch a ride back with Lisa and Justin ... is that okay?" She looked at Justin and he nodded.

Moments later, the over-nineteen contingent of the team headed off. Charlie stared after Arianna, trying not to look like a wounded puppy. He couldn't figure out whether he was glad she wasn't driving back with Zach or miserable because Zach's offer had rung with a definite tone of possession.

Charlie and Sadie, weighed down with the equipment bags, followed Beulah to her truck. David was over by Hannah's Suzuki and everybody had to wait while the two of them kissed goodbye. Finally, Beulah shouted, "All aboard for Micah Camp. Now." David ran over with a small grin on his face and Charlie felt like hitting the guy. It didn't seem fair that David had already lucked into having a girlfriend.

Sadie told Charlie, "You still owe me five bucks. Don't forget."

"No way. Arianna isn't even going back with us."

"Don't burn your bridges." Turning to look at David, Sadie narrowed her eyes, "Watch out, David. Kissing like that could mess up your little contract with God."

Beulah was behind the wheel. "Get in the truck and quit sniping like grade-schoolers."

Back at Micah Camp, David and Charlie headed for their cabin. When they came through the door, Ethan was sitting on the sofa with a sketch book open in his lap. His iPod was on the table. He pulled out his earbuds as David walked straight through to his room, whistling quietly. Charlie plopped into a chair. Ethan pointed to David's closed door, "Why is he in such a good

273

mood? I thought you were at a baseball practice not a Bible meeting."

Charlie chewed at his bottom lip, "He's got a girlfriend."

Ethan closed his sketch book and reached for his iPod. He stood up and asked, "Ya ... who?"

"That Hannah girl who works in the kitchen."

Ethan whistled. "Wow ... if you like girls, she's a hot one." He stared at Charlie for a moment, "What's up with you?"

"I think Arianna might like this Zach guy who's on the team. She went off with him and a few of the other players. She didn't even drive back with us."

Ethan headed towards his door. Charlie frowned, "Have I done something to piss you off? It seems like every time I walk into a room, you walk out."

"I have work to do, kid. My dance will not choreograph itself," Ethan explained as he walked away.

❧❧❧❧

Sitting in her chair in the grief group circle, Izzy said, "I've been thinking about my mother's death ... and how the ways we cope with one loss have an impact on how we deal with others." She glanced around at the faces that surrounded her. "I never understood my mother until she was gone and then, of course, it was too late. She seemed such a cold and controlling person. After she was gone, I read her journals and discovered that nothing could have been further from the truth. She was passionate in her writing, concerned about me and interested in so many other things. I had no idea."

The group had reached a point of coalescence that allowed Izzy to let her guard down slightly – to explore her own issues. She went on, "I had a lot of anger towards my mother when I read her journals. I kept asking myself – why didn't she let me know her? I thought I had dealt with my resentful feelings until the fear of being that angry and disillusioned again resurfaced with another grief. I was invited by someone close to me to read Caleb's journals. I didn't want to do it and I turned the invitation down flat. I was afraid."

She smiled at the group. "Well, I faced that fear. After our first meeting, I went home and started reading Caleb's journals and they've been wonderful. Funny and sweet ... sad at times. But my feelings were nothing like what I went through in reading my mom's diaries." Izzy smiled as she said, "I wouldn't let Liam talk about Caleb's journals before. But now that I've started reading them, I want to share the experience with anyone else who loved Caleb."

After a few moments of silence, Bethany took a deep breath and looked around the circle. "I've been thinking about something. When I was seventeen, I had a baby that I gave up for adoption. Then I moved on with my life. I never spent a moment grieving for that child. The whole thing was just over and done with." She glanced at Izzy before she went on. "Or at least, that's what I thought. A few years ago, I almost drowned in a boating accident. When I woke up in the hospital, all I could think of was that baby. I thought I heard it crying and I even thought for a while I wanted to have another baby." A quick grimace passed over her face. "Saner minds prevailed and I got on with life. Lately, I feel ready to grieve for the young girl I was back then. I never even looked at the baby and I don't know if it was a girl or a boy." Bethany paused for a moment, her head tilted to one side. Then she went on, "I read somewhere about kids trying to find their real parents and parents trying to find kids they gave up. It got me wondering why doing something like that never even crossed my mind."

Into the quiet that wrapped itself around the circle, Helen said, "I put about five times the proper amount of a very strong vanilla into the whipped cream that was to go on the gingerbread for tonight's dessert. People all around the table were gagging. My daughter spit her food right out on her plate." She was silent then and the people in the circle waited. When it came to Helen, the group had a hard time knowing if she was finished talking or not. She looked up from studying the toes of her shoes, "I realize that story might not fit the gravitas of this group but I've shared it, anyway."

Alison stirred in her chair and said, "I am sick of being stuck in the blaming stage of things." She sighed, "I want to wake up one day and not blame Bradley for everything from a snag in my stocking to climate change. That may sound funny but it's exactly what I'm doing. I'd like to be able to look back and laugh at myself someday."

Later when the meeting ended, Alison touched Kieran's arm and asked, "Could I stay behind a few minutes after the others leave. I'd like you to hear my confession." Kieran nodded.

When the door closed on the last group member, Kieran pointed to one of the chairs. "Let's sit down."

Alison sat primly in the chair across from him and folded her hands in her lap. He cringed at the idea that she might start a rote – *Bless me Father for I have sinned* – litany. But she didn't She cleared her throat discreetly and said, "My sacramental marriage ended."

He waited but when no other words came, he felt the need to challenge this woman. "Is that a sin? Surely you've never believed the end of the marriage was your fault. Why ask forgiveness for that?" He stopped speaking and hoped that the trust built up in the group was enough to allow such an approach.

"Maybe it was my fault. According to my soon-to-be ex-husband, I couldn't get beyond certain hang-ups in the bedroom."

"This is your confession, not his."

She echoed his words, "So, why ask forgiveness for that?" She was silent for a moment. "I felt such intense anger towards him for leaving me. I've blamed him for everything that's gone wrong since the moment he told me he was leaving. And I was complacent. I never thought to look too closely at the perfect little life I was living. I will ask forgiveness for those things."

They spent a few minutes discussing Alison's insights into where she had missed the mark before and after her marriage broke down. Finally, Kieran bowed his head as he reached for her hands. "God, the Father of mercies, through the death and resurrection of his Son has reconciled the world to himself and sent the Holy Spirit among us for the forgiveness of sins; through the ministry of the Church may God give you pardon and peace, and I absolve you from your sins in the name of the Father, and of the Son and of the Holy Spirit," as Kieran made the sign of the cross to bless her, Alison repeated with him, "Amen."

After she had gone, Kieran sat in the chair in the empty church and reflected on the beauty of those simple words of absolution that allowed God's forgiveness to flow through him to another. He was humbled by the experience. The bounty of God's mercy was available in so many ways beyond this sacrament – doled out, freely given every single day. He felt sad for those who believed something so abundant could be contained, or withheld or solely dispensed by flawed human beings. And even though the sacrament was only one of many ways to find forgiveness, for those who believed, Reconciliation was powerful.

THIRTY-ONE

A voice rang out through the crowded, stuffy hall, "Hey, Father." The hour was early and the place already smelled of overheated coffee and hotdogs.

Kieran stood on the stage between the Bingo machine that sounded like an out-of-control popcorn popper with its seventy-five balls whirling around inside and a large lit up board dotted with holes. He had been pulling the balls from the machine, calling the numbers and setting them into the board for five games now. It seemed like he was getting the hang of it and he hoped that nothing else would throw him for a loop the way an elderly woman in the first row had when she raised her voice to ask him, "Are you going to drop your balls or what, Father?" He quickly learned that meant turn the machine on and get calling.

He stared out across the tables filled with people wielding fluorescent Bingo dabbers like plunging daggers over their paper cards, and said, "What can I do for you?"

"What do you call a sleep-walking nun?" A man at a table near the back of the hall yelled.

A person on the other side of the hall shouted, "A roamin' Catholic." Then someone else rang a huge cowbell and everyone burst out laughing.

A cranky voice spouted off, "Shut the door, it's frigging cold."

Another responded, "Why you always sitting so close to the door if you're always cold."

The Dipsy-Doodle Days, Big Jackpot Bingo was underway. As Kieran grabbed the first ball, he checked the sheet in front of him and said, "Okay ... we're playing a combo game now. Going for the letter X, folks. First game is going to be two lines any way and your first number is under the B ... fifteen."

He got to the third number, obeying the screams that had come at him during the last game telling him to slow down. A woman down in front of him shouted at the stage, "Speed it up, will you? We don't want to be here all night."

Out on the floor, wearing cloth aprons with deep pockets, Ethan and Sadie sprinted from one end of the hall to the other selling Bonanza game cards and raffle tickets. For the third time, a woman beckoned to Ethan. When he arrived by her table, she told him, "Sweetie-pie, I just love to see the way you sashay over here. Give me another couple of cards."

Stopping for a quick breather near the concession stand counter loaded with trays of baked goods, Ethan beckoned Hannah over, "Get me something cold to drink, okay? I'm going to lose my voice out there." He fanned himself, "These people are crazy." He looked at Sadie, "Did you see that woman try to slip a five-dollar bill in the waist band of my pants?"

Sadie laughed as she leaned her elbows on the counter and her bangles jingled down her arm. She called out to David who was filling the hotdog machine, "Got a handle on that lust thing yet, Davie?"

He looked back at her and said, "Ha, ha ... aren't you getting sick of the same old line?"

Hannah glared at Sadie as she handed Ethan a can of soda. He popped the top, drained the can down by half and looked over at Sadie. "Lay off David or you won't get to help with my dance video." Spotting Charlie heading for the concession, Ethan pushed away from the counter and moved in the other direction.

David had come forward to stand beside Hannah. Someone had screamed Bingo and that was a signal for people to rush from their tables to the concession stand. They watched Sadie run after Ethan as people waved their hands in the air for cards. David could hear her saying, "Okay, okay. He won't hear another word from me, I promise." He looked at Hannah and smiled right before they were deluged by a long line of hungry and thirsty Bingo players who were in a hurry and not inclined to be too polite about the fact.

Charlie was working with Brigit to check the numbers on the winning cards. Before that, he had been near the table where Arianna sat with Beulah and Bethany. He'd gotten her tea and a huge cupcake and he was hanging out beside her as she bounced eagerly on her chair, grabbing Beulah's arm and gasping, "I need O seventy, again." When she screamed Bingo, got up to wave her arms and danced him around in a circle with her, he had a hard time resisting the urge to touch her long hair and look into her eyes shining with glee.

"Hey, Father," another voice rang out. Brigit leaned against a wall and smiled across the heads of the crowd. "How do you make holy water?"

As Kieran shrugged, someone shouted back, "You boil the hell out of it." The cowbell rang and the laugher let loose.

Helen sat at the table with Beulah and Bethany, playing her cards and fuming at the way Hannah was draping herself over David in the concession stand. She hardly noticed when she dabbed the last number on her card for two postage stamps. Beulah pointed wildly at her, "Wake up, Helen. You've got a Bingo."

At the break, Kieran came down from the stage for a cold drink. Brigit joined him near the back wall. "Well, Father, how are you holding up?" She grinned at him.

All he could do was shake his head and raise an eyebrow at her. "You might have warned me about the cowbell."

"And spoil all the fun?" she asked. "I did tell you the Big Jackpot Bingo had a tradition of giving St. Bertha's priest a good roasting."

One of the guys from the Lion's club was up on the stage with the mike. He spotted Kieran against the wall and called out, "Hey, Father, you're going to love this joke." He strode to the front of the stage as he began, "The Pope was on a trip to New York –,"

Interrupting him with groans, several people in the crowd yelled, "Not that old one."

Ignoring the catcalls, he went on, "A driver picks him up at the airport. The Pope asks – *Would you mind if I drive? I never get to drive in Rome.* The driver shrugs and says– *Sure, Holy Father, you drive, you're the boss.* The Pope is speeding along having himself a great old time when he sees red lights in the rear-view mirror. The driver says – *You better pull over, Holy Father.* So, the Pope pulls over. The cop comes to the window, a big and burly Irish cop, and he recognizes the Pope right off – *Excuse me Holy Father, I'll be right back.* He goes to his car, radios in and asks to speak to the Captain – *I've got a big problem. I've pulled over an important person.* The Captain asks – *What do you mean? Important like the mayor?* The patrol cop says – *More important.* The Captain asks – *Important like the governor?* The patrol cop says – *More important.* The Captain asks – *Important like the president?* The patrol cop says – *More important.* The Captain loses his patience and yells – *Come on man, you're having me on. Who's more important than the president?* The patrol cop shrugs and says – *I don't know but he's got the Pope driving for him.*

Never having heard that one, Kieran let out a loud and genuine burst of laugher at the punch line and earned himself the goodwill of the crowd. Unfortunately, those feelings weren't shared by the man who shouted at him during the jackpot game, "Pipe down a bit there, Father. You don't have to yell into that mike. We're not all deaf old coots out here, you know."

With great relief, Kieran spoke his final words of the evening as he smiled across the hall at Brigit. She was standing at the end of a long table with her clipboard in hand checking the numbers on the Bingo card lying in front of her. She gave him the thumbs up and he called out, "That's a good Bingo. Pay that one lucky winner five hundred dollars."

⋇⋇⋇⋇

The storm clouds that had hung over Dearborn for most of Dipsy-Doodle Days were swept away by a stiff Saturday night breeze. Sunday dawned with clear skies over a world brushed sparkling clean and shiny new. All that was left to remind people of the rain were the puddles and muddy ruts near the massive trucks, trailers and RVs belonging to the carnival midway show. The vehicles were lined up at the edge of the field that separated the two downtown strip malls. Cords snaked everywhere and generators droned.

By eleven, when the midway rides came to life, the sun was shining and the whole area began to fill up with people. The population of Dearborn, totally bummed by the soggy parade, rained-out baseball games, blown-over vendor booths and a cancelled bike rodeo, seemed to decide that coming out in droves was the only way to redeem the weekend.

The rhythmic clack of wheels running on metal tracks blended with the whooshing of air brakes and the clank of safety bars being banged into place by the ropey-muscled arms and weather beaten hands of carneys dressed in their leather vests and oil-stained jeans. Tinny music drifted from the merry-go-round with its garishly-painted ponies and competed with the moans coming from the two-story haunted house, gloomy in shades of black and grey and overhung with a spider web netting.

The smell of popcorn and fried onions wafted between the rides and the game booths. A seagull squawked loudly and swooped down to pluck a chunk of discarded hotdog bun from the overflowing trash can. In every direction lights flashed, rides spun and twisted, parents pushed strollers and held the hands of little ones, teenagers ambled along with schooled expressions of boredom and excitement, and sticky-faced kids of all ages ran back and forth wild with sugar, thrills and chills.

Lisa-Marie stood by the little airplanes moving round and round in their static path. She waved to Sophie whose mustard-stained face alternated from wide-eyed wonder to frowning worry.

Justin was also watching Sophie. He looked up when he heard his name. "Hey, Justin ... Justin ... up here." Tabby and Robbie flew overhead encased in a shiny black car at the end of a waving octopus arm – going up and down and around, changing direction and doing it all over again.

Fiona waved to the kids overhead as she made her way to Lisa-Marie's side. Nick was close behind breaking a path through the crowd as he pushed Aidan in the stroller. The baby was wearing a headband with sparkling stars bouncing wildly on antennas over his head. Fiona pinched off chunks of pastel-blue cotton candy from a large funnel filled with the spun confection. She was eating it with obvious pleasure. "I love this stuff," she told Lisa-Marie. "Guess it's not the best example from Dearborn's doctor but some days you have to live it up."

She pointed to the merry-go-round and tapped Nick on the arm, "Let's take Aidan on there."

Nick frowned, "He's too little to sit on one of those horses."

"You have to stand up there and hold him on the thing."

"Why me?"

She laughed, "I'm sure to get queasy after eating all this cotton candy."

Looking skeptical, he said, "Okay, but you're not very safety conscious for a doctor."

Fiona chuckled, "Like I said, you have to live it up some days." As they walked towards the carousel, Fiona told Nick, "This whole thing reminds me of the country fairs we had out on the reserve when I was a kid. Well, minus the packs of crazed dogs running everywhere."

Across the parking lot, near a ring-toss booth with its walls and ceiling adorned with plush animals of all sizes and shapes, Wynter and Mike avoided the hawker who smacked his hand against his leather apron and beckoned them forward, "Three tosses for two bucks. Win that pretty girl of yours a stuffed monkey." The man pulled a smiley-faced monkey out from under the shelf and made it jump wildly up and down.

Mike laughed and waved the guy off as Darlene Evans hailed them from the dart booth further down. She was clutching a long, green, stuffed snake under her arm. "Wynter Snow ... just the gal I was hoping to see." She met them halfway between the two booths. Laying a hand on Wynter's shoulder, she said, "I'm putting together a committee to liaise between the high school and the town council to initiate a community anti-bullying strategy." She smiled broadly and leaned closer to be heard over the wild whooping, clapping and beating of the music coming from the Karaoke stage, "I thought you were just the right person to handle working with high school kids and sitting in stuffy council meetings. What do you say?"

Taken aback by the offer, Wynter looked at Mike who only smiled and lobbed the decision-making ball back into her court. "It sounds interesting, Darlene. I am looking for things in the community to keep me busy."

Darlene smiled, "Great. Come and see me any afternoon at the Town Hall. I'll give you the whole lowdown."

Zach and Arianna caught up to Mike and Wynter in front of Micah Camp's food wagon. Hannah and David were inside the wagon enjoying their first lull since taking over from Charlie and Sadie. Hannah leaned on the counter as the smell of hot oil and frying onions spilled out around her. Talk turned quickly to the ball tournament. "We didn't do so bad," Zach said. "One loss, one win and one cancellation that we could have won if the game hadn't been rained out."

Arianna flicked a side glance his way, "Ya ... not so bad but not that great either."

Justin and Lisa-Marie walked up with Sophie swinging along between them. Zach hailed Justin, "Arianna thinks we could have done better at the tournament. What do you say?"

Justin smiled at David up in the food cart, "David and I did our part. Don't know about the rest of you minor leaguers." Arianna gave Justin a playful slap on the arm as Lisa-Marie told Hannah, "Sophie is starving again."

Sophie called up to the counter, "I have fwies."

Hannah grinned, "One order of fries coming up."

Robbie's voice screamed from nearby, "Sophie, Sophie ... look at us." He and Tabby were in a brightly coloured teacup, spinning for all they were worth as the ride clacked and clanked around on its tilting circular track.

Charlie had come off his shift in the food wagon to walk a large circle around the midway with Sadie. He was on careful alert for any sign of Arianna. Eventually, Sadie wandered off with some other kids from the camp. He was standing alone near the Karaoke stage when he spotted Arianna over by the food booth he'd left not twenty minutes earlier. Zach stood by her side.

The baseball tournament had been one long torture session for him as it became increasingly clear that there could really be something between Arianna and Zach. The number of times they stood close together, with eyes meeting and arms touching added up to more than friendly baseball comradery.

He watched as Zach slipped an arm around Arianna and she smiled up at him. Out of the corner of his eye, he could see Jeremy manning the soundboard at the bottom of the stairs to the Karaoke stage. A lull in business meant the stage was still. Without pausing to think about what he was doing, Charlie crossed over to Jeremy. "Can you cue up that Bruno Mars song?" He tapped his fingers impatiently against his leg, "You know the one ... *girl, you're amazing Just the way you are.*" He sang the last few words.

Jeremy raised an eyebrow at him as Charlie ran up the few steps to the stage and reached for the mike. "Urr ... listen up." He was taken aback for a second by the way his voice boomed out over the midway and by the number of people who turned to stare at him. He gazed across the faces of the crowd and fixed his eyes on Arianna. "I've got a song going out to a special girl."

Moms and dads with strollers, tired parents clutching onto hot and frazzled toddlers, even teenagers stopped to stare. "*Oh, her eyes, her eyes Make the stars look like they're not shining.*" His voice was okay, almost reminiscent of Bruno himself, but his desperate ardor was the thing that lent a gripping quality to his delivery and kept people in place, listening and looking around to spot the girl he was singing to. "*And when you smile, The whole world stops and stares for a while.*"

Arianna had noticed Charlie on the stage right away. Zach had been oblivious at her side as he chatted to some guys he knew from high school. She had felt an uncomfortable thump in her stomach at Charlie's starting dedication. When he got to the line about *lips he could kiss all day if she'd let him*, she stopped glancing over her shoulder to see if a more likely candidate stood behind her. She knew he was staring at her and he was singing to her.

When the song ended, Charlie clutched the mike to his chest. His eyes were glued to hers while a strange pounding echoed in his ears. He felt suddenly exposed to the crowd like he was naked. He put the mike back in its stand and rushed off the stage to the sound of clapping and cheering. Weaving quickly through the crowd, he was by Arianna's side at the food cart before it dawned on him where he was going or what he was doing or what he could possibly say.

Zach was waving goodbye to his friends. He pulled Arianna closer and said, "Let's go over to the game booths. I'll win you a stuffed gorilla."

Arianna looked at Charlie's face and moved away from Zach. "I've got to talk to Charlie for a minute. I'll meet you there." Zach smiled, walked away and disappeared into the crowd. Taking Charlie's arm, Arianna drew him over to the side of the food cart.

When their eyes met, his voice was hushed as he said, "I sang the song for you."

She nodded, "I know."

Misery welled up inside him at the uselessness of his gesture. "I needed you to know." The next words rushed out, "You are amazing, Arianna ... don't laugh, okay."

"I wouldn't laugh, not ever." She leaned closer to him and in that moment, he felt like he was in the song. *Her hair Falls perfectly without her trying.* "I know how you feel. I loved a guy once who didn't feel the same about me. It was so hard. I wouldn't laugh, not ever." His head bent with the weight of his grief. Arianna touched his arm, "Thank you, for the song and for making me feel so special."

Then she was gone, walking away to join Zach. His dreams of Arianna were over. He would never be able to take a deep breath again without the pain. He leaned against the food cart to get his bearings. Then he walked around the back and up the stairs. When he opened the door David and Hannah were holding hands. He sighed heavily. "I'll work the wagon if you guys want to go."

They both turned to stare at him. Hannah said, "We have another hour in our shift." She looked out at the riotous fun all around on the midway and smiled as she clutched David's hand tighter, "Are you sure?"

Charlie nodded and squished into the corner to let them get by. When they were gone, he walked over to the counter where a small hand was reaching up to give him a five-dollar bill. "I want a corn dog," the kid said. Charlie pulled one from the machine and dropped it into a paper holder. The kid stared at him, "Hey ... you're the guy who was singing up there." He pointed over to the stage. Charlie nodded as he handed over the batter-wrapped wiener and took the kid's money. Dropping the change into his pocket, the kid, whose mouth was already crammed with corn dog, said, "My mom said you should be on Canadian idol."

Charlie watched as the kid ran off into the crowd. His heart was broken. He'd never love anyone else the way he loved Arianna. A barren landscape of years spread out in front of him with nothing to look forward to but becoming a lawyer or a teacher or maybe even a Canadian Idol.

Soon enough, Charlie had other things besides his heartbreak to occupy his mind. The food wagon should have been manned by two people. Charlie was now flying from hotdog machine to pop dispenser, throwing bags of chips into grubby hands, taking money and making change so fast he had no time to think of anything else.

THIRTY-TWO

E than came out of the drive at Micah Camp to walk the five-minute commute along the gravel logging road to the sawmill. He was headed for another day of hard labour with Reg chewing his butt out every hour on the hour. These days, the boss man was hitting maximum overdrive on the badger scale. But in the grand scheme of things, Reg was the least of his worries.

He was using the camp video equipment for the preliminary taping of his dance demo rehearsals and what he had seen so far was shit. Plunking a camera on a tripod and dancing in front of it was static and one-dimensional. He was frustrated. Nothing on the tapes was turning out the way the moves looked in his head. His success on this project had gotten tangled up in his mind with the heartbreak of never having Charlie. If he couldn't have one, he had to have the other.

When he got within sight of the sawmill yard, he spotted Justin leaning into the driver's window of Lisa-Marie's red Jeep. The sight of the two friends together like that twigged a memory for Ethan. He picked up his pace and sprinted to the vehicle. As he got within hailing distance, he called out, "Lisa ... I've got something to ask you."

Justin glanced at him with a raised eyebrow but Ethan ignored the look and pushed past him to get in front of the window. "You know a guy who does filming, right?" He snapped his fingers, "A guy named Tyler."

Justin backed away and waved at Lisa, "I better get in there. Reg will have a coronary if I'm not sweating away at my desk when he comes in. If I don't see you before you head off on the Las Vegas trip, have fun and play a few of the slots for me."

Ethan tapped his hands on the edge of the open window as he waited. When Lisa-Marie turned her attention to him, he said, "I can pay. I need to hire someone to film my dance demo." The manic tap, tap on the window continued, "I wouldn't try to cut my own hair, right?"

Lisa gave him a strange look. "Ya, no ... me neither. Tyler's back in Vancouver now but he's coming up to do some filming in a few days. I won't be here because I'll be in Vegas for Wynter's bachelorette party." She stopped and her tone changed, "Not a word about that. It's a surprise. Get your phone out, I'll give you Tyler's number."

After he had cued in the number and checked it with her a second time, Ethan said, "Do you think he'd want to do it?"

Lisa-Marie nodded, "He'd probably be happy to make a few bucks. He loves filming and he'll have the equipment from the movie job." She stopped talking and stared at Ethan's drum beating on her window until he pulled his hands back and shoved them in his pockets. "He's good ... not only at the filming but at putting together a finished piece from a few takes."

Ethan was about to pivot and walk away. Lisa-Marie had the vehicle in drive. He looked back at her. "Justin did a great impression of a jealous guy when Zach made it sound like you and Tyler are a hot item."

She began to turn the wheel, "Justin's a friend and I work with Tyler. Nothing else to tell, Ethan. Sorry not to be more interesting."

⁂

Beulah opened the outdoor oven and reached for the wood paddle to pull the bread out. She glanced behind her for Charlie but he was still on the steps of the bakery shed. "Pick up the pace. The bread won't wait for you."

Though the kid did speed up, Beulah would have had to be blind not to notice he was down in the dumps. At break time, he flopped onto the old sofa with a thump and sat staring straight ahead with his arms crossed over his chest. Beulah leaned against the nearby wall, sipped her coffee and said, "You look like the sorriest excuse for a guy I've seen in a while."

As she glanced out the window to the rushing water in the nearby stream, she heard Charlie say something under his breath. It sounded like – *I'm not what you think I am.* She chuckled, "I don't know about that. What I think you are is a heartbroken guy who liked a girl who didn't know he was alive." Charlie glanced at her with a mixture of surprise and humiliation on his face. "I saw your Karaoke performance." Beulah raised an eyebrow, "Not exactly a secret the way it happened right in the middle of the midway and all. I put two and two together. You've been mooning over Arianna since that first day you met her." She straightened up and finished her coffee as she glanced at the clock on the wall. "If being a baker doesn't work out for you, a career in the music business might be worth considering. You've got a good voice."

Charlie leaned forward and words rushed out, "I never meant to get up there like that, Beulah. I never meant for her to know. It just happened." His shoulders slumped. "Before I knew what I was doing, I was on the stage and singing and looking right at her." He hung his head, "And afterwards, I had to tell her that the song was for her."

Tightening her features to hide the grin that was threatening to take over her face, Beulah said, "I've done some strange things in the name of romance, but I'm glad to say that I've never gone in for public serenades." She shrugged, "Better to have loved and lost than never to have loved at all." Charlie didn't respond. He continued to slump on the sofa. Taking pity on him, Beulah asked, "Is it the first time you've fallen for someone?"

"First and last," Charlie muttered.

Beulah had learned a thing or two about young people over the last few years – first with Lisa-Marie and then with some of the kids she worked with on the ball field and here at the bakery. They blew things out of proportion but the intensity of what they felt was real ... they weren't faking that. The thing was, they didn't understand how much harder the rest of life was going to be. You could tell them – *hey, it's no big deal. Don't sweat the small stuff.* But it isn't small to them. This is the big stuff of their lives. She spoke gently, "A good looking guy like you, come on, you're going to fall for a ton of girls. Some will work out and some won't and that's sort of how the world of love goes ... round and round." She smiled, "Hey, maybe there's a song in there somewhere."

"You don't get it. My life isn't so easy when it comes to girls."

Something in the tone of his voice and the slump of his shoulders caught Beulah's attention. She stood still and waited. Charlie took a deep breath, "I'm the T of LGBTQ." He stared up at Beulah, "You know, transgendered." While Beulah processed that piece of information, Charlie added, "A guy up here," he tapped his head. "But down here," he pointed to the fly of his jeans and shook his head, "I'm transitioning, but I don't know how far I'll go with that."

Beulah frowned. "I wouldn't have guessed that about you ... if it's any consolation." She tipped her head to the side, thinking. "And you like girls?" She paused before adding, "You like girls but I'm guessing not the way I like girls."

"Oh, for shit sakes, I'm not a lesbian." Charlie scowled, "How could I be? I'm a guy. And I'm not a crossdresser either." He rubbed his hands up and down the legs of his jeans. "It's complicated, like I said, it feels way too complicated. How will I ever meet someone who understands?"

His head slumped again and he picked at the edge of the cording on the couch cushion. Beulah sat down beside him. She crossed her arms over her chest, stretched her legs out and studied the toes of her joggers. When the quiet had gone on for a while, she said, "We're all people looking to be accepted for who we are." She tapped the left side of her chest, "It's what's in here that matters. It's not about how you make the parts fit ...it's about how you love. And that is always going be complicated."

⚜⚜⚜⚜

Kieran passed Brigit his burger wrapper and she stuffed it into the paper restaurant bag. They were in his car on the Island Highway. Having left Dearborn at seven a.m. for a morning meeting down Island, they were now tackling the three-hour drive back. Smiling at her, Kieran said, "I'm glad to find a travelling companion who doesn't mind eating burgers on the go."

Brigit laughed, "It's something I got used to in my cop days."

He had enjoyed attending the refugee committee meeting with Brigit. The participants were all friendly and not apt to make a big deal of the fact that a priest was attending the meeting. Hearing a member from one of the sponsored families speak was eye-opening and he felt grateful to have been born in Canada. He was especially proud of Brigit's easy way of dealing with the other group members and her passion for the work they were doing. At first, he had wondered about her having been a police officer but the more he got to know her, the more he could pick up certain traits that spoke loudly of her past. Her voice could command a room when she wanted it to and as she spoke, her bearing demanded attention. She carried herself in a way that indicated vigilance. Not much got by this woman.

He glanced over at her. "Tell me why you stopped being a cop."

"It's a long story and not very uplifting." Her head was bent as she sipped from the straw that stuck out of a paper to-go cup.

"We've got time and I can take a hard story."

"I was naïve, I suppose." She put the cup in the holder and crossed her arms over her body. "The Haitian community I grew up in was filled with strong women. I had good role models – my mom among them. I thought I could do anything if I set my mind to it." She paused to look at him and then returned her gaze to road. "I had friends who thought I was crazy when I was

288

busy at university and pregnant and planning to keep the baby. But their opinions didn't faze me. I chose to be on my own. I wanted a child. I valued my education. It didn't occur to me I couldn't do it all."

Picking at a thread on the cuff of her sweater, she went on, "I'd always dreamed of being a police officer. After getting a degree in criminology, I applied to be a Toronto City cop. I got through the training and I hit the streets." She smiled at the memory. "I loved being a cop. I still miss that life. So ... why did I stop?"

Kieran tapped the brakes, maneuvered a tight curve and shook his head slightly as he said, "Before I decided on the priesthood, I was out of the forces and following the exact same path – a degree in criminology and then a career in the police force. I had the RCMP in mind."

Brigit stared over at him for a moment. "I could see you as a cop. It's an odd coincidence, isn't it? Both of us here now working at jobs so different from what we planned." Brigit sighed and took up her story again. "Like I said, I was naïve. People told me the academy would be brutal because of all the sexism. Well ... brutal isn't the word. You probably know this, but there are men in the world who hate women." She waved her hand, "What they feel is not just occasional resentment or bruised egos or professional jealousy ... it's full on hate." She was quiet for a moment. "The academy was bad but I toughed it out."

When her silence filled the vehicle, Kieran said, "Come on, you've come this far. Don't stop now. I see all those strong women who influenced your life every time I look at you."

"Okay ... you're right. In the police department, the harassment was worse. I thought I would get used to the daily grind of it but I never did." She stared out the passenger side window as she spoke. "For female cops the low-level hostility never stops ...the nude photos in desk drawers, lewd drawings, innocent come-ons that create real fear, accidental gropes here and there. Where I was stationed, not all the guys participated but enough of them did and a few too many in higher positions ever to make complaining of any use." Her fingers continued to work the loose thread. "I'm a fighter and I get pissed off when people are being taken advantage of. I went to bat for another female officer one time too many. They hounded me out on a bullshit claim that I was unstable. So, I tried to fight it." For the first time since she had started to speak, her voice shook. "That's when things got ugly. I stood my ground because I couldn't see any other option. I didn't eat properly, I didn't sleep. Tabby was with my parents and I basically forgot about her. I had to fight. I was going to lose everything – my job, my apartment, my sense of self."

Brigit's shoulders slumped a bit as she dealt with a sudden rush of emotion. "I lost it all anyway. I was ruined, emotionally and financially by the time I gave up and moved in with my parents. They convinced me to take the paltry settlement money the department was offering. Once I knew they had beat me ... well, it did something strange to me. I started giving up on everything." She took a deep breath before continuing. "But, like I said, my mother is a strong woman. She sat me down and made me listen to her. She said I needed to get myself together and move on - for Tabby's sake. So, I did. I got the job at Micah Camp and came out here. End of story."

They covered a few more miles and a roadside bathroom stop before Kieran said, "I'm sorry, Brigit. I'm sorry for you and Tabby and I'm sorry that there are so many damaged men out in the world."

"I'm glad you asked me to talk about it, Kieran." He felt her eyes linger on him for a moment as he paid attention to the road. "I haven't told that story since I came here. Even back in Toronto, I was selective about what I told my parents and, of course, I had to speak in an objective way for depositions. Just the facts and all that."

"Do you have different feelings when you talk about your past now?"

She nodded, "Yes ...time does heal. I suppose I've been coming to that conclusion for a while."

"Is that why you plan to go back to policing someday?"

She smiled at him, "I guess it must be."

❦❦❦❦

Justin mopped his forehead with the sleeve of his shirt as he held the phone to his ear. The sawmill office was like an oven. The rain that had threatened to derail Dipsy-Doodle Days a couple of weeks ago had morphed into full sunshine without even a breeze over the waters of Crater Lake to cool things down. He was on hold with a guy in Cedar Falls who, at the last moment of finalizing a large order for alder flooring, had decided he wasn't sure about his measurements. He'd gone off somewhere to find his notes.

Standing behind his desk close to a fan near the open window, Justin watched as Reg approached the tall metal filing cabinet that stood against the wall. For reasons that God only knew, the boss had decided to rearrange his side of the office right before quitting time. The way Reg's arms were out, he looked like he was either going to attack the cabinet or dance with it. "I'll help you with that, Reg," Justin told him. "Give me a minute to finalize this order. I don't know where this frigging guy has gone. I've been on hold for five minutes."

Reg waved an arm at Justin, "You stay right there on that goddamned phone and get the order. The day I can't move a fucken file cabinet is the day I better hang up my hat." The toothpick in his mouth moved wildly as he pushed his sleeves up, bent his knees and wrapped his arms around what he called the mother-humping beast.

Mike walked into the office with Ethan right behind him. "Quitting time, boss." Mike called out. He looked at Justin and jerked a thumb towards Reg, "What the hell is he doing?"

Suddenly, Reg's arms dropped away from the cabinet and he backed up, clutching at his chest. He was making a strange grunting sound. Justin dropped the phone on the desk and moved forward. "Jesus, Reg ... what is it?"

Straightening up slightly, Reg swayed on his feet, "Whoa ... I felt like I had a fucken hand right inside my chest squeezing."

Given Reg's pallor, the sweat on his forehead and his own description of what he had felt, Justin knew what was happening. The realization hit him like a freight truck. The guy wasn't going to have a coronary someday, he was having a cardiac incident right this moment. "You've got to sit down, now, Reg." He turned to Mike, "Get that guy off the phone and call 911." He swung around to Ethan, "Bring me the first aid kit though I don't know what use the bloody thing is going to be."

Reg was standing straighter. He had his balance. He waved Justin back, "It's nothing. Stop your goddamned panicking." He looked at Mike who was on his way to the phone, "Don't even think of touching that phone."

Mike ignored the boss. Speaking into the phone he said, "Get off the frigging line, we've got a medical emergency here."

Justin gripped Reg's arm, "You are having a heart attack." He called over to Mike, "When you get them on the phone, tell them we're going to need a med-evac chopper right away." Propelling Reg towards his office chair, Justin told him, "You're going to sit down right now or you'll have more than a coronary to worry about. I'll sock you in the jaw if you don't do exactly what I tell you to do."

"Ya, ya ... okay." Reg sat down. "You might be onto something. The pain's not backing off." Justin pulled Reg's hat off and loosened his collar. He plucked the toothpick out of his mouth and threw it in the garbage can.

Mike walked across the office with the phone, "I've got the 911 operator. She wants to talk to you."

Justin reached for the phone as Ethan slid the first aid kit onto the desk and flipped open the lid. Turning his eyes to the open kit and holding the phone to his ear, Justin told the operator Reg's symptoms. "No ... we don't have any baby aspirin in the first aid kit. Negative on the portable defibrillator as well." He listened for another moment and then said, "Right ... got it."

He passed the phone back to Mike and held his hand up for quiet, "I've got to take his pulse." After doing that, he looked closely at Reg to assess his condition. He was conscious, leaning into the pain in his chest as he slumped in the chair. His breathing was shallow, probably due to the pain. Justin signaled for Mike to give him the phone again so he could relay the information to the 911 operator. Handing it back to Mike, he explained, "They want us to stay on the line. You take it. Let me know if they have any other instructions."

Mike nodded and told Ethan, "Get your cell phone out and call Liam. Tell him to get up here right now." Ethan pulled out his phone and ran his finger down the directory of numbers on the wall by Reg's desk.

"Listen up now Reg ... the chopper is on its way," Justin spoke in a steady voice. "You've got nothing to worry about, man. You take it easy and we'll get you through this."

Reg shook his head slowly as he whispered, "Death from moving a fucken file cabinet is a bad way to cash in my chips. Hope it doesn't come to that."

"You aren't cashing in anything, Reg. You hear me, hang in there."

Ethan shoved his cell phone back in his pocket as he said, "Liam's on his way."

Mike spoke into the phone, "Right." He called out to Justin, "Chopper's ten minutes out."

Justin alternated between watching the minute hand crawl its way around the clock and checking Reg's condition. He felt absolutely useless. "Keep breathing, man. Don't go under on me." He kept repeating the words to Reg until he heard the whirring of the chopper blades coming in suddenly out of nowhere. The next thing he knew, Liam was in the room with the paramedics right behind him. Then he was standing back and watching like everyone else.

It seemed like no time at all passed before Reg was on the stretcher, wearing an oxygen mask and being pushed out the door. They all followed to the yard to watch as the chopper rose into the air, banked and became a smaller and smaller speck as it flew away. Liam stood with them and said, "You guys did good." His tone was a bit shaky but filled with pride.

Justin's shoulders slumped, "I can't believe the number of times that I joked he'd have a coronary. And he's been showing the signs for weeks and giving us a bullshit line about heartburn. I should have seen it coming."

"I know what you mean," Liam said. "I told Izzy months ago I was worried about him."

Mike shoved his hands in his pocket as he spoke, "What could any of us have done even if we had taken his symptoms more seriously? He wasn't going to listen. You saw it yourself, Justin. You had to threaten to punch him out before he'd sit the hell down."

Ethan had been quiet through the whole event – doing whatever he was told to do but looking stunned. He beat a tattoo of sound against his legs with his work gloves as he said, "I think we've just been through that shit storm Reg is always warning us about."

⁂

Later that night, Liam awoke from a nightmare sweating and shaking. Izzy shook him gently and called his name. He tried to catch his ragged breath and pull himself out of the dream. He could see Caleb's body on the stretcher; a white sheet was pulled over his face. The watch on his exposed wrist glittered in the sunlight flickering off the chopper blades. But then Reg was on the stretcher and then it was Liam himself laid out flat staring up at those spinning blades. He rolled over and pulled Izzy close to him. She whispered, "Hey ... breathe. It's going to be okay."

He did what he was told. He'd been in the aftermath of nightmares enough to know the drill. But he couldn't turn off the thoughts. Caleb had died on the woodlot and they hadn't been able to save him. They loaded him on a stretcher and took him away. Bethany had nearly drowned and they flew her away in a helicopter. Reg was showing all the early signs of a heart attack and he was flown away, too. But Liam was still here. He slowly named all the people who mattered to him, one-by-one like a litany, accounting for each one. Everything was going to be okay. He said it over and over to himself until sleep slid in from the quiet and took him away.

THIRTY-THREE

Justin stood back from the saw and made sure he was in Mike's sightline before he waved his arms over his head. After a moment, Mike gave him the thumbs up, pressed a few buttons and the high-pitched whirring sound ramped down as the revolving blade of the saw began to slow. Removing his ear protection and pushing his safety glasses up on his head, Mike came down the few stairs from the platform where he stood to operate the saw. He walked over to Justin, "What's going on?"

"I got a message from Liam. He's coming up to talk to us."

As they began to walk towards the office, Mike said, "He must have some news about Reg."

Justin nodded, "I'll make some coffee. You go and get Ethan from the yard."

Later, when they were all gathered around the lunch table, Liam said, "Reg had triple bypass surgery last night. I heard from Josie right before I came up that he's resting as comfortably as can be expected ... for Reg." He smiled and the other guys' expressions all indicated they understood what roping Reg into a hospital bed might look like. "He'll be down Island for a couple of weeks. Josie tells me that he'll need to take things easy for at least three months after that."

Taking a drink of coffee, Liam made eye contact with each of them. "Izzy and I want to thank you. Your reactions demonstrated quick thinking and working together in an emergency. You kept your heads. That's more than a lot of guys would have done." He paused before adding, "And we appreciate the way you came in today and got back to work as usual."

Ethan spoke up, "Seemed like Reg would appreciate us busting our butts even if he wasn't here to see it."

"Reg worked hard lining up the orders we've got on the go." Justin added, "We don't want to let him down."

Mike drummed his fingers on the edge of the table as he spoke, "It makes you think, that's for sure. The way he was laid out on that stretcher."

"We're getting a bottle of baby aspirin for every first aid kit," Justin stared at the one that hung on the wall of the lunchroom. "A portable defibrillator would be a good idea, too." He frowned, "I felt useless waiting for that chopper to land, wondering if Reg's heart was going to stop and he'd die right in front of me."

Ethan stared at Justin, "You seemed totally on top of everything, man. Cool as a cucumber. I felt like pissing my pants I was so scared."

Reaching out a hand, Mike laid it on Justin's back, "If I ever go down, out on that saw, I want to see your face hunched over me and hear your voice telling me to hang on, help is on the way."

Pushing his empty cup aside, Liam said, "With Reg not coming back for at least three months, what are we going to do about *Crater Lake Timber*?" Silence greeted his words. He looked at Justin. "Izzy and I would like to offer you the job of running the place." The expression on Justin's face made Liam hold up his hand. "Hang on. Think about it for a minute. Ever since you started at the sawmill, you've been learning the business from the ground up. You've been shadowing Reg and active in the day-to-day management. You know the ins and outs of the selective logging operations and the sawmill side of things. You've got an engineering degree and industrial first aid. You are more than qualified."

Doubt clouded Justin's features. "Shadowing Reg is one thing. Running the whole show is something else."

"Believe me, I know that," Liam told him. "I followed Caleb around this place tighter than a shadow for years. But when he died, I wasn't half as qualified for the job as you are right now."

Justin crossed his arms over his chest and leaned back in his chair. "They've called me for a second interview on that Western Forest job. I think I've got a shot at it. The money's good, but that isn't the only thing I'm after." He met Liam's gaze, "I wanted to swim around in a bigger pool."

"Western Forest isn't going anywhere and you'll only look better with the experience you'll get running this little pond."

Justin glanced at Mike who was trying to keep his face neutral on the proposal but not doing a good job. He gave it another moment of thought. "Okay, but the minute Reg wants his job back, he's got it. And Mike's got to run the sawmill side of things."

Mike held up his hand, "Whoa, man. I operate the saw. I don't want to do paperwork or deal with clients."

"You won't have to," Justin told him. "I'll manage the paperwork and the clients but I want you in charge of everything that happens with those saws. I want to know that when I line up an order, you're ready to make sure it gets filled."

"I can do that." Mike reached his hand across the table to Justin and they shook on the deal.

Justin told Liam, "Mike will need a raise."

"I guess that will be your first executive decision," Liam said as he stood up. "That along with getting your portable defibrillator and your baby aspirin."

Ethan leaned across the table to pluck a toothpick from the glass jar on the table. He passed it over to the new boss. "Thought you might need this," he said with a grin. Justin laughed as Ethan did his Reg imitation, "We got a shit storm of work coming down on us boys. And there's going to be hell to pay if any of you bloody slackers even think of trying to get out of here early. I'll be kicking your ass so far up that woodlot there won't be a fucken thing left of you but your boots sitting out in that goddamned yard."

✄ ✄ ✄ ✄

Jeremy stopped by the paper and soap shop in the hopes of seeing Paula. Ever since they had shared a coffee together, he had been trying to run into her to recreate the experience or, with any luck, move things forward. As he entered the shop, he didn't find Paula but he saw Sadie holding Noah's hand and heard her telling Lisa-Marie, "Seriously ... I don't feel well. I have to leave."

Lisa-Marie shook her head, "No way. I have my hands full with managing the shop. I'm not Josie. I can't keep an eye on paper and soap production and babysit Noah at the same time."

"Please ... Paula will be finished her class in an hour." Sadie now had her free hand on her stomach like her condition was worsening.

"Oh, go then," Lisa-Marie told her. "I don't want you making everyone else sick."

As Sadie passed him in the doorway, Jeremy had an idea. He went into the shop. "Hey, Lisa. How are things going?"

"Not great." She had hoisted Noah up on her hip and was staring over towards the soap vats where a couple of kids in black aprons were waiting for her. "Sadie's ditched on me and I need to supervise this batch of soap but I can't very well have Noah hanging over the vat while I do it."

Jeremy held out his arms for the child, "I'll take him to the computer lab. I'll text Paula that he's with me."

"Thanks. I'm really scrambling here. I've run the shop before but never with Josie out of town and she always had me working on the easy days. I don't want to screw up this batch of soap."

An hour later, Paula came into the computer lab where Jeremy was dragging Noah around in a rolling chair. Noah had an intense look on his face as he gazed at the screen of the cell phone clutched tightly in his little hands. Jeremy was leaning over a computer, instructing one of the residents, "It's just coding, it's not rocket science." Holding Noah's chair with one hand, he reached across to the keyboard with the other. His fingers rapidly punched a few keys and he straightened up, "There, that should get you back on track."

He turned and saw Paula staring at him. Pushing Noah in front of himself, he crossed the classroom toward her. She glanced from Noah's rapt attention to Jeremy's face, "I got your text but I never imagined you had students, Jeremy. Someone should have come and got me to take him." Paula plucked Noah out of the chair and pried the cell phone out of his hand. He howled with outrage.

She handed Jeremy his phone, "Thanks, I mean it. He can be a little dynamo at times. I hope he behaved."

"Once he got his hands on that phone, he sat in the chair like Captain Picard on the Starship Enterprise." He cringed. Star Trek remarks had killed more than one of his budding romances and comparing Noah – who seriously lacked hair for a kid over two – to Captain Picard might rub Paula the wrong way.

"I loved that show." Clearly oblivious to her son's bald head, she smiled down at Noah.

Ignoring the voice from behind the computer screen calling his name, Jeremy walked Paula and Noah to the door. "I'm taking my girls to the *Beach Road Café* for fish and chips after work. Why don't you and Noah join us?" Paula hesitated and Jeremy said, "They want to meet the woman who came up with the scheme to swap housework for the WiFi password." He grinned at her.

"I was going to take Noah to family swim at the pool tonight. It's sort of lonely at Mom's place on my own."

Jeremy slapped his forehead, "I'm sorry. How is Reg?"

"He's going to be alright but Mom's staying down Island with him for another week."

Leaning against the door jamb, Jeremy tickled Noah and got a smile out of the kid. He looked at Paula, "My girls love the pool. Have dinner with us first and then we'll all go swimming."

"Okay, it sounds like fun. But you have to promise to protect me from them if they get hostile over the WiFi thing."

❧ ❧ ❧ ❧

"I'll have to set this up ... come at it slowly," Kieran told Izzy.

She nodded, "Tell the story any way that makes sense for you." She sat quietly and waited. They had come to a crucial stage in the counselling process. They had already handled surface issues and had built up a high level of trust. Kieran was ready to go deeper.

"Okay ... I grew up Catholic, went to parochial schools and attended church every Sunday. I was an altar boy." His eyes met Izzy's, "I liked hanging around the church. Home was chaotic and the rectory was quiet. There was always a warm meal and there were shelves of books. Even as a kid, I loved to read." His voice deepened with emotion, "Sean was jealous and he wanted to go with me but I wouldn't let him. He thought I wanted all the fun to myself but that wasn't the reason. I always brought home more than half of any food I got, and I gave it to him. Sean was like a part of me."

Any mention of Sean was always accompanied by emotion. Into the silence, Izzy asked, "Why leave Sean out?"

"I was protecting him." Kieran's hands clenched in his lap. "I paid a price for hanging out at the rectory and I had to protect Sean from that." Deep in the memory of that time, Kieran's eyes were far away. "One day when Sean tried to follow me, I told him straight out - *to get the food, you have to stand by Father O'Malley's chair while he puts his hand on your bum and uses his other hand to play with his wiener.*" Kieran raised an eyebrow and despite the weight of the story, a wry look covered his face. "Sean thought my warning through for a minute and then you know what he said?" Izzy shook her head and he added, "*Doesn't sound so bad. Better than a smack on the head from Dad. If we both went, we'd get double the food.*" Kieran's hands clenched again, "But I didn't let him go. Being in the rectory wasn't as a bad as a smack from Dad, that was true. But that didn't mean it was fun either."

"The words you used to describe to Sean what was happening at the rectory ... what the priest was doing ... you must have been young."

"I was eight and it went on for a couple of years. Then we got a new priest and he never wanted kids hanging around the rectory. Sean always said he was a miserly old bastard who couldn't even be bothered to have a fiddle with his woody in exchange for giving a kid a bit of food. Then Sean would laugh and roll around on the ground grabbing at his pants. He was definitely one to see the humorous side of things."

When Kieran spoke in Sean's voice his whole demeanor changed. Izzy noted the good-natured indulgence with which he must always have dealt with Sean, even when he was a child of eight and Sean only a year younger. The abuse story was so bound up with Sean that Izzy concentrated closely on discerning the separate threads. Drawing now on one thread over another, she asked, "Do you remember how you felt, at the time, about what happened at the rectory with the priest?"

Kieran forehead creased in thought. "I don't remember feeling much of anything. I was mostly thinking about the hot food that would soon be on the table and which book I would pick out next. Later, if I ever thought about it at all, I mostly felt pity for the old guy." He looked at her and his intensity told her he needed her to understand. "He was so lonely and desperate in a pitiful, creepy way, and though it couldn't ever make up for what he'd done, he always tried to even the score with the food and the books."

Probing gently, Izzy asked, "Did all of this begin to bother you when you were studying to be a priest yourself?"

"No ... and not when I was starting out in the priesthood either." Kieran was shaking his head as he spoke, "You don't understand what it was like for me in the seminary or interacting with other priests. When it came to matters below the belt, anything that had ever happened to many of those men had been buried beneath layers of concrete. I had a strong hunch that half of them were breaking their vows of celibacy. I'm not saying they were pedophiles, though a few did show signs of the disorder. Some of the men were gay, others were in relationships with women. So, there was a lot of guilt. Then there were the ones who seemed so sexually stunted they were either addicted to porn or so afraid of their own bodies they could barely get out of their clothes to shower." He let out a deep breath. "The pretense of celibacy led to a culture of secrecy and shame when it came to anything having to do with sex. Any gathering of priests was the last place where what happened to me in that rectory would ever have been discussed."

"When did it start to be an issue for you?"

Staring out the nearby window, Kieran said, "I told you about those closed doors that started to open in my mind after Sean died?" He glanced at her for affirmation. "I was surprised when these memories showed up. Remembering made me drink."

Kieran was thoughtful, deep in a process of making sense of his past. "I know that when I hit my teens, I had a difficult time, running wild and getting in trouble. But that was common for most boys in our town. One night, Sean and I broke into a gas station and I got caught. When we heard the sirens, I pushed Sean out of the back window and told him to run like hell. A local cop took an interest in me and got me into a sports program so I could blow off some steam. He said he had his eyes on me, so I better not screw up again."

He shifted in his chair but his hands remained clenched. "The only thing I can come up with is that what happened with the priest strengthened a belief I learned at home ... nothing comes for free. My dad always used to say - *you wanna dance, you gotta pay the band.*"

In his father's voice, Kieran's body tightened with stress, as if he were waiting for a blow to fall. He went on, "I lived my life like there was this ledger somewhere and I had to fill my side of the page so everything could come out right."

A plea for understanding filled the room and Izzy leaned forward in her chair as Kieran kept speaking. "I remember, in the seminary, feeling desperate to believe that God's love was unconditional, but I never bought it. When Sean died, I saw that no matter what I did myself or let others do to me, that ledger would never come out even. When I lost the ledger, I lost all sense of being able to control anything. Everything fell apart. But it wasn't until I stopped drinking that I figured out I was pissed off."

Izzy reached across and gently touched Kieran's clenched hands. She sat back and said, "I suppose it comes down to how we make sense of events in our lives, doesn't it? Like an onion, the outer layer of meaning you assigned to what happened in the priest's sitting room was that it amounted to nothing more than a simple exchange you went through to provide for you and Sean, to meet your basic needs. And like Sean said, it was better than a smack in the head from your dad. Peel that layer back and underneath, you discover the whole experience was contributing to a core belief system ... a faulty one."

"Ya, and under that I found anger." He leaned forward and rested his bent elbows on his knees. His stared at her over his folded hands. "Being turned into an object was the worst part. The priest didn't see me; I could have been anyone or any warm piece of flesh. I wish Sean was alive now so I could tell him that getting a smack in the head from Dad wasn't nearly as bad as the embarrassment and degradation of standing in that room and not being seen." He shook his head slowly. "Our old man was a real bastard for eye-contact. At least when I got a smack from Dad, I knew he saw me."

THIRTY-FOUR

T yler had Micah Camp's video camera on its tripod, one of his own cameras on a skid and a huge handheld one on his shoulder. Ethan had commandeered the living room of the main building by posting signs at every doorway - *Do Not Enter - Taping in Progress.* The large sofas, chairs and tables had all been moved to the back of the room, leaving the area in front of the huge brick fireplace open.

Tyler gestured with his fingers to Sadie, "Move those cords back and then get over here. I need you by that camera on the right." He motioned to Ethan, "Run through the moves once for me before we start filming."

Wearing tight pants and T-shirt, Ethan was dressed all in black. His ashy blond hair and pale skin provided a sharp contrast. Calling to Hannah, he said, "Let's go, beautiful."

Tyler cued the music and the opening notes slammed through the empty room. As the song progressed, he folded his arms over his chest and tapped his booted foot. Ethan spun past him. Then, with exaggerated sensuality, he slid his body against Hannah's as the lyrics of the song intoned - *look into my eyes and I'll own you.*

David stood in the dining room watching as the song ended. He was the only resident in the building and he was allowed in simply because he had to work. Even though most of the residents were off on a trip to Victoria for the long weekend, Roland had laid down the law to those left behind that they were not to go anywhere near the main building from two until six Friday afternoon. David's eyes widened at Ethan's moves and Hannah's outfit. She was wearing a very tight, black skirt and a shirt opened two buttons down the front. She had explained to him that her role was simply to be a live prop for

Ethan's dance moves. He took a deep breath as he stared at her. She was a very hot-looking prop.

Ethan jumped up from the floor where he had done a dramatic arched backflip into a split as his finale move. He caught his breath as Tyler walked towards him. "Okay, man. That's impressive. I'm going to run through it with only the handheld on this take and lay in some time markers." He stared up at the high ceiling. "The sound's okay in here but we'll do way better laying in the music track afterwards."

At the end of the second take, Ethan stood close to Tyler mopping his forehead with a towel and watching the small screen on the camera. "Ya, I see what you're saying."

They walked over to Hannah. Tyler pointed at her shirt, "What do you have on under that?"

Surprise edged her voice as she looked down at her shirt. "My bra."

"Ya, I guessed that. What kind of bra?"

Frowning, she said, "Black with some lace."

He looked her up and down for a moment. "Great, take the shirt off. It's in the way and we need to turn up the heat." Walking away, he called over his shoulder at Ethan, "I'm going to run all three cameras on you this time. Remember what I told you about not going too deep into the corners. I don't want to lose you in the shadows."

Hannah looked towards the dining room. David had gone back to work. "I don't know, Ethan –,"

"Come on, this isn't going on YouTube. A handful of people are going to see this video. Don't take this the wrong way, but they're going to be looking at me." Tucking his shirt in tightly at the back, Ethan pressured her, "Do what he says, Hannah. Tyler knows what he's talking about and this change isn't just for effect. My hand is pulling your shirt askew every time I do that slide up your body. It looks like crap on the tape."

"Okay, okay," Hannah conceded as she unbuttoned her shirt and slid it off her shoulders.

He gave her the once over. "You're no more exposed than you were for that beauty pageant dance. And you look yummy." He leaned forward and kissed her cheek.

The next time David came from the kitchen to the dining room to sneak a look at the taping, he saw Hannah with her shirt off; her back was arched as she looked over her shoulder at Ethan. He was gyrating his hips behind her and raking his hands up her body as he touched his lips along her exposed neck. The lyrics blasted – *kiss me till you're drunk and I'll show you* –

David's mouth went dry and his heart started to thump – *all the moves like Jagger* – echoed through his head. He wasn't sure whether he should be pissed off at the way she was exposing herself for everyone to see or simply glad he was one of the onlookers.

Packing up his gear later, Tyler leaned close to Sadie and whispered something in her ear. She laughed. Ethan who had been moving the living room furniture back, looked up in time to see Tyler lay a hand low on the girl's back as he spoke to her. Using his hip to give the chair a last nudge into place, Ethan walked over to Tyler, grabbed the guy's arm and pulled him away a few steps. "Party's over, man. I'm impressed with your work and I can't wait to see how the finished product comes out." He glanced over at Sadie, "But hands off the hired help. Look for someone your own age."

Tyler gave him a long, slow look that lingered at Ethan's crotch before rising to his face. "Like you?" he asked.

Ethan smiled, "If I'm your type."

Nodding with a grin of his own, Tyler said, "Meet me over by my van when we finish up. I know somewhere we can go."

✻✻✻✻✻

Coming out of the doors of the main building, Hannah pulled David around the corner. Her long hair fell around her face and swept over David's arm as she pushed her body against his. Her hands locked around his neck. "That dance was so wild. I'm hot everywhere. I knew you were watching." She grinned at him, "Did you like what you saw?"

David's hands slid up her back and drew her closer. They kissed and his response went from the slow burn he'd felt while watching her dance to full out conflagration. Before he knew what was happening, her body was molded to his; he was pulling her even closer and found no resistance in her at all.

Hannah gasped words against his mouth, "Come on, I know where we can go." She grabbed his hand and walked quickly down the trail towards the boat shed. Once inside the building, she spun around and backed him against the wall. He was kissing her again and this time his hands were sliding up inside her shirt. Then he was touching the black bra she'd worn as she had shimmied, slid and crawled through Ethan's dance video.

She pulled at his belt, undid his jeans and whispered in his ear, "We're doing this ... we're really going to do this." As her hand brushed against him, he shuddered with the shock of it. Suddenly, she stopped and though he desperately wanted her to continue, she was now unbuttoning her shirt and sliding it from her shoulders. Driven by her own unchecked feelings, she

303

released the black bra, kicked off her shoes and stepped out of her skirt.

She pulled him down onto the ground with her and everything became a blur of bare, hot skin and pounding excitement – he felt a condom pressed into his hand and he fumbled around with it. Before he had time to panic about not knowing what to do next, she was helping him and clumsily guiding him inside her. From far, far away he heard her cry – a sharp, strange sound that came too late for him to stop. He moved with an urgency that blocked out everything but searing need.

When he did stop, only moments had passed but they felt like an eternity to David. Gasping for breath, he looked down at Hannah. All around her head, her hair splayed over the boards of the floor and her clenched hands were by her side. She was making small, sniffing sounds. "Hannah," he said her name quietly, then again, "Hannah, are you okay?"

Her hands came up to push him off her body. She rolled away and sat up, grabbing erratically for her clothes. "I better get going."

He touched her arm but she flinched away from him. "Wait ... say something. Was it okay?"

She had slithered into her underwear and was doing up her bra. She turned to look for her shirt. He handed it to her and watched as she shrugged her way into it. "No ... it wasn't. This was my first time." She wiped at her eyes. "I'm not blaming you."

Feeling like a fool with his shirt open and his pants off, David quickly removed the condom and pulled on his clothes. She was already moving towards the door, "Hannah, wait. Did I hurt you?"

He could see tears running down her face and shining in the light from outside the door. "It's not your fault. I wanted to do this as much as you did."

With his misery now in exact proportion to the elation he had felt only moments before, David said, "Why didn't you tell me. I thought ... the way you kissed me and said we should come down here ... I thought you had –,"

"Done it a ton of times?" she asked him. "That makes me sound like a slut."

He shook his head, "I didn't mean it like that. I've never done anything like this before. I had never even kissed a girl until I met you."

Hannah bowed her head as she leaned back against the door. "I just didn't want to be a virgin anymore. I didn't know having sex would be like that. I'm sorry, David. I've got to go now." She turned, went out the door and ran up the path towards the parking lot and her car.

Lisa-Marie and Arianna sprawled on one bed. Wynter sat on the other with her long, tanned legs stretched out in front of her and her back against the headboard. It was almost midnight and their first day in Vegas for Wynter's bachelorette weekend had been nonstop fun.

They had arrived at the Mirage in the early afternoon, spinning around and giggling as they took in the volcano outside and the razzle-dazzle inside. They had dropped their luggage in the room, donned bikinis and headed poolside. Lisa-Marie had reserved a cabana for the afternoon. They were lucking out with the weather – the temperature was uncharacteristically cool for August – only in the high 80s. They laughed at that as they lounged in and out of the shade. Lisa-Marie had brought Wynter a special tiara to wear that said Bride-to-Be – Viva Las Vegas. She wore it proudly because anything would go with a fluorescent yellow string bikini on a fashion model body.

They had wandered the strip and the nearby casinos, eating, drinking and enjoying themselves. Lisa-Marie had stopped at the Nike of Samothrace statue near Caesar's Palace. "It's Izzy's statue. She told me about it being here ages ago." She forced them all to get their picture taken posing under the wings of the statue in front of a huge fountain and its dazzling blue pool.

They were now in for the night, lying in the room, playing a party game for which Maddy had sent Lisa-Marie the link. They had already shared hilarious stories about their worst ever period mishaps, bra disasters and their most embarrassing situation related to a bodily function. Staring at her phone, Lisa-Marie moaned as she said, "This is really bad." She glanced dramatically at the other two, "How did you lose your virginity?"

Responding to a chorus of groans, Lisa-Marie sat up crossed-legged on the bed and said, "Okay, okay ... I'll go first. My story is crappy, though, I warn you." She made a face as she said, "I was fifteen, working a summer job at Subway. He was the night manager – with an acne-covered face and big ears. It happened in the walk-in cooler and, if you try to picture that setting ... boxes overflowing with rotting lettuce, the smell of cold cuts, me sprawled out on a crate ... the experience was about as bad as you can imagine." She sipped from her glass of wine and glanced over the rim at Arianna and Wynter. They were staring back at her in shock. "Someone say something. I can hardly end up dying of embarrassment five years after the fact."

Arianna spoke up, "I'll go ... but ... I don't know how to say this."

Lisa-Marie stared at her, "Come on. It can't be as bad as my story."

"I haven't ... actually."

Frowning, Lisa-Marie asked, "You haven't actually what?"

"Done it." Arianna rushed on, "I feel like I'm cheating at the game." She held up her hand, "Wait ... I've got something. One time, when Dylan was still finding himself," she made air quotes with her fingers, "we went to the boat shed together. I would have done it with him in a minute but he couldn't ... I felt sorry for him and I wanted him to like me so I went down on him."

Wynter made a sympathetic noise and Lisa-Marie wrinkled her nose and said, "Hmm ... that sucks."

Wynter and Arianna stared at her and then they all started laughing hysterically, rolling on the bed and holding their stomachs. Finally, Lisa-Marie sat up and choking down a laugh, she looked at Arianna. "What about you and Zach? I thought maybe the two of you were getting it on out in that library bus."

Arianna shook her head. "We've come close. I like him, a lot. I want to be sure." Glancing over at Lisa, Arianna said, "He's nice. But I'm not telling you anything you don't know. You dated him."

Lisa-Marie guessed that Arianna had assumed more about her relationship with Zach than was true. "I never slept with Zach. He is nice, though." She changed the subject by pointing over at Wynter, "Your turn bride-to-be. Fess up. When did you do the dirty deed?"

Wynter grinned. "I thought you'd never ask." She stared up at the ceiling looking as if she were about to sing a hymn. "Mike and me, out on the west coast in a tent with the waves crashing on the shore." She sighed heavily as she looked over at them, "It was the most romantic night of my life."

Shouting, "Oh my God," Arianna and Lisa-Marie began to heave the multiple pillows from their bed at Wynter. She dodged around the flying objects as she said, "Did I say there was a full moon and Mike brought roses and my favourite chocolates?"

Having run out of pillows, Lisa-Marie fell back on the bed. "Okay, that's it." She threw her hands up in the air. "No more of that game. You guys make me feel like the skank who got mistakenly invited to the Disney Princess Party."

"Hey," Arianna said, reaching out a foot to nudge Lisa-Marie's leg, "I don't think my story qualified for princess status." She rolled over onto her stomach. "Have you ever thought about how you hardly ever see the brown Disney princesses?"

Wynter and Lisa-Marie gave her a blank stare. Arianna went on, "You know ... Pocahontas and Mulan and Jasmine and that black girl ... Tianna.

Stores always shove them on the back of the toy shelves and they never get in any of the cool commercials."

Shaking her head, Lisa-Marie stared at Arianna, "That is something I hadn't given much thought to. Now I won't be able to walk down a toy aisle in Walmart without trying to see if they have a brown Disney princess on display. Thanks for that."

Hugging a stray pillow to her chest, Wynter sighed. "This is so much fun and we still have Lady Gaga to look forward to tomorrow night."

$$\maltese\maltese\maltese\maltese$$

Zach drummed his hands on the kitchen table at Justin's cabin. "Doesn't look like Ethan's going to show. Should we start without him?"

Justin shrugged, "He must have got delayed with his dance video thing. He was having it filmed this afternoon, right?" He looked over at Mike for confirmation.

"That's why he said he needed the afternoon off."

Taking a drink of his beer, Zach said, "It sure is quiet out here for a long weekend."

"It's always quiet out here," Justin told him. "That's what I like about the place. But lots of people are away."

Zach nodded, "Arianna and Lisa-Marie went to Vegas for the bachelorette weekend."

"Izzy and Bethany and Brigit are chaperoning a bunch of Micah Camp kids down in Victoria," Justin told them. "Tabby and Robbie are with them."

Mike frowned, "Who's left?"

"Liam and Sophie next door. Nick and Fiona and their kid over at the Saltbox. Skeleton crew at Micah Camp. I heard that Roland has gone to Vancouver for the weekend." Justin tore open a bag of potato chips and tossed a handful into his mouth.

Mike shuffled the cards a few times and laid the deck down in front of him. "Doesn't seem right without Ethan. Who knew the guy was going to become such a big part of poker night?"

"I'll be glad when his frigging dance demo thing is finished. Ethan has been twitchy the last couple of weeks." Justin said as he shook out a few more chips.

Zach pointed at the deck, "Deal the cards, bro. We got nothing else to do out here."

Mike picked up the deck and began to deal. "Poor, Zach. Are you bummed because Arianna's away?"

Zach's voice dropped, "I'm not going to bullshit you guys. I really like her."

Mike chuckled and raised his eyes to the ceiling, "Praise the Lord. I never thought I'd see you cow-eyed over a girl. Isn't it always the other way around?" He glanced over at Justin. "And what about you? Have you found the guts to pull the plug on Lauren, yet? Just asking because of the wedding guest list."

Justin picked up his cards. His voice had a hard edge. "You may be about to enter married bliss with the most gorgeous girl in the world, Mike, but that doesn't give you license to ask that sort of question."

Mike held his hands up in surrender, "Okay, but I've got to tell you, that attitude says a lot."

They were taking a break a couple of hours later when Mike said, "I wonder if Ethan is all freaked out about Reg." He looked at Justin, "That could be making him twitchy. I've had a few sleepless nights myself. What happened to Reg ... makes a guy think."

Justin was over by the counter pouring a drink. "Life is short, man."

Shaking his head, Mike agreed, "I know. That's exactly what I've been telling myself. I hate all the wedding tension around my house. Father Kieran said Wynter and I should do what makes us happy. It's our wedding, no one else's." He chugged his beer and added, "I think we should move out now. The Lady Brit is ready."

Zach returned from the bathroom in time to hear Mike's words. He sat back down at the table and said, "Don't do that, Mike. Seriously. It will mean starting things out on a bad footing with Mom. She'll never get over it if you move in with Wynter before you guys get married." Leaning back in his chair, Zach's eyes lit up. He smacked his hands down on the table and his chair thumped on the floor. "Elope. I told you to do it ages ago. Then you'll be married and you can move out and all the tension is gone ... poof." He snapped his fingers.

Mike punched Zach in the arm, "Ya ... like that won't make Mom think Wynter and I started off on the wrong foot."

"Mom brought this on herself. Come on, Mike, be a man of action for once. Where is the best place in the world to get married?" Zach paused and looked from Mike to Justin. "Vegas. Where is your fiancé right now?" He tapped his finger against his temple a couple of times, "Think ... Vegas."

Justin laughed, "How much have you had to drink, Zach? That is one crazy ass idea." He slammed his hand on the table. "But I like it."

Mike folded his arms over his chest, "Do you think I don't want to be married to Wynter right now and have all this wedding bullshit behind us? It's not that easy to get married. Shit ... Wynter has a whole binder of notes and lists and forms and stuff."

Zach's fingers had been flying over the screen of his phone. "It's apparently not that complicated in Vegas. You can get a marriage license for sixty bucks US. The place you get the license is open twenty-four hours a day. All you need is your driver's license or passport. You can get married as soon as you have the license." He was still tapping on the phone. "Hey, listen up, there's this Elvis impersonator who's licensed to marry people. When you book with him at the Viva Las Vegas Chapel, you get driven to the chapel in a 1955 pink Cadillac that used to belong to Lucille Ball. I say you go with that. I can book it right now online. Want me to do it?"

Mike grabbed Zach's phone. "Stop talking like such a fucking idiot."

Zach snatched the phone back and laid it on the table. He put his hands up in the air. "Settle down. Listen ... hear me out. Why not? It could be awesome. Something for a hometown boy like you to remember your whole life. You love Wynter. It's a grand slam gesture and girls are always impressed with something like that."

Mike stared at Zach. He looked over at Justin and got nothing more than an affirmation about the grand slam gesture. He stood up and walked tight circles around the small cabin. He came back to the table, sat down and took a deep breath. "We'd never be able to book something like that on such short notice."

Zach chuckled as his fingers flew over the phone again, "It's August in Vegas, man. The place is as hot as hell. I don't think that's going to be a problem."

Mike looked at Justin, "What about work?"

"If being the boss has any perks, Mike, one of them should be the ability to get time off. It's a long weekend. If we have to, we'll shut the place down on Tuesday, too."

"I can book the chapel, the Elvis impersonator, everything for Sunday afternoon. It's only a click away, man." Zach grinned.

Mike hesitated, then he took a slug of beer and said, "Do it."

Within half an hour, Zach had booked flights out of Comox for noon the next day. "We can get some sleep and be out of here first thing tomorrow morning with plenty of time to get there." He had reserved a bridal suite at the Mirage and a limo to pick them all up after the wedding for a ride on the strip.

Zach frowned over his phone, "The girls are sharing a room down there, right?" He looked at Justin, "We better get another room."

Mike began to shake his head, "Shit ... the wedding dress. Wynter will be heartbroken if she doesn't get to wear that dress."

Justin laughed, "That's the easy part. It's over at Beulah and Bethany's. We'll sweet talk Beulah into giving it to us before we leave in the morning."

Looking down at his own clothes, Mike said, "What about us? And we need our passports." He frowned, "I don't want to go anywhere near home. Mom will take one look at me and she'll know everything."

Zach smacked Mike on the back, "I'll take care of that. You and Justin get the dress. I have to take my truck back to town, anyway. I'll go home, pack some stuff and meet you guys somewhere."

Justin grinned, "Okay ... let's hit the sack. Looks like we're going to Vegas, boys."

THIRTY-FIVE

Pushing through the crowds at the doors of the Lady Gaga concert, Wynter leaned close to Lisa-Marie to shout, "Oh my God ... that was so good. She's so amazing in person." They were coming down a bank of stairs with a view to the open expanse of foyer which was filling quickly with the concert goers pouring out from several doors. Wynter stopped and tugged at Arianna's arm on one side of her and Lisa's on the other. "Is that ... is that ...," People began to push and they had to keep moving down the stairs. Lisa-Marie and Arianna had followed Wynter's gaze and they were too stunned to answer.

Against the back wall, holding up a huge sign that read – *Wynter Snow will you marry me tomorrow?* – stood Mike and Justin and Zach.

By the time the three girls had made their way across to the guys, they were all talking at once and Wynter was in Mike's arms. Zach held up his hand, "Hold it. Not here. We've reserved a table."

When they were seated in the restaurant with a large bottle of champagne nestled in an ice bucket near the table, Mike reached for Wynter's hand. "I want to marry you tomorrow, right here in Vegas. It's all arranged. Please say yes."

Tears brimmed in her large eyes. "But Mike ... what about your family and all our plans and my dress?"

Zach leaned forward, "Don't worry about the family, Wynter. All Dad wants is for Mike to be happy and Mom will get over this."

Justin grinned, "And we have your wedding dress."

Half-joking, Lisa-Marie said, "That's great for Wynter. Arianna and I didn't exactly pack for a wedding."

Mike pulled a roll of money out of his pocket. He laid in on the table. "We've been here since three this afternoon hitting the casinos. For some reason, I couldn't place a bad bet. I've paid for all the wedding expenses. Take this and buy a couple of fancy dresses and anything else it will cover."

Wynter took a deep breath, "You've arranged everything?"

Mike leaned forward to kiss her. "All you have to do is be in the lobby at two o'clock tomorrow afternoon wearing that dress."

"You didn't look at it, did you? Because if you did, that's it ... no wedding." Wynter's lip trembled.

Zach and Justin both started laughing. "He didn't get a glimpse of it. Beulah packed it in the box and wrapped about two pounds of duct tape around it."

As Wynter smiled, Arianna said, "Where is this wedding taking place? You have to say more than be in the lobby at two o'clock."

Zach shook his head. "It's all a surprise." He looked at each of them in turn as he said, "You girls are going to love it."

Not that many hours later, Wynter stood in the middle of the room she shared with Arianna and Lisa-Marie and spun around so they could check that all was as it should be with the wedding gown. The dress was airy, falling in gentle folds to the floor. Gossamer lace overlay ornamented the fabric beneath that draped and shone through in luminescent layers. The back was bare except for the lace. The train fanned out in a semi-circle against the carpet. Wide, gathered shoulder straps gave way to a deep V in the front.

Wynter's wheat-coloured hair was done in thick spiral curls and woven through with sparkling stars and tiny, pink flowers. The hotel hairdressers had gone the extra mile for the bride and her two attendants when they heard the story of Mike's surprise arrival. The fact that he had toted along Wynter's dress and never once glanced at it, gave the story an extra dose of poignancy.

Elopements in Vegas were normal occurrences but Wynter's happiness was catchy and people simply wanted to do all they could for her. The same treatment followed them into the high-end boutique store that supplied Lisa and Arianna's dresses. They wore layers of sheer fabric over a slip-like material that draped to their knees in the back and became shorter in the front. Arianna chose a deep pink and Lisa-Marie opted for a less dramatic shade of purple. Mike's roulette winnings paved the way and Wynter took her time in the jewelry store choosing matching gift necklaces for Arianna and Lisa-Marie.

At one o'clock, Arianna had answered a knock on their hotel room door. She'd been greeted by a woman from the hotel with a long florist box balanced in her arms. The bouquets were delicate arrangements of white roses and gardenias trimmed with pink ribbons. The smell that wafted into the room was divine.

In a fever pitch of excitement, the three girls waited in the lobby at two o'clock. The mirrored walls reflected the light from the massive chandeliers overhead and lit Wynter like a display in a jeweler's case. Everyone stopped to stare and cameras clicked and flashed as if it were some sort of media event.

Suddenly, Mike was in front of Wynter in a black tux offering her his arm. Justin and Zach were behind in matching suits. The wedding party walked out the glass doors as the pink Cadillac convertible drove up with a limo close behind. The driver of the Cadillac, Elvis himself, glittering like a diamond in his white suit girded with a thick gold belt. "Miss," he said to Wynter in a deep, Elvis voice as he offered her his arm. He escorted her to the Cadillac. Mike got in beside her. The rest of them piled into the limo and the two vehicles began their procession along the boulevard.

As they pulled up in front of the Viva Las Vegas Chapel, Wynter threw a hand over her mouth to cover a squeal of delight. Her and Mike's names were on the marquee in bright lights. The pink Cadillac drove them right down the aisle of the chapel. Zach, Arianna, Lisa-Marie and Justin clapped wildly as Elvis offered Wynter his arm and walked her to the front. Before officiating at their wedding, he sang a heart-felt rendition of – *I Can't Help Falling in Love with You.*

Only a few minutes were needed for Wynter and Mike to tie the knot and sign the marriage papers. Then Elvis swung his guitar across his body, waved his hand in the air and screamed, "Everybody dance," as he rolled right into a rousing rendition of *Viva Las Vegas.*

Laughing and chatting, the three couples made their way to the Doo Wop café next to the chapel for photos, root beer floats, hamburger sliders and ice cream. Wynter cut the small wedding cake with its Elvis cake topper and she and Mike fed each other a piece. Then they were in the limo for multiple rides up and down the Vegas strip, waving to people and drinking champagne. They ended the celebration with dinner at Top of the World, spinning above the bright lights and glitz of the city that never sleeps.

❦❦❦❦

As they got out of the limo outside the hotel, Lisa-Marie held up her hand, "Wait ... we need a photo." She passed her phone to one of the door men and ran over to squish in beside Justin for the shot. Their movement towards

313

the large glass doors that opened into the hotel lobby was slowed by the number of tourists who asked Wynter to pose so they could snap a picture. One older lady said, "You look just like a Disney Princess."

Arianna clutched at Lisa-Marie's arm, "Did you hear that? I bet you anything if I were standing there in the very same dress, that woman wouldn't be saying those words to me. No such thing as a brown Disney Princess."

Lisa-Marie pushed Arianna out in front of her and shouted, "Stand back everyone. I present to you ... Vegas' one and only ... Princess Arianna." She got into paparazzi mode and snapped Arianna's picture with her phone over and over. Soon a big crowd was gathered around taking photos. Lisa-Marie laughed as her friend posed and smiled. While she waited for the crowd to thin, she hit a few buttons on her phone to do a Facebook posting of the shot of the four of them by the limo. She was creating quite an impressive photo journal of the whole day.

When they finally made it through the doors to the massive lobby and over to the bank of elevators, Justin stepped close to Wynter and leaned forward to kiss her cheek. He reached out to shake Mike's hand as he said, "Get your new wife up to that bridal suite."

Zach nudged Mike with his arm, "Congratulations, man."

Mike stared at Zach for a minute. Then he stepped forward and wrapped his arms around his brother. When he stood back, he said, "I wouldn't have had the nerve to do this without you. Thanks."

After a few more rounds of hugs and kisses, Wynter could be seen flashing a million-dollar smile and waving madly as the elevator doors swished closed on the bridal couple. Zach dropped his arm around Arianna and said, "Let's find a place to dance." He looked over at Justin, "Do you have your phone? I left mine in the room. I need you to Google the best dance spot in Vegas." He smiled down at Arianna. "I've got moves to prove to this girl."

Justin pulled his phone out of his pocket and turned it on. The thing started pinging and chirping like one of the slot machines in the nearby casino. Lisa-Marie raised an eyebrow, "Better check those messages. Sounds serious."

Staring down at his phone for a moment, Justin went from smiling to frowning to looking resigned and ill. Digging in his pocket, he extracted the plastic card that would get him into his room. "Change of plans. I'm beat. I'm going to the room." He turned and walked away.

Arianna, Zach and Lisa-Marie watched as he disappeared into the crowd. Glancing at Lisa-Marie, Arianna said, "That was weird."

Lisa-Marie nodded, "I'll make sure he's okay. You two go ahead. I'll text you later if we want to join you." She looked at Zach, "What room are you guys in?" He told her as he dug his door entry card out of his pocket and passed it to her.

❧ ❧ ❧ ❧

Lisa-Marie banged on the hotel room door. "Justin, let me in." It had taken her ten minutes to find the room. First, she'd taken the wrong elevator then the wrong turn.

Justin opened the door with his phone in his hand. "You didn't need to check on me, Leez. I don't want to wreck the night for you."

She pushed past him to walk into the room. "What's up?" She sat down in a swivelling armchair, kicked off her heels and tucked her feet underneath her. With her heart thumping, she asked, "The text messages ... they aren't about your mom, are they?"

Shaking his head, Justin sat on the side of the bed and stared at the screen of his phone. "No, not my mom." He looked at her, "Lauren. Fifty text messages with photos." Lisa-Marie bit her lower lip and just stared at him. "She found out I'm here in Vegas ... with you." He shrugged, "Apparently, she's stalking your Facebook page."

"Oh, crap. I'm always messing up my privacy settings." She shrugged helplessly, "I'm sorry."

Justin waved off her apology. "I'm only about halfway through reading them." He held the phone up, "There's some real gems here." He shook his head, "She never gave a shit about me, not from the beginning ... all the way back to that first summer. That guy I saw her with wasn't her cousin."

The implications of that revelation hung in the air between them until Justin dropped his eyes. She knew she should be a friend and tell him to delete the rest of the messages without reading them. Hitting him with an *I-told-you-so* was useless. It wouldn't change anything or make her feel better. But the wounded part of her that still felt the pain of his rejection would have its say. "I never thought she was right for you. I told you that but you wouldn't listen."

His stared over at her for a moment, looking like a guy who had been kicked when he was down. He shrugged, "Ya ... I suppose I deserve that. You also said you'd never love me again if I chose her. I guess you were right about that, too." He looked over at the mini bar. "Maybe you should go. I think I'll get drunk while I read the rest of my messages. When you knocked, I was on number twenty. It includes a few choice photos of Lauren with some guy she met in Ottawa last year. She told me she had lost the charger for her cell phone. That's why I couldn't get ahold of her for two days. Apparently, she was this guy and preferred not to be disturbed."

A strange ringing started in Lisa-Marie's ears. Her stomach rolled oddly and her hands clenched. Two years ago, when Justin broke her heart, she had thought nothing could ever feel worse. She knew now she was wrong about that. Watching his heart break over Lauren was way worse. Tears welled up in her eyes and rolled down her face.

Justin got off the bed and crossed the few steps to her chair. He pulled her up and into his arms, holding her, stroking her hair and whispering, "Why are you crying? What a mess." He led her to the bed where she perched on the edge. He sat down beside her and held her close.

When her tears stopped, he tipped her face up and stared into her eyes for a moment. Then he bent his head and his lips touched hers. She started to fall down the slippery slope that would dump her into bed with a guy who was in the middle of going through an ugly breakup with his girlfriend of three years. He'd being saying for weeks that the relationship was over, but he had failed to make the effort to end it. Deep within herself, Lisa-Marie could hear Emma's voice - *he brought this on himself* - and she paid attention. She pulled away and got quickly off the bed. "No ... I can't do this. It would be a mistake."

Justin's head dropped into his open hands. "Things are over with Lauren. I'm sorry, Leez." He raised his head as he said, "You're right. I'm so messed up by all of this." Standing up, he added, "Three years is a long time to be running down the wrong path."

Lisa-Marie felt like they were in a weird standoff. If he was waiting for her to say something, he'd be waiting a long time. Finally, Justin walked over and drew her into a hug. He spoke against her hair, "I don't know what I would do if you weren't here. Please stay. I won't do anything stupid, I promise. I need you here with me."

Stepping back, Lisa-Marie said, "Delete all the messages. Don't read any more of them and promise you won't talk to me about her at all." Justin nodded. Another thought occurred to Lisa-Marie. "What about Zach?"

Justin shrugged, "You have his key. He'll have to find a different place to sleep."

❈❈❈❈

Left alone in the glitzy lobby of the Mirage, Arianna and Zach stood in awe. Automatic doors swished as arriving and departing revellers allowed the heat and noise of the Strip to rush in. Flashing lights and dinging sounds of slot machines accompanied the hoots and hollers of happy gamblers. Arianna looked at Zach and asked, "Now what?"

Grinning, he took her hand, "Forget about dancing. We're going to see some of the Vegas highlights."

She grinned back, "Like what?"

"Volcanos, light shows, waterfalls, the Eiffel tower, the Statue of Liberty, the pyramids ... you name it. If it's here, we'll see it."

Arianna looked down at her fancy dress and heels, "Like this."

Looking at his watch, Zach said, "You have five minutes. Start moving. Go and change. I'll wait here for you."

"Give me ten ... it takes five minutes to get from the elevator to my room."

Hours later, footsore and happy, they were back in the lobby. Zach held up his empty hands, "I'm homeless. I gave my room key to Lisa-Marie."

"Come up to my room. We'll see if she's there."

Inside the room that Wynter, Lisa-Marie and Arianna had been sharing for three days, the aftermath of their whirlwind departure for the wedding ceremony was evident. Lisa-Marie was not in the room. Arianna kicked off her shoes as she said, "If she isn't here at three o'clock in the morning, I don't think she's coming back." She flopped down onto one of the huge beds. "Oh, that feels good. We must have walked ten kilometers."

Stretching out beside her, Zach said, "Probably more. This has been some day."

Arianna turned and pointed a finger at him as she asked, "Favourite part of the wedding?"

"The hamburger sliders in the Doo Wop room." He pointed back at her.

"Dancing in the aisle to Viva Las Vegas."

Nodding, Zach agreed, "Ya ... that was fun."

"Best part of being in Vegas?"

Zach pointed at her and said, "You."

"Ahh ... you're sweet. I've got to say Lady Gaga."

He made a face and reached over to push her arm, "Thanks. But then again, what guy could compete with Lady Gaga."

"Craziest thing that happened in Vegas?"

"Lisa-Marie taking my room key so I end up here with you." Zach smiled at her.

Arianna pushed him in the arm, "All of you guys showing up in Vegas."

They both laughed. Zach pulled her close and soon they were kissing. By the time he moved away, flopping onto his back and breathing heavily, his shirt was unbuttoned and Arianna's top was on the floor. "I want you, Arianna. If you don't want me, say so now, okay."

With her own breath hitching and her body alive like one of the popping, squealing slot machines down in the lobby, Arianna took the moment Zach offered her to think. If she slept with him, the experience wouldn't be like Lisa-Marie's story of the rotting lettuce smell and an uncomfortable crate. She was in a cozy bed in a Vegas hotel. On the other hand, she wasn't going to have Wynter's love-of-my-life romantic night with the sound of the waves crashing on the beach. But this guy beside her was nice. He respected her, he cared about her and she liked him a lot. She felt the time was right but she'd have to be honest with him about a few things first.

Resting her hand on his naked chest, Arianna said, "I want you, too, Zach. But you need to know a couple of things about me." She took a deep breath, "This will be my first time." She saw his eyebrow go up as he stared at her. "And having this first time with you doesn't mean I want a relationship when we're both at UBC. I don't want to mislead you. I have years and years of intense schooling in front of me and that has to be my priority."

He glanced over at her. "I really do like you, Arianna." When she looked away, an expression of resignation settled on his face. "Maybe we'll meet years from now when you're a doctor and I'm running some highly successful business. Then I'll tell you how I never forgot this night with you in Vegas, that no other woman I ever met made me feel the way you did. And you'll say – *hey, it was the same for me.* We'll fall into bed together and live happily ever after."

Arianna grinned, "Who knew you were such a romantic? It must run in your family."

Zach slid off the bed, turned to her and held out his hand, "I want to do this right. I need a shower. I don't want this casino smell on me when I make love to you. Come with me."

THIRTY-SIX

Kieran stopped at the entry to the Micah Camp kitchen. David was standing by the sink washing pots. "Hi," Kieran said, "Is Brigit around?"

Without looking up, David shook his head, "She went to the greenhouse."

Sensing something in the slump of David's shoulders as he scrubbed away like his life depended on the outcome, Kieran walked through the doorway. He glanced around, "No Hannah today?"

"Nah ... she's out sick." David threw the pot scrubber down into the sink and the water splashed up in an arc. He stared at Kieran for a moment before he asked, "You know the Bible, right?"

"I hope so. It's a big part of my job. Why do you ask?"

David picked up a tea-towel. He plucked a pot out of the dish drainer and started to dry it with quick swipes. "Forget it."

Kieran moved a few more steps into the kitchen and closer to the sink. He leaned against the counter, "You asked about the Bible for a reason, right?"

Holding the pot like a shield, David said, "I was taught not to trust Catholics."

Not overly surprised by the words or the sentiment, Kieran said, "I guess having Jesus in common isn't enough to make people trust one another."

As he clunked the pot down on the counter and tossed aside the towel, David's words rushed out, "I need to talk to someone who understands about God."

"I do have an understanding of God." Keeping the width of the counter between them, Kieran sat down and asked, "What's up?"

The young man's eyes darted out to the dining room and then to the door near the pantry. Judging the coast to be clear, he rushed out his words, "I had sex with a girl the other night down at the boat shed." He glanced quickly at Kieran and then away. "It seemed like she wanted to; she was all over me. I thought she had done it lots of time. But then, afterwards, she was crying. I guess I hurt her because it was her first time." He met Kieran's gaze, "I didn't know."

Kieran was silent. David went on, "Maybe if I had ever done anything like that before, I would have figured it out in time to stop. But everything happened so fast." Now that he was talking, it seemed like a dial inside him had been set to high. "I signed a covenant when I was fifteen saying I wouldn't have sex until I was married." His hands gripped the edge of the counter and after a moment, he raised his eyes to Kieran. "From the moment I saw Hannah –," he stopped suddenly and slammed his hand down on the counter. "Shit ... I didn't want to say that the girl was Hannah."

"I was pretty sure you were talking about her. I have seen the two of you together a few times. The chemistry between you was obvious."

"I didn't care about anything but being with her." David's face clouded with confusion, "Everything happened so quickly and I felt so great." Angry disbelief edged his words, "For a few seconds, I couldn't believe what a load of crap I had been taught about sex being dirty and wrong. Nothing ever felt that right." The confusion on his face crept back. "But then she cried and wouldn't talk to me. Now I feel like I never should have broken the covenant and I'm getting what I deserve." His voice took on a didactic tone, "Sex can only be right in marriage. Even Catholics think that, too, don't they?"

Kieran chose his words carefully. "The point of holding marriage up as the gateway through which a couple passes before they have sex is to emphasize that marriage means maturity and commitment. As you and Hannah have found out, sex is a powerful force. But, David," he waited for David to look at him before he went on, "Sex is not dirty or bad. The things that can turn sex into something it shouldn't be are wrongful intent, selfishness, demanding your own satisfaction and outright cruelty. Marriage isn't an inoculation against any of those things. Marriage can't guarantee a couple will act with love towards one another." Kieran paused before he added, "When it comes to sex, God created such powerful feelings for a reason."

David's shoulders slumped as he said, "To torture us?"

Kieran's face wore a rueful expression, "It sure feels that way some days. When adults advise young people to wait, there's a reason but it's not because sex is bad or dirty. It's because sex is so powerful and being that close to someone, in that way, has consequences."

"We used a condom."

"Well, that's good. But I'm talking about emotional consequences, too. Talk to Hannah. If you listen to each other, you might both be able to learn from this experience. And don't be so hard on yourself. God understands the motivation and the regret."

David made a face, "If that's true, then your God is someone I've never met."

"You asked to speak to me because I know the Bible, right?" David nodded and Kieran went on, "Peter denied Jesus three times and yet Jesus forgave him. If your God isn't a God of forgiveness, then what kind of God do you believe in? That is something to think about." He stood up and reached across the counter to pat David on the arm, "I doubt this is as serious as denying our Lord when the chips were down and the going was rough."

✻✻✻✻

Nick looked up from his desk at the sound of a knock and said, "Hey, Ethan. I haven't seen you in my office for a while."

Standing by the door, Ethan pointed to Aidan who was asleep in the playpen in the corner of the room, "I thought we could talk but it's a bit weird with your kid in here."

Nick shrugged, "He's a baby, he can't understand anything you're saying and he's sleeping, anyway."

"It's the whole you and a baby thing."

"Ya, tell me about it."

Ethan closed the door and came partially into the room. "I did something stupid."

Nick got up from his desk and walked over to sit in one of the two counselling chairs. "Are you going to sit down and talk about it or would you like to me to read your mind?"

Ethan sat down and bit at the corner of his lower lip. He stared at a spot on the floor past Nick's chair. "I hooked up with a guy I'd just met and afterwards I felt ... bad." He frowned, "Don't get me wrong ... the sex was insanely good. That wasn't it." He frowned, "Shit ... I don't know what's wrong with me."

With a frown of his own, Nick said, "If you don't, I sure don't." Pausing to give Ethan a closer look, Nick asked, "Are we talking about a consenting partner, old enough to make the choice?"

321

"Oh, ya ... he was consenting and consenting and consenting –,"

"Okay, I get the picture." He made a rolling motion with his hand, "Keep going. Talk it out."

"I've been in this dry spell as far as getting laid ever since I got here. Maybe that's all it was. Scratch the itch."

"If that's all it was then what brings you here? Something's bugging you."

Ethan sighed, "Maybe it was the whole Reg thing."

Nick's eyebrows went up, "You've lost me.

"Mortality, Nick. Seeing Reg clutching his chest like that. Makes you wonder. You never know when your number might be coming up."

"Let me get this straight," Nick spoke slowly, "you had consensual sex with a guy you just met to deal with existential angst about death?"

"When you say it like that it does sound lame. It was about Charlie."

Nick paused while alarm bells went off in his head. He went on in as calm a voice as he could master, "What has Charlie got to do with this?"

"Don't freak out, Nick. I haven't seduced Charlie with my irresistible charms." He sat back in his chair. "But I did fall for him and I tried to do everything right ... be the guy's friend, be authentic ... but none of it mattered. I never even got to declare the passion I had for his pouty lips. Charlie doesn't go for guys." Ethan took a deep breath, "When I realized that, I felt completely crushed."

He got up and wandered the room with his hands gesturing widely. "I fell right into all the stuff you and I talked about ages ago in counselling ... back into the hopeless drama of loving someone and never being able to have him. I was giving an Oscar performance." He looked at Nick for a moment, "To be honest, I surprised even myself." Back to pacing, Ethan went on, "I was lapping up the misery, getting as fat as an old eunuch on the impossibility of it all. I made myself sick with it. Couldn't eat, could hardly sleep." Coming back to his chair, he sat down and laced his fingers together, bent his hands and cracked his knuckles. "I threw myself into making the dance video. I felt like I was possessed. And I was good, the dance video was great. I had *the moves like Jagger* and then some. When I finished dancing and this hot guy was telling me to meet him at his van, I couldn't wait. I thought I might tear his clothes off before we got there."

Still frowning with confusion, Nick said, "Connect the dots for me, Ethan. How does this sexual encounter that was satisfying on one level but bad on another tie into your drama over Charlie?"

"The more I wrapped myself in the heartbreak of never being able to have Charlie, the less I wanted to be around the kid. He even asked me one night what he'd done to piss me off? Ironic, right?" Regret weighed down Ethan's voice. "I was thinking of him every minute but it wasn't him anymore. I made him into this fantasy object. It was wrong for me to use Charlie to drive myself so crazy that I couldn't think straight. That's what is making me feel bad, Nick." Ethan crossed his arms over his chest. "I wasn't thinking straight. When I run off with a hot guy for steamy sex, I want to be thinking straight."

❧ ❧ ❧ ❧

Helen rushed through the doors of the church and took a seat within the circle of people gathered for the grief group. She addressed the hushed arc of faces, "I wasn't going to come at all. But here I am." Total exasperation could be heard in her heavy sigh and seen in her drawn face. She folded her arms tightly around her body, crossed her leg and sat with her foot jiggling up and down.

Kieran glanced at Izzy and saw the slight rising of her eyebrow. She sat forward and said, "Helen ... you seem upset. Would you like to tell us what's going on?"

The erratic jitter of Helen's foot increased as she thought about speaking. After a moment, words burst out of her. "My oldest son and his fiancé eloped to Las Vegas on the weekend." The words skittered around the group as she delivered them, hung in the air and found no purchase. No one knew whether to smile congratulations or offer condolences and for once, it seemed the group was completely comfortable with not having to say anything at all. With her frustration growing in direct proportion to the silence in the group, Helen burst out, "Craig says it's all my fault. I drove them to it. He says he told me a hundred times this would happen ... like it's my fault I thought that girl wasn't right for Mike ... like a mother has no say in something of this sort ... like I don't have a right to keep my kids safe." She glared around the group. "I want to know what other people think. Craig isn't always right. I've been married to him long enough to know that."

Kieran frowned as he said, "The purpose of the group is not to offer that kind of feedback. But I'm sure everyone is fine if you want to continue to talk this out. We're here to listen."

Helen looked around the group as she said, "I know they aren't kids. Mike's twenty-four. It's just that they have nothing in common. She grew up in a commune, whatever that means. She was off in Europe posing for fashion magazine photos last year when Mike was here plugging away at the sawmill. Does that sound like a perfect match?" Without pausing for an answer, she went on. "She has all this money and ideas that are way too highfalutin for a small-town boy like Mike. He spent Christmas with her in Cuba. Christmas ... she doesn't even understand that Christmas is a time to stay home with your family. Mike wasn't even here when," her voice faltered and she choked out the words, "The accident happened." The folded hands in her lap flexed and locked together. "She's sure to break his heart. She'll leave him. It's only a matter of time."

At some point, the oomph of anger had drained from Helen's body. She was now sitting back in her chair and tears were glistening in her eyes. Izzy passed the box of Kleenex and it circled the group as it had several other times during their gatherings. As Helen drew out a tissue, she said, "It all comes back to the kids that died in the car crash." Her shoulders slumped and she began to cry in earnest. After a few moments, she blew her nose and pulled herself together. Helen looked around the group as she said, "I feel so stupid and sad." Sitting up straighter she said, "Sorry for hijacking the group like this. Can someone else talk?"

The group was silent for a minute. Then Gordon said, "I'll go next. All I want to say is that Susan's parents hated me for years. They never thought I was right for her. Their attitude was a sad thing because they missed so much of what we would have loved to share with them."

Alison cleared her throat as she looked around the circle. "I've learned a lot about myself by going back over some of the hardest times in my life. One thing I know for sure is that no matter how much I wanted to, I couldn't hold onto Bradley or stop him from doing what he chose to do. The only thing I can do, is look at myself."

Bethany sat forward eagerly to address the group, "Not long ago, I said I had never thought about trying to find the child I gave up for adoption. After saying that, I couldn't help thinking about it all the time. So, I did some research. Then I decided. I was scared but I went ahead and put my name and contact information in the adoption registry. I am now officially searching for the child I gave up twenty-six years ago this October sixteenth."

THIRTY-SEVEN

Fiona took Aidan from the car seat and reached for the diaper bag. She was running late. She had agreed to bring the baby to the drop-in daycare in Dearborn because Sadie was studying for a test and Nick had clients. Arianna was working at the addiction center. Liam was off in Cedar Falls. Izzy and Lisa-Marie had gone down Island on an overnight shopping trip, taking Sophie with them. That tapped out all the family and friend resources.

She pushed open the door to the daycare and stopped at the registration to sign Aidan in. Tapping her fingers on the counter, Fiona waited for the woman who ran the place to break up a scuffle between a couple of toddlers. Seeing her at the desk, the woman waved, "Be right there, Dr. Wells." Directing the toddlers to separate corners of the play area, she walked over and checked the calendar on the desk. She frowned, "Hmmm ... how long were you planning on leaving Aidan today?"

"I don't get off until six," Fiona told her. Nick wouldn't be able to pick up the baby any earlier because Fiona had his car. They had agreed that the car seat would stay in Nick's Mazda because they both got sick of asking Liam to show them one more time how to install it properly.

The woman made a face and checked down the list again, "I've got a full house, Dr. Wells. I'm sorry. I can't take him for the whole day. You could bring him back at two. One of the babies is getting picked up then."

Fiona narrowed her eyes, "Two? I need to be at the clinic right now. There are sick people waiting for me."

With a helpless shrug, the woman told her, "I'm so sorry but it's regulations. We could get shut down if we have more kids in here than we should and I'm at my max on babies."

Fiona put a screaming Aidan back in the car seat. She pulled out her phone and texted Nick – *unbelievable – the drop-in daycare is full – no exceptions – not even for the only doctor in town – help*. She waited a moment to see if he would reply but he was probably with a client. She stretched her arm into the back seat to secure Aidan's soother in his mouth, buying herself a few moments of silence as she drove the short distance to the clinic.

When she came through the back door, the receptionist was already waiting for her with a patient file in hand. The woman said, "Oh my ... give him to me." She reached for Aidan. Exchanging baby for file, Fiona walked to her office to get her stethoscope.

Three appointments later, she had a moment to glance into the reception area. Aidan was sitting in the playpen normally used for the babies of patients who needed the respite for a solo trip into the examining room. The girls at the desk were keeping an eye on him.

She finished up with her next patient and as she left the examining room, the receptionist met her in the hallway. "I've cancelled your next two appointments. You need to go to the addiction center. They've got a resident who had a seizure in the bathroom. He's stable now but it's better for you to examine him there than have them bring him here." As she turned to walk away, the woman added, "Oh ... and your husband is here to pick up Aidan."

Fiona met Nick in the hall. He was holding Aidan and smiling at her. She gave him a spontaneous hug of gratitude. "I'm sorry to call you at work. I was desperate. I've got to go to the addiction center. The car's out the back."

He followed her out to the parking lot and dangled a set of keys in front of her, "I'll need my car since I've got Aidan. You can drive Gordon's." He grinned at her as he pointed to the pea-green Pontiac Le Mans that was wedged between a Honda mini and Nick's Mazda. The vehicle looked like a barracuda lounging next to minnows.

Fiona's eyes widened, "I've never seen a car that long. It's all nose."

"They don't make them like that anymore. Your text sounded urgent so I didn't want to go all the way to Liam and Izzy's to ask if they had a vehicle I could borrow. Gordon seemed to be the only one at Micah Camp who didn't mind lending his car. When I saw it, I understood why."

Fiona reached for the keys, "Okay ... I'll give it a spin but how do you even see the road over that hood? Are you heading right back to the camp?"

"No, I've cleared my schedule for the rest of the day and Gordon doesn't need the car back until tomorrow. He said he'd catch a ride to Dearborn with Paula. I think I'll hang around town. I haven't done that in ages. I might take

Aidan for a walk on the seawall. The stroller's in the car, right?"

Fiona nodded as she dug in her purse. "Take my keys to the Lady Brit apartment in case he needs to nap or something. If you're going to be here all day, hang around until I get off. We can have dinner together." She grinned at him, "We'll celebrate. Apparently, my husband showed up at the clinic today."

Giving her a strange look, Nick took the key. "First an undisclosed baby and now a husband. You are full of surprises."

"According to my well-informed receptionist, you're the man."

He laughed, "Right. Dinner sounds good. I'll order that pasta dish with the scallops and crab from *The Sea Shed* and you can pick it up when you get off."

※ ※ ※ ※

Wynter had been unpacking china for what seemed like forever – there were boxes of the stuff. What on earth could her grandmother have wanted with all these dishes? She unwrapped a set of two small jars each complete with its own sterling silver lid and also found a caddy for the pair to rest in. She glanced across the kitchen island with its dark granite countertop. Hannah sat on the bench of the window seat with her knees drawn close to her body. She clutched a pastel throw cushion to her chest. Wynter held the caddy up, "Look at this, Hannah. It's too much."

"What is it?"

Wynter touched the tiny figures on the top of the silver lids, "Jam and honey jars. There's a strawberry on one and a bumble bee on the other."

Hannah shrugged and stared down at the pillow. She plucked at the thick fringe around its border. Wynter had been pleased when Hannah showed up at the Lady Brit earlier asking if she could hang out for the day and help with the unpacking. But Hannah hadn't been much help so far. Setting the china jars aside, Wynter walked over to the window seat and sat down. "What's up?" she asked.

With her head bent and her hair hiding her face, Hannah hesitated for a moment before she said, "Can I tell you something?"

"Sure ... we're sisters now, right?" Wynter smiled. "I love the idea of having a sister."

Hannah's shoulders shook and her voice was thick as she said, "I did something so stupid." She glanced at Wynter before resting her face on the cushion. "Let's just say I'm not a virgin anymore."

Into the silence that stretched out after this revelation, Wynter asked, "David?"

Hannah nodded, "In the boat shed at Micah Camp after Ethan's dance thing." Her wound up body gave a small shudder. "I started it. I wanted to do it. Only, I didn't know ..."

"Oh, Hannah ... I'm sorry." Wynter laid her hand on the girl's arm for a moment.

"I kept thinking of how Shawna and I talked about what it would be like to go all the way with a guy." Hannah's breath hitched as her words rushed on, "And now she's never going to know. Ever since she died, I've been thinking about how it could have been me and how I didn't want to die never knowing anything or doing anything." She hugged the pillow tightly. "I knew it would probably hurt the first time but the whole thing was more awful than painful ... fast and desperate and not hot and exciting the way it all started out."

"Did you tell David how you felt?"

"Some ... but everything felt so awkward afterwards. I left him there and ran out. And I haven't talked to him since or even gone to work. I feel so stupid." Sitting up straighter, Hannah said, "How am I going to face him?"

"He probably feels worse than you do. He seems like a nice guy. Talk to him. You'll feel better after you do that." Wynter paused for a moment and considered her words before she asked, "Did you guys use protection?"

Hannah waved her hand, "I brought the condom." Her nose wrinkled, "Maybe it was the whole dance thing. It seemed like everyone was on fire after we were done. David and I sure weren't the only ones with sex on our minds." To Wynter's look of curiosity, Hannah added, "I saw Ethan walking out with Tyler, the guy who did the filming. And over by Tyler's van they were all over each other." Tossing the pillow onto the pile with its companions, Hannah got up from the window seat. "Hope he had a better time than I did." She looked over to the china still to be unpacked. "Let's talk about something else. I'll help you with the rest of those dishes."

About an hour later, Wynter was standing on a tall-backed dining room chair receiving moss-green curtain panels from Hannah and feeding them along the ornate metal rods that spanned the length of the side windows of the gallery. "What will you put in here?" Hannah asked as she passed the next panel into Wynter's waiting hands.

"We're not sure yet." Wynter grinned, "Maybe a kid's playroom" Before Hannah could respond to that, they heard the most delightful sound of chimes ringing through the lower floor. Wynter dropped the curtain over the back of the chair. "That's the main door at the front of the house. Aren't those chimes awesome?"

Hannah followed Wynter out of the apartment and into the main entry. Wynter opened one of the large double doors and her and Hannah's faces both wore looks of stunned surprise. Helen Sampson stood on the top step with a small cake box in her hand.

Wynter recovered first. "Helen ... come in." She ushered her mother-in-law into the Lady Brit.

Helen stood in the center of the entry and looked around in awe. She took in the gold-toned walls above the dark wainscoting; the tall vase in muted, burnished copper that sat in the middle of a long table against a wall; the cream-coloured carpet thickly bordered with flowers, lying on the shining hardwood; the curved stairway that wound up to a wide hall and the door of the upper unit. Light spilled down on her from tall windows on the second story. "Oh, my," she said in a hushed tone.

"Our apartment is over here." Wynter went ahead leading the way.

Once inside, they walked past built-in book shelves and a few small dark tables adorned with lamps. The creamy shades complemented the floral pattern on the high-backed chairs and sofa. Coming into the kitchen with the bank of windows facing out to the view of the ocean, Helen stopped to touch the white ceramic chicken that sat on the edge of the dark counter. She looked at Wynter and said, "This is amazing."

"I wanted so much for you to like it." Wynter glanced around the room with a large smile on her face.

"I brought a coffee cake." Helen held up the box.

Hannah grinned, "I'm starving. Let's have it right now. Wynter and I just unpacked about ten boxes of dishes so she has no shortage of plates."

Wynter made the coffee while Helen wandered the lower floor with Hannah who stopped often to point things out to her. Wynter got out a pedestal cake plate, coffee cups, a cream pitcher, a sugar bowl, a matching coffee pot for serving, and three dessert plates. A few minutes later, she called out, "Everything's ready." She poured the coffee as Helen and Hannah joined her at the table.

Helen sat down and touched the fluted green edge of a dessert plate. The rest of the dish was covered with multicoloured flowers. In a hushed tone, she said, "Is this Spode?" She turned the plate over and whispered the words, "Chinese Rose." She set the plate back down carefully on the table.

Wynter passed Helen a delicately patterned pitcher, "I know you like cream."

Helen took it with a look of reverence on her face. "You didn't need to go to such a fuss for me." She pointed with her free hand to the dishes.

Hannah laughed as she bit into a piece of cake, "She has tons of the stuff. There's even a soup tureen."

"These dishes belonged to your grandmother?" Wynter nodded as she reached for the cake. Helen stared from the bright flowers of the china to the light fixture in the hallway. Visible from the kitchen, it hung from the hall ceiling like a heavy bowl of glass fruit. She sighed. "Well, everything is beautiful, dear."

She took a piece of cake and sipped her coffee. She glanced across the table at her new daughter-in-law. "I'm sure my dropping by must be a shock." She held Wynter's gaze for a moment. "I came here today because I wanted you to know how sorry I am. Words don't seem to be enough. I've made a mess of things and I've been unfair and unkind to you." Helen sighed, "And because of that, I didn't get to see my oldest son get married. And I never got to see your wedding dress."

Helen saw the emotion that flooded the young woman's face. Wynter's eyes shone bright with tears as she took a shaky breath and said, "I'm sorry, too. I wanted the big wedding with family and everything. I didn't want to disappoint anyone. But when Mike showed up in Vegas and he had everything arranged, I couldn't say no. He worked so hard to make the day perfect and I love him so much."

"I understand. You were right to follow your heart." Helen turned to Hannah. "Your dad told me I would end up driving you away with my words and actions but I couldn't stop. The accident made me so afraid for all of you, all the time. I thought if I could control everything, I could keep my kids from getting hurt."

Resentment tinged Hannah's words, "Geez, Mom ... I wanted you to see that I was afraid, too. I miss Shawna all the time. You made losing her all about you and acted like what I felt didn't matter."

Helen touched her daughter's hand, "I let you down. I'm sorry." Hannah struggled for a moment then she accepted her mother's apology with a shrug.

Wynter looked from Hannah to Helen as she said, "I want to tell you guys something. You might think growing up in a place like the Peach Valley Commune was so different from everything in Dearborn, but it wasn't. The things I remember are all about family. When I left there, I didn't think I'd ever have that kind of feeling again. And I missed my mom." Tears welled up in Wynter's eyes. "But from the first time you invited me into your home, Helen, I've had that feeling of family again. I want so much to be part of what you have." She dabbed at her eyes with a napkin. "And I love Dearborn ... the way people recognize each other and help each other out. Those are the things I want." Wynter went on, "And the other thing about the Peach Valley Commune was that there were lots of kids. I want that, too. But, like I said, I miss my mom and I have a lot to learn about so many things."

This last part was too much for Helen. Her eyes filled with tears. Hannah shook her head, "Oh no ... stop it, the both of you. I'm going to cry now, too."

Helen stood up and opened her arms to hug Wynter. Hannah came around the table to join in the embrace as the door on the side of the gallery opened and Mike, followed by his dad and Zach came into the room. All three of them stopped and stared. Craig's voice was leery as he asked, "What are you doing here, Helen?"

Letting go of Wynter and Hannah, Helen walked over to Craig. "Mending fences." She patted his arm. She turned to Mike and gave him a tight hug.

As she stepped back, Zach grinned at her, "Nothing for your son who is like a pig being led around by the ring in his nose?"

"Oh, you." She hugged him, too. Wynter had come to stand beside Mike who wrapped his arm around her waist and Hannah was leaning into her dad. Helen looked at the faces of her family and smiled. Turning to Mike and Wynter, she said, "I am thrilled to welcome Wynter into the Sampson family. I have one request and one question."

Mike raised an eyebrow but Wynter smiled. "Anything, Helen. Ask away."

"Okay, the request first." She smiled at Mike, "Your father and I would like to throw you two the most amazing wedding reception and I already know exactly what I want to do with the cake." She glanced around the room they stood in. "I think this place is the perfect venue." She looked around in wonder, "Your first home together. Wow."

Mike looked at Wynter. She grinned and he said, "We agree to that request. What's the question?"

Helen looked up at Craig for a moment and then turned to the newlyweds. "Are you legally married in Canada?"

Zach laughed as he dropped an arm around his brother's shoulder, "With the Elvis chapel and Lucille Ball's pink Cadillac convertible ... how could they be otherwise?"

Later that evening, with the house to themselves, Mike and Wynter lay at opposite sides of the claw-footed bathtub that dominated the middle of their ensuite. A window was open and they could hear the rhythmic swoosh of the waves rolling up the beach. The dark trees were silhouetted against the midnight blue of the sky. Emptied wine glasses sat on the ledge and Elvis' voice crooned in the background – *I can't help, falling in love with you.* Wynter sighed, "I can't stop listening to that song since the wedding."

Mike's attention was taken up with the shifting pattern of the bubbles that barely concealed his wife's breasts. He smiled, "Good thing we didn't get married in the Johnny Cash Chapel. I don't think I could stand to listen over and over to – *I hear the train a coming ... a coming down the track.*

Wynter giggled as she slid her foot up along his leg. "Are we legally married in Canada?" she asked.

Not able to concentrate on much more than the slow travel of her foot, he said, "I have no idea. I suppose we'll have to Google it."

❧❧❧❧

Fiona came through the door of Rosemary's apartment on the upper floor of the Lady Brit with a large bag from *The Sea Shed* and a bottle of wine. She glanced at the note on the dining room table – *I'm getting Aidan settled. Set things up for dinner. I'm starving.*

When Nick came out of Rosemary's second bedroom, he was greeted by the smell of food and the table laid with steaming bowls of seafood in béchamel sauce layered over pasta, thick chunks of sourdough bread, plates of Caesar salad and full glasses of wine.

Near the end of the meal, Fiona laughed as she said, "I wasn't sure I was going to be able to park Gordon's car. I took two spots just to swing the nose around." Carrying their wine glasses to the sofa that commanded a view of the foam-tipped waves lit by the half moon, they settled down close together. Sighing, Fiona tucked her feet under her legs and leaned into Nick.

He drank his wine and recognized the signals. Since the first time he and Fiona had slept together, he'd always been able to read her. There had been a couple of nights, at the Saltbox, when he sensed her openness but she didn't stray across the boundary established by his claim to the upstairs bedroom. Maybe she sensed his reticence. Until she was back in his life, he hadn't realized the emotional toll taken by the way she had left him in Vancouver. Or maybe she felt as he did – that Aidan was such a whirlwind in their lives, they were not capable of doing more than cooperate in caring for their son.

When Fiona moved closer to him and turned so she could rest her hand on his chest, he didn't resist. Her fingers soon brushed along the collar of his shirt to stroke his neck. When she pulled his lips down to hers, he didn't stop her.

The kiss began tentatively – exploring, rediscovering, deepening until he lost himself in the feel of her. By the time they came up for air, he had drawn her up against him in an embrace that made his pulse hammer.

Her eyes glittered with desire as she said, "Will you come into the bedroom and make love to me?"

He hesitated, "Is that wise?"

She moved away to get a better look at his face. "I'll be honest with you, Nick ... wisdom is not my main motivator." His lips twitched with the smile he was holding back. "It might be unwise to say no to a desperate woman."

"Are you that desperate?"

The gaze between them deepened with intimacy. She moved closer, breathing her words almost against his lips, "There's been no one since that last day in the hotel with you."

His hands slid up her arms. "If that is the criteria for desperation then we are in the same boat. I haven't been with anyone else either."

Fiona raised an eyebrow in surprise. Right before their lips met, she said, "I'm finding our mutual desperation quite the turn on." Several kisses later, she disentangled her body, rose from the sofa and said, "The bed, now." From the doorway, she called out, "There are condoms in my purse."

He picked up the bag on the way to the bedroom. Dropping it on the night table, he watched her pull her shirt over her head and unhook her bra. He pointed to the purse but his eyes stayed on her curves, "You're certainly prepared. Did you plan to seduce me tonight?"

As she stepped out of her panties, she laughed, "I'm a doctor, Nick."

THIRTY-EIGHT

C losing the file on her desk, Alison checked her watch. Her client session with Ethan wouldn't start for fifteen minutes. She smoothed her hair. She hadn't bothered to put it up this morning when she stood in front of her tiny mirror in the trailer bathroom. Reddish curls highlighted with darker auburn tones hung loosely around her shoulders. Before leaving for work, she'd pulled a silk scarf from her drawer and looped it loosely around her neck. It had always seemed a bit loud to her but now she fingered the fringe along its edge and enjoyed the way wearing it made her feel.

She looked out her window at the sun reflecting off the water in a brilliant display that made the whole surface one huge disco ball of sparkling light. The view of lake, trees and mountains was so different from the prairie landscape she had loved all her life, but this new view was growing on her. With the end of summer not that far around the corner, she wondered if she would miss the quickening excitement of fall harvest and the encroaching cold of a Saskatchewan winter. Time would tell, she supposed. All she knew right now was that she felt suddenly and inexplicably comfortable in this new environment.

She wasn't sure when this sense of wellbeing had crept up on her, but it was a welcome sensation. Her participation in the grief group had provided much for her to reflect upon. Sharing openly her own experiences of loss and being present as a witness to the pain of other group members had put many things into context for Alison. Moving back into the flow of church life was comforting. Her friendships with both Brigit and Gordon were becoming meaningful social outlets. And she was finally beginning to feel competent in her career counselling position at Micah Camp.

More than anything else, Alison had to attribute her sense of wellbeing to the discovery of how much she enjoyed being on her own. After so many years of living with and for others, she found she was relishing the joy of eating when and what she wanted, the pleasure of pursuing her own interests, the excitement of choosing her own friendships, the comfort of having the whole bed to herself, and even something as mundane as the reward of handling her own finances without consulting anyone else. When Bradley left her, she never imagined that she would end up feeling relieved and happy about the new direction her life was taking.

❦ ❦ ❦ ❦

Ethan strolled into Alison's office looking refreshed and energetic. He sat down across from her desk. "Did you see the video?" he asked. When he had received the zip file of his dance video from Tyler, Ethan had been overcome with gratitude for the work the guy had put into the editing. The mixing of various camera angles and the cutaway and close-up shots were superb. The professional quality of the final product made him look even better than he was. Ethan still felt a twinge of guilt over what had gone on between him and Tyler in the van down at the deserted end of the lake. But he had to conclude, based on the work Tyler had put into the editing, that he'd been as on fire in the back of the van as he was on the dance floor.

He held up a piece of paper, "I've got the reference letter from Reg. I just have to pull everything together and send the package to Toronto."

Alison couldn't stop herself from grinning. "I did watch the video, Ethan." She frowned for a moment, "I don't think Hannah needed to have her shirt off but I suppose that was up to her." Her face brightened again, "The moment I finished watching, I sent it off to my brother." Ethan sat up straighter in his chair. He had never seen Ms. Kirk grin and the effect was slightly disconcerting. She reached for the dance school brochure they had looked at weeks earlier when she had suggested he apply. She waved it in the air and her grin became a smile. "My brother is owed a large favour by a woman who is on the board of this school."

Ethan's eyes widened as he breathed out the words, "No shit ... you're kidding me?"

"I am not kidding you. He got the video to her and she watched it right away. I got a call from her this morning."

Ethan was now on the edge of his chair with his hands clasped in front of him like he would fall to the floor on his knees in prayer, "Oh, please, please, tell me she liked it."

Alison regained some of her own composure as she said, "She not only liked it, Ethan, you are to carry on with submitting your application package but you're booked for an interview and audition," she glanced at the calendar on her desk before she looked back at him, "a week from today."

A stunned moment of silence followed her words then Ethan was off his seat and whirling her around the office as he sang, "*I've got the moves like Jagger, I've got the moves like Jagger.*"

※※※※

The moment Roland opened the floor for new business, Alison spoke up, "I'd like to talk about getting funding ... travelling expenses and stipends ... nothing outrageous, to bring in some professionals who can speak to the residents on different career options."

Roland pinched the bridge of his nose for a moment before responding, "Alison, if you have a funding request that is not part of your current allocated budget, I would appreciate seeing the appropriate forms before we meet as a group."

Nick obviously thought Alison's issue had been dealt with by Roland's response because he began to speak. Alison's voice cut him off. "I am sorry for not filling out the forms. But since I've brought it up now, I don't see why we can't discuss it."

Sitting back in his chair, Nick eyed Alison with surprise. He spoke to the group, "Surely we aren't going to run around funding guest speakers for every little thing that might interest the residents."

Maryanne waved her hands in a sweeping motion, "I wouldn't want to set a precedent for bringing in paid outsiders. The next thing we know all the teachers could be out of work." Roland ignored Maryanne's concern. Their English instructor was always one to deliver a dramatic statement with theatrical punch.

Watching the way Alison stared at Nick, Roland realized with surprise that she wasn't going to back down. Her voice rang out across the table as she said, "Nick, I believe my request deserves as much respect as your last one ... hiring someone to lead an overnight kayak trip down to the end of the lake."

A ripple of suppressed laughter circled the table. Nick's request for the kayak trip had been tabled at the last meeting for further study into costs and liability issues. Roland watched Gordon and Jeremy give Alison a couple of thumbs up. He had been surprised enough when, at a previous meeting, Jeremy had presented a list of resources for Alison's skills group idea. This second episode of staff solidarity was nothing short of stunning.

With good humour, Nick smiled and said, "Point taken, but I'm not letting go of the kayak trip."

THIRTY-NINE

Fiona re-read the email on the screen of her laptop. Rosemary was still doing her *Doctors Without Borders* work in Uganda, but she had sent this email in which she made Fiona an interesting offer for the fall. As she glanced back at the screen, words jumped out at her – *share the practice with me ... feeling the need to slow down ... we could do some good work together.*

Fiona closed the top of her laptop and checked the clock. She was down to the last five minutes of her fifteen-minute lunch break. She finished the sandwich she had found on her desk when she collapsed into her chair between appointments. The staff at the clinic looked after her well. They kept her organized, on the move, well fed and dosed with caffeine. Everything the girls at the desk could do for her, they did. She was sure they'd take her bathroom breaks for her if they could. The team was great. She could learn so much staying here and working with Rosemary. Together, they could divide up the more peripheral work like community outreach and even put a few preventative medicine strategies into practice.

Aidan could grow up around family. Her dad and Cynthia would be home soon and she knew they were both itching to be involved in Aidan's life. She was attached to Liam and Robbie. The only thing that made her hesitate was Nick. He was Aidan's father and bringing the baby here and introducing Nick to his son meant far more than she had realized it would. She hadn't anticipated the way he would rise to the challenge of fatherhood. Nick had demonstrated complete commitment to the child they had brought into the world. Taking Aidan away again after a few months would be beyond cruel.

She sighed as she pushed the plate away. The night she and Nick spent together at the Lady Brit had rekindled the one thing that had always worked

338

for them. She was keenly aware of pulsing desire when she thought about him. She wanted to be with him. But what if he started screaming commitment again and all she wanted to do was run? Her receptionist poked her head into the room, "I've got your two o'clock appointment in examining room one, Dr. Wells."

She got up from behind the desk. She'd have to decide soon. Rosemary wanted a quick reply. Fiona took a deep breath and pushed all personal issues into the background as she headed out to greet whatever health concern awaited her behind door number one.

⚜⚜⚜⚜

David had his head down and was polishing his way across the stainless-steel counter toward the sink. Hannah had finally come back to work but she'd avoided meeting his gaze since she arrived in the kitchen. They'd gone about the work of getting lunch ready and cleaning up. He had considered and then rejected about a million ways to start a conversation with her because every single one sounded more lame than the last.

When Hannah leaned over the counter and said his name, he was so sunk in misery he could hardly believe she'd spoken to him. She said, "I shouldn't have run out the other night like I did, I'm sorry.

David's face turned red. He couldn't look at her. "I'm the one that's sorry. I never meant to hurt you." Confusion settled in his eyes, "I didn't know what I was doing."

Hannah shook her head, "Don't blame yourself." She quickly brushed the tears from her eyes. "I've felt sort of crazy for months ... since my best friend died. Those feelings made me rush into something I wasn't ready for and I dragged you along with me. None of what happened was your fault."

"I like you a lot, Hannah. Does that matter?"

She tucked a strand of hair behind her ear as she spoke, "Yes ... it matters. I'd feel even worse about everything if you didn't."

Knowing the answer before he voiced the question, David couldn't help himself. "Can we start over?"

Hannah shook her head. "I don't think that's a good idea. I'm sorry because I like you, too. I need to figure out what's going on in my own head before I can be with anyone else. I'm going away for school in a few weeks anyway. Can we just be friends until I go?"

⚜⚜⚜⚜

Ethan walked into his cabin after his shift at the sawmill and spotted Charlie

339

sitting on the sofa with a rolled-up piece of white paper in his hand. He sat down in a chair across from the kid and gestured towards David's door, "Is he here?"

Charlie shook his head while he banged his open palm with the paper roll. "Nah ... still over at the kitchen."

Hunching forward with his hands on the knees of his work jeans, Ethan stared at the floor. "I wanted to tell you that I'm sorry."

"For what?"

"For giving you the cold shoulder the last few weeks."

Charlie shrugged, "You were busy with your dance video."

"Ya, well, that's true." Ethan pulled his ball cap off and smacked it against his leg. He raised his gaze to Charlie's face as he shook his head, "But it was more than that. I was into you, man. Shit, I'm still into you." A dramatic sigh escaped Ethan's mouth as he continued to slap his hat against his leg. "When I found out you like chicks, I didn't deal with it well."

Charlie's head had gone back in surprise and his eyes had widened as Ethan spoke. Now he just stared. "You were into me?"

Ethan looked up at the ceiling, "Don't freak out or anything. I'm harmless."

"I wouldn't freak out." Charlie stared at the paper in his hand. "I know you're cool."

The outside door opened and David walked into the cabin. He started on his regular route across the living room towards his bedroom. Then he stopped, turned and sat down in one of the armchairs. With one eyebrow raised, Ethan directed a quick glance at Charlie who simply shrugged in response. David looked at Ethan and said, "I heard from Hannah that your dance video worked out and you got an audition at the school you were applying for. Congratulations."

Charlie stared at Ethan, "Is that true?"

"Yes, it is." A grin lit Ethan's face.

Rising from the sofa, Charlie dropped the paper on the coffee table and high-fived Ethan. "That's great."

When he sat down, David pointed to the unfurled art work on the table, "What's that?"

Smoothing the page flat, Charlie said, "It's a collage I made with Izzy." David and Ethan craned forward as the three of them studied the paper covered from edge to edge in magazine pictures of smiling girls with long black hair, one layered over the other in a kaleidoscope of glistening tresses and white teeth.

Ethan tipped his head to one side to examine an upside-down girl, "Sort of erotic from a certain angle." He shook his head, "I'm still bummed I got Nick for a counsellor instead of Izzy." He pointed at the collage, "Did making that help?"

Charlie pulled a face, "Like a purge or something. I don't know. Maybe."

David frowned, "It's a bit weird." He looked at Charlie, "No offense." Charlie waved the remark off and rolled the paper back up. Staring over at Ethan, David said, "I go to Nick. He knows about how to handle crap that happened when I was a kid but he's pushy. In practically every session, the guy makes me so angry I feel like punching him out."

Ethan laughed, "Ya, that's Nick alright." He paused to give David a searching look. "You've got to stand up to him. He expects it." Pointing to the collage in Charlie's hand, he added, "Izzy likes the artsy stuff, but Nick thinks it's good for a client to push back at him. He can take it. Think of it like a purge." Charlie grinned and in a moment even David had a smile on his face.

Taking that smile as an invite, Ethan asked him, "What's happening with you and Hannah?"

David's mouth twisted as he said, "I blew it with her. She only wants to be friends, now. She's going away to school soon anyways."

Getting up from his chair, Ethan gave his ball cap another couple of smacks against his leg. "Well, that would be this entire cabin of guys batting zero on the romance front. I've got first call on the shower." He looked over at David, "What's on the menu for dinner?"

"Brigit's spicy jambalaya."

Ethan did a few fancy dance moves on the way to the door of the bathroom. "Oh, la, la," he sang out. "I think I've died and gone to heaven. Who needs romance when you have spicy jambalaya?"

⚜⚜⚜⚜

Robbie and Tabby sat with their backs against the railing of the boat-shaped, top platform of Sophie's play structure. Two sets of identical knobby knees were drawn close to their bodies, matching sets of bruises and scratches adorned their legs. "It's cool up here." Tabby told Robbie as she picked at a scab on her shin.

"Shush –," Robbie pointed past the railing to a grouse pecking in the nearby salal. They watched the small, chicken-like bird move leisurely up the hill. "Grouse have the best camouflage. That bird is almost the same colour as the ground."

341

"Being up here reminds me of the boat in the museum in Victoria." Tabby pointed to the flag pole at the prow of the structure, "Sophie loves the dragon windsock." Tabby and Robbie had found it for her on the trip to Victoria.

"*Puff, the magic dragon lived by the sea.*" Robbie grinned, "She loves that song." He looked out across the waters of the lake towards the mountains. "I asked Liam to come on the hike up to the Cat's Cradle."

Tabby looked over at him, "Ya ... how come?"

Robbie's brows knit together as he said, "I don't know. I just want him to come."

"I can't wait. I've never stayed overnight in a tent before." She smiled, "My mom is sending me with four chocolate bars." She rested her chin on her bent knees. "The summer will be over soon. What do you think we'll do in the fall?"

"Keep going to the band school in Cedar Falls once a week to play soccer."

"Check," Tabby said. "Skating?"

Robbie echoed, "Check. We could take a junior hunter training course."

"What?" Tabby looked at him with wide eyes, "We'd never shoot anything."

"Course not," Robbie told her. "At least not unless we had to. It's not so we can hunt. They teach all kinds of stuff about animals. Learning about firearms is a safety thing if you want to be around animals."

"Okay ... I guess." Tabby got up to hang over the railing and swing her arms. She looked back through the slats at Robbie and said, "I want to read *The Hunger Games* books. Katniss hunts with a bow. That would be cool."

"Maybe ... I was going to pick this book about a guy who runs a game preserve."

Tabby stood up and circled the platform stopping to stand by the flag pole. "I would read that if you read *The Hunger Games*." She sat back down cross-legged on the deck. "What do you want to be when you grow up?"

"Working with animals for sure."

"Like a vet?"

"No ... a vet would have to be inside too much. A conservation officer maybe."

"It rains a lot around here. I'd like to work inside."

"You could be a vet then."

Tabby's face wore a thoughtful look for a moment as she spun one of her curls around her finger. "It would be okay if people only brought in cats or dogs or rabbits. But what if someone brought in a snake?" Her nose wrinkled with distaste.

Robbie grinned at her, "Don't be a baby. A snake's nothing. What if someone brought in a tarantula or a rat?

Tabby made a face, "That's gross. Definitely not a vet." Her head tilted to the side as she considered her options. "I might like to run a book store or I could be a travel agent. They get to go to lots of cool places." Tabby jumped to her feet. "Come on, first dibs on the tire swing."

Robbie got up too, "Okay, but if I push you first, you have to push me, too."

❦ ❦ ❦ ❦

Reaching high over his head into the green leaves, Liam plucked beans from the vine as he said, "Robbie asked me to come on the overnight hike up the Cat's Cradle." He threw a handful of beans into the bucket at his feet.

Izzy stood beside him, working her way in the other direction around the teepee-shaped trellis. He glanced at her and smiled at the way her hair was piled on top of her head. A scarlet runner bean flower was trapped in her black locks. He admired her tanned arms as she reached to pick her own handful of beans.

Concentrating on the job, she said, "It's a good idea. I know the kids would be fine with Justin but it will be even better with you there." She parted the vines with care as she added, "I'm sure it will make Brigit more comfortable about the trip. She told me a couple of times she wasn't sure if Tabby should go."

Izzy stopped picking for a moment and looked out over the garden. Liam followed her gaze. The bean trellises sat on a rise. Spread out in front of them was a lush abundance of August growth. His gaze was drawn to the thick row of Swiss Chard in shades of red, orange, yellow and cream. The curling leaves bordered a bed overflowing with summer squash. Deep green zucchini speckled with white sheltered under the vines that crept beyond the rock wall meant to hold them in check.

When Izzy looked back at him, she said, "It's hard for Brigit when we make a decision for Robbie that is the opposite of what she wants for Tabby."

Liam turned back to the picking. "I wouldn't get involved, Izz."

Crouching, Izzy gathered the beans close to the ground as she said, "Easier said than done." She changed the subject to ask, "Who else is going on this hike?"

"Arianna and Zach, Lisa-Marie and that guy she works with. They want film footage of the old mine site up there. Me and Justin and Tabby and Robbie. It's a good-sized group for an overnighter. Enough people to carry stuff so we won't starve. I'm on for the breakfast." Liam stood back from the trellis. "I think we've got everything we're going to get from this one."

They headed for the next teepee. Izzy's bucket swung at her side. "I wonder what Lisa's plans are for the fall." She glanced over at him. "It would be nice if she discovered a reason to stay home."

"Do you think having Justin around all the time makes that more or less likely?"

A line etched its way between her brows. "I don't know. It would be awful if in doing something right for one of them, we were hurting the other."

Touching her arm, Liam said, "We can't think like that. Once we start down that road, we're sure to do the wrong thing."

"I suppose." Izzy pushed her hair back from her face. They picked along in silence for a while. When they had circled the trellis, Liam dumped another handful of beans into his bucket and said, "Let's take a break before we tackle the raspberries. It's hot out here."

They carried their buckets over to the steps of the garden house and sat down in the shade. Izzy stretched out her legs. "Justin seems to be doing well with his new job." She frowned, "Do you think Reg will come back?"

"When I was visiting him the other day, he told me why he was driving everyone so hard at the sawmill."

Izzy looked at him with curiosity, "Why?"

"He lost some money on an investment. He was trying to make it back. Josie took a strip off him about how he hadn't told her and how she didn't care about the money. She's not going to let him overdo it." He paused, "It wouldn't surprise me if Reg didn't come back."

Izzy frowned, "Are they okay for money?"

"Josie seemed to think so. They're selling the house. Paula's moving out anyway and they don't need a place that big. The market's good in Dearborn right now so she thinks they'll do well."

Liam watched the bees buzzing in and out of the nearby patch of golden oregano gone to flower with delicate purple spires. He sighed, "I keep thinking I'll see Pearl strolling down the path."

Izzy reached over and held his hand. "Loss ... it sure takes a while to deal with that emotion. I'm going to miss the grief group now that we're finished. I enjoyed facilitating again. Kieran and I worked well together and everyone seemed to get a lot out of the sessions." Izzy glanced down at their joined hands. "I had an email this morning from a potential client for the fall."

"How are you feeling about the private practice?" he asked her.

"It's starting out slowly but I'm fine with that. I've enjoyed this summer and having the time to do things around the garden and go down Island shopping and supervising that trip to Victoria. I'm glad Bethany agreed to come along. She's doing much better."

"That's a relief."

"I'm looking forward to your dad and Cynthia coming home." Izzy's smile turned to a frown. "But then what happens with Fiona and Aidan. And what about Nick?"

Liam rubbed his chin slowly, "More than a few things up in the air with this family."

The sound of good natured shouting came from the direction of the play structure behind the cabin. Izzy looked over in the direction of the noise. "I never expected Tabby and Robbie to enjoy Sophie's play structure so much."

Liam chuckled as he reached for Izzy and pulled her close. He plucked the red flower out of her hair and kissed her. "It's a nice place to hang out. We should try it sometime."

Izzy pushed him away, laughing, "I don't think so. I'll stick with my cliff deck." She stood up and reached for her bucket of beans. "Hey, that reminds me. I've found someone to redo the fire pit. A couple of guys from Dearborn. They're going to start in September." She gestured with her hand towards the raspberry canes. "Come on. We better get this picking done."

FORTY

Zach slid the packs to the tailgate of his truck and attached extra, empty water bottles to each of them. He smiled over at Arianna as he worked, "I've taken the heaviest stuff but yours is no girly pack. Are you up for it?"

She grinned back at him, "I'll make you proud."

They waved as Justin's truck pulled off into the gravel at the trailhead to the Cat's Cradle. His black Chev was closely followed by Liam with Tabby and Robbie almost hopping on their seats. Leaning against the truck, Zach told Arianna, "Liam put me in charge of the dinner tonight. I've got a dozen of everything for good measure. The meal is foil-wrapped, fully cooked and frozen in individual serving packages of chicken cordon bleu, southern fried potato wedges and carrots that will be steamed to perfection in the juices by the time we haul our food away from the edge of the fire." He pointed at her pack. "I put the brownies in your pack."

"Impressive," she said as she leaned against the door of the truck beside him. This was going to be their goodbye trip. Arianna was leaving for Vancouver the day after they got back. She realized she'd miss Zach. Vegas had been nice but sharing her bed in the library bus with him had given a whole new meaning to the word *nice*. Getting used to having him around would not be difficult. She forced herself to stop that kind of thinking and focus. She was going to be a doctor.

They milled around the trucks checking Justin's master list of who had what – hatchet, rope, compass, walkie-talkies, first aid kit, sunscreen and sunglasses, extra layers of clothing, flashlights, matches and more matches, the rocket stove, water bottles, tents, sleeping bags, food and drink. Each item got a check. Eventually they were only waiting for Lisa-Marie and Tyler to show

346

up. Justin looked at his watch and frowned. "We said we'd meet at noon, right?"

Arianna shrugged, "I texted her but she isn't answering. She must be driving."

By the time Lisa-Marie pulled her Jeep off the gravel road at twelve-twenty, Justin was not in the best of moods. He and Leez had barely spoken since they came back from Vegas and he still felt raw from the deluge of Lauren's text messages and the tension they had caused in his complicated relationship with Lisa-Marie. He'd been keeping to himself and she'd been letting him but there seemed to be a tremendous weight of unspoken things between them. He came up to the driver's window and asked her, "What's up?"

She got out of the Jeep. "We're late. Let's not make a big deal out of it."

He stared at her, "Why are you snapping at me?"

"Forget it," she said, as she went to the back of the vehicle to grab her pack.

"Did you get the stuff I texted you about?"

Lisa-Marie pulled a bag forward. "Ya ... but I need a couple of minutes to load my pack."

With a frown on his face, Justin picked up her pack and hefted it to check the weight. He had assigned Lisa-Marie and Tyler the job of getting and carrying a few cans of pop for the kids, as well as trail mix and energy bars for eight people. "You're supposed to split the load with him," he jerked his thumb towards Tyler who stood by the passenger side of the Jeep hauling out his camera gear.

"He's got enough to carry." Soon everyone was milling around and she was busy introducing Tyler.

Justin gave the guy's hand a quick shake. Then he took the bag of added supplies and called Zach over. "We'll have to split this stuff up. Leez's pack is already too heavy and apparently, the camera man is fully loaded down."

"No worries," Zach told him. They were delayed another five minutes while he and Zach rearranged their loads to carry the extras. As Zach did up the ties on his pack, he leaned close to Arianna and said, "Justin is steaming over that Tyler guy."

Arianna grinned, "What's new? It's always like this with him and Lisa. Two years ago, he was all steamed up about you." She grinned, "Maybe he and Tyler will be great friends in another year or so, too."

When they were finally assembled at the trailhead, Justin told them, "We've got a two hour hike to the lower summit. There are a couple of rest

347

spots on the way and two good streams for refilling the water bottles. We'll eat a late lunch when we get to the lower summit, then if everything looks clear, we'll make the hour hike to the top."

Tyler adjusted one of the camera bags over his shoulder. "Where is the mine site?" he asked.

Catching Justin's impatience, Zach said, "I'll point out the turnoff as we go by."

Robbie had warned Tabby about a tricky section of trail about forty minutes into the hike. "You stay close to the rock wall and you'll be good." But halfway across the ledge that wound along the edge of a cliff, he looked back as he pointed out an eagle swooping in the sky over their heads. "Look, Tabby," he called. But he could see her light arcing wildly as she leaned her shoulder into the rock and moved one foot carefully past the other.

"I have to watch my feet." Her voice shook.

He slowed right down and when she caught up to him, he said, "You okay?"

She only nodded at him with her eyes wide. Robbie signaled to Liam who was behind Tabby, "We are going to go slow on this part." Liam waved his understanding. They caught up with everyone else at the first break spot.

Flopping on the ground by the stream close to Tabby, Robbie asked her again, "Everything okay?"

She smiled, "Ya, I'm glad we're past that spot though. It was really high up." Robbie smiled back at her but her words made him nervous. The upper summit was way higher; the trail was narrower and more exposed. She might not be able to do it and he didn't want to have to tell her that.

The hike was harder than Lisa-Marie had anticipated. The weather was great but her legs were feeling the strain of the climb. When the group got to the first stopping point, she had a difficult time adjusting her bad mood to the high spirits displayed by the others. Liam passed by and reached a hand out for her water bottles, "Give me both of yours. I'll refill them for you." She smiled as she handed them over. "We've finished up with the steepest part," he reassured her.

She rested and caught her breath. Tyler sat down close to Zach and Arianna and soon the three of them were chatting and laughing. He was getting on great with people. Well, everyone except for Justin who was managing to avoid the guy while pretending not to. But to be fair to Justin, Tyler was getting on her nerves, too.

Lisa-Marie should have expected Tyler would be late getting out of the hotel to meet her. Then he had dragged his way through the grocery store, making them even later. And she'd told him a couple of times to go light on the film gear because he'd have a full pack to carry, but he hadn't listened. They'd had an argument on the way out from town when she explained that she'd worked it out with Justin that everyone would go to explore the mine site on the way down, after the hike to the peak and the overnight stay. He'd wanted to do the mine right away and skip the rest of the hike. She had given him a cold stare, "You agreed to an overnight hike."

Her irritation had other roots, as well. She had seriously underestimated how difficult she would find it to be around Tyler and Justin at the same time. Seeing the two of them together was like folding the pages of her life into a fan. Things that should never have touched were now side by side.

When Justin got them all up and moving ahead on the trail again, she felt like she'd hardly had time to catch her breath. But the next section of the hike wasn't as steep and she started to enjoy herself enough to unsling her camera and take some shots of three deer picking their way delicately through the scrub brush below them. The trail widened out in spots and she walked along with Tabby and Robbie for a while. They were still in the trees but she could see flashes of bare ground higher up as they rounded corners, and she knew they would soon get above the tree line.

Zach called back to Tyler, "You can see the *Eagle's Talon* site down below from this section of the trail." They were soon all gathered around Zach and Tyler gazing across a slope of waving purple fireweed to the old copper mine below. Lisa-Marie could barely see the outline of worn wood around the dark opening to the mine but the area was mostly overgrown trails backing onto dark trees. She was taking a few quick shots of the fireweed slope when she heard Tyler say, "I want to get some footage. This is the perfect spot and the light is great."

Justin stared at his watch with obvious impatience. The guy had been filming for ten minutes and that didn't count the five it had taken him to get his gear organized. They were getting so off-schedule he worried that they wouldn't have a shot at the peak today. A hike that should have taken about an hour to this point had taken them two. Their first break had stretched on and now this guy was holding them up again.

Standing near Tyler when he finally lowered his camera from his shoulder, Zach pointed to a trail that veered away from the main one. "You have to make sure you get on the right trail to get down to *Eagle's Talon*. If you miss the turn, you'll end up at the old *Bear Creek Mine* and that is definitely not where you want to go. The mine entrance is in bad shape. It's way too dangerous."

Justin was getting everyone lined up to move on. He called out to Zach, "Save it for tomorrow. Let's get moving. It's not like anyone will be coming back this way without the rest of us. That's the plan."

When the group reached the second break spot, at the start of the alpine meadows, everyone was starving. Justin was forced to bring out the sandwiches he was carrying. Robbie passed around a large bag of Cheezies. The kids drank a pop and Liam made some tea on the rocket stove. The weather was warm and the spot was beautiful with rolling hills and the tops of trees banking away from them on all sides. There were small pools dotting the area and around those pools were clusters of yellow and red wildflowers poking out of the scrubby green and doubling their presence as they were reflected in the mirrored surface of the dark water.

They didn't reach the summit of the lower peak until after five. And though the higher peak was outlined clearly against the blue sky and the dipping cradle approach was totally clear, Justin knew even before Liam approached him that it was too late in the day for them to make the last section of the climb.

They had all collapsed on the ground to rest on their packs when Liam stood beside Justin and said, "We can't risk it so late in the day. It's going to take at least an hour each way with so many people and we need to go slower for Tabby. Robbie says she's more scared of heights than she's letting on."

Justin nodded his agreement as he stared up at the peak, "Okay, but I doubt we'll ever see more perfect conditions." He turned to the group and called out, "Let's set up camp. We'll try for the higher peak first thing tomorrow morning."

As Lisa-Marie struggled to put up her small tent, she noticed Tyler resting nearby. Taking a closer look at his pack she realized he did not have a tightly rolled tent roped to the back. She glanced quickly around. Justin's tent was up and he was already using the hatchet to chop the scraps of wood everyone had been gathering on the trek up and dumping into a huge sack that Zach carried over his back like he was Santa. Arianna and Zach were just about finished with their tent. Liam was inside the one he would share with Tabby and Robbie calling out from the flapping door, "Hey, you two ... we still need to bang in the pegs."

She let her tent sag down and walked over to Tyler. "Where are you planning to sleep?" she asked him.

He grinned up at her, "You've got a tent, right?"

"You're not sleeping in my tent."

He frowned, "Why not?"

Justin approached them, swinging the hatchet by his side. He looked at Tyler lounging on the ground. "Where's your tent?"

"Didn't bring one."

"I'd rather carry a tent than sleep under the stars but to each their own." Justin walked away and started to gather rocks to encircle the camp fire.

Tabby and Robbie moved about the area collecting armfuls of scrub brush branches. Zach knelt by the carefully laid pile of kindling Justin had chopped. He dropped small chunks of resinous wood over the pile from the Ziploc bag in his hand. "Fir sap," he told Justin. "It's a dynamite fire starter."

Later, everyone cheered when Zach divvied out the individual foil packets of gourmet chicken nestled among potato wedges and herbed carrots. The fact that Tyler had brought neither plate nor cutlery was no problem. Liam had an extra fork and Tyler ate right out of the foil boat. The extra servings disappeared quickly. Arianna passed around the chocolate brownies as Liam brewed the tea.

With her knees drawn up near the fire and her pack to lean on, Lisa-Marie enjoyed the liminal blue of the sky. She sipped the steaming mug of tea Justin had brought her and watched for the first star. The fire was down to a few crackling branches. They didn't have a ton of fuel and everyone wanted to have a hot breakfast in the morning, so they decided to let their campfire go out now.

Arianna sat down beside her. Warming her hands around her own mug, she said, "Tyler's nice."

Lisa-Marie frowned, "Do you think so? I thought he was acting like a jerk, holding everyone up all the time."

"I didn't even notice." She shot a sly look Lisa's way as she added, "It seems like only you and Justin have a problem with him."

Making a face, Lisa-Marie changed the subject as she pointed to Arianna and Zach's tent, "Seems like you and Zach have moved along down the relationship line since Vegas. Has our brown Disney Princess found her Prince Charming?"

Arianna grinned as she shook her head, "I'm glad the first time was with him but it isn't going to be a long-term relationship. I'm too busy with school."

Lisa-Marie nudged her friend with her shoulder, "That's what they all say."

Across from them, Tyler sat poking at the last of the burning branches with a stick causing sparks to zing up into the sky. He spoke to no one in particular and thus managed to get everyone's attention. "I was at the hotel in Dearborn last night talking about coming up here and some guys told me a weird story ... all about this Cat's Cradle place and how it's supposed to be haunted." He stared as the dying fire as if mesmerized.

Tabby leaned forward, "Tell us what they said."

Robbie reached behind her to tap her shoulder and she jumped. She looked at him beside her and said, "Cut it out."

Tyler shrugged, "I don't want to freak anyone out. Those guys were probably pulling my leg because they knew I was going to be hiking up here."

Insistent, Tabby said, "Come on ... you have to tell us now."

Tyler sat up straighter. "Okay ... well ... the story goes like this. A mom and dad took their only daughter ..." he stopped talking to stare at Tabby. "Seems she must have been about your age. How old are you?"

"Eleven," Tabby told him.

"That's exactly what they said ... the daughter was eleven. They hiked up here for an overnight." He glanced around. "It wouldn't surprise me if they camped right on this spot. Anyway, they got their camp set up and had a fire and some dinner." He paused again to look around the circle until his wide-eyed gaze fixed on Tabby. "Just like us. Then they crawled into the tent to go to sleep."

Arianna nudged Lisa-Marie and gestured with her chin towards Tabby. The girl's eyes were huge as she hung on Tyler's every word.

He dropped his voice as he went on so people had to lean forward to hear him. "The girl slept for a while but woke up hearing a strange sound ... a sort of a weird scratching, scrabbling, moaning kind of sound." Tyler had his hand in the scrub brush and he was dragging his fingers through it and making a wooing sound in his throat. "She shook her mom – *Mom, I hear a funny sound.* Her mom said – *go to sleep. It's probably the wind.*

Tabby whispered to Robbie, "That is so what my mom would say."

"The girl tried to sleep but she noticed that it wasn't windy out at all. Then she heard that scrabbly, scratchy, moaning sound again." This time Tyler's moaning was lower pitched. "The girl shook her mom – *I hear it again.* Her mom shushed her – *go to sleep, it's nothing.* But once more the sound returned."

Lisa-Marie caught herself shivering as Tyler scratched at the brush and moaned. She turned to raise an eyebrow at Arianna who was grinning.

Totally into the role, Tyler wagged his head back and forth as if he'd like to stop right there but had no choice except to go on. "The third time her daughter disturbed her, the mom just got mad." A muscle in his jaw twitched. "Finally, the kid was so exhausted she fell asleep."

Getting a bit of a lilt in his voice, Tyler went on, "The next time she opened her eyes, it was morning. Her mom was still asleep but her dad wasn't in the tent. She crawled out to see if he was getting the fire going and making breakfast. He was nowhere around." Tyler's face contorted as he looked out beyond the camp and into the dark. "But she could see a trail running through the scrub brush. By now, her mom was awake, too. Together, they followed the trail until it led them over to the edge of that cradle drop," he pointed his finger in the direction of the trail down into the cradle. "They peered in but they couldn't see anything." Shrugging, he said, "The dad didn't come back and eventually they hiked down and called 911. The next day the dad's body was found stuck in a crevice down there. A wild animal must have got to him because he was torn up bad."

Tyler was quiet for a minute, letting that information sink in. He sat forward. His voice was sober and his eyes were intense, "But here's the weird part ... according to those guys at the hotel who told me the story, every time people camp up here, someone hears that scratching, scrabbling, moaning sound. Some people say it's the ghost of that dad trying to get back to the tent."

Tyler leaned against his pack and looked up at the stars. "Probably those guys were just having a joke on me, like I said."

Zach was pretending he could hear sounds behind him and Arianna punched him in the arm, "Cut it out." She grinned over at him.

Tabby looked around the circle until her eyes came to rest on Robbie. "There's no such thing as ghosts," she told him.

Liam got up as he said, "Right you are, Tabby. Let's head to bed."

People began to dig around for their flashlights. One after another, they made bathroom treks into the nearby darkness carrying the ice cream bucket that had banged its way up to the summit tied to Liam's pack. "Toilet paper in there when you're done," he had explained. "We pack out everything we bring up here."

Justin smiled when he overheard Tabby telling Robbie, "Don't you dare leave the tent all night. I mean it."

Crouched near the dead fire, Justin watched Tyler and Lisa-Marie in conversation with one another. The guy's voice carried as he said, "You aren't serious about making me sleep outside, are you? You don't want the ghost of that half-eaten dad finding you all alone in your tent, do you?"

A familiarity in Tyler's chuckle and the way he looked at Leez rankled Justin. He stood up and walked over to join them. He glanced up at the sky and the clouds rolling overhead. "We'll get some rain tonight." Looking at Tyler, Justin added, "You can bunk in with me."

Before Tyler could say yes or no, Lisa-Marie spoke first, "He can sleep in my tent. It's no big deal." She didn't want Tyler spilling his guts to Justin in the lonely hours of the night. Who knew the guy was such a storyteller? Leaving the two of them standing there, she walked away, relieved Tabby of the ice cream bucket and shone her flashlight along the ground as she moved off into the dark.

Justin was waiting for her when she came back. Everyone else had disappeared into the tents. His voice was low, "I thought you said you and Tyler just work together?"

"We do work together. What are you trying to say?"

His voice dropped even more, "You seemed pretty quick to offer him a spot to sleep. I'm not going to lie in a tent a few feet away and listen while you screw him."

A surge of something she had no time to name rippled through her and skittled down her arm in pings of firing sparks. Before she could stop herself, she slapped his face. She ignored his stunned expression and said, "You have no right to say that to me." Turning in a huff, she flicked open the flap of her tent and crawled inside.

Oblivious to everything, Tyler lay on his back with his hands folded behind his head. He had his earbuds in and his foot was tapping to a beat only he could hear. She felt like kicking him. She scooted to her side of the tent and unlaced her boots.

He glanced over at her as she slid fully clothed into her soft flannel sleeping bag. He flashed his familiar come-on smile at her. "I could keep you company in there ... for old times' sake."

Bunching her extra sweater under her head for a pillow, she said, "Absolutely not ... those people out there are like my family. And even if they weren't, I wouldn't."

He reached across and brushed a piece of her hair out of her face, "I can be so quiet."

She pushed his hand away. "Stay on your own side of the tent, okay. We have work to do tomorrow. Let's not mess that up."

He rolled over and muttered, "Fine by me." Before she even had a chance to still her breathing, she heard him snoring.

Hours later, when she awoke alone, she crawled out of the tent and into the morning light. She saw that Liam had erected a lightweight, metal grill over a small fire. He was flipping pancakes in one frying pan and grilling bacon in another. Robbie and Tabby were huddling in thick sweaters by the side of the fire, eating with their fingers off the same plate and drinking hot chocolate out of the same mug.

Tabby called out, "Lisa, guess what? Robbie says he woke up all night thinking he heard the ghost. I didn't hear anything," she said with a big grin.

Liam smiled at Lisa-Marie, "You'll want to get a sweater. The cloud cover is pretty low and it's chilly." He pointed to the frying pan, "The next order is yours. Hand me your plate."

When she located the dish and passed it to him, she asked, "Did you guys see Tyler anywhere?"

Liam tossed a pancake onto her plate. "He's off somewhere taking some footage of the peak through the mist."

Tabby laughed, "When Tyler got up he said we had to make sure everyone was accounted for because he was sure he heard that moaning all night."

Soon everyone was up and milling around. Liam was dumping batter into the pan and flipping fresh pancakes as fast as he could. Justin boiled water for instant coffee and he delivered cups around the circle. He deliberately ignored Lisa-Marie, so Arianna handed her cup along and said, "Take mine. I'll share with Zach."

When Tyler returned to the group and cleaned up all that was left of the food, he drew Lisa-Marie aside. "Let's head down to the mine site."

She stared at him. "That isn't the plan. Everyone's waiting to see if this weather will lift so they can try for the peak and then we're all supposed to go to *Eagle's Talon* together."

He was staring at the screen on his camera as he spoke, "I'll wait another fifteen minutes but then I'm going."

Lisa-Marie fought the urge to stamp her foot with frustration. She couldn't let him go on his own. They were here to work and she had to take stills of the mine to go with his footage. She pulled her tent down and packed up her things as she tried to figure out how to handle the situation.

When fifteen minutes had passed, Tyler signalled to her as he gathered up his cameras. Everyone else was still enjoying the view of the sun on the higher peak. She walked over to Liam. "Tyler wants to go down to do the filming at the copper mine. I have to go with him."

He looked at her steadily, "That's not a good idea, Lisa. It's always better to go with a group. And I had planned on asking you to stay behind here with Tabby if we get a shot at the peak. She's scared and I don't want to risk her panicking up there."

"It's work, Liam. I don't know what to say."

He looked at the ground for a moment. "I think you should wait but it's your choice. I'll stay with Tabby if the others get a chance to make the climb." Glancing at her, he said, "Get one of the walkie-talkies from Zach in case you run into any trouble."

Suddenly, Justin was in front of her jerking his thumb towards Tyler, "What's he doing? We agreed to wait to see if the cradle will clear."

When Lisa-Marie didn't answer, Liam said, "He wants to head down to the *Eagle's Talon* now."

Justin looked at her. "No ... you aren't going with him down there on your own."

Clenching her hands at her side, Lisa-Marie managed to stifle the urge to slap him again. Her eyes narrowed as she said, "You don't get to tell me what to do." She picked up her pack, stopped to get the walkie-talkie from Zach and headed down the trial behind Tyler.

Robbie sat near Tabby watching the light around Justin go crazy. He would have been scared if Liam weren't there. It was a kind of light that made him think anything could happen and it was hard for him to watch. Tabby asked him, "What's going on?"

"I don't know."

"Robbie ...," her voice was quiet. He looked over at her. "I don't think I can do it." She pointed to the mountain peak. "I'm scared."

"Don't worry. No one is going up there today. The clouds aren't going to lift."

While they waited, Liam asked, "Do you guys know the story about the cairn up on the higher peak?"

Zach had his arm around Arianna. He shook his head. Justin shrugged. Robbie said, "Tell us if it doesn't have to do with ghosts," he grinned over at Tabby.

"If you make it up there and get to leave a message in the cairn, the story goes that whatever you wish for will come true." Liam smiled at the memory of the one time he and Caleb had made it to the top. They had stood in the bright sun and gusting wind as they exchanged their slips of paper. After reading each other's messages, they had folded them up and stuffed them into the cairn. "I can tell you for a fact that I know of one case where things happened exactly that way."

Liam leaned down to grab his pack as he told Justin, "I don't want to wait anymore. The fog isn't going to lift and I'm worried about those two on their own at the mine site."

Taking one last glance at the peak, Robbie hefted up his pack. He really wanted to see that magical cairn and put his wish inside it.

The low cloud slowed their descent. It was dense on the skin and hung over the trail, crowding close and limiting their vision. Even so, in what seemed like a fraction of the time it had taken the day before, they were back at the spot near the overlook to the mine. Zach was out front and he pointed down a trail shrouded in swirling shreds of low-hanging cloud. "This one goes to *Eagle's Talon*," he told them.

As everyone started to follow Zach, Robbie clutched at Liam's arm, "Lisa-Marie didn't go that way." He spun around until he was facing the other trail down to the old *Bear Creek Mine*. "They went this way."

Liam called out, "Zach, hold up." He turned to Justin who was bringing up the rear of the line. "Robbie says they took the wrong turn."

Worry etched its way across Justin's face. Zach and Arianna came up to them. "What are we waiting for?" Zach asked.

As Robbie's eyes pleaded for someone to believe him, Liam told Zach, "We think they might have taken the wrong trial."

Zach looked down the trail to the *Bear Creek Mine*, "Why?"

"I feel it, can't say why." Liam replied. He came up with a plan in quick order. "Zach, you and Arianna and Tabby check out *Eagle's Talon*. I'll go to *Bear Creek* with Robbie and Justin. If you don't find them, head right back down to the trucks. You've still got one of the walkie-talkies, right?" When Zach nodded, Liam went on, "If you don't hear from me and Lisa's Jeep is still down there, call for some help. The cloud cover is getting worse and I don't want people wandering all over the mountain in this kind of weather."

Tabby shook her head. "I want to stay with Robbie." Tears made her large eyes glisten. Then she looked at him, "You come with us, okay?"

Robbie stepped towards her, "Lisa is down that way, I know she is. They need me."

Tabby stared at him for a minute and then she said, "Okay." Arianna stepped forward, dropped an arm around Tabby's shoulders and squeezed her close.

Justin, Robbie and Liam heard Tyler shouting Lisa-Marie's name long before they made it to *Bear Creek Mine*. The mist swirled around their feet and clung damply to their hair and faces, frustrating their attempts to get down the steep trail in a hurry. Finally, they emerged into the clearing near the site. Through the eerie shadows of low cloud, they could see the mine entrance vaguely outlined against the rock face. It was partly covered by an old metal grillwork that had fallen to one side. Thick fern, moss and draping lichen hung down from the rough timbers that topped the entry. The camera gear had been tossed to the side of the rock face beside Lisa-Marie's pack and

Tyler was outlined against the dark entry to the mine. Hearing Justin call his name, he turned and waved his arms wildly as he shouted, "Help ... help us."

Justin moved forward ahead of Liam and Robbie. He grabbed Tyler by the shoulder. "Where is Leez?" his voice barked out the question.

Tyler was shaking and a dribble of cocaine mixed with mucus ran down from his nose. "She went in ahead of me. I ... I was getting my cameras ready. She was there, I could see her right inside the entrance and then she was just gone, man. I don't know. She just disappeared."

"And you stand up here doing some blow. Are you fucking crazy? Why didn't you use the walkie-talkie?"

Tyler looked back at the dark opening to the mine, "Lisa had it." Justin's face twisted with disgust and Tyler backed away mumbling, "The blow ... it was for courage, man."

Robbie spoke quickly to Justin, "She's not dead and she's not far down there. She must be knocked out or something."

As Justin stepped toward the mine entry, Liam stopped him. "Wait. We need to go carefully ... move in slowly. We don't want more than one injury to deal with. From what Tyler's saying she must have fallen through something." Liam turned to Robbie and passed him the walkie-talkie, "Get ahold of Zach and tell him we found them. He's got to get to where he has cell service as fast as he can and call search and rescue to let them know we've got a member of our party injured at the old *Bear Creek Mine* site. Have you got all of that?" Liam waited for Robbie to repeat the messages back to him and then he waved at Tyler, "You stay with Robbie for now. We'll call you if we need you."

Liam unhooked a coil of rope from the side of his pack. "I'm thinking you should go, Justin. You're more agile than I am. But you're going in prepared." Justin was already on the ground, dumping things out of his pack, lightening his load and leaving only the first aid kit, his sleeping bag and some water.

Liam nodded, "That's good. Whatever she fell through, it might be only a narrow opening." He anchored the rope on an exposed chunk of concrete footing near the entry. He passed it to Justin and helped him loop it around himself and secure it around his waist. "Okay ... that should be good. Assess the situation. Come back out if it looks too dangerous to go after her. We'll wait for search and rescue." He stared into Justin's eyes for a moment, "You okay?" Justin nodded. "Go on then. I'll keep a close watch on this end of the rope and listen for you."

Manning the walkie-talkie and sitting beside Tyler, Robbie tried not to listen as Tyler babbled. He knew from one quick glance at the guy's light that he was over the edge, freaking out. After that, Robbie didn't look directly at him again. Tyler chewed manically on the edge of his thumb as he mumbled. "Have you ever seen that movie, *Flight?* Denzel Washington could never have landed that plane if he wasn't stoned." He dropped his head into his hands. "I got stuck in a drainage pipe when I was a kid. Bunch of us were playing there and I got stuck ... couldn't get out. I thought they all ran away and left me." He rolled his head in his hands, "There was no fucking way I could go down that hole." Robbie sensed the guy's gaze as he added, "You get that, right?"

Robbie nodded as the walkie-talkie crackled to life with Zach's voice, "Search and rescue can't get a chopper up here until this cloud cover burns off. They think it will be soon. We're almost at the trucks. Arianna can drive Tabby home and I'll hoof it back up to you guys as fast as I can. Over."

Robbie depressed the button and said, "Okay, Zach. Got it. Over."

Entering the gloom of the mine, Justin could see he was walking on very old timbers. An attempt had been made to close off the incline shaft by laying out a series of beams. Shining his flashlight further back into the dark, he could see the spot where the worn wood met the hard-packed earth at the top of the tunnel. Beneath his feet, the timber was spongy, covered in moss and ferns and clearly rotting away. He carefully lowered himself down on all fours and then flat onto his stomach. He slithered forward. Almost immediately, he came to the gaping hole Leez had fallen through. His guts rolled over as he trained the light down the opening. A few meters down he could see the hard-packed incline shaft with its broken-up minecart tracks disappearing into the dark at what looked like a thirty-degree slope. Calling back, Justin told Liam, "I can see where she fell through. I'm going down. It's about three meters and then I'll be on the incline shaft. Watch that rope."

Turning himself around and holding the rope, he slid through the hole and shimmied down onto the slanted path. He pulled the flashlight from his pocket, got on his butt and jammed his feet against the minecart tracks to steady himself. He began to crab walk down the incline with one hand guiding him and the other aiming the flashlight ahead into the dark. He spotted her about seven meters in front of him. A portion of debris from a collapse of the tunnel had stopped her forward progress. Beyond the pile that only half blocked the path, the broken tracks stretched away into the darkness.

Justin scuttled the last bit of the way to Lisa-Marie's still body. Shining the flashlight on her neck he checked for her pulse. She was alive. He took a deep breath. The walkie-talkie lay on the ground beside her. It must have fallen out of her pocket. He picked it up and depressed the button,

"Liam, can you read me?"

Robbie's voice came back at him, "Just a second, Justin."

Then Liam came on, "Go ahead, over."

"She's unconscious but she's alive. I'm going to assess her condition and do what I can with the first aid kit. Over."

"Okay, keep me posted. Over."

Lisa-Marie was coming to and moaning softly. Justin propped the flashlight so it shone against the wall, spilling light over her and he did the best evaluation he could. Her low moans turned to sharp yelps of pain when he got to her wrist and he knew it was broken. She couldn't move her shoulder on the same side without screaming in pain. He supposed her collar bone was fractured. The blood on her face came from a couple of minor lacerations where she had smacked the side of her face up against the pile of debris. She had a large goose egg size lump on her head and a more serious cut running down the back side of her shoulder. The blood had soaked through her ripped shirt and sweater.

Justin pressed the button on the walkie-talkie and reported his findings before he got started. Liam's voice came back, echoing in the narrow space of the tunnel, "Do the best you can. They can't get a chopper up here until the clouds lift."

Leez called his name. She recognized him. That was something. He did his best to stabilize her wrist. Dealing with the collar bone was harder because he had to stop the bleeding and dress the wound on her shoulder. Her cries were sharp and plaintive as he worked and at one point he knew she lost consciousness for a few moments. He then set about getting her in the most comfortable position he could and cleaned up the cuts on her face. By that time, she was lucid enough to ask, "Where am I?" Her voice trembled with fear.

"You fell down into the old mine. A chopper is on the way. As soon as the clouds burn off, it'll land and some good-looking search and rescue guys will hike in here with a stretcher and carry you right out." He tried to smile at her. "I can't give you anything for the pain, Leez. I'm sorry. Your wrist is in bad shape. You might need an operation. You have to hang in there and be tough."

He kept her warm and tried to keep his mind off the gaping tunnel that disappeared into the dark beyond the pile of rubble they hunched against. If Lisa hadn't come to a wrenching, tumbling stop right where she had, if she'd tipped the other way in the tunnel and kept going down the incline shaft, he probably never could have gotten to her without getting killed himself.

It seemed as if hours were going by, though his watch told him a different story. He kept Leez awake but she mostly moaned pitifully. The walkie-talkie crackled to life, "The chopper is going to land in that flat space right above the trail to the mine. It's coming in now but the guys have to hike down to you. Are you, okay? Over."

Holding the walkie-talkie close to his mouth, Justin said, "I'm good, Liam. Thanks. Over."

Time lost its meaning for Justin in the semi-dark, stuffiness of the tunnel as he tried not to think of how the dirt above him could collapse at any moment. It could have been hours, but only twenty more minutes had passed when Liam's voice came over the walkie-talkie telling him the search and rescue paramedic was coming down. Moments later a guy in rappelling gear with a narrow rescue litter attached to his back arrived at Justin's side. He quickly assessed Lisa-Marie's condition then told Justin, "You did a good job. I'll wait until we're topside to put in an IV. Let's get her out of here, okay?"

Justin felt like screaming himself when he heard Lisa shriek as she was moved onto the litter. The paramedic told her, "I'm sorry, sweetheart. Don't hate me. We've got to get you out of here and this is the only way."

Together Justin and the paramedic maneuvered the litter up the incline. When it was in position, they hooked it to the rescue line that snaked down from the opening above. A second paramedic was stretched out flat on the timber cranking on the pulley that would allow him to hoist the litter up through the hole.

By the time Justin got out of the mine, the last traces of the low clouds that had draped the site in ghostly white shadows had disappeared. Now the whole area looked different. He felt as though he'd been underground for days and had emerged to a world reborn.

The fifteen-minute hike up the trail to the chopper wasn't easy but with six guys and the right equipment it was doable. When they transferred Lisa-Marie from the litter to a real stretcher, she had lost consciousness again. Justin had a few moments to stare at her face which was as white as the blanket tucked under her chin. The IV bag swung in an arc as the guys slid the stretcher into the chopper. Jumping down, the paramedic who had been down in the mine shaft with Justin told them, "Central dispatch is telling us to take her straight to the airport in Cedar Falls. They'll have a plane waiting to fly her to Victoria." He slapped Justin on the arm, "You guys get yourself safely out of here, okay?"

FORTY-ONE

David sat forward in his chair and his voice went low, "Back off ... I'm warning you."

Nick's eyebrows rose but he held his ground. "It's a simple question, David."

Getting up, David walked over to the window of the counselling office. He took a deep breath and turned back to Nick. "I don't want any simple questions from you about what I believe in."

Spreading his hands in a gesture of innocence, Nick said, "I'm not sure we're going to make much progress if there are things you won't talk about."

David sat back down. "You don't get to rip apart all my beliefs and call it counselling."

"Tell me how you think I'm doing that?"

Staring straight into Nick's eyes, David said, "You're trying to lead me in a particular direction and I don't want to be led by you when it comes to my faith in God. I'll decide when I question anything about religion."

Nick nodded slowly. "Okay. How do you feel about the rest of our counselling work ... talking about what happened when you were a child?"

"I'm okay about that part of things. Talking about that stuff with you is helping me."

"And what if the indoctrination part keeps you from making progress?"

David narrowed his eyes at Nick, "Don't call my faith indoctrination. I know you think what I believe about God is a crutch I'm going to lean on so I don't have to face up to the hard stuff I need to talk about. You've thought that since I first walked into this office. But you don't have a crystal ball. You don't know that for sure."

"Fair enough." Nick leaned forward in his chair, "But I do reserve the right to revisit the question. For now, though, you're in the driver's seat when it comes to talking about God." He paused for a moment before he added, "I respect you for speaking up, David, and for doing it without recourse to rote scripture quoting or hedging. You've been very clear and to my way of looking at things, that can only help our counselling process."

※ ※ ※ ※

Tabby walked into the cabin soaked to the skin. Robbie was right behind her. Brigit stared at her daughter dripping everywhere, oblivious to all except whatever joke was making her and Robbie laugh their heads off. She felt an irritability she knew was rooted in her fear about what had happened up on the Cat's Cradle. Sure, it was Lisa-Marie who had fallen down an old mine, not Tabby. But the whole thing got to her. She never should have let Tabby go on that hike.

Hands on her hips, she demanded, "What on earth happened to you?"

Tabby barely glanced at her, "I fell out of the canoe." She called over her shoulder to Robbie, "I'll get dry clothes on and we can go back out."

"How did you manage to fall out of the canoe?"

Tabby headed to her room as she said, "We were trying to hook onto a sunken log and I fell out."

Brigit held her hand up to stop Tabby's progress. "Hold it. That sounds dangerous. I want to talk to you." She turned to Robbie, "Tabby is not going back out in the canoe today."

Robbie lifted his eyebrows when Tabby stamped her foot and splashed more water onto the floor. She looked at Robbie and said, "Don't go." She glared at her mother. "I am too going back out in the canoe."

Brigit's voice rose, "Go to your room and get changed." She pointed at Robbie, "You go home, right now."

Head down, Robbie left the cabin. Tabby stomped into her bedroom and slammed her door. She was out in a few minutes, dressed in dry clothes. "How could you?" she shouted at her mother. "You can't order Robbie to leave like that." She searched around for a pair of dry runners. "I'm going to find him."

Brigit sat down in the armchair. "You are not stepping out of this cabin until we talk." After an intense moment of defiance, Tabby threw her shoes into the corner, flopped down on the sofa and covered her eyes with her folded arms.

"Being out on the lake and falling out of a canoe doesn't sound safe to me."

With her voice aimed to the ceiling, Tabby said, "We were close to the shore. We were wearing life jackets. It's no big deal."

Brigit shook her head in frustration. "Easy to say that now but people do get hurt. Look at what happened to Lisa-Marie on that hike. I'm your mother. I'm starting to think I've put far too much faith in Liam and Izzy's judgement. They let Robbie run around and do anything." Getting nothing but silence from her daughter, Brigit's tone hardened, "I'm in charge of you and things around here are going to change."

Tabby sat up suddenly and stared at her mother. "What's that supposed to mean?"

"I'm going to be keeping a closer eye on you and you will be going to school in Dearborn in September."

Tabby's face went from sullen anger, to outrage and finally to desperation. "No ... I won't do it." Tears overflowed her eyes and poured down her face. "Why are you doing this to me? You'll wreck everything."

Brigit sat forward in the armchair; she was surprised by Tabby's shift from defiance to heartbreak. Feeling somewhat heavy-handed, she took a deep breath, got up and moved over to the sofa to sit next to her daughter. "How about telling me why you're so against the idea? I can't see how going to a new school could be as bad as you're imagining. You'll get used to it and I bet that in no time, you'll be telling me how much you love it."

The tears weren't stopping and Tabby's voice was thick and choked up as she said, "You wouldn't understand. You walk around everywhere like you still carry a gun or something. You don't see things."

Shaking her head in confusion, Brigit asked, "What things?"

Tabby's hands had gone up to cover her face and her voice was muffled, "People staring all the time. You don't get it. I don't want people staring at me." Her shoulders started to shake with fresh sobs. "And I couldn't do it without Robbie and he won't even be there because no one is going to ruin his whole life by making him do something he doesn't want to do."

Sighing heavily, Brigit rubbed Tabby's back. "Honey ... you have to brush stuff like that off. You're being too sensitive. So what if people stare?"

Tabby dropped her hands and gave her mother an accusatory look. "I knew you wouldn't understand."

While Brigit was waiting for the storm of fresh tears to settle down to hitching breaths, she decided to take a different approach. "Do you think you are going to stay here at Crater Lake forever? You can't hide out from the world."

Tabby was so shocked she simply stared at her mother's face, "What do you mean? Why can't I stay here forever?"

"Tabby ... honey ...," Brigit struggled to find the right words. "When I took this job, I never planned for us to stay here for more than a few years. It's been wonderful and I love it here, too. But I'm not going to be a cook forever. I want to be a police officer again someday."

As Tabby took in her mother's words, her face went slack with shock. And suddenly she was sobbing in earnest. She threw her arms around her mother and gasped, "No, no .... Mom ... please don't say that. Please."

Taken aback by her daughter's reaction, Brigit held her and stroked her hair, "Calm down, Tabby ... take it easy."

Pulling back, Tabby caught her breath. She begged, "Don't do it, Mom. Please ... it makes me too scared. I can't stand it. I'll go to Dearborn for school, I'll do anything, we can leave here if you want but promise you won't be in the police again ... please, promise." Her desperate words dissolved into heartbreaking sobs.

Brigit pulled her close and hugged her. "Okay ... stop crying, Tabby. It's going to be okay." She shushed Tabby like she was a small child again and tried to figure out what to do. When Tabby had finally calmed down and was sniffing quietly, Brigit offered a compromise. "I promise we won't make any changes for two years. And I won't say another word about the school issue. You can decide. But, Tabby, two years isn't forever, okay?"

Tabby sniffed and asked, "Can I go to my room now?"

❄❄❄❄

Kieran answered the knock at his door with a surprised look of pleasure, "Hey, Brigit. I didn't know you'd be in town today."

His surprise turned to concern as he studied the trapped look in her eyes. She stared at him and said, "I need to talk."

He ushered her inside and watched her take a seat at the kitchen table. He pointed to the coffee pot. "Do you want a cup?" he asked. She shook her head, so he sat down across from her and said, "What's up?"

"Tabby and I had a set to and I ended up telling her I didn't want to stay being a cook at Micah Camp forever ... that I want to go back to being a cop someday." She looked up at him and he saw tears brimming in her huge, chocolate-coloured eyes. "She got so upset, Kieran. I had no idea she would react that way. She cried and cried and begged me not to say that I would be a police officer again." Staring down at her hands clenched on the table top, she added, "And it wasn't just kid stuff. She was terrified of seeing me go back to that life."

"That must have been hard for you."

"At first, I didn't know what to do." Brigit's wide brow was wrinkled with concern. "I promised her we wouldn't make any changes for two years." She took a deep breath and held his eyes with hers. "I knew the last part of our time in Toronto was hard for her but I must have rationalized a lot of it. She seemed so young then and my parents were always there for her. When I decided to take the job at Micah Camp, I was mostly worried about dragging her so far from her grandparents and the neighbourhood in Toronto." A tear slipped down her cheek, "I didn't think what I had gone through could have had such an impact on her."

Kieran reached out his hands to wrap them around hers. "Hey ... you made a hard choice uprooting and coming here and you did it for Tabby. And she's done well, right?" Brigit nodded. "Did she seem okay with your idea to wait two years?"

"Yes ... she calmed down. Two years seems like forever for a kid but it isn't. It will fly by. I think she's mostly happy right now that the pressure is off on the school issue."

"You aren't ready to leave yet anyway ... are you?"

"No ... I wouldn't want to make a change for at least two years. I want to be on a firm footing, financially. I'm thinking of one of the police forces in the lower mainland or Victoria and living in either of those spots is expensive."

Kieran let go of her hands and sat back. "You have the time now to explore Tabby's fears with her and work on those issues. She was old enough when it all happened, to remember being afraid. And I can tell you from my own experience, that she will need to share those memories and face those fears."

Brigit glanced at the clock on the wall. "I better get back to the camp. I've got the van and I said I wouldn't be long."

Kieran walked her to the door and when she turned to thank him, he opened his arms and held her for a moment. Her curls brushed against his chin as she hugged him back. She stepped away. "Thanks, Kieran. Thanks so much for being here to listen."

He returned her smile. "It's my job, but it's more than that, Brigit. We're friends and it's my pleasure to be here for you."

As Brigit drove back to Micah Camp, she realized she felt better. Tabby's level of distress had seriously shaken her. She had been overwhelmed by the thought that she had nowhere to turn. Then she had known that she could go to Kieran.

She thought of the hug. She was surprised how nice it had felt to have a man's arms around her – to press her cheek against the roughness of his sweater, to breathe in the smell of him, to lean on his unyielding, muscled chest. The strength in his body was reassuring. That physical contact made her realize that a friendly embrace wasn't the only thing she had gone without for quite a while. Smacking her open palm against the steering wheel, she smiled. She had enough on her plate with an eleven-year-old daughter to raise. A man, in or out of bed, was the last thing she needed.

FORTY-TWO

*D*ear Emma:
    I'm in the hospital. I fell at the old mine. It was so foggy and I was pissed off at Tyler. He made a bunch of trouble about going down the mountain before everyone else and then he acted like all he had to do was shoot some film of the opening to the mine. Geez ... obviously, we had to go inside. But it turns out we took the wrong freaking trail and we weren't even at the right mine. Then I fell and Justin was there and I was in so much pain. Then I was here in the hospital and Izzy was with me. I know there must be a lot more to what happened – I still don't remember exactly how I fell – but the doctor says that's normal.

    I was freaking out about my camera but Izzy says Liam brought it home. I think I slapped Justin but I'm not sure why. Maybe I was crazy in pain or something. And then after the surgery on my wrist, I got it in my mind that something had happened to Sophie. They had to give me a shot to calm me down.

    They're going to let me out of the hospital tomorrow. I got a bad knock on the head but all the scans they did say I'm okay. I've got a pin in my wrist and my broken collar bone hurts like mad. Thank God, both of those injuries are on my left side. I have ten stitches on the back of my shoulder. You guessed it, my left side.

    Justin keeps texting me and phoning and I can't talk to him because I don't know what to say. Emma, I'm so confused. I know he's not with Lauren anymore, but he never broke up with her. He had the whole summer to end the relationship and he didn't. I can't live with always being his second choice.

Izzy stopped by the hospital that evening. Earlier, she had been glad to get Lisa's text saying she would be released the next day. Though Izzy had enjoyed staying with Jim and Marlene, she was ready to go home. Lisa was sitting in the chair by her bed when Izzy came into the room and dropped a to-go bag from White Spot on the hospital tray. "One Big-O burger. I'll get a chair and keep you company while you eat."

When Izzy was in her chair across from Lisa-Marie, she knew something was wrong. "What's up? Shoulder or wrist?"

Lisa-Marie stared down at her hands folded tightly in her lap, as she said, "When I get out tomorrow, I'm not going back to Crater Lake with you." She looked up suddenly, "I'm sorry to have kept you hanging around down here for nothing."

Izzy took a deep breath. "I would have stayed here to be with you, regardless. You've had surgery, Lisa. That's a big deal. You've been scared and in pain. No one should go through that alone." Looking closely at the young woman in front of her, Izzy saw that she was pale and that she had dark circles under her eyes. For all her twenty years, Lisa could well be the young, pregnant girl Izzy had first befriended. If anything, she looked more fragile now than she had then. Izzy spoke gently, "You're going to be pretty uncomfortable for the next while between that wrist and your collar bone. Where else would you want to go?"

"I've been texting with Maddy. She's got this show coming up at a gallery on Granville Island. She uses my photos and does some artsy things to them. She wants me to be there. I'm going to her place in Vancouver for a while. She's coming over to get me tomorrow." Lisa-Marie fiddled with the ties on her hospital robe as she spoke.

Izzy reached out and touched her hand. "Tell me what's really going on?"

Lisa raised her tear-filled eyes, "I can't be around Justin right now. Tell Sophie that her mom has to work. She's used to that." The tears brimmed over and her voice choked.

"I can do that, if you're sure that's what you want."

Nodding her head, Lisa-Marie held Izzy's hand and wept silently.

⚜⚜⚜⚜

Justin looked up from his desk and saw Izzy walk into the sawmill office. His eyebrows rose as he said, "Hey ... we sure don't see you up here very often."

She stopped inside the doorway. Her hand went to her throat for a moment and she stood still as if she were catching her breath. Then she shrugged, "I can't remember the last time I came up here." Her voice fell slightly, "It all looks the same."

Pushing things aside on his desk, Justin said, "Everyone knows you don't like the place."

A slight frown flickered over her face before she asked, "Do you have a minute?" He nodded and she pulled a chair from near the wall over to his desk. She sat down. "Caleb loved this place. He was so happy here – being in this office, working out on the woodlot, tinkering with the saws and sitting at that desk." She sighed, "If Caleb's ghost is wandering around Crater Lake, this is where it comes to rest every night." Her shoulders moved with a slight shrug, "When I came in, you made me think of him ... the way you were sitting at the desk." She held her hand up, "Not the Caleb I knew ... the one who built this place when he was in his twenties. I never met that Caleb but I've been getting to know him from some old scrapbooks he kept."

She changed the subject. "I came up to tell you that Lisa didn't come back with me."

Justin leaned across the desk, "Why? What happened? Is she okay?" Worst-case scenarios flashed through his mind – maybe the knock on the head Leez had taken was more serious than everyone thought.

"She said she couldn't see you right now. She's gone to stay with Maddy for a while."

Stunned, he sat back in his chair and placed his hands flat on the desk. Izzy had no judgement in her voice but he felt a surge of gut-roiling guilt all the same. "Did she say anything else?" he asked. Izzy shook her head. "Does she have any idea how close a call she had?"

"She knows she fell. She remembers that you were there with her but as far as her accident being a close call, no ... I'd say she has no idea."

"Maybe that's for the best," he said as he stared at the desk.

He had wanted to rush down to the hospital in Victoria every single day since he had stood on the trail from the *Bear Creek Mine* site and watched as Lisa-Marie was flown away in the chopper. He'd told Liam as they hiked out to the trucks in the dying light, that he planned to drive straight down to Victoria that evening. But Liam had advised him to wait, saying Justin was tired and it had been an ordeal for all of them. Because the drive to Victoria would take seven hours, Liam had told Justin he should get a good night's sleep and see where things stood in the morning. Though the situation was serious, Liam had convinced him that the paramedics were right – Lisa had been lucky.

The next day, Justin learned that they were keeping Leez in the hospital for surgery on her wrist and that Izzy had gone down to be with her. He still planned to go but he had to clear up a few things at the sawmill first. Everything went against him – one thing happened after another. They were floundering without Ethan out in the yard. A large order got put on the wrong truck. He spent all day straightening that out with two angry customers demanding to know where the hell their lumber had gone.

By the end of that day nagging doubts had crept in. Leez hadn't returned any of his texts. All his calls went straight to voice mail. He began to rationalize ... she was in the hospital, she had to have surgery and tests because of the knock she'd taken on her head. He tried to convince himself that she would hardly have the time or the energy to be texting anyone.

Finally, yesterday, he'd received a few cryptic words – *I'm okay ... just overwhelmed.* That seemed reasonable. But she still didn't answer when he called. And now she wasn't coming home at all and he wasn't going to have a chance to tell her any of the things he wanted to tell her.

After Izzy left the sawmill office, he forced himself to concentrate on clearing several items from his ever-lengthening to-do list. One of the main things he was learning about the job of running Crater Lake Timber had to do with time management. There was no leeway to let today's work slide into tomorrow because, as Reg always said, tomorrow was just a shit storm waiting to happen.

Later that evening, sitting in his rocking chair as the light faded from midnight blue to black, Justin thought about needing to tell Leez how sorry he was. He couldn't shake the feeling that every bad thing that had happened to her since she came to Crater Lake could be laid on his doorstep. And now she wasn't coming home because he was here. She wouldn't be with Sophie because of him. He felt bad about that but he didn't know how he could change anything. This was his home, too. He couldn't leave here, not even if he thought it would mean Leez would come home.

With a heavy sigh, he got up and turned on a light. He shuffled through the mail he'd picked up from Beulah earlier. He saw the letter from his mom among the flyers and tore it open. He had to walk back to his chair and sit down. She wanted to see him. She was asking him to come and visit her.

FORTY-THREE

Nick walked out of the bedroom of his cabin buttoning his shirt. He, Fiona and Aidan had stayed here the night before after having dinner with Alex and Cynthia and handing their Saltbox back to them. Aidan was sitting on a blanket on the floor playing with some toys. Nick pointed at his son, "He's got that sitting thing down solid."

Perched in the nearby armchair, Fiona smiled. She reached down to pass Aidan his giraffe and he began to gnaw on it as he turned his attention from one parent to the other. She looked up at Nick. "I have to tell you something."

Here it comes, he thought as he moved over to the sofa to sit down. He'd tried to prepare himself for this moment but he couldn't wrap his head around it. She was going to leave him again and this time, she was going to take his son with her. He'd kept quiet, he hadn't put any pressure on her for fear she would bolt but now he wondered if that had been the wrong strategy. He leaned forward, "Okay ... I'm listening."

"Rosemary has asked me to stay and share the practice with her." Fiona kept her eyes on Aidan as she said, "I've decided to say yes."

Nick's world tilted back to a normal axis and he could breathe again. "You've decided to stay?" He needed to hear her say it again.

"I have." She gave him that serious look. "When I thought about her offer, I realized that I couldn't take Aidan away from you. Not now. When I brought him here and practically threw the poor kid in your face, I didn't know what was going to happen." She shrugged helplessly, "You're a good guy. But that didn't mean you'd want a child or have any aptitude for fatherhood." She gazed into his eyes, "Aidan deserves to have you in his life."

Grateful for what she was offering him, Nick wanted more. He couldn't stop himself. He had to ask, "What about you and me? Is there ever going to be an *us*?"

Fiona pointed at Aidan, "There's a you and me in him." A slight smile curved her mouth, "There's an us in the bedroom, for sure."

Nick squared his shoulders and took a deep breath before he said, "I want something more than running between two or three different places and only now and then getting into the same bed with you."

Twisting her braid around her hand, Fiona sighed. "What are you suggesting?"

"I want us to live together."

The quiet that settled down around them after that statement was broken only by the small squeaking sound coming from the toy giraffe in Aidan's mouth. "We'd need to find a place in Dearborn."

"I don't have to live at Micah Camp to work here."

Aidan started to fuss. He looked on the verge of pitching himself backwards and landing on his head. Nick reached down and picked up his son. He held Aidan in front of him so the baby could dance on his dad's knees. Fiona smiled, "I found a notice under the door at Rosemary's apartment the other day. The forest company that owns the apartment on the first floor is looking to sublet it for a year. What do you think? It's already furnished and everything – two bedrooms plus an office."

Nick looked at Aidan, "What do you think, kid? Do you want to live with Mom and Dad in the Lady Brit?" He glanced over at Fiona. "It sounds good to us."

⚜⚜⚜⚜

Brigit looked up from chopping vegetables to see Tabby standing in the doorway. Her daughter was wearing a dress that Brigit had bought for her on the Victoria trip – a sleeveless one with a flaring skirt ... all in a dark fuchsia pink that complemented her colouring perfectly. She'd done her hair and had clipped into her curls a barrette with spiraling ribbons that matched the colour of her dress. Brigit looked closer and realized that Tabby had put on some lip gloss and she was wearing the pearl stud earrings she'd gotten from her grandparents ages ago. She had a lightweight, white sweater over her arm.

Brigit was stunned. Tabby was dangling her white sandals from the fingers of one hand but even in her scuffed runners she had morphed from a tweener to a teen with one change of clothing. The words – *be careful what you wish for* – ran through her mind as she simply stared at the beautiful girl in front of her.

Tabby watched her mother's face and her own eyes narrowed, "I thought you'd be happy ... you ordered me to wear a dress the last time I went to a party at Robbie's." She flounced out her skirt and stared down at herself, "It's okay, right?"

Brigit came from behind the counter and across the kitchen to hug her daughter. She stepped back and said, "You look lovely. Is Robbie coming over to walk with you?"

Tabby shook her head, "I'm going to walk over with Nick and Fiona and Aidan."

Brigit smiled and shooed Tabby out the door, "Away you go. Have fun. I'll be over after I get the crowd here fed."

⚜⚜⚜⚜

Cynthia was standing in the living room of the Saltbox taking in the view. The lake was lit with light flickering and sparkling in the path of the sun. She felt Alex's arms go around her waist and she leaned back against him. "So, you enjoyed the trip?" he asked her.

She sighed, "I loved it. The whole thing, including the tea drinking and the fish eating." She was thoughtful for a moment. "I learned so much ... not only about the pipeline issue ... I discovered more about people on this trip than I have ever learned at any other time in my life." She glanced back to get a look at his face, "And I think I have a better idea about you."

Alex chuckled, "You've got me all figured out, hey?"

"Not quite ... I doubt that I will have enough time in this life for that. We aren't exactly spring chickens." She smiled with pleasure, "I'm glad to be home and happy to see Aidan. He's grown so much. He's already sitting up."

She pulled away and turned around as she said, "Something is up with Fiona and Nick." Cynthia's lips pursed with displeasure, "If she tries to take Aidan away, I'm going to give her a piece of my mind, no matter what you say."

Alex eyed her with a grin on his face, "You are starting to sound like the right partner for a warrior." He leaned forward to brush her lips with his own. "Rest easy. I talked to her for a couple of minutes last night and we're not going to lose our grandson any time soon."

"Whew ... that's a relief because I wasn't sure how I'd come out in an altercation with Fiona."

"She's not as tough as she seems." He glanced over at the clock on the

374

kitchen wall. "We better get going over to Liam and Izzy's. We don't want to miss our own welcome home party."

Nodding, Cynthia glanced back out the window. A breeze had come up and leaves from the nearby alder tree were skipping along the ground out near the hedge line of japonicas. "Summer's almost over." She followed Alex to the door. "I guess your friend will be arriving in a couple of weeks. I'm looking forward to meeting him."

Alex passed her the walking stick that was leaning against the porch wall, "Ya, well, Calvin Grey Eagle is not everyone's kind of Indian."

Cynthia frowned as she went down the stairs to the path, "I don't know what that might mean."

⚔⚔⚔⚔

Bethany glanced over at Beulah as soon as they got on the trail. "I know you must be dying to ask me about the email." The previous evening, she and Beulah had been sitting in the living room together. Bethany had her laptop open on her knees. She had checked her email, spotted a new message and opened it. Her loud gasp had caused Beulah to look over at her with concern. Bethany had waved her hand for silence and read on with increasing shock. She had then closed the laptop lid with a thump. Getting up from her chair, she had told Beulah, "Don't worry about me. I received an email I need to think about. Don't ask me anything." She excused herself, saying she was going to take a bath.

Out on the trail, Beulah lifted a shoulder in a half-shrug, "Yes and no. I don't pry. You're looking at the reformed Beulah. You've taught me well enough when to back off. I might be an old dog, but I can learn a new trick now and then."

Bethany raised an eyebrow before she started to speak. "One night at the grief group, I talked about the baby I gave up. I had read an article in a magazine at the dentist's office about how people try to find kids they gave up and how some kids are also searching for their birth parents." She took a deep breath, "I was stunned by the idea. I tried not to think about it but, of course, the more I tried not to, the more I did." Her words sped up, "I went online and checked out what I'd have to do to find the child I gave up and I ended up entering my information into the adoption registry." She stopped walking and when Beulah looked at her, she said, "The email last night was from my son. Sergeant Steven Hayes. He put his name in the registry ages ago searching for me. He's been back from Afghanistan for a year. He wants to meet me."

Beulah brushed her fingers through her hair and her grey spikes stood up to attention. Her eyes were narrowed with concern as she asked, "Well ... that is huge news. How do you feel about meeting him?"

Bethany's mouth turned up in a small, only slightly shaky smile. "I want to, Beulah. I'm ready. And meeting my son isn't just something for me to clutch onto." Beulah waved her hand as if to deny her own unexpressed opinions about her wife's past behaviours, but Bethany's tone demanded attention. "No ... don't do that. Don't act as if you don't know that I've had lots of trouble finding my way." She stopped to get her breath before going on. "I need you to know that this is different. I've learned a lot from being part of the grief group. I won't say I'm ready to meet my son ... because I have no idea what the experience will be like. But I do know this, I'm ready to face the challenge. And I'm sorry I didn't tell you I was going to take this step because I know it is big." Bethany took a shaky breath. "I should have included you. But I'm still learning how to do that so it isn't like I'm asking for permission. I need to practice standing up for myself while also being a partner. It's hard."

Beulah nodded and started to walk again. She paused only to glance at Bethany and say, "If you're ready, I'm ready to support you."

FORTY-FOUR

Izzy slipped the pile of worn exercise books back into the bottom drawer of the desk in the workshop. She leaned her elbows on the scratched surface and rested her chin on her folded hands. As she stared out the window to the view of the garden path, she felt quick tears on her lashes. She wasn't sorry she'd read Caleb's journals but she did feel sad to come to the last pages.

She dabbed at her eyes with her fingertips. No one would ever fill the space Caleb's death had left in her. The love she had for Liam was as strong, as deep, but different. Because for Liam, she was different. Caleb hadn't needed her to be the woman Liam needed.

Caleb was the only person she had ever met who didn't need people to be anything for his sake. That aspect of him had tested her love. She had yearned to be indispensable. But Caleb's completeness in himself had given them all a far greater gift. He became their compass; he was the force to which they oriented themselves. For her and Liam and Beulah and Bethany – the only way to be true to Caleb's memory was to carry on his legacy of acceptance and compassion ... to be, in their own unique ways, that compass for others. As such, they were not there because they had all the answers or because they could tell others what to do. They led by example. They did their own work, they made commitments to love and family, and they didn't give up on each other.

She heard Liam's step near the door. He came into the workshop and pulled up a chair close to the desk. The bottom drawer was still ajar. He smiled at her. "Being up on the Cat's Cradle the other day reminded me of the time Caleb and I climbed up to the summit." Izzy turned her chair to face his. "We both put messages in the cairn." He searched her face for a moment. "I can tell you what Caleb's message said because it came true." Her quiet attention gave him permission to go on. "There was a Thomas Jefferson quote – *I like the dreams of the future better than the history of the past.* And under that he wrote ... *I want to love Izzy every day for the rest of my life.*"

Her eyes shone suddenly with tears. She took a deep breath before saying, "He shared that with you and you remembered?"

Liam nodded, "We both shared our messages before we put them in the cairn. Mine was –,"

Izzy threw her hands over her ears, "Don't tell me. It's bad luck"

Liam gave her an odd look. "I never thought of you as the superstitious type, Izz."

She got up from the chair. "I'm not, but that doesn't mean I'd mess with the magical cairn on the Cat's Cradle."

He closed the space between them and tipped her chin up so he could search her eyes. "Are you okay?"

"Better than okay. I love you, Liam."

❧❧❧❧

Aidan carefully picked up a piece of banana from his tray and pushed it against his mouth with the flat of his hand. As banana squished through his fingers, he grinned and kicked his feet.

Sophie looked across the crowded table of people to the high chair where Aidan sat. "Auntie Fi," she said, pointing at Aidan, "Why him still a baby? Him been here a long time."

Fiona laughed, "It takes a while for a baby to turn into a big kid like you, Sophie."

Nick helped himself to more of the fried chicken Bethany had brought over to the potluck lunch to welcome Alexander and Cynthia home. "It looks like you're going to get a chance to see him get bigger, Sophie." The child frowned as Nick glanced at Fiona. "Shall I tell them, or will you?"

"Well, I guess I'll have to now." She smiled around the table. "I'm going to be taking on a half-share of Rosemary's practice."

Liam gave her a searching look, "You're staying, then."

Fiona nodded. "You're looking at Dearborn's other doctor." Nick raised an eyebrow at her and she added, "Nick and I are going to move in together."

Cynthia smiled across the table at Nick. "Congratulations to both of you," she said.

Izzy passed Robbie the basket of buns as she looked at Liam. "Where is Justin?"

"He said he'd stop over later for cake. He was up at the sawmill all morning."

Izzy frowned, "I hope he's not going to get crazy about production like Reg."

Beulah reached for a bun as the basket went by. "He had a letter from Vancouver in yesterday's mail."

Cynthia glanced over at Tabby who sat next to Robbie. "You look nice today, Tabby. That's a lovely outfit. Did you dress up for our homecoming?"

The girl smiled shyly, "My mom says clothes make a statement."

Robbie dropped his half-eaten bun on his plate and stabbed a piece of chicken with his fork. "That dress is stating that you won't be wanting to hang backwards off the tire swing."

Fiona wiped Aidan's face as she asked Cynthia, "What was the best part of the trip?"

Glancing over at Alex, Cynthia grinned as she spoke, "Hands down, nothing else even came close ... we were in the canoes dragging the crochet chains out across the channel. The water was choppy and the spray was coming over the sides and whipping off the paddles. And these giant, bobbing spools of colour were winding out behind us while people cheered from the shore and drums sounded from the other canoes. It was something to see." She rubbed her arms as she said, "But cold. I wasn't prepared for it to be so chilly out on the water. One of the grannies passed me a cup of hot tea from her thermos." She sighed, "I never tasted anything so wonderful."

Sophie slid off her chair and climbed up on Alex's knee. "When I have a feather for my hair, Grandpa?" She touched the feather that dangled down over his ear.

Across the table, Izzy touched Liam's arm, "Did you hear that? She said feather." Pausing, Izzy added in a quieter tone, "She's not doing the *r* thing anymore."

Liam smiled, "You look disappointed."

"Geen gapes was one of my favourite Sophie-isms."

Alexander pushed his plate away and told Sophie, "You have to find one."

"Where I find a feather?"

"You have to pay attention when you're outside. Look carefully at things. Notice what's around you." Then he gave her a serious look of warning, "But you can't keep the first feather you find. You give that one away. The next feather you find you can keep."

Sophie's face was a picture of deep thought as she considered Alex's words. She tipped her head to one side and said, "I have to find two feathers?"

Alexander smiled into her eyes, "Yes ... then I'll have to call you Sophie two-feathers."

⚜⚜⚜⚜

Robbie stood over by the nearly depleted dessert table and took the last piece of cake from one of the plates. He was wishing Tabby hadn't decided to wear a dumb dress today because he wanted to show her how the eagle he had carved on Pearl's grave marker had turned out. To do that, they'd have to go off the trail and into the bush. As he bit into the cake, he remembered the face she had made at her mom when Brigit had shown her the new dress down in Victoria. Tabby had whispered to him that she would rather be stuffed in a coffin with one thousand spiders than ever wear that dress.

He hadn't seen Tabby for two days, ever since her mom pointed at the door of their cabin and told him to leave. He had wanted to go over the next day but Liam had said he should give Brigit a day or two to cool off. And now that Tabby was here, she was acting weird – wearing a dress and not saying much and her light was strange, too – all jumbled happy, sad and scared. He found it hard to look at her.

He chewed and savoured the rich chocolate flavour of the cake as he watched Tabby come up from Sophie's playroom and look around. She spotted him and walked over to the table. "Thanks a lot for ditching me to finish the puzzle."

Robbie made a face, "I've built it with Sophie a hundred times. I can see Belle and the Beast dancing in my sleep."

Tabby stared at the cake in his hand, "You'll explode if you keep eating." She smoothed the skirt of her dress as she spoke.

He swallowed quickly and asked, "What happened with you and your mom the other day. Did you get in trouble?"

Tabby looked away from him and gave a small shrug, "I told my mom why I didn't want to go to school in Dearborn and she said she wouldn't bug me about it for two years."

He frowned. She wasn't telling him everything. "What else happened?"

She darted a few glances around the room. Then she pulled Robbie by the arm through the French doors and down to the sunporch. She whirled around to face him and the skirt of her dress spun in a brilliant pink circle. "She said she's not going to stay being a cook at Micah Camp forever. I wasn't going to tell you because I don't want to cry."

Robbie was stunned. How could Brigit even think something like that? He swallowed hard; the cake in his stomach rolled oddly.

"She wants to be in the police again." Tabby's voice shook and fear-filled eyes locked on to his. "What if something happens to her? I begged her not to do it. I told her I'd go to school in Dearborn or we could even move if only she wouldn't do it."

The light around her sparked and glittered. Robbie closed his eyes for a moment so he could think. When he opened them, he had made his choice. "If she does that, you'll have to leave here. I'll go with you. We can watch her together and I'll know if something is going wrong."

"You wouldn't be allowed." The sudden hope on her face had given way to resignation.

"I'll go, anyway. We'll be thirteen in two years. I think Liam and Izzy will let me go to school wherever I want and if they say no, I'll make my dad say I can." Robbie's expression turned sad for a moment. "It would suck because I never want to leave here ... but I'll do it."

Tabby gazed at him for a moment as if she couldn't believe her ears. He saw her light arcing all over before she threw her arms around him and hugged him with all her might. When she stepped back, Robbie felt stunned and he stared at her. Then he kept staring. After a moment, she frowned, "Why are you looking at me like that." She smoothed her dress again and said, "Cut it out, okay? You're looking at me like I have cake all over my face or something."

Robbie stared at her again. He tilted his head and narrowed his eyes and stared some more. When he spoke, his voice was urgent. "I can see your light like a kind of outline around you but it isn't telling me anything ... nothing at all."

Tabby's eyes widened, "Why? Am I going to die or something?"

"Don't be dumb."

She whooshed out her breath with relief before she asked, "Is it just me?"

"Good point," Robbie told her, "I'll check." He walked up from the sunporch to the dining room and casually scanned the people milling about the living room.

Tabby nudged him, "What do you see?"

"I see everyone else the way I always do." He glanced back at Tabby again. The light was there but it didn't mean anything anymore. It didn't flicker or change or arc around her. All he saw was a low hum.

Tabby recovered from the shock of Robbie's news first. "It might change back but maybe it's better like this. Maybe you're not supposed to know everything about me."

Up in the kitchen they heard Izzy say, "Hey, Brigit ... glad you could make it."

Tabby's mom laughed as she replied, "Better late than never."

Tabby took a few steps towards the kitchen then stopped. She turned to look back at Robbie. "Bet you don't know what I feel right now." He put his palms up in a gesture of confusion. He didn't know and it made him feel lonely.

⁊⁊⁊⁊

Moving through the crowded living room, Izzy reached Justin's side and put a hand gently on his arm to get his attention. "Hey, just checking in ... how you doing? Beulah mentioned you got a letter in yesterday's mail." A wry look settled on her face, "Not much privacy around here when it comes to things like that."

Justin shrugged, "No problem. The letter was from my mom. Good news. She wants to see me and her doctor thinks she's ready. I'm going down later in the week."

"Hey, that's great."

"That's why I was up at the sawmill all morning. Trying to get everything in order so I can be away a few days."

She gazed at him for a moment. "Do you have other plans when you go to Vancouver?"

"Seems like it's not only the mail that isn't private around here." He knew Izzy would accept equally his choice to keep his own counsel or a choice to share. "I won't try to see Leez, if that's what you mean." With sympathy in her eyes, Izzy patted his arm before she moved on.

Justin sat down on the sofa and tried to relax. All around him were the sounds of people connecting, caring, interacting. He was here for a reason – these people mattered to him and he mattered to them. But he couldn't shake the feeling that he was staring into the room from the outside. None of it made any sense without Leez. He felt disconnected and lost. Sophie came up the stairs from her playroom and climbed onto his lap. She was holding her bunny close to her face. She leaned into his body and said, "I miss Mama."

He nodded, "I know. I miss her, too." He rubbed her small back.

A loud knock on the door that led out to the garden turned heads and hushed conversations. Reg walked through the entry into the living room. The toothpick was going full speed in his mouth as he waved to everyone. "I'll save you all the trouble of asking how I am." He laid one hand on his heart and pointed a finger at Justin with his other. "I took a licking but still kept ticking thanks to that guy." He jammed the ball cap up and down on his head a few times before telling Justin, "Got that something you were asking me for. It's out on the porch."

Justin moved Sophie off his knee and sat her on the sofa. "You wait here. I'll be right back. I've got a surprise for you."

Moments later, Justin returned to the living room carrying a small, golden bundle of fur that wiggled in his arms. He sat down beside Sophie and said, "This is for you. From your mom." He put the puppy in Sophie's lap. He had decided only at the last moment to assign credit to Lisa-Marie for a gift she knew nothing about.

Sophie's eyes lit up with wonder as she looked from Justin's face to the wiggling dog in her lap. "From Mama?" The puppy reached its small paws up her chest to lick at her face. "For me?" she looked at Justin and he grinned at her.

She slithered off the sofa holding the puppy close. Standing in the middle of the room with the golden lab in her arms, she looked around and announced, "This my new dog ... from Mama." She smiled brightly as she set the puppy on the floor and said, "Come Baby Pearl, come." She walked down the stairs to her playroom chatting a mile a minute to the dog who trotted along behind her.

FORTY-FIVE

The day Justin and Robbie made it to the summit of the Cat's Cradle was picture perfect. The early September sun shone on the distant peaks that surrounded them. The snow that nestled in the deep crevices, never giving up its hold at this higher altitude, glittered and dazzled with sparking light.

Justin turned to Robbie and raised his hand. Their palms smacked against each other and echoed a slap into the quiet that surrounded them. "We made it, kid." Justin smiled as he pointed over to the cairn. "Let's do this."

They walked the few steps to the cairn that nestled against a rock outcropping. In their hands, they held the slips of paper with their messages. All their attention was bent on the words of the wishes they were making. Robbie read his silently one last time - *Please let Tabby belong here.* He nodded slowly as he looked at Justin.

Justin was down on one bent knee. He was folding his message as he repeated the words like a litany to himself - *Send Leez home.* When he had written the message early that morning before he and Robbie had started off on the hike, he had thought of adding the words - *to me.* But he had decided against it. He didn't want to jinx anything by being selfish.

When both their messages were folded into small bits of paper, they dropped them into the cairn and Justin moved the rocks that covered the opening back into place. Looking up, Robbie pointed to the eagle that floated overhead, wafted by the air currents so its wings barely moved. He and Justin stood for a moment to take it all in.

They gazed in wonder at the coastline far below with its folded inlets dipping in and out to form rippling blue tendrils like the hair of a mighty giant laying her head down to sleep. Beyond that, the sun glinted off the open Pacific.

Justin laid a hand on Robbie's back, "Let's go home."

ACKNOWLEDGMENTS

Many thanks to my husband, Bruce. Cicero says: *If you have a garden and a library, you have everything you need.* I will ask for one more thing – someone to share my library and garden with. Thank you for being that someone.

More than ever, I'm grateful for the opportunity to work with a wonderful friend and editor. Louise, our process reminds me of Arthur Plotnik's words – *You write to communicate to the hearts and minds of people what's burning inside you, and we edit to let the fire show through the smoke.* Many thanks for letting the fire shine through my words.

For my grown children, their spouses and for my grandchildren – my life is enriched by your presence in ways that would probably surprise and hopefully delight each of you.

Thanks to friends far and wide. Every writer needs to know she is part of a circle of 'real' people. You may become part of a fictional character now and then but I promise, the process is painless and it will do you no harm.

Thanks to Guy and Debbie Mitchell for lending us their compass. We should get our own.

The Chain of Hope Brigade was a real event though inserting Alexander and Cynthia into the action is an author invention. Excerpt from: Coastal First Nations Website – Article – *First Nations Complete "Symbolic Blockade" of Douglas Channel in Opposition to Enbridge Northern Gateway Pipeline* – June 2014. "A flotilla of boats from the community began the journey at 2:00 pm after inclement weather delayed their launch. Gitga'at women paddled a canoe across the channel in the pouring rain, carrying a giant spool of multicolor crochet wool, interspersed with mementoes and fishing floats with messages written on them. *The community came together and everyone crocheted, to show our full support for the Gitga'at way of life, to stand up for our coast, the whales, our traditions, our food and for the future Gitga'at that will use our territory for generations to come,* said Jodi Hill, a member of the Gitga'at First Nation and Chain of Hope participant. *We stand today to take care for generations we will never meet, just as our ancestors stood up for us. The crochet line means something to us all now. We won't stand for Enbridge or the government that supports them.* The paddlers laid a crochet chain more than 11,000 feet long from Hawkesbury Island to Hartley Bay. *This chain is made of wool, but it's stronger than steel*, said Grand Chief Stewart Phillip, President of the Union of BC Indian Chiefs. *First Nations will do whatever it takes to protect our communities from the dangers of oil spills because we have everything to lose. The BC and Canadian governments ignore this message at their own peril."*

Unreserved Podcast – Sept. 20, 2015 – host Rosanna Deerchild – *Unreserved looks back 25 years at the Oka Crisis* – cbc.ca – from the stories told on this podcast, I decided that Fiona would have been at Oka as a child with Alexander and that she would see and experience certain things.

Trans Bodies, Trans Selves: A Resource for the Transgendered Community – Oxford University Press – 2014 – an invaluable resource that helped me come to a greater understanding of the issues Charlie would face as well as what his parents might feel.

ABOUT THE AUTHOR

Francis Guenette has spent all of her life on the west coast of British Columbia. She lives with her husband and finds inspiration for writing in the beauty and drama of their off-grid, lakeshore cabin and garden. She has a graduate degree in Counselling Psychology and has worked as an educator, trauma counsellor and researcher. *No Compass to Right* is her fourth novel in the Crater Lake Series. She is also the author of the stand-alone novel, Maelstrom. Francis blogs at http://disappearinginplainsight.com. Please stop by and say hello.

DISAPPEARING IN PLAIN SIGHT
First book in the Crater Lake Series

Sixteen-year-old Lisa-Marie has been packed off to spend the summer with her aunt on the isolated shores of Crater Lake. She is drawn to Izzy Montgomery, a gifted trauma counsellor who is struggling through personal and professional challenges. Lisa-Marie also befriends Liam Collins, a man who goes quietly about his life trying to deal with his own secrets and guilt. The arrival of a summer renter for Izzy's guest cabin is the catalyst for change amongst Crater Lake's tight knit community. People are forced to grapple with the realities of grief and desire to discover that there are no easy choices – only shades of grey.

WHAT THE REVIEWERS SAY ABOUT DISAPPEARING IN PLAIN SIGHT:

I devoured this story, felt attached to the characters, and was sorry when it was over.

I couldn't put this down!! I was drawn into the lives of the complex characters.

Disappearing in Plain Sight is a stellar accomplishment for Francis Guenette.

I found it a touching read, at times bringing tears to my eyes.

A story of real life problems and the often unforeseen consequences of the choices we make.

Written with tenderness, you will find yourself feeling personally involved and wanting to delve deeper and deeper.

Disappearing in Plain Sight is one of the best novels I have read in years: the writing is beautiful; the characters are believable and all are people I would love to have a chance to know; the plot is complex and compelling and kept me turning pages well beyond when I should have been asleep on more than one night. I certainly will be looking for more work by this author

I highly recommend this to everyone, especially for those who can use a little bit of healing and compassion

This was a thought-provoking book and healing. I also enjoyed the writer's celebration of the beauty of people, nature, friendships and so much more. I read it in three sittings as I didn't want to leave the setting or characters for long.

The beautiful prose made me yearn for the rugged west coast of Vancouver Island, BC, Canada.

THE LIGHT NEVER LIES
Second Book in the Crater Lake Series

As circumstances spiral out of control, Lisa-Marie is desperate to return to Crater Lake. The young girl's resolve is strengthened when she learns that Justin Roberts is headed there for a summer job at the local sawmill. Her sudden appearance causes turmoil. The mere sight of Lisa-Marie upsets the relationship Liam Collins has with trauma counsellor, Izzy Montgomery. All he wants to do is love Izzy, putter in the garden and mind the chickens. Bethany struggles with her own issues as Beulah hits a brick wall in her efforts to keep the organic bakery and her own life running smoothly. A native elder and a young boy who possesses a rare gift show up seeking family. A mystery writer arrives to rent the guest cabin and a former client returns looking for Izzy's help.

Life is never dull for those who live on the secluded shores of Crater Lake. Set against the backdrop of Northern Vancouver Island, *The Light Never Lies* is a story of heartbreaking need and desperate measures. People grapple with the loss of cherished ideals to discover that love comes through the unique family ties they create as they go.

WHAT THE REVIEWERS SAY ABOUT
THE LIGHT NEVER LIES:

Holy patoly, what a read!

Guenette is a craftswoman who lets her work see the light of day only when she is sure it is as good as she can make it. Another five stars and I'm pleased that there's a further work in the Crater Lake series in the pipeline.

Far from falling into the pitfall of a second installment not being as good as the first, this book is marvelous and emotional, well-crafted and populated with characters that could be friends, family or neighbors.

What an amazing read, I couldn't put it down. I laughed out loud. I cried. The author does an amazing job of bringing the reader into the story.

Having recently read and very much enjoyed Francis Guenette's debut novel, "Disappearing in Plain Sight", and having been sad to leave the feisty characters behind, I was delighted to discover that the author had a sequel up her sleeve, though I was a little nervous as to whether it could match the first book. I needn't have worried – it was every bit as good, broadening the cast of characters to include all ages and stages of life, from the newborn to the dying. A satisfying, moving and memorable book which, like its predecessor, I'll be recommending far and wide.

Guenette tests the limits of her characters personalities, none of whom are saints. Kudos, that her characters behave realistically, both the adults and the teens. This is a worthy book and a great series thus far. I am looking forward to book three.

The writing is wonderful, particularly in terms of settling the reader into the landscape of Crater Lake and the secluded area of Northern Vancouver Island, Canada. Guenette also has a talent with characterisation, storytelling ability and complex relationship conflicts which are the real backbone of this novel.

CHASING DOWN THE NIGHT
Third Book in the Crater Lake Series

One might be excused for assuming that an idyllic life unfolds for those who have chosen to live and work near the shores of Crater Lake. Nothing could be further from the truth.

Long-time resident, Izzy Montgomery juggles the stress of a new job with her burgeoning home life. Family dynamics go into overdrive when Alexander and Cynthia launch plans to build a home nearby and Liam's sister, Fiona shows up to do an internship with the local doctor. Lisa-Marie and Justin are back for the summer and sparks fly. While crusty, old Reg keeps sawmill production booming, Beulah runs the organic bakery and plans the *First Annual Caleb Jenkins Memorial Ball Tournament*. Bethany discovers her own hidden talents working with young people at Micah Camp.

As a nine-year-old's dreams reflect a dangerous reality, many encounter issues from the past. This is a novel for all those who work at building family ties by strengthening the traditional and creating the new. *Chasing Down the Night* explores a wide-ranging emotional landscape while highlighting the many aspects of day-to-day, rural life. Tears and laughter are inevitable.

MAELSTROM

A shot is fired into the still night air and a young woman dies on Suicide Ridge. A dangerous game has begun. Over the course of one blistering, hot week, winds of change sweep through an isolated valley in small town America.

Sheriff Bert Calder, with the help of Mayor Amos Thatcher, has held the town of Haddon under his thumb for twenty-five years. As things spin out of control, Calder works the angles, ensuring he can make the most of the upheaval that is to come.

Rafael Destino, facing his own mortality, races against time to gain control of the railroad – a lifeline essential to the town's survival. His goal – to financially destroy Thatcher, the man he believes responsible for the death of his beloved sister. His tool – adopted son Myhetta. But how far down the road of revenge will Rafael push the young man who owes him everything?

Myhetta is poised on the edge of controlling Destino Enterprises, the job he has been groomed for. While money, power and influence are his to command, the past continues to torment him.

In a clash of powerful men, with fathers pitted against sons, no one will be left unscathed. *Maelstrom* is a page turner that speeds along like a runaway train.

WHAT REVIEWERS SAY ABOUT MAELSTROM

A wonderfully diverse cast of characters make this story memorable. Good and bad, they are all well-portrayed and realistic.

This is one of those novels that sucks you into the whirlwind of events from page one onward! I literally could not put this book down. The characters got into my head!

With Maelstrom, Francis Guenette has created a thrilling suspense story with local flair. I was drawn into the story immediately and thankfully invisibly! It is up to the reader who to trust and who to fear; don't be afraid of changing your take on things along the way! A thrilling suspense with twists seemingly too real for comfort.

The title of this thriller is appropriate on several levels. The plot is a maelstrom of conflicts. The characters are embroiled in a maelstrom of emotions. The events could be described as nothing else besides a maelstrom.

If you are looking for a book that will take your breath away and leave you on the edge of your seat, look no further! Maelstrom will propel you into a vortex filled with hate and prejudices where the only way out is to find trust and love within your own family.

Recommended for the reader who prefers a study of how it is to be human in an isolated township and an arid setting. This is hard lives, hard survival, in an 'unforgiving' landscape.

www.ingramcontent.com/pod-product-compliance
Lightning Source LLC
Chambersburg PA
CBHW020507020726
47493CB00001B/222